THE ORC OUTCAST'S MIRACLE

ORC MATES OF FAEDA

BOOK THREE

AURORA WINTERS

ISBN: 978-1-963552-09-6

CONTENT WARNINGS

All content warnings can be viewed on Aurora Winters's website at www.AuroraWintersRomance.com/books/content-warnings.

PRONUNCIATION GUIDE

I want to preface by saying that however you want to pronounce the characters and locations in my novels is absolutely fine by me. But if you would like to know how I read them in my own head, I have a pronunciation guide on my website here:

https://www.aurorawintersromance.com/books/
pronunciation-guide

CHAPTER

ONE

GOVEK

His bones rattled and the blood in his veins scorched as he charged into the hall.

"Where is she?" His roar thundered. It echoed off the crystal leaves of the Rove Tree above him and rained down to skewer silence into the worthless frames of every male present.

Deadly silence that catapulted him into more dread.

The imprint that connected him to Miranda was like an inferno in his chest. The bright white light of the Fades scorched behind his eyes, rippling with intensity, fueled by his rage.

He could not calm himself. He couldn't control his magic.

He couldn't bend it to his will to find Miranda, and not one of his wretched brethren spoke up to tell him where she had gone!

He bounded over to the nearest table—a thick slab of

wood that was wider than he was tall, thicker than the length of his massive hand, and as old as the woods themselves. He would render it to fucking *cinders*.

The orcs who had been seated there scrambled and leaped out of the way, leaving behind bowls of stew and cups of mead.

"Tell me where she is!" His words punctuated as his fist struck the middle of the table. His magic flamed out of control and burst from his knuckles on impact. Bolts of white current skittered like lightning across its surface, leaving a crack in its wake, searing his rage into the tabletop. The bowls of stew bubbled from the heat; the clay goblets of mead shattered. The scents of overcooked meat and fermented honey combined with scorched wood and burned his nose, his eyes watered.

Miranda's scent wasn't among them. He could not scent her here. She was gone.

Gone.

He whirled around to face the table with the humans and their mates. The women shrieked and clambered away as their orcs leaped to protect them. Their eyes were wide, their tiny fangs bared, their fists bunched. They stood frozen in shock and fear.

When they should be fucking *talking*.

"Where is she?" She should be with them. They should have protected her.

She'd screamed for help. He'd felt it. Now he felt nothing, and he could not focus his magic enough to *find her*. Light exploded behind his eyes as terror-laced agony shot through his body.

Where was she? *Where was she?* He could not calm. His

magic refused to obey. It crackled in his palms, prickled between his fingers.

"Calm down, tough guy."

That's what she would have said. And she would have touched his cheek and taken his hand and dabbed at the cuts on his palm.

Govek trembled as he turned his hand over, the magic pulsed with the beat of his heart and light danced in the veins of his wrist. His claws had sunk so deep into his flesh it was a wonder he couldn't see bone. Blood pooled in his palm, spilled over, and dripped to mar the jagged burned lines he'd scorched into the ancient wood table.

He gnashed his teeth.

"Govek! You must be calm!"

His father's shout had him almost keyed up again. How *dare* Ergoth tell him to be calm when his *mate was missing*!

And in pain.

He could feel it through the imprint that rumbled in his chest. The scatter of her broken plea still jittered over his flesh. He'd felt her screaming for him.

He had to find her. *Now*.

Instead of waiting for these fools to answer him, Govek barreled toward the exit. He would find her by scent alone.

"Govek, what have you *done*? Look at this table! Explain yourself." His father's voice was clipped and left no room for argument. In any other situation, Govek would have stood and accepted whatever punishment he was due for committing such an atrocity.

But not this time.

The imprint flooded his body with thrumming anguish, demanding he atone for his mistake—for believing Miranda would be safe in the hall without him.

After he found Miranda, he would come back and rip his brethren's limbs from their torsos for not protecting her.

Rip himself apart too. He'd left her too. *He'd failed her.*

"Where are you going? You cannot just *leave*, Govek!" His father bellowed as he started toward the doors. "I command you to stay and take responsibility for your actions here."

Like fuck he was staying here. He was going to find Miranda.

"*Govek*. Stop. *Now.*"

The magic-laced command from his father prickled through Govek's already scorched veins, and he was forced to halt. His muscles refused to budge.

His father's magic flashed deep into his bones and held him firm. The bitter, familiar stench of it mixed with the burning wood and Govek's stomach twisted, threatening to bring up his last meal.

Govek's thoughts flashed with acknowledgment. Confusion. Something about this scent was . . .

"Stop fighting me, Govek." His father's voice brought Govek back to the present.

"I must find Miranda first," he grated, and barely managed to turn his head to look at his father. The male stood atop his platform, his chin high, his eyes pricks of golden light. *"Let me go."*

The magical hold danced in Govek's veins. Stinging his muscles with every twitch. His bones felt like they would crack under the pressure.

"No. You will stay and wait and atone." Chief Ergoth rested his hand atop the back of his wooden throne. "Look at you. Do you think Miranda will even *want* to come near you in this state? You'll *terrify* her."

Govek tried to slink his claws away or cover his teeth, but he couldn't move. His father's magic was too powerful.

"Agol, go and fetch Sythcol. I believe we will need his clearing magic to calm things."

"Miranda is hurt." Govek grated through the clench of his teeth. "Someone must go to aid her."

"She cannot possibly be. We are within the bounds of Rove Wood Clan. Under the canopy of our Great Tree." Ergoth swung his hand up to indicate the crystalline leaves above. "No harm could come to any woman here."

"She is. I feel it in the imprint—"

"That imprint," his father scoffed, and the sound raked fury through every scrap of Govek's body. "I'm not convinced what you are feeling is *true*, Govek. You have barely known her for a quarter moon. It's simply not possible."

Govek trembled against the bounds of his father's magic as his anger rose. He *knew* what he felt toward Miranda. There was no mistaking it.

His body quaked, his magic blistered, his will fought against his father's strong, unyielding magic, battering it with his own might.

"Calm down, tough guy." He shut his eyes, focused on the light in his mind, focused his rage into a pinpoint, pushed it into his father's hold.

And it budged.

All went still in his mind as shock radiated higher than his anger.

"Govek," his father said low and deadly, a tone Govek had never heard before.

But he did not stop. He pushed against his father's magic again, forced it to release the tips of his fingers.

"Fine, Govek, you win. I'll send someone to look for Miranda. Now be still," Ergoth said quickly. "Good, Agol, you're back. Send your son a message to find Miranda and bring her back here as soon as possible. Sythcol, hurry it up with the clearing."

He wanted to send *Wolvc* to Miranda's aid? Fuck the Fades to the depths. He would *never* allow that to happen.

No other male would touch his mate. Govek let his rage build and shoved hard at his father's magic again. This time his whole left arm popped free.

"Govek, don't fight me. You will only hurt yourself in the attempt!"

"I only want to find Miranda." Govek caught Sythcol's gaze from the corner of his eye. The slender, pale green male had been on his way to his post near the back of the hall but paused to look upon Govek with wide, blinking eyes.

This male was the only one in the clan whose magic could rival his fathers. The only one who could fight Ergoth's might.

Or at least he'd *thought* he was.

"My chief, perhaps you should release him," Sythcol said, shocking Govek.

"Are you questioning my decision?"

"N-no, my chief. It is just—"

"Govek!"

She called again. Miranda *called*.

And Govek's magic spiraled into a frenzy, churned up by the force of his imprint, by the heat of his rage, by the bone chilling depths of his terror.

He had to save her. *He had to.*

The light of the Fades exploded in his mind and his

father's holding magic was caught in the inferno and burned out with a searing, electric jolt.

He was vaguely aware of his father's cry of pain as the magic between them severed, of voices rising in shock, of clattering and commotion as orcs leaped out of his path as he bolted for the door.

He would find Miranda.

His rage broke free from his control.

He would rip apart any being who'd touched her.

CHAPTER

TWO

MIRANDA

Miranda fell back and hit the floor.

The vent crashed in above her.

She writhed, but a heavy weight pressed her down. She contorted her body as she scrambled to escape. Jutting screws cut deep into her flesh. The metal was so hot. She couldn't breathe. Couldn't move. Couldn't get out!

Accept it.

Oh god, she didn't want to accept it. It *hurt*. Everything hurt. The burning, the cutting, the clawing. *The screaming.*

The screaming of her babies.

Oh god, she had abandoned them. She'd escaped from the vent and just *left*.

Stop. Breathe. Clear your mind.

She tried. She flexed her legs, hunched her shoulders, and dug her fingers into the metal.

Was this metal?

No, it was soil.

She breathed in deeply. She sucked in the pungent aroma of the world around her into her sinuses. The real world. The world her body was *truly* in right now.

Faeda.

Rich pine, crisp frost, and decomposing leaves.

"What is *wrong* with you!? I told you she had to *drink* it."

Her ears burned and her mind felt muddled. She tried to rise to her knees but couldn't manage it.

"Be *quiet*."

There were people here. She was not in a vault. Not in a vent.

She was not on Earth.

"She's *fine*. Just pick her up and carry her back to the hall like we planned."

The hall. That sounded familiar.

Miranda tried to open her eyes then. The vent faded.

She parted her eyelids. As she focused on what was around her, everything blurred and swirled until she felt sick. She squeezed her eyes shut and took gulping gasps through her mouth to keep from vomiting.

"She's coming to! You said it would last."

"I said she was supposed to *drink* it, you fool!"

"But she didn't drink anything in the hall! What were we supposed to do?"

The hall. The hall of Rove Wood Clan.

Where Govek was.

Govek's words thumped with every beat of her heart, soaking into her veins. *"You are not in a vault. You are safe. In the woods of Faeda. With me."*

She managed, "G-Govek—"

A hand slapped over her mouth as another gripped her

arm. The sensation struck the confusion from her mind. The crisp scent of frost and clean air, the icy night breeze. She blinked rapidly. The ground below her was covered in blurry leaves and pine needles.

"Let her go, you fool!" The hands left her cold. It was *cold*.

It hadn't been cold in the vent.

She was so dizzy. Why was she so dizzy? And why were things blurry? What had these males tried to make her drink?

They'd gotten it in her *mouth*. "Y-you poisoned me?"

At Miranda's words, the two voices went silent.

She became acutely aware of the wetness on her top and chin. She scrubbed at her mouth with her dirty hands. The gritty mud was foul, but it covered the scent of the bitter liquid, and her mind cleared a little more.

"Let's *go*." One of the voices hissed, distorted by the hushed tone. She heard the stomping of their feet retreating into the brush, growing quieter with each passing second.

"You're just going to leave me here?" She tried to sit up, but she was still too damn dizzy. "Help me!"

She put her forehead to the cold, damp dirt, taking deep breaths. "Govek! *Please* . . . you said you'd be able to hear me."

What in the hell was going on? The disorientation was so sharp she wondered if she was in the woods at all, but one thing was very clear: she was not in a vault. She was not trapped in a vent.

And she'd gotten out of those agonizing memories on her own. It was stupid and irrational, but that little sliver of power gave her hope.

The seer had been *right*. She could *heal*.

The cracking of branches sounded, hard thuds hitting mud. Growing louder.

Someone was coming!

She let out a hard exhale that took some of her tension with it. Govek had heard her. She managed to get to her hands and knees. The effort was so enormous that she trembled from it.

"Are you alright?"

Her lungs seized. It wasn't Govek.

"What are you doing out here?"

She recognized this voice. It was the same one that had *just* been here.

They'd come back and were pretending like they hadn't known she was here? Why? It didn't make sense.

"Here, let me carry you back—"

"Don't touch me," Miranda snarled, ready to rip this male's eyes out if he came within striking distance. She looked up to his face, trying to force her blurry vision to return to normal.

"I only want to get you to the hall," the male said.

"If you touch me, I'll scream bloody murder and everyone in the clan will hear it," she snapped. She blinked rapidly, shook her head. Squinted. "*Wolvc.*"

"Uh . . . yes. Yes, I am. You can trust me."

"*I'm not going to trust the guy who did this to me,*" Miranda snarled, and Wolvc scampered away from her. She would have grinned if she hadn't been about to puke. "What the fuck is wrong with you? How dare you? Govek is going to *slaughter* you when he finds out."

"Miranda!"

That voice registered as clearly as one of the Rove Tree's crystalline leaves.

Maythra.

The older woman came to the edges of Miranda's vision, blurry but distinct. "Miranda, you've been attacked. You're confused."

"Attacked by *you.*"

"No, of course not. Let us help you."

"You must think I'm a complete idiot. I *heard* you. *All* of you." She hadn't. The voices had been garbled and male, but Maythra had shown up far too quickly for her *not* to be involved in this.

"I-I don't know what you mean, Miranda," Maythra managed, though the trembling in her voice betrayed her. "We found you here. Come, let my son carry you back to the hall."

"Your *son?*"

"Rogeth," Maythra replied. "Wolvc is here too, but since you aren't comfortable with him—"

"I'm not *comfortable* with either of them. Or you." Miranda's stomach churned, and she pressed her forehead back into the dirt, gasping. Using the clean, fresh scent of the fallen leaves to help clear her nausea. The cold prickled at her hands and knees as the damp soaked into her gown.

"Rogeth," Maythra whispered. "Get her. Wolvc, go in front to intercept him."

"How *bad* do you think my hearing . . . Intercept *who?*"

"Dear, you're delusional. Please, just let us help."

"You mean Govek, don't you?" Miranda's mind flitted around and put together the pieces. "You're *trying* to make him lose his temper."

"Miranda, we would never—"

"You want him to go crazy after seeing me hurt and attack in front of the clan," Miranda said, surprised by how quickly all the pieces fell into place despite how dizzy she felt. "You *want* him to be despised by them."

"Miranda, you don't *know* him. He has *earned* his reputation all on his own."

"Sure, on his own, with a lot of help from *you*." Miranda rose to a crouch, rage giving her strength. "*You* cut up those animals, didn't you?"

Maythra's voice was laced with genuine confusion. "What *animals*?"

"The animals Govek hunts. The animals that everyone says he *tortured* when he didn't."

"He does torture them." It was Rogeth who stepped forward now. "I'm the best butcher in this clan and even I can barely save them."

"If you were really the best butcher, you would know that those wounds were made *after the animal was already dead.*"

Rogeth fell silent.

"Why would you *do* this? Create such an elaborate rouse? What could you possibly hope to gain by making Govek seem like a *monster*?"

"He *is* a monster. They'll all remember after this," Maythra said, her slender body trembling.

"Remember?" Miranda managed, bile rising in her throat.

"Yes, *remember,*" Maythra raged. "You've been distracting him with your vile cunt, letting the clan *forget* what he is. Letting them think that perhaps with you at his side, he might be manageable, but *I* know the truth. I know that there is no controlling that *monster.*"

Miranda's head swirled and her vision went blurry again. Fuck, how long was this stuff going to *last*? "You *drugged* me. You're crazy." Another thought punctured. "How long have you been framing him?"

"I *never.* He has done *all* of it!" Maythra screamed, her voice so high and shrill that the two young orcs backed up a step. "Every last fucking thing! He's been vile since *birth.*"

"From birth?" Miranda sucked air between her teeth to quell her nausea. "What do you mean?"

"Corine knew it. She *felt* it when he was still in her womb. He's the reason she abandoned us all." Maythra actually began to cry.

"You . . . you think *Govek* is the reason his mother left." Her heart seized.

"Of course, he is. She would never have abandoned her *mate* or young Tavggol," Maythra said between growing sobs. "She loved them with every fiber of her being, and then *Govek* was conceived, and *everything* changed."

Miranda shook her head. The forest was growing clearer. "You really think an *infant* could drive their parent away?"

Maythra scrubbed at her eyes. "You weren't *here*, you don't *know*. You didn't see it. Corine was my closest friend. And she could not even tell *me* the whole truth of it."

"What did she tell you then?" Miranda asked carefully.

"*Nothing*," Maythra exclaimed. "She only looked pained and conflicted, and I thought it was just a rough pregnancy and then she came to us in the dead of night immediately following the birth and begged my Zayvor, my *mate,* for his aid. To be her guide back to Estwill."

"She wanted to leave after the birth? Could something have happened immediately *before*?"

Maythra's face contorted with rage again. "Our chief had *nothing* to do with his mate's betrayal! He is a good, strong, elegant leader, and Corine abused him terribly! Why, he told me that by the end she wouldn't even *look* at him."

That was enough of an answer on its own. She glanced at the two orcs who had edged to the outskirts of the clearing. Neither of them would meet her eye.

"And then they were *gone*," Maythra sobbed. "I never saw either alive again. Only days after orc warriors found my Zayvor in the woods in bloody *pieces* and Corine had disappeared. This clan has never been the same. My Zayvor was the strongest male in the Rove Woods. His magic rivaled that of even our great chief."

Miranda's stomach dropped with pity even through the nausea, even as logic gripped her. "But how could you blame *Govek* for that? It's more Estwill's fault than his. He was just a baby."

"How can you believe that? If he hadn't been born, they never would have left!"

This woman was a slave to her own grief. There was no logic with her. "I am sorry for your loss. Truly." She glanced at Rogeth. "And you, too. It must have been horrible to lose your father like that."

Rogeth flinched. "He . . . wasn't . . ."

Miranda blinked in confusion, though she realized Rogeth was far too young to have been born around that time. He was younger than Govek.

"I have honored their legacy. By raising the babes of this clan whose mothers refused to do the duty. I alone take on the role the conquests of Oakwall Village abandoned. I am *mother* to this entire clan," Maythra said haughtily, as if the original agreement between conquests and orcs wasn't for the male to raise the babe on his own.

Before Miranda could even think of how to respond, the

thundering sound of feet and the cracking of branches sounded in the distance. Getting closer.

"He's coming!" Wolvc yelled as Rogeth's still blurry form took shelter behind him. Coward.

"No!" Maythra screamed, as Miranda got to her feet. "It must be in the hall! We have no witnesses!"

Too bad, Miranda thought as Govek's brutal, hulking form burst through the underbrush and hurtled into the clearing.

He skated to a halt and the sight of him took Miranda's breath away.

He was gone. His eyes were glassy pricks, glowing in the darkness. His breathing was labored and his muscles were bunched, ready to spring into action. His fists were tight, ready to swing.

His gaze landed on Miranda, piercing her right through. She froze and her rational thoughts winked out. He looked like he was ready to rain pure carnage down on them all.

And she wanted to let him.

That single moment of hesitation was enough permission for Govek. He ripped his eyes away from her, found Wolvc, and slammed into him. The young male barely had time to flinch before Govek's fist connected with his jaw.

The crack ricocheted off the trees and reverberated all the way up Miranda's spine. Blood exploded from Wolvc's mouth as he fell. Govek followed him down and raised his fist again as Maythra screamed for help.

Miranda wanted to let Govek vent his fury and get revenge on her behalf, but it wasn't fair. He would regret this to the depths of his core just as he did everything else.

"You stole my mate."

Oh lordy, him and his fricking *voice*. Unfortunately, he seemed too far gone to notice Miranda at all. All his attention was focused on the male that cowered beneath him.

Govek hesitated and his grated words revealed why. *"I challenge you, Wolvc. Stand up and face me."*

Wolvc coughed and choked. Unable to get up. He only held up his hands to fend Govek off. "I—yi—" The sound came out garbled and strange. His jaw hung oddly loose. "Y-yield."

Govek's face contorted and Miranda's heart fell right out of her chest.

His fist rose, tightened, muscles bunched. *"I'm not fucking done."*

He would kill him.

Miranda lost every sense of reason she had and rushed in. She grabbed the fist that was in the air and yanked it to her mouth. Govek's attention snapped to her and adrenaline spiked down her spine. He was so terrifying, but the surprise loosened his muscles enough for her to pull his fist down and unclench his hand. She extended his finger, drew it to her mouth, and licked from his knuckle to the tip of his claw.

Everything seemed to go still, from the males, to Maythra, to the wind in the trees. But most importantly, *Govek* froze.

His mask of blind rage fell from his face and something closer to complete disbelief settled over his features.

"What the fuck?" Rogeth said and almost gained back Govek's attention.

She sucked his finger into her mouth. She kissed and licked him carefully, trying not to cut herself on the sharp edge of his claw. The taste of salt and burned wood washed over her tongue.

Govek's eyes bulged, and he shivered. *"Miranda."* His hand twitched as if trying to get it away from her. *"Not safe."*

"Is that so?" she asked softly around his digit.

"Miranda!"

It was Maythra who called for her this time. For fuck's sake, had she really not given up? Her two orcs were retreating. Rogeth supported Wolvc's weight as they loped through the woods.

Miranda glowered at the woman. "Fuck off, Maythra. He's not gonna go crazy. Except for my *cunt*, of course."

Govek twitched, eyes wide as he slid his gaze between the two.

"He's a *beast*, Miranda." Maythra balled her skirts in her fists. "One way or another, we will—"

The threat made Govek tense again, but Miranda had no problem soothing him. She stroked his arms. Pushed for him to look at her instead of the vile woman. "Hey, tough guy."

He swallowed thickly and his eyes flickered over her.

"My tough guy." She continued to rub him. "I'm okay. See? I'm just fine."

He shuddered, almost made a move to step past her.

"They didn't hurt me," she said quickly. "But my stomach hurts. I feel sick. Can we go?"

"They grabbed you, Miranda."

"Yeah." She stroked up to his jaw. There was no denying it. She knew she smelled like them where they'd grabbed her arm and covered her mouth. "Yeah, they did.

And I want to get away from them. Let's just leave. Let's just find a quiet place to calm down. Okay?"

Govek growled, still undecided.

"Please, Govek?" Miranda murmured. "Please don't attack them. It would make me upset if you did."

His face twisted with anguish. It made guilt roll through her stomach. But still she pushed.

"I wouldn't like it if you attacked them. Can't we just let them be for now? Once you're calmed down, we can talk about what to do, okay?"

Govek took a deep, shivering breath and closed his eyes. Then he nodded.

"Why don't you pick me up, tough guy?" Miranda said. He lifted her before she'd even finished. "Let's go calm down. Together."

"Yes," Govek whispered, and Miranda touched her forehead to his, gently stroking her hands through his hair. He cradled her into his frame and began to walk away.

She only glanced back once to find Maythra still standing there, shaking and glowering, before she ran off to find the two other orcs.

CHAPTER

THREE

GOVEK

Govek's blood raced, his teeth gnashed, his heart pounded behind his eyes. His body felt too small to contain his rage, and he worried the force would break him apart at any moment.

His vision flashed with images. The scent wafting off Miranda was maddening. They had *put their hands on her*. They had touched his mate. He was going to rip them apart. He would sink his teeth deep into their flesh until their blood gushed against his tongue.

His stomach rolled, and he was certain he would vomit. The images wouldn't *stop*.

"Set me down here."

Miranda's voice cut through the fog but didn't clear it. He managed to get her safely to the forest floor before he curled in on himself, clenched his hands to his scalp as if the pressure might squeeze the thoughts from his mind.

"Govek?" Her soft hand tenderly stroked his arm,

leaving torrents of prickles in their wake. "Talk to me. What are you thinking?"

"Carnage," he managed between the rolling madness. His muscles bunched up with the longing to charge back toward the males and slaughter them. To paint the trees with their blood.

He sucked in a breath and Rogeth's stench overwhelmed him.

Fuck. She smelled so fucking—

"Govek—"

Her call ended in a yelp as he yanked her into his arms again, forced her to his chest. He needed to get that fucking scent off her or he would lose the last miserable scrap of his sanity.

It was the worst over her mouth. Rogeth's pungent odor lingered on her lips. His shaking increased as he lowered his head to her.

He couldn't wait to give her a bath.

He slanted his mouth over hers and sucked at her lips, laved his tongue over her. He drank down Rogeth's tainted, bitter musk and replaced it with his own.

It worked too blasted well. Miranda moaned against him and returned the kiss with gusto. She squirmed against his body as he pressed her into the tree. She must have thought he was trying to woo her, because she kept tempting his tongue into dueling. Distracting him from his goal of removing the scent from her flesh. It was on her cheeks too, down under her chin, near her neck.

Only when he broke away to lick across her cheek did she manage breathlessly, "What are you *doing*?"

"Marking," he snarled, and *fuck*, this wasn't the kind of mark he wanted. His body buzzed with need. He longed to

drag his fangs across her neck and sink them into her flesh, brand her fragile skin with his bite. Force a mark upon her that could never be undone. The instinct was strong, vivid, *alive.*

Like it had been all those moons ago with Yerina.

He pushed the bitter memories from his mind and concentrated on Miranda. On kissing her tender lips. On making her tremble and squirm.

"Govek, hold on." She splayed her fingers through his hair, turned her head away so she could speak. He laved his tongue over her cheek in response, and she let out a little whimper of pleasure that shot right through him. "Govek, wait. We need to get to the hall."

The hall? *Fuck* that. He'd just escaped from his father's clutches. He would not be going back.

"Govek, we need to head off Maythra before she tells everyone lies about what happened."

Fury swarmed his mind until he felt like his limbs were buzzing. He pulled back to search her face. "What did they do to you?"

Her eyes went huge, but she didn't hesitate. "They were trying to frame you. They wanted to get me back to the hall so you'd see me with them and attack. I think they thought this would force Karthoc to rescind his order to make you the chief."

"No," he snapped. "What did they *do to you*?"

Her brow furrowed with confusion until he reached up to touch her face. "They . . . they threw some kind of liquid on my face that made me feel dizzy and disoriented."

"You *smell* of them, Miranda. *They touched you.*"

"They only touched me briefly to silence me. Just once on my face and arm."

The confirmation only made it worse. He slunk back from her, his anger raging like an inferno.

"Govek, hold on." She stepped closer.

"*Go,*" he rasped. The word felt like jagged glass tearing up his throat. He wrenched away from her so fast his head spun and he actually staggered. He went to his knees in the harsh icy dirt. The wet chill soaked into his pants and cooled his heated flesh. He needed to calm, *calm*—

"I'm not safe. *I'm not in control.*"

"Govek—"

"*Go!*"

Her breath hitched.

Fuck, *fuck*! He'd scared her. He'd ruined this. She really would abandon him now.

But she didn't. Instead, she came around to face him and leaned down close. She reached out to hold his shoulders firmly in her warm grasp.

Fuck, Rogeth's scent on her face was still there, right under her chin. His eyes fixed to the spot.

"I'm not going, Govek." Her words were clipped. "If we're going to survive, it will have to be *through* this. You can't control yourself forever."

The agony of that truth rippled over him and cooled the rage with his sorrow. She was right. He couldn't control himself. He didn't deserve to have a mate.

"Govek, look at me."

He couldn't. He couldn't face losing her.

"Look at me."

The demand from his mate couldn't be denied, and he snapped his gaze to hers. His mind raced as he braced himself against the emotions she would be feeling. Terror, disappointment, disgust . . .

But looking up, all he saw was . . . determination?

He searched her features. He was still breathing hard, still buzzing with need, and still on the brink of losing his Fades-blasted *mind*.

"I know *exactly* what you are, Govek." Her voice hit him like the swing of a fist to his gut. "I know you are an orc. I know your magic is fueled by your emotions and you're having a lot of bad ones right now. I know you've lost control and done horrible things that rack you with guilt."

He bowed his head, eyes prickling.

Warmth cupped his cheeks as she used her hands to bring his face up. Forced him to meet her eyes. She stroked her fingertips along his jaw. The soft pad of her thumb soothed over his lips. She caressed the crook in his nose, his tusks.

He shivered under the force of her generous touches. His mind reeled to that not-so-distant day in the outer woods where she'd examined him, learned his features.

Her eyes were so gentle and warm and *giving*. She held his gaze as she pressed her thumbs into the hinge of his jaw. Her stare burrowed deep into him. She wasn't learning his features this time. She was learning his *soul*.

And he could hardly stand it. It cracked his defenses apart, shattered him with the same force he'd used to shatter the table in the hall.

He could do nothing but crumble.

He leaned into her embrace, tucked his head into her chest as she bent down to hold him, soaking up her warmth, her light, listening to the beat of her heart as it thundered in his ear. Her scent—sweet, clean honey drenched in sunlight —flooded him.

He was drenched in that light too. It was so kind and gentle and *consuming.* It drowned out the burning blaze the Fades used. Her sunlight flooded his magical energy until it started to ease away.

"I have you, Govek," she whispered into his ear. "I have you. I'm not going to let you go. I will always be by your side. I will always defend you and support you, just as *you* have always defended and supported me."

Fuck, his guts twisted, and his voice was so thick he barely managed, "I couldn't protect you from them. From Wolvc and Rogeth and *all of them.*"

"You *did,* Govek." She wrapped her arms around his head, his face nestled firmly into the warmth of her chest, and he went boneless. "You made it to me in time. You heard me call, and you came. You did *everything* right."

He let out a half sob, half laugh that made his frame shudder against Miranda and she tucked her cheek into his hair. Grounded him. Soothed him.

The tide of emotions ebbed. The light of the Fades was replaced with her. Miranda.

"We're going to get through this." She stroked his hair, running her hands down his back. "Together. I promise."

CHAPTER

FOUR

"I am sorry, Miranda."

Govek's eyes were red rimmed, and his cheeks were damp as he kneeled before her.

He was past the storm, but still needed support. Her chest felt tight and hot and so *full*. He'd given her so much when she had fallen apart in the past, and now she could do the same for him.

"You have absolutely nothing to apologize for." She rustled his hair as he got to his feet. "What just happened to us was . . ."

The bitter, sweet scent of the horrible tincture caught her again and made her a little dizzy. The reminder of what had happened with Maythra lodged in her stomach. She looked down at her bodice to the wet spot at her neckline where the red discoloration revealed the extent that the woman and her cronies had gone to destroy this male she adored so much.

Rage spiked in her gut, and she clenched her jaw.

"We will get you to a bath now," he said quietly, his eyes on the stain.

But she shook her head, determined. "No. I don't want to wash away the evidence."

"Evidence?"

"Maythra and those orcs aren't going to get away with trying to frame you."

His face went flat. "Miranda. We shouldn't bother."

She blinked. "We what?"

"It isn't worth it. No one will listen, and it will only lead to more frustration and anger. Believe me, I have been through this before."

She couldn't tell if her stomach was churning more from fury or sorrow. "Govek, I know no one has been on your side in the past, and I'm so *so* sorry you had to go through that alone, but you have me now. Next to you. Supporting you."

He shook his head. "You cannot get your hopes up—"

"Look, you might be able to put it behind you, and I commend your ability to let things go, but I'm not like that. They *attacked* me, Govek. I want justice. They aren't going to get away with this shit."

"In the morning then—"

"No. Right now. Morning will be too late. It will give Maythra the whole night to spin whatever story she wants."

"That doesn't matter."

"It *does*," she insisted. "Time *does* matter, Govek. We need to get to them before they draw their own conclusions. *Please*."

He growled low, threatening, but she crossed her arms and narrowed her eyes until he finally said, "Fine."

Her irritation soothed and the tremor in his voice caught

her. She tugged him into a tight hug, gave him a gentle kiss, and scratched her hands along his scalp to the nape of his neck.

She would have her justice. And Govek's too. And with it would come . . .

The seer's words flooded her mind.

"You want to spark your healing. That's what you need to do."

She would heal, and then she would find her babies. "Are you ready, Govek?"

He sighed heavily and opened his eyes to meet hers. "Yes. I'm ready."

She smiled and turned quickly to search the woods and find the lantern light that would guide their way back to the path.

Too quickly.

Her vision swam, spinning, lurching. Her stomach rolled, her skin went clammy, and bile rose up in the back of her throat.

She staggered, leaned forward, and vomited onto the icy forest floor.

"Ah, fuck! Miranda!" Govek rushed to her side. His hot hands soothed her back and gently stroked the nape of her neck as he pulled back her hair.

She spat and rose up slowly, taking deep breaths of the crisp night air. Even in the dark she could see the orange leaves glittering from frost. Their edges tinged with ice crystals.

At least until her vision blurred and her head spun, and her stomach threatened to bring up everything else it had in it.

"We will return home, Miranda." His tone left no room for argument.

But she argued anyway. "No. The hall."

"You are *ill*. We need to get you back to where you can rest. Then I will fetch Hovget for you."

"No." Her tongue tasted awful. "That's too long. We have to beat Maythra."

If they even could. Maythra was probably already at the hall telling everyone that Govek was an uncontrollable monster. Saying he had come out of nowhere and attacked Wolvc for fun.

The vile woman would not get away with this.

She would have her justice even if she threw up the entire way there.

She couldn't get justice for the ruin of Earth, but she could get it for this.

Is . . . is that what the seer had meant when he said this would spark her healing? If she got justice for what happened with Maythra, she could use the relief of that victory to help ease her grief long enough to dredge.

"Miranda."

His tight voice brought her out of her head and into the woods. The darkness and stillness of the incoming winter swirled around her. "Let's get to the hall. I'm fine."

She wasn't. He knew that, and so did she.

"But you're *hurting*, Miranda." His voice was a low rumble. His skin was fire against her fingertips. "You're ill. I ask only that you consider logic. Your gown will still be tainted in the morning. Maythra's tales will be told whether you confront the clan now or not."

"Govek, if you don't want to go to the hall, that's fine, I understand. But I'm going," she said firmly.

A muscle in his jaw ticked, his body went stiff as his fists balled. He wanted to fight her. She could read it all over his face.

But then he looked down and he sagged. "All right. I will go with you."

"Thank you." She exhaled with relief.

"Can I carry you there?"

"Absolutely you can." She'd barely gotten the words out when he swung her up into his arms and began to walk through the woods. The warmth of his skin was so starkly contrasted against the chill of the night.

"Govek has his arms so far open it's no wonder you fall into them at every opportunity."

The seer was right about that. Govek was like a rock for her—stable, comforting, and calm. He helped her see reason when all she wanted to do was barrel headfirst into the unknown. He dragged her back to sanity whenever the horrors from Earth caught up with her.

"I think you're too good for me," she said into his neck.

He snorted with disbelief. "You must truly be delusional."

They'd just made it to the path. The lamplight illuminated Govek's features and dappled his green skin. The firm set of his jaw. The slight crook in his nose. The wind rustled the trees above, sending a rainfall of orange leaves around them.

"Thank you, Govek," she said softly.

He stopped walking to search her face. "For calling you delusional?"

She chuckled. "For everything. You've done so much for me I'm gonna have to spend the rest of my life and probably a good portion of my afterlife paying you back."

He sucked in a slight breath, his chest puffing out against her frame. She blinked as his face slacked and a smile played at his lips. "Do you mean that?"

Her heart began to hammer. Dang, he looked so good when he smiled. His happiness made the whole world light up. The torchlight backlit him, coloring up his dark green hair like a halo, illuminating his features, softening his eyes.

She leaned in to kiss him.

"There he is!"

Miranda whirled and found five orcs rushing toward them. All had masks of fury written on their green faces. Tall, tense, fists bunched as if ready to fight.

None of them had anywhere near the muscle Govek did, but the one in the lead had more than the others and Miranda recognized him by his strong jaw and steely eyes in a gut-clenching instant.

Agol. Wolvc's father.

"Govek," Agol snarled as soon as they were within hearing distance. Govek gripped Miranda tight and his claws slunk out against her dress. "You will come with us to the hall. Now."

"This is about Wolvc attacking me, isn't it?" She couldn't imagine the guy was in very good condition right now. His jaw had been mangled.

But he'd deserved it.

"*You* attacked *him*," Agol said so low and deadly it shot up Miranda's back like lightning. "Maythra has told us everything. You will come with us *now*."

Agol had a right to be furious, but Miranda still bristled. "She clearly left out some important details. Govek attacked because Wolvc was attacking *me*."

One of the backup orcs scoffed loudly. "He was attacking *you*?"

"Yes," Miranda said. "Both he and Rogeth drugged me with something while I was in the woods."

"That isn't what Maythra is saying," Agol said.

"I'm sure," Miranda said dryly. "What she's saying is lies."

One of the orcs she didn't recognize snapped harshly, "Who are you to call our eldest woman a liar?"

Govek growled low and threatening.

"Unhand her!" Another orc stepped forward like he would try to take her by force. Govek's growl turned to a snarl.

"Don't you *dare* touch me!" Miranda glowered at the male and, surprisingly, he stopped. "I've been manhandled by enough orcs tonight." She turned to Govek. "Let's go, Govek. You can carry me all the way there, just like we planned."

Govek's face contorted, his throat worked, and his eyes flickered.

And then he nodded.

Miranda breathed a sigh of relief and stroked the back of Govek's neck before looking at Agol. "All right, it's settled. So, let's go."

CHAPTER

FIVE

"Wolvc, Rogeth, and Maythra came upon Govek attacking Miranda in the woods."

Agol's testimony rang through the hall and made Govek's head roar. His skin blistered, and his claws dug deep into his palms.

The hall was deadly silent. The three long tables were filled with over a hundred Rove Wood orcs. All of whom kept their glares firmly on Govek. The roasting fires burned hot, heating the room to dizzying temperatures. And the crystalline leaves of the Great Rove Tree they were within reflected the scene below.

He was surrounded. There was no escape.

Miranda made a loud scoffing noise that drew the attention of most, but she seemed unperturbed by the skewering of the male eyes. Her hair was wild, her clothes were rumpled and damp, and there was a smudge of dirt on her forehead that Govek longed to wipe away.

She was breathtaking. Her eyes mirrored wisdom beyond her years. Her back was set straight with determination. She narrowed her sharp gaze on Agol.

"That is the truth my son and Rogeth told to me," Agol said in the face of Miranda's disbelief. He towered over her from where he stood atop Chief Ergoth's wooden platform, but Miranda met his eyes nonetheless. "That is what Maythra said."

"I'm sure she did." Miranda waved her hand as if batting off the topic. "And she was lying."

Her argument caused whispers to roll through the clan.

"You've been doused with vorial herb. You don't know *what* happened to you."

"So, you're discounting my word now? I don't even get to tell my side of the story?"

"No one is saying that." Govek's father stepped into the fray, his hair in a tight, neat queue. His violet robes perfectly fitted. His expression was easy, ready to take on this great matter with his usual grace.

He'd been raging at Govek just a few moments prior. Demanding he stay and atone for the atrocity of splintering the table, which was still smoking. Govek could see the black, spiderweb like cracks from where he stood. He shivered.

And Miranda tightened her hold on his hand.

Chief Ergoth stepped in front of Agol on the platform. He and Miranda stood below, craning their necks to see them.

"Miranda, I vow you will get to speak your side once Agol is done. My clan, please remain calm. Sythcol, will you release more clearing?" Chief Ergoth appeared regal and calm. All traces of the drink that had once addled his mind were gone.

Govek's stomach twisted as the lead conjurer picked up his work again. Sythcol sat at a small table near the platform, surrounded by shelves of herbs and tinctures. His black hands moved gracefully over a wooden bowl of incense as he swirled the smoke up and cast the familiar scent of copal into the air. The smoke spiraled up into the leaves of the Rove Tree and disappeared.

The clearing magic whispered in Govek's veins. It swirled up his thoughts and a sense of calm descended heavily in his mind.

His hand tightened around Miranda's and he soaked up her warmth. Her support was sweet and strong. It flattened out his anger like a heavy leather hide smothered out flames.

She offered better aid than the clearing ever had.

"Please, Agol, go on," Ergoth said.

"They came upon Govek attacking Miranda. She'd been drugged with vorial and was mostly unconscious. Wolvc and Rogeth rushed to aid her, but Govek intercepted before they could reach her side. Govek struck my son with a magic-laced punch to the jaw that has splintered the bone. Hovget is yet unsure if it can be mended."

Govek went so cold, he thought he might lose his feet.

Wolvc may *lose his jaw*.

He was a fucking *beast*. An abomination of the Fades—

"Oh wow."

Govek blinked toward Miranda, who only appeared wryly amused by these vicious truths. She shook her head as if in disbelief.

But what was there not to believe? He *had* struck Wolvc. He *had* destroyed the young male's jaw. He *had* infused his brutal strength with magic to make the blow more deadly.

"They were forced to retreat and raced to find Hovget at his healing house. Wolvc is there now, and his outlook is grim." Agol's fury blazed down Govek's spine as their eyes met for the split of a moment.

The angry voices in the clan rose again, grumbling talk of what to do with Govek now, of how to handle this new atrocity he had committed, of how dangerous and vile he was, of removing Miranda from his side.

His teeth gnashed and his blood pulsed hot in his head.

"Govek." Miranda's murmur caught him up, and he managed a breath.

She gave his hand a quick squeeze before speaking loudly. "That is *not* what happened."

"You may now speak your side, Miranda," Ergoth said before raising his hand toward Sythcol. The lead conjurer doubled his efforts, and Govek almost coughed as a plume of copal swallowed up his head.

His anger dulled and his senses dimmed. He sucked in the clearing, using the magical smoke to quell his fury, to soothe his emotions, and help him to concentrate—as it was meant to do.

It took a moment for him to realize that Miranda had gone up onto the platform. She stood at the edge, so beautiful it made his chest tight. Her brown waves of hair flowed down her back; her hazelnut eyes flashed to him before looking to the orcs behind him.

"I was speaking with the seer in the woods when———"

"Hold a moment," Chief Ergoth said. "You spoke with seer Evythiken? When?"

"Earlier this evening, right before Maythra attacked me," Miranda said.

"But the seer is not here. How long ago was this exactly?"

"He was in the woods only a few minutes before Maythra attacked."

"Minutes? What is a minute?" Chief Ergoth asked. "And you saw the seer in the *woods*? At this time of the eve?"

"Yes, I *did* see him. And talked to him. And a minute is . . . it's a measure of time. It's just a few moments." Miranda glanced to Govek, clearly struggling, but he had trouble finding the words to help her explain.

"Miranda, the seer is *unwell*. He does not go out at night. Are you *certain* that is what you saw?"

"*Yes,* I am one hundred percent certain that I talked to the seer."

"One hundred . . . *percent*?" Chief Ergoth glanced toward the clan as if looking for someone to explain. "You aren't quite making sense, Miranda. Perhaps we should leave your account to when the vorial has worn off. I believe the herb has muddled your mind."

"My mind is *fine*. I want to speak," Miranda insisted.

"Of course, I would never seek to silence you."

The door to the hall opened. The sound was muffled to Govek's ear. Slightly distorted. The copal caught him as he turned his gaze and found Wellia had entered and was hurrying to the platform.

"Ah! Wellia, please, come up and examine Miranda. We won't keep you. I'm sure your mate needs your aid while he is mending Wolvc. Can you tell us if vorial was what drugged her?"

Miranda nodded. "Sure, yeah. Come look."

Wellia went up the steps and over to her. Her curly hair bouncing, her dark eyes alight with concern. She looked into Miranda's eyes a moment, leaned in to smell.

"Yes, you were drugged with vorial." Wellia's tone was gentle, and it smoothed Govek's battered senses. Thank the Fades, Miranda was finally getting aid. "Are you woozy or disoriented?"

"It's not too bad since I vomited."

"Disoriented?" Chief Ergoth cut in. "What kind of disorientation?"

"Vorial is usually a sleeping aid, so sometimes, in extreme cases, it can blur between our dreams and the waking world and make us see things that aren't there," Wellia explained, taking Miranda's chin gently in her palm and looking over her lips. "Can you open your mouth so I can check your gums?"

Miranda did so without hesitation.

"It can make one see things that are not there. Miranda, about the *seer*—"

An icy chill fell over Govek.

"What are you saying? That I imagined talking to him?" Miranda jerked her chin out of Wellia's grip. "I spoke to him *before* I was drugged. Bring him here and ask him."

"Calm, please," Ergoth said quietly. "I did not mean to upset you. I am only seeking to understand. To help us *all* understand. You were drugged in the hall, so everything you heard and saw after you left might be distorted."

"I wasn't drugged in the hall. They threw the drug on me after I spoke with the seer in the woods."

The clipped nature of Miranda's voice registered. She was upset. He should do something, but the clearing was so strong that Govek struggled to fight it off.

"You said you felt better now that you have vomited. Does that not mean you ingested the drug?" Ergoth asked, looking between her and Wellia.

Wellia stayed quiet, but her expression spoke volumes.

"You came here together," Chief Ergoth said. "He was the only one, aside from yourself, to touch your food, was he not?"

"He . . . he was, but my *food* wasn't drugged. Wolvc and Rogeth threw the tincture on me. That's how it got on my dress. I only ate a few bites of my food, so it couldn't have been in that."

"Then why did vomiting help your symptoms?" Chief Ergoth asked.

"It . . . I mean, some got on my lip," Miranda sputtered. "Govek couldn't have drugged me. He was with *you*. Right before he came to save me, Govek was here with you in the hall."

"Govek left the hall in a rush quite a while ago."

The copal swirled high into Govek's mind, as he tried to make sense of the timeline.

"We all saw him leave, didn't we?" Ergoth addressed the clan and many voices rose to confirm.

"B-but—but that's not right. It wasn't that long ago at all. It couldn't have been. *I* only left the hall a few minutes ago."

"I ask again Miranda, what is a minute?"

"Govek," Miranda said, and her tone cut through the clearing. She sounded lost. Confused. Her face was pale, and her eyes were desperate.

He fought against the copal but could not find his voice or move from his place.

"Look." Miranda turned back to Chief Ergoth. "I got

some of it in my mouth because they threw it all over me. Here, see, I still have some on my dress."

Wellia bent close to Miranda's chest. "There is some here, yes."

"What?" Ergoth's clipped tone betrayed his tension, but his face was still a congenial mask. "Let me see."

Ergoth got far too close to Miranda, near to her breasts. Govek began to blister all over again.

"It's just here." Miranda pointed to the splotch on the front of her gown. "Right in this area."

"I don't see . . ." Chief Ergoth reached out and placed a hand on Miranda's hip.

His woman jumped in surprise.

Govek's rage *exploded*. Light burst behind his eyes, and he broke from the clearing.

He charged to the platform and leaped up, pounding the wood slats so hard they shook beneath his feet.

The clan began to rage.

"Govek, *control*—" His father snapped, but Govek had already snatched Miranda away from all of them, caging her close. "Agol, help her!"

"Stay away from her," Govek snarled, tightening his hold. Miranda's warmth radiated through his muddled mind.

"Unhand her, Govek!" Agol demanded.

"Don't you dare."

Miranda's snap quieted the hall and made Govek shiver. She clung to his arm, stroking his cheek. He sucked in a deep breath of her honeyed bliss.

"It's okay, tough guy," she said. "Just stay here by me. We'll get through this."

He sighed heavily into her hair, the clearing calming him much faster than he usually would.

"Govek . . . what's *wrong* with you?" she whispered.

"Miranda, he isn't safe," Chief Ergoth said.

"I decide what's safe."

"He was the one who drugged you!" Agol said loudly, and the clan began to clamor again.

"I've heard enough," Chief Ergoth said. "In light of my son's lack of control, I have no choice but to confine him until a judgment can be held."

Govek went cold.

"Confine him?" Miranda looked between his face and his fathers.

"Govek will be held in magical quiet beneath the Rove Tree. Govek, go with Agol and Sythcol. Do not fight this."

Fuck *fuck*. He wanted so badly to fight, but his rage had soothed, and the clearing magic had his mind muddled and compliant. Copal swirled in his nose and his arms around his mate loosened.

"Govek, *no,* don't you dare. Ergoth, he hasn't done anything wrong. You can't just lock him up like this."

"No matter the circumstances, he *did* attack a member of this clan," Chief Ergoth said, and Miranda tensed against him because that fact couldn't be denied.

He'd ruined Wolvc's jaw. *Fuck.*

"Govek, *please*," Miranda whispered to him.

What could he do? He could not fight this. It was the way of the clan. At least Miranda would be safe from him.

"I must. I cannot fight them. It will only make things worse."

"Govek, *what is wrong with you?*" She searched his face, and his mind blistered with confusion.

She'd asked that once already. *What was wrong with him?* She wasn't making sense.

The vorial really must have had her completely muddle up.

"Wellia," he said thickly. "I ask that you care for her."

"Of course."

"Govek, *stop* it. This isn't right."

But it had to be. It was the only thing that made sense. He leaned in, sucking in her scent one last time and nearly coughed on Rogeth's pungent odor. "She smells of him."

The words escaped him before he knew they were coming. The copal scent faded as the reminder that Rogeth had *touched his mate* slammed through him. Fury burst through him all over again.

"She smells of him?" Agol's voice was quiet, but punctuated further through the cloud.

"Govek, I smell nothing," Chief Ergoth said. "And my decision is final. Agol take him."

"Rogeth *did* touch me! He covered my mouth when I tried to scream for Govek's help!"

A wave of whispers rolled over the clan, spilling into Govek's senses. Rogeth had touched his mate. *He had touched her.*

"Allow me to scent her."

Agol's request shot lightning down Govek's spine. He looked into the males appealing face. His determined brow was creased from many seasons of stress being the lead guard.

His job was not an easy one, and Govek had made it even more difficult. But despite that, Agol had never treated Govek badly and had only ever followed Chief Ergoth's orders.

For that reason alone, Govek let Miranda go, allowing Agol to approach.

"Agol, you do not need to go that far. It is unseemly to treat Miranda this way. She should have a bath and rest—"

But Agol ignored Govek's father and leaned in close to Miranda. Govek balled his fists and had to look away. Liquid warmth pooled in his palms.

"*She does smell of him*," Agol said, stepping away, eyes wide on Miranda in shock. "Rogeth *did* touch her."

The clan burst into chaos.

"Quiet!" Chief Ergoth nearly roared over them and Govek was shocked by his father's lack of control. "Sythcol, *more clearing*. I order you all to silence."

The clan fell to quiet, but it was more stunned at their leader's unusual outburst than from a result of the magical incense.

Govek dragged Miranda close again, leaned in, and used her scent to drown out everything. Including the clearing.

Miranda leaned against him in relief. "Don't you dare let yourself get locked up for this, Govek," she whispered.

"I'm sorry."

"He attacked a male of this clan," Chief Ergoth argued, loudly.

"He was *defending me*." Miranda straightened and looked toward the males seated with their human mates. All of them were huddled close together. "Would *you* want to be locked away for defending your mate? While the one who attacked her walked free?"

Govek held his breath, shock radiating through him as the orcs voiced their agreement with Miranda.

His father's face flattened; his eyes flashed in a way that made Govek go cold. "A *binding* then."

Govek's breath faltered.

"What's a binding?" Miranda glanced between them.

"A magic our own Sythcol created that prevents an orc from committing any acts of undue violence," Chief Ergoth answered.

"I remember . . . you told me about that." Miranda touched Govek's chest. "Govek?"

Govek clenched his jaw at the explanation. It made the spell sound so *simple*, but left out so many important details.

"Govek will be bound against all strife and violence. Unable to harm anyone or anything, unless, of course, they willingly *ask* to fight him," Chief Ergoth continued.

"What if someone attacks *him*?" Miranda asked.

Ergoth shot her an annoyed look. "You are new here, Miranda, so you do not know, but there are *none* here who would attack Govek without cause—"

"Would Govek be able to defend himself or not?"

Ergoth hesitated a moment before finally answering. "No. He would not. But, again, no one in this clan resorts to such violence."

"And yet Maythra attacked *me*," Miranda said low.

Ergoth's face twisted. "As *you* say."

"My chief, I do not think . . ."

Govek blinked toward where Sythcol was now standing before his worktable at the far left corner of the hall. His slender frame tense, his blackened hands clenched. His light green eyes flickered with uncertainty and his jaw was held tight.

"Sythcol, these are my orders."

"But we discussed—"

"These are extenuating circumstances," Ergoth said firmly. "Or are you going against the will of your chief?"

Sythcol, surprisingly, straightened his back. "You should

remember that the binding, when left in place for too long, causes *extreme* pain. It goes against my conscience to impose such a thing on another."

Govek blinked in the face of Sythcol's defense.

"Are you *serious*?" Miranda asked.

Rage flashed in Chief Ergoth's eyes when he looked toward Miranda, and Govek felt the urge to hide her behind his back. "In Govek's youth, when his magic and might were uncontrolled, we *were* forced to make difficult choices, but Govek has since recovered from the pain with no ill effects, correct?"

"Yes," Govek said, desperate to quell Miranda's worry. Far better to be bound then separated from her. "And it takes three or four days now before pain sets in. I have enough experience to stave it off."

"Stave it off?" Miranda's lip trembled slightly.

"All will be well, Miranda." He looked to his father. "I am willing to be bound."

"You see," Ergoth said, addressing Sythcol. "Govek has consented. Sythcol, step forward."

"You'll be doing the same to Rogeth, Wolvc, and Maythra, right?" Miranda asked then, her voice clipped. "It's only fair."

Sythcol looked stricken but before he could answer Ergoth said. "It will not work on Maythra, as the binding was not created for humans, but Rogeth and Wolvc will receive it."

His father's quick agreement, along with the slight grin on his face, had Govek unsettled. But before he could puzzle over why his father was so pleased with this, Sythcol was before him.

Sythcol came to stand before Govek and placed his blackened hands forward. "Are you . . . ready, Govek?"

Fuck, Govek had not had this magic forced upon him since he was in his late teens, before his second growth cycle. Sythcol was so much *smaller* than him. Nearly a whole head.

It was no wonder the male had created the binding. Govek was so much larger than any other orcs in Rove Wood.

He was a danger to them all.

"I am ready," Govek said low as he closed his eyes.

"Miranda, please stand away."

He felt her touch leave him and before long a tremendous heat bloomed in his chest. It spiraled embers down his limbs, blistered through his fingers and toes, erupted waves of heat in his mind.

Govek was burning alive, and he clenched his teeth at the familiar sensation. He would not shout. He would *not*.

The pain slowly ebbed and Govek forced it to the back of his mind, separated it away. Used the practiced skills from his youth to recover his senses.

He rolled his shoulders. The heat was down to a tingling warmth, and with enough concentration, it would barely simmer.

At least for now.

"I trust you will let me know if it becomes too much," Sythcol said and Govek's brow rose at the male's concern, but he nodded.

"Are you okay?" Miranda stroked his arm. The touch felt a bit raw but Govek would never refuse it.

"I am well," he assured his woman. "Rest will do me good."

"Then go, Govek," Ergoth said. "Tomorrow is the trade, so we will hold a full judgment on this matter day after tomorrow. All who wish to take part should be here after the morning meal. Spread the word. Now let us go to Rogeth and Wolvc. We will bind them now. Agol, lead the way."

Govek took Miranda's arm and let her lead him out into the icy chill of the night. It helped to cool the fire in his blood, the thundering in his heart, the confusion in his mind.

Sythcol had argued against the binding. Even though he'd been the one to invent it. Govek shook his head.

"Are you really okay?" Miranda asked softly. "Does it hurt?"

He glanced down at his beautiful woman, tension easing. "I am well, Miranda. It will be fine."

She nodded, soothed his arm. "Don't worry, Govek, we *will* get justice for this."

Govek tensed in the face of her conviction, unsettled and unsure how to respond.

"We *will* win."

He tucked her against his side and bustled her back to his home, but his thoughts were focused on one simple truth.

He had *never* won a judgment before.

CHAPTER

SIX

MIRANDA

G ovek leaned back in his chair at the kitchen table, eyes half-mast, mouth slack, stomach bulging. Light from morning was barely breaking through, and out the window she could see frost covered every leaf on the path.

"Woman, if you keep cooking like that, I'll grow too round to hunt," he said and such pleasure radiated through her that she abandoned the packing and went to his side.

He dragged her down to straddle his lap, and her skirt bunched up around her hips.

God, he felt good. He was so warm it made her muscles relax. The stretch of her thighs spread around his made her want to sink down into him. She wiggled closer.

"Careful with your tempting or we will be late," he grumbled even as he wrapped his massive hands around her waist and pulled her against him. She squirmed helplessly as need pooled between her legs. The want to drown out all her worries in him was darkly tempting.

But they couldn't.

"How long until they leave for the trade?" she asked.

"Not long." He loosened his hold on her as his expression tensed.

"Are . . . you sure you're feeling up to it?" she asked, probably for the thousandth time since they'd returned from the hall the night before, which earned her a deep scowl from him.

She couldn't help it. That binding looked *horrible*. Govek had shuddered all over. His breathing stopped and his face contorted.

"Couldn't you fight the binding off?" she asked softly. "The same way you fought off your father's hold on you last night."

He shifted under her, swallowing, "I . . . was only able to break out of my father's hold because I was so desperate to find you. My rage and terror built to a heinous peak allowing my magic to break the bind."

"Don't call your magic heinous, Govek," she said firmly.

He let out a huff. "Even if I *did*, what good would breaking free from the binding do? If anything, it would prompt my father and the clan to take further, more extreme, action."

Miranda sighed heavily. He was right. "I'm just worried about you. I don't want you to be in pain."

"You needn't worry." His eyes went soft and her heart fluttered. "I've long learned to work past the pain. I barely feel it now."

She brought her hands up to his face and smoothed out his brow with her fingertips, rubbing the hinge in his jaw till it slacked, caressing the slight break in his nose.

"How did you get this again?" she asked.

"From my trial into adulthood. It is a rite of passage for hunters in this clan." His voice was low and lazy as she continued to stroke his face. "I took down a wild boar on my own."

"You mean like a pig?"

"Yes. A very *big* one. An adult is one and a half times my current height and has pointed tusks that can skewer you through with a single shake of its head. They are one of the most difficult beasts to take down."

She shuddered. "Oh gosh, that's . . . terrifying." He snorted. "The other hunters must have been really impressed with you. How old were you?"

"Seventeen summers." He glanced away from her. "And . . . they would have been . . . had they still been here."

She tipped her head. "What do you mean?"

He shifted beneath her. "When I was eleven, most of the hunters relinquished that title. Those with apt skill left the Rove Woods to join the war efforts, and the few who stayed stepped into more . . . *suitable* roles."

"More suitable?"

"Fishing or trapping. Things that did not require the use of claws or teeth."

She stroked back his hair. "So you learned how to hunt on your own?"

He nodded. "Geblon, the lead hunter, had shown me a few things before he was sent to the war when I was fourteen. He taught me how to stalk large game and kill clean, told me of hunter traditions and ceremonies. I have worked to honor him since, respecting their ways and holding seasonal ceremonies on my own as best I can."

His saddened gaze was trained on the window, out into the woods. She crumbled and wrapped her arms around his neck, pulling him against her.

"So . . . they *abandoned* you?"

He stiffened against her. "They did what they had to for Faeda, and they worked hard to prepare me to take on the mantle of hunter before they left."

"Take on the mantle of hunter? So, you started hunting for the *entire* clan when you were fourteen?"

"Yes."

He said it so easily, like it wasn't any huge thing to be the sole hunter for a clan of three hundred orcs when you'd barely hit puberty.

She pressed her forehead against his, took a few deep breaths to quell the tightness in her throat and the prickling of her eyes.

They were all assholes. Every last one of them.

And the unfairness of the night before proved that. Everyone had turned against them. Not a single person wanted to listen to their side.

But she would make them listen. Her eyes trained to the little bag of evidence she'd collected for the judgment. The roll of parchment where she'd written down all her notes.

She'd show the whole clan that Govek wasn't the monster he'd been made out to be.

She'd get justice for this. For Govek *and* herself.

And once she did, the seer could dredge with her.

"It is time to leave for the trade, Miranda."

She pulled back and found him tense with worry. She rubbed his shoulders. "It's going to be all right, tough guy. You just gotta speak your peace to a couple people from Oakwall and I'm sure the truth of what happened between you and Yerina will get around on its own quick enough. Then we'll trade a few things, schmooze, and come on home."

"Sch…ooze… what?" He raised an eyebrow.

"Chit chat. Make friends."

"I don't see what that has to do with 'oozing.'"

She laughed. "Oh my god, Govek, *no,* it's *schmooze.*"

His eyes twinkled, and her stomach flipped over. She kissed his cheek, thankful beyond words he was mostly back to himself after last night.

"What exactly is the clearing?" She remembered how quiet and still everyone had gotten every time the pungent incense had flooded the room. The smell had been overwhelming, but it clearly had an altering effect on the orcs.

And it was not for the better.

He adjusted her slightly, sitting up. "It aids in concentration and maintains peace. You needn't worry. It will not affect you. Like bindings, Sythcol created it to only effect orcs."

"Aids in concentration . . ." she mused, thinking on how the air had felt so still and cold. "Is that really all it does?"

He gently removed her from his lap so he could stand. "Yes."

"Then how come you couldn't even talk?"

"Part of the magic stops outsiders from speaking their opinions. Only those with pertinent information are allowed to have a voice during judgments." He finished packing.

"But you *did* have pertinent information," she said, watching him work. "Do you use it for all judgments?"

"Yes, and some announcements as well. Likely my father would have used it for Karthoc's announcement had he known it was coming." He packed a water flask before tying his bag up tight. "The clearing also allows my brethren to draw conclusions easily. Once their minds are made up, they are *resound*." His voice grew low again and he wouldn't look at her. "*Nothing* can change their minds."

"That doesn't sound good," she said. "It sounds like that means people's opinions can be swayed based on who gets to speak first."

His fists balled up so tight his hands shook.

"Govek . . . who gets to speak first?"

"The parties who are wronged speak first."

So that meant he always went last?

Her heart ached for him, and she moved in to take his hand in hers. Trying to soothe it so he wouldn't cut himself.

He sighed heavily and relaxed. "We must go now, Miranda."

"Okay," she said, eyeing her little pile of evidence again.

Things *would* be different this time. She was the one who was harmed in this, so she would get to speak first.

She would get justice. For her *and* Govek. They would fight for this together. They *would* win.

"Miranda."

He stood at the door and propped it open for her to go through. She filled her lungs with the icy morning air and stepped out into the woods.

"All right then, let's go get our 'oozing' done," he said.

The bubble of turmoil popped in an instant and laughter burst out. "Oh my god, Govek, it's *schmooze*. You know what? No. Keep calling it ooze. I'd rather Oakwall think we're weirdos."

He snorted his agreement. They walked in silence for a

long while, feet crunching on the icy ground. The cold began to penetrate her cloak.

"Gosh dang, it's cold. So fricking cold. Why is Faeda so freaking *cold*?"

"It's near winter, Miranda."

"Well, why don't you hurry up and make it spring for me then?" She shot him a look while warming her fingers with her breath.

He swung his cloak out around her shoulders and yanked her into his heat.

The temperature under his cloak was at least twenty degrees higher, and she almost groaned with pleasure. "Oh wow. Okay, yeah, this is way better." She moved his arm around her back so she could curl into his side. Walking was a little awkward, but well worth it.

"I'm glad you approve." His voice was tinged with delight, but his face was still tense.

She pursed her lips and moved his hand up from her waist. "Plus, it has the added benefit of being able to cop a feel."

"Cop a what—?" He broke off in a choke as she pushed his hand to her boob. His fingers twitched, stroking her chest, and she shivered.

"We can get all naughty, and no one would ever know."

"I think they would know, Miranda," he said, though he didn't move his hand away.

"Even better. We can just let them be jealous." She paused in the stride to bring his hand up to her mouth and kissed his palm.

He melted, his tension finally ebbing as his lips quirked.

"*There's* that smile I've been looking for all morning." She beamed up at him, only to blink when his smile turned soft, gentle. There was a warmth in his eyes that took her breath away and her heart skipped.

"My son."

All sweetness vanished as Govek removed her from his cloak to face his father. The male looked extra regal today, with deep blue silk robes lined with gold trim. His long white hair had been braided intricately into patterns down the sides of his head and back. His expression was placid and easy, but there was a sharpness to his gold eyes. A cutting depth that made Miranda instantly uneasy.

The winter chill grew colder as Chief Ergoth approached. The trees groaned, and the leaves swirled around them like a cage.

"My son. I understand you would like to accompany Miranda to the trade, but it isn't appropriate after all that occurred last night." Chief Ergoth kept his eyes on Govek. "Rogeth, Wolvc, and Maythra have agreed to remain in their homes until the judgment tomorrow. I request you do the same."

Govek's grip on her tightened. "No."

"Govek." A deep sigh escaped the chief. "Be reasonable."

"I have your blasted binding, Father. That has always been enough in the past."

Ergoth's eyes darkened, and Miranda glanced behind him. There was a bend in the path, and she assumed that the party of orcs readying to go to the trade was waiting just beyond it.

Ergoth continued smoothly. "I've already told Oakwall you will be named chief before the next trade commences."

Miranda's gut twisted, and she snapped her eyes to Govek's face. His expression flattened. He'd told her already of his father's plan to make Govek a figurehead. Chief in name, but with no real authority. The power would remain with Ergoth.

They'd both agreed to let his father believe they were going along with this little plot. Who knew what Ergoth would do if he discovered they would let Karthoc merge Rove Wood Clan with Baelrok Forge?

Ergoth continued, "I also explained that, even through this change, I will be the one to maintain the trade. So Govek, you needn't push yourself in this. I know that the binding is a trial to hold."

"I am *fine*."

"Govek didn't do anything wrong," Miranda said. "And I want him to come to the trade with me. He shouldn't have to hide in his home like he's the guilty one."

Ergoth's eyes flashed, but it was so quick Miranda couldn't read it. "My dear, I apologize for how turbulent your arrival to our fair clan has been. I assure you that once Karthoc and his warriors have left our woods everything will return to normal, and you will settle in well here. But for now, please, allow me to assign you a different male to escort you today, so Govek can rest at home."

Miranda heard a low rumble from deep in Govek's chest and knew his anger was mounting. She stroked the back of his hand to soothe him.

"I've told you no so many times now, Chief Ergoth, and yet you still try to get me to be with another orc. For all your genial talk of fairness toward the women of your clan, it certainly doesn't feel that way."

Ergoth straightened and hid his hands in the long opulent robes. "I am truly remorseful you feel this way. I mean no disrespect. Of course, it is your *choice* to go with whoever makes you feel the most comfortable and I am only trying to find a solution that will ensure comfort for all within the clan, including Govek."

"I think Govek can speak for himself." Miranda looked up at him. His coloring was off and his face was tense. "Govek? Do *you* want to go home while I go to the trade by myself?"

"No." The word was clipped and instant.

Ergoth bowed slightly. "Then I concede."

Miranda blinked, flummoxed that it was such a quick reversal.

Then the chief said, almost absently, "I hope Yerina does not attend today's event."

Before she or Govek could think of a response, a booming voice sounded behind them.

"Good *morning* to you."

Karthoc. With what looked to be *most* of his fifty warriors.

Gosh, they were huge. About as tall as Govek, nearly as burly, with disheveled hair and rough strewn clothes and scars covering almost every inch of their bodies. Some were even missing ears or eyes.

Had they been invited to the trade? Miranda glanced up at Govek, but he appeared just as stunned as she felt.

"What are you doing here, Karthoc?" Ergoth snapped, his expression bitter with shock. "I thought we agreed your warriors would only come into the clan when invited."

Miranda rose her brows at Ergoth. Apparently, all his bluster about hospitality didn't extend to his own kin.

"Well, we *have* been invited. To the trade at least," Karthoc said with a grin that flashed his massive sharp teeth. None of his warriors tucked up their jaws like the Rove Wood Clan orcs did.

How would Oakwall respond to that? Had they seen warrior orcs like this before?

"W-What?" Chief Ergoth stammered. "You can't. I won't allow it. The peace with Oakwall is more important than your selfish *wants*, nephew."

Karthoc's grin only widened. "Well, it isn't *my* want you are speaking of now. But the want of *Oakwall*. They themselves have invited us."

Karthoc then pulled out a tiny piece of parchment with scribbled Faedish writing that Ergoth quickly snatched out of his hand.

Miranda glanced up at Govek, finding him tense, jaw tucked up, eyes stuck to the note. She stroked his arm to soothe him, though really, she wanted to know what was in the message just as bad as he did.

"I would like to speak to you in private, Karthoc," Ergoth said between clenched teeth, and Miranda blinked at the usually composed male's rapid shift into fury.

"Of course, dear uncle," the warlord said smoothly, a grin on his face as he followed Chief Ergoth away. His warriors continued to mingle on the path and watched their leaders casually.

One of them, huge and scarred with a deep gash in his neck, nodded to Govek and Govek returned the gesture before he gripped Miranda's elbow and turned her away.

"What was that about?" Miranda asked.

"That is Brovdir, my cousin. Karthoc's younger brother."

"No, no. I mean *Karthoc*. He's going to the trade? Did you know?"

Govek glanced at her before picking up the pace slightly. "I . . . knew that he *wanted* to attend the trade. I told him to seek aid from Viravia. I don't know how speaking with her could have resulted in him openly attending the trade, though."

"Hmm." Miranda glanced back. Ergoth was obviously livid, but Karthoc looked smug. "I guess your attendance isn't going to be the highlight after all."

Govek blinked, considering.

But before he could find a response, they had rounded the bend and the sight of fifty or more orcs making ready came into clear view.

There were massive carts piled high with baskets of vegetables and barrels of fish. Crates of tinctures were being loaded carefully into smaller two wheeled wagons. She couldn't see any animals that might pull them. No horses or elk.

The atmosphere was pleasantly busy as people bustled about. Everyone seemed to either be distracted by chatting or occupied with tasks. They hauled goods by hand, adjusted wooden wheels, stacked and organized crates made from twigs and branches.

Current day Faeda was almost like medieval Earth. Back before noxious fumes had broken down the atmosphere. When the sun wasn't so deadly, and the water wasn't so toxic. When animals could live freely without human intervention and plants didn't struggle to survive outside of farms and greenhouses.

Miranda's mood shifted; her chest ached.

"Miranda?"

She snapped out of her self-pity and gave Govek a reassuring smile. "I'm okay. Where do we go?"

"Let me see about finding you a cart to ride in," he said, glancing around.

"I don't see Viravia." Miranda searched the crowd of mostly green bodies.

"She wasn't able to make it today."

Miranda spun around and she came face to face with a woman right about her age with golden hair and a pinched nose. She wore a plain cotton gown and a thick wool cloak that was wrapped tight around something buried underneath. Something that appeared to be resting in a sling over the woman's shoulder.

Miranda's heart twisted.

The woman glanced at Govek hesitantly before saying, "I'm sorry for sneaking up on you. My name is Savili. My mate Iytier and I returned early from the seasonal communion when we heard from Viravia that you were here with Govek. She told me I should help you out today."

"Oh, uh . . ." Miranda said, still distracted by the bundle in her arms. "Govek can help me, but thank you for the offer."

"Oh, of course, Govek will help you. I'm certainly not saying he shouldn't," the woman said quickly. "I just wanted to be on friendly terms. Viravia said you've had a rather rough start to things."

That was certainly an understatement.

"I don't want to muck around where I'm unwanted." Savili bounced her bundle slightly. "I just wanted to welcome you to the clan, and let you know that not *everyone* is like Maythra."

"Well, thank you." Miranda wondered briefly if this new woman knew about everything that had happened the night before or if she only knew about the argument they'd had with Maythra outside Viravia's house.

But suddenly that little bundle was *cooing*, and that was all Miranda could think about.

"Uh, sorry, is that your baby?" Miranda's throat was tight.

Savili smiled. "Yes, this is Haysik." She pulled her cloak back and Miranda's heart skittered right on over itself.

The baby was likely the cutest thing Miranda had ever seen in her entire life. Chubby green cheeks, bright eyes, fuzzy dark hair, little pointed ears, and black nails.

A baby. An *orc* baby. Probably around ten months old, judging from what she could see. How long had it been since she'd held a baby? She'd mostly taken care of the toddler-aged kids but had covered the infant room enough times to be well practiced.

"Govek." The clipped voice came from an approaching orc. He was slender and tall, though not quite as tall as Govek. His hair, bound to his head in a bun, was white, but he seemed to be around Govek's age. His cold, light green eyes narrowed briefly on Govek before he looked to Savili. "Are you well, my mate?"

"I'm fine, Iytier," Savili said dryly. "Play nice."

The male huffed. Miranda glanced at Govek and found him looking pointedly away.

"Would you like to ride on our cart, Miranda?" Savili adjusted the baby in his sling. She tried to cover him back up, but he protested, getting squirmy. He clearly wanted to look around. "Govek, I thought you could help Iytier pull it today."

"I don't—" Iytier started, but Savili shot him a scathing look. "Yes, that's fine," he grumbled.

Apparently, the orcs pulled the carts and Govek just got himself volunteered. Miranda would have laughed had Govek not looked so stricken. "You okay? I'm fine with just walking with you if you'd rather do that."

"No," Govek said quickly. "You will ride. It's too far for you."

"We just hiked around for days on end through the woods. I think I can handle a few miles on a path."

Savili tipped her head. "Miles?"

"She means leagues," Govek said.

"Ah, I see," Savili said, with a nod. "Viravia mentioned you were from a very large village over the mountains. What was it called?"

Oh god. How to answer that one?

Thankfully, Miranda was saved from a response by the baby starting to fuss.

"Haysik," Savili said warningly. "You have to stay in my arms right now, sweetie."

"Can I . . .?" Miranda cut off, unsure, but Savili cast her a smile that gave her courage. "Can I hold him?"

The woman blinked. "Oh, of *course*." She untucked the babe from her cloak, but kept him nicely bundled in a wrap. He hesitated to be pried from his mother's arms, but Miranda had more than enough experience with pass-offs.

"Hello, Haysik," she said, bouncing and smiling at the little baby when he started to fuss. "Well, hello, how are you? You look so sweet. Oh here, what's this?" She scooped up the tassel of her cloak and waved it in front of his eyes. "Ooh, how neat. Look at it wiggle."

The baby stopped his fussing and grabbed hold of the tassel. He pulled on it with tiny green fists and started to babble.

"You really are good with children," Savili said. "Viravia said you worked with them."

"I did, and he's *precious*," Miranda gushed, adoring the weighty warmth of him, the clean, milky smell. She stroked his hair as he yanked up the other tassel.

An orc called out from the party. "Sounds like it's time to load up. Come, Miranda. I'll help you get settled."

Iytier grumbled something under his breath, but one look from Savili stopped his fight. Miranda looked to Govek to check if he was equally perturbed.

And instead found him staring at her fixedly. Her *and* the baby.

Her stomach did a flip at the telling expression and her thoughts turned warm.

Even as her gut twisted up.

She couldn't really think about having her own children right now. She still wasn't convinced she deserved that kind of happiness after what happened on Earth.

But . . . seeing Govek's face so warm and soft as she cradled little Haysik, the twisting of her stomach turned into a little flutter.

Now was not the time to dwell on this, so she brushed Govek's arm, jarring him out of his stupor. "You ready?"

"Yes," Govek said decisively before following her through the crowd.

CHAPTER

SEVEN

GOVEK

G ovek raked a hand through his hair as he followed his mate and Savili over to Iytier's produce wagon. His gaze stuck on Miranda as she bounced the little one.

The babe was so *tiny*. He should have expected that one would be, but he'd never been close to a son for an extended period, especially one so young.

"You can come right up here, Miranda." Savili gestured to the ladder near the front on the side. The cart was loaded with crates, but they'd been stacked to make a comfortable looking bench nearest the pull handles. "I'll go up first and you can hand Haysik to me."

"All right," Miranda said brightly, but Govek could hear the hesitation in her voice. See the slight clench of her fingers around the child's body.

She looked good holding a babe. *Very* good.

Fuck.

"You're going to let *him* pull your wagon?"

Govek turned. The other women were watching as they stood in a little circle near the fish carts. There were only five of them, all younger. The elder women rarely attended on the colder days. Their mates were all busy readying the supplies, but stopped to watch closely.

Hilva, a bare chit of a girl, stood with her hands on her hips, so slender and petite, and Govek found her bluster more amusing than irritating. At least she wasn't shrinking away and averting her gaze like the handful of other women who watched him take his place next to Iytier.

"Who pulls our cart doesn't concern you, Hilva," Savili shot back, and Govek blinked with surprise.

He'd known Savili nearly all his life. She'd grown up in Oakwall, and Iytier had pursued her for a long while before she finally came around. Govek had watched their relationship bloom over the seasons and had crossed paths with her a few times since she had made Iytier her mate.

But Savili had never once spoken to Govek directly. He had not thought she was quite so brave as this.

Hilva huffed, but the rest of the women had already abandoned her so she had no choice but to rejoin her mate on the fish cart near the back.

Govek took his place at the front of the wagon, holding the wood bar aloft slightly so Iytier could duck beneath. The male's face was flat and unhappy.

Savili's reaction to him was surprising, but Iytier's cold demeanor was not.

Tavggol had been Iytier's closest friend.

And Govek had failed to arrive at Clairton in time to save him.

Govek's hands clutched around the grip bar, putting

concerted effort into not crushing the thing. He concentrated on his mate's chatter instead.

"Will his teeth come in sharp?" Miranda asked Savili. She was close enough behind him that if he reached out, he could brush the back of her head. It comforted him.

"The baby teeth don't. Thank Fades, because he's such a gusty eater. I expect he'll be breastfeeding for a long time to come."

Miranda laughed, but it was cut off by the sound of one of the orcs near the front announcing that it was time to head out. Chief Ergoth had taken his place on the first cart, and Govek craned his neck to see Karthoc and his warriors taking up the rear. Karthoc's expression was incredibly smug.

This would be a trade to remember. Govek couldn't decide if he was lucky to witness it or not. But his time for musing was over and the line of wagons began a steady pace.

"I'm surprised orc babies are the same size as human ones since orcs are so big."

"They get their growth spurts once they hit puberty. Until then they're pretty much human size. Otherwise, I don't know how I would manage. My arms would have fallen off already to say nothing of the *birthing*."

"Yeah, I can imagine that it's not particularly fun," Miranda said lightly, even as Govek's stomach twisted. How would *he* manage watching her go through such pain?

Then he shook his head. This was not even something he should consider.

"I also imagine that a lot of insanity goes on with only boys running around. I once cared for a group of seven three-year-old boys for an entire shift—er, *day*. The place looked like a natural disaster had torn through. There was freaking poop *on the ceiling*."

Savili laughed—a genuine one—and Govek noted that Iytier shifted his head to listen, his expression lightening. "Oh Fades. I've never had it *that* bad. But I bet you and Roenia could compete. She has five children."

Fades, Estoc had *five* sons? Govek hadn't known that. It was a wonder he'd ever had time to join their fishing trips.

"Govek."

The sharp tone Iytier used instantly brought Govek's attention back to the task of pulling. Was he being too slow?

"I apologize."

"For what?"

Govek bristled, but managed past his anger. "I apologize for being distracted. It will not happen again."

There was a brief pause before Iytier said. "That's it?"

Anger bloomed in Govek's throat, but he managed a thought. "*And* for listening in on your mate's conversation."

He could feel Iytier's glower lingering on him, but he refused to give into the male's ire. He would *not* lose control this day. He would not risk being seen as a beast in Miranda's eyes.

He'd worked so blasted hard to win her. He'd do anything to maintain her trust.

"Fades help me."

Govek shot a brief glance in Iytier's direction before saying, "Was there something *else* I was meant to feel remorse over?"

"I cannot believe you, Govek. This is exactly why everyone—"

"Iytier."

The warning call came from Savili and he glanced back

to find she was now skewering her mate with a much hotter glare than the one Iytier had used on him. The male all but balled in on himself as he went silent.

Govek sighed raggedly, already exhausted by the brooding male. "It's a long trek. Speak plain, Iytier."

Iytier blinked and straightened himself. Govek readied for the onslaught of accusations and tried to convince himself that nothing Iytier said could make him feel more guilty than he already did about Tavggol's death.

"Why did you leave for Clairton without me?"

Govek tripped.

"You are so shocked? You honestly think so little of me?"

Of course, he was shocked. Iytier's specialty in magic was *gardening*. How could a male that grew strawberries in snow patches ever think to hold his own against soldiers of the Waking Order?

"I did not think you wanted to come," Govek said dumbly.

"Of *course*, I wanted to come," Iytier hissed. "Tavggol may have been your brother, but he was my closest friend. And I wanted to support *you* as well. I *thought* we were friends, but it's been made clear to me this past season that was not the case."

Govek was doubly shocked. He would have fallen right over had the wagon not held him aloft.

Iytier was *Tavggol's* friend. Not his.

"I also can never forgive you for simply going off to Estwill of all horror drenched places, without even *bothering* to send a message to us at the seasonal communion. I know you wanted distance from us all to mourn after Tavggol's passing, but I never thought you would be so stupid as to—"

"Iytier." Savili's threatening tone sounded past the ringing in Govek's ears. His mind clattered to put together everything Iytier was telling him.

"I apologize, Govek," Iytier said less begrudgingly. "I am just . . . we already lost *Tavggol*. If you were hurting so badly you were contemplating *martyring* yourself, you should have . . ."

Martyring himself? What?

Govek went cold, realizing it was not such an odd conclusion to draw. Viravia had called him a martyr too, on the night he'd left for Estwill.

The male sighed heavily, wiped a hand over his perfect, pale green face. "I am sorry. This is my own guilt talking. You asked for space, but I *never* should have given it. At least not for so long."

Govek's brows pinched. "I never asked for space."

Iytier's eyes rose to meet Govek's gaze. "What? Of course you did. Chief Ergoth made the announcement right after you returned from Clairton. He told us . . . what happened there."

Govek's gut pitched, and he could no longer meet the male's eyes. The pain of that day in Clairton was too great. It boiled inside him still.

"Chief Ergoth told us you did not feel safe to be among other orcs, that your control was in tatters, and that was why you did not come into the clan or allow anyone to visit you."

His mind was reeling. "My father told me *you* asked for space."

"What do you mean *I* asked for it?" Iytier's eyes were wide.

"He told me . . . after Clairton . . . he said the clan had passed a unanimous judgment that . . . I was not allowed to enter the borders of the clan . . . unless it was to get supplies or deliver meat."

"You're fucking kidding me. We never held a *judgment* over this," Iytier said. "Chief Ergoth told you we did? Are you serious?"

Govek could only nod. His throat was too tight.

Iytier shook his head, looking away.

The rest of the walk was done in silence.

CHAPTER

EIGHT

"*My father told me* you *asked for space.*"

The words rolled steadily through Miranda's mind, even as she bounced little Haysik on her lap and chatted pleasantly with his mother. She tried to enjoy the lush autumn scenery. The day was absolutely stunning— bright sun streaked through the red and orange leaves, blue sky peeked through the branches, glittering frost covered the shady areas.

It was so beautiful and . . .

And Govek's father had lied to keep Govek isolated.

Miranda took deep breaths and glowered toward the cart where Ergoth was seated at the front of the line. She reminded herself that screaming at him would do nothing.

Especially with the judgment coming up the next day.

She and Govek *would* win. They had to.

"Let's get down," Savili said, alerting Miranda to the fact that they had stopped. Savili took her baby, leaving

Miranda feeling a little empty as she stood up on the crate of apples she'd been sitting on and looked around.

They'd made it to the trade.

The space was massive and open, probably as large as a football field on Earth. The white and gray trunks of birch trees, which lined the entire exterior, arched high above their heads, perhaps thirty feet, looming and leaning and *intertwining* with each other to create a roof that Miranda suspected was tightly packed enough to stop rainfall from coming in. The branches above were barren of leaves which allowed her to see the woven pattern—like thatch work but spiraling out in points that looked like sun rays—more clearly.

In the center there was a round opening that let in light, but Miranda couldn't see what it illuminated on the ground because there were so many tall orc bodies roaming around, mingling among each other, unloading boxes.

A human man appeared in the crowd and called out. "Chief Ergoth, Warlord Karthoc, *welcome*."

"Miranda."

Govek's soft call brought her back to his attention, and she discovered that Iytier had begun unloading the cart at the back. She stepped to the edge where Govek was and let him lower her to the ground.

"Are you okay?" she asked, noting the tightness in his face, the clench of his fists.

"I'm fine."

He wasn't, and it was a stupid thing to ask anyway. He'd just found out his father had lied to him and the *entire* clan.

"Welcome, welcome!" Boomed the man's voice again and Miranda whipped around. He was a tall human with a heavy-set frame and kind eyes. His clothing was much the same as that of the orcs—cotton shirt, woolen pants. The only difference was that he wore a brown jacket where the orcs had cloaks. Or at least, the orcs from Rove Wood Clan did. The warriors barely had any clothing on their torsos at all.

The human approached Karthoc without a scrap of hesitation, as if the orc male didn't dwarf him. Ergoth rushed over to intercept but it was too late.

"I am glad to see you and your warriors here, Warlord. I have told my people what to expect so feel free to mingle openly."

"Your generosity is—"

"Headman Gerald," Ergoth said, his voice a little louder and more clipped than usual. "I would like to speak with you in private."

"Of course, Chief Ergoth." The headman looked more amused than worried over Ergoth's anger.

"I would like to join in on this conversation as well," Karthoc interjected.

"You don't need to—" Ergoth started.

"I insist," Karthoc said with a wide grin. "After all, I should verbally cement our agreements before any of my males proceed. Wouldn't you agree, Headman?"

"Of course, Warlord. Right this way. We can talk in private over here."

Miranda couldn't help but be pleased with how frustrated Ergoth looked. Oh, to be a fly on the wall for that conversation.

"What do you think, Miranda?" Govek asked.

"I think that headman is going to give Ergoth a run for his money." Miranda kept her voice low so no one but Govek could hear.

"I meant about the *trade*."

Oh gosh. She'd pretty much forgotten where they were. "Ah, it's, um . . ." She looked around again, really not able to get a good view now that she was on the ground. There were just too many orcs and people mingling about.

"Can I lift you?" Govek repositioned to stand directly behind her.

"Okay . . .?" Miranda agreed and he scooped her up by the waist like she weighed nothing.

All the way up to his fricking *shoulder*.

She gasped out a laugh as he plunked her down. "Govek, oh my gosh!" She giggled, warm and giddy. He was so dang *strong*. His shoulder was so wide her scrawny butt fit on it quite comfortably. He wrapped an arm around her thighs to keep her steady and she clung to the top of his head, weaving her fingers through the short strands.

Her stomach flipped as he shot her a little smirk. His teeth were all tucked away, and his face was squat, and she leaned down to kiss his forehead even though it tipped her off balance. He tightened his grip so she wouldn't fall.

She cupped his face. "My tough guy, carting me around like I really am a rucksack." She leaned close to his ear. "Or should it be a 'fuck sack'?"

Govek snorted and covered his face as his shoulders shook from silent laughter. She clung to his head to keep her balance even though his grip on her legs was more than enough.

"For Fades will, woman." His grin was huge and his jaw was slightly lowered as his tension eased. "Just look at the *view*."

She obeyed and lost her breath.

The branches of birch trees that lined the perimeter had

been bent and formed into tables that spanned the outside. Humans, both male and female, were setting up goods to display. Everything from blankets, to trinkets, to wood carvings and *massive* shoes fit for orc feet.

The ground was packed with springy green moss, dotted with tiny purple flowers. At the center, where the opening let in light, there was a thick but short tree with golden yellow leaves and a white trunk dotted with carvings. Its roots spiraled through the moss like spiderwebs for twenty or more feet before disappearing beneath.

"Wow," Miranda breathed. "This is incredible . . . what's written on that tree?"

"The Honor Tree displays the original treaty that brought peace between Oakwall Village and Rove Wood Clan."

"It's amazing. Everything here is amazing." She glanced behind her to find most of the orcs were unloading the crates and piling them up. "You guys don't have tables?"

"No, we stand before the goods of the humans and indicate we have a trade to deal. If they are keen, they wave us forward to negotiate. Then we come back here to fetch our goods for them."

"I see. Very organized."

"Yes. It was created as such to prevent fear or distrust."

Miranda hummed, watching as orcs approached humans with warm greetings and groups visited amicably. Fear and distrust didn't seem to have much place now.

"What the . . ."

Miranda glanced down at Govek and followed his eyes across the mossy clearing. A massive orc warrior was walking up to a table packed high with bread and pastries.

Miranda looked between them. "What's going on? Wait, isn't that your cousin?"

"It is," Govek said quietly, distracted as he watched. The woman behind the table, a short girl with a full frame and dark curls, straightened and waved him over. She greeted him with enough gusto that it was clear she *knew* him.

Govek snorted. "So *that's* what Karthoc meant. How on Faeda did Brovdir come across Trinia?"

"Trinia?"

"Yerina's younger sister."

Oh frick.

"How the fuck did they even meet?" Govek asked as Trinia's smile warmed at something Brovdir said. They were too far for Miranda to hear properly. The woman leaned over her table a bit when handing him a pastry, pushed her breasts up, and tipped her head so her neck was elongated.

"Govek. A word." Karthoc drew their attention away as he stomped over. Govek lowered Miranda back to the ground. Ergoth was watching smugly, and the headman was nowhere to be seen.

The warlord's face was a mask of contorted fury. Gosh, she'd forgotten how big Karthoc was, only slightly smaller than Govek.

Govek tucked her tightly into his side.

"Govek," Karthoc's deep rumbling voice lacked the pleasant qualities Govek's voice had. "I need to speak to you. Privately. *Now.*"

She felt Govek tense, and she took a moment to look around. She found that Savili was chatting with Iytier as he unloaded produce from their cart.

"That's fine. I'll go ask Savili to walk around with me,"

Miranda said. Govek was still tense so she patted his hand and teased. "I'll go get some 'oozing' done."

Govek made a shocked choking sound and she peeled herself away from his side. She flashed him a reassuring smile before she turned to join Savili.

"Did your woman just say she was *oozing*?" Karthoc asked and Miranda had to cover her mouth to keep from bursting with laughter. She looked back only once, just long enough to see that Govek was pinching the bridge of his nose, eyes squeezed shut, and a slight smile at his lips.

She grinned and went to join the other woman.

GOVEK

"What the fuck happened last night, Govek?"

The pleasant chatter of the humans and orcs died away as his cousin narrowed his dark eyes. His hulking frame was menacing. His fists were balled to strike, his teeth were bared.

"Perhaps we should take this to privacy." Govek looked toward the humans' tables. None of them seemed to notice Karthoc's fury yet, but Govek was certain they would soon enough and he had no idea what effect it might have on the residents of Oakwall.

"We're doing this *here*. Right now," Karthoc said darkly, and Govek knew better than to argue again. "Ergoth says that you struck Wolvc outside of a challenge. Tell me that isn't true."

Govek could say nothing, and his silence was enough for the warlord. Karthoc's scowl deepened. "Fades *spit*, Govek, what were you *thinking*? How could you do something so insane? Do you know the kind of trouble you've caused for me?"

"I would not think it would be of much consequence to you," Govek said.

"Of course, it is! It ruins every Fades-blasted plan I had set. *Ergoth* is forcing my hand with this wretched judgment your clan is holding tomorrow. He wants me to enact the punishment I would give one of my warriors who attacked without a challenge."

Govek's stomach dropped.

"I'll have no choice but to send you to Avokil, Govek. To the fucking *foothills*."

To the front lines of the war.

Govek's head swam. His thoughts blurred. He sought out Miranda in the crowd, followed the sound of her voice on the wind. Stuck to her smile and laugh as Savili familiarized her with the trade.

Fuck *fuck*. He would lose her.

He could *not* let that happen.

"I can't change it, Govek," Karthoc continued, "Your bastard of a father made sure that all the warriors within earshot could hear it. I can't show you favoritism, even if you are my cousin."

"I don't expect you to."

Karthoc sighed raggedly, pinching the bridge of his nose. "Tell me there is *something* that could sway this judgment, Govek. Tell me *why* you would attack this male."

Govek managed to breathe past the tension in his gut. "He drugged and tried to harm Miranda."

Karthoc paused, stunned into silence.

"He and Rogeth, as well as the human Maythra, drugged Miranda with vorial root extract to make her lose consciousness and I lost control when I happened upon the scene."

"Fades mercy. No fucking *wonder* you lost your blasted mind. I would have done far more than rip his jaw off."

Govek tensed at the reminder of what he had done. Fuck, the feel of that crack under his knuckle, the scent of blood, Wolvc's pain-laced voice.

Miranda's call for aid.

It roared through him.

He wanted to attack Wolvc again.

"I assume you have proof that your words are the truth and not theirs?" Karthoc asked, tension leaching into the tone.

Govek inhaled deeply, thinking of Miranda's little bag that she called "evidence." "It may not be enough. The final judgment is put to a vote and my brethren—they have traditionally never been on my side, no matter what truths are presented."

"Fuck, Govek." Karthoc raked a hand through his hair. "If we can't prove that they attacked your woman first I will still have to order you to the foothills. Why would they do something so heinous?"

"I don't know. Miranda overheard a bit and thinks they were trying to get her back to the hall. They thought that if I saw her there, unconscious, I would go on a rampage and prove myself to be unworthy for the role of chief in Rove Wood."

Karthoc scoffed. "Fucking lunatics. All of them. They think that would will stop me from merging the clans? From unseating Ergoth off his crooked little throne? The fools had better think again. This whole fucking judgment is just to swindle you out of your own birthright. *You* are meant to be chief of Rove Wood Clan, Govek. Ergoth should have stepped down long ago."

Govek gulped, trying to find the words to tell Karthoc he had no intention of becoming chief here. That, at best, he would stay behind in these woods when the rest of his brethren left for Baelrok Forge.

"This has all gotten so Fades-blasted wretched. It was supposed to be fucking *easy.* Ergoth gets shoved out, you take his spot. Simple. Now I've got my fucking seer breathing down my neck about staying here indefinitely and a whole massive judgment to oversee and no end to this stay in sight."

The seer wanted the warriors to stay in Rove Wood?

"But fine. So be it. Ergoth thinks my patience will run out first? Ha! He's in for a Fades-cursed season. I'll just bide my time here and wait him out. See what kind of hole he digs himself in trying to get me to finally give in to his foolish demands. At least the seer will be happy."

Govek stomach churned threateningly. So Karthoc *wasn't* going to be leaving then?

What exactly was the warlord's game?

One thing was certain, Govek wanted *no* part of it. "Karthoc, I have no intention of taking on the role of chief."

Once again, Karthoc was stunned. His jaw slacked. His dark eyes bulged. "You must be *jesting.* I thought a few days would have helped you to see *reason.*"

"I've never wanted that power. And the only thing that matters to me is Miranda's safety. Something that I cannot ensure among these males. Look at what they *did* to her last night. And not a single fucking one of them believes her."

"All the more reason to *want* to be chief," Karthoc hissed. "You should be fucking *clamoring* to get power over these wretches who have treated you so foul for your entire life. You should want to get revenge on them."

Govek shook his head slowly. "Get revenge? What good would that *ever* do?"

Karthoc sputtered, looking for words, blinked when he couldn't find them.

But Govek could. "Getting revenge would not undo any of the damage. It would only prove me to be the vile abomination they claim I am. Something I've tried to do my *entire* life without a glimmer of success. I give up, Karthoc. I refuse to spend even one moment more trying and failing to change their minds."

Miranda cared for him. Miranda did not think he was vile.

And that was more than enough.

Fuck, he wanted her now. He turned to go. Scanned the crowd to find her.

"Wait. Govek, stop. I . . . apologize."

It was Govek's turn to be stunned. He snapped his gaze back to Karthoc.

The male sagged. "Look, Govek. I . . . fuck, this isn't . . ."

Govek waited, throat tight.

"I . . . need you to be here to help train the magic wielders I've found, Govek."

His hope extinguished in a quick burst.

Karthoc continued, undaunted. "Ergoth *won't* do it the way I need. I need them to be *strong*. As strong as you were at Clairton. With these seventeen males, we could turn the tides of the war."

Bile burned the back of his throat. "You think what I did at Clairton was *on purpose*?"

Karthoc rose an eyebrow. "Wasn't it?" Shock burrowed so deep in Govek's gut he couldn't find words and Karthoc waved him off. "It doesn't matter if it was on purpose or not. It was *incredible*. That kind of power will win us the war."

Fuck, that stung. "So, I really am just a weapon to you."

"No, Govek, that isn't what I—"

"I am not capable of this task you would have me put to, Karthoc. I can *barely* control my own magic. I won the day for you at Clairton because I completely lost my *mind*. I do not even recall most of what I did in those moments. It's a blur of red and wails. I am not fit to teach *anything*."

"Govek—"

"You think the orcs of Rove Wood treat me unfairly? That they don't see my potential? I believe it is *you* who does not see how *horrific* this potential of mine could be if left to run wild. Your own drive for power has made you *blind*, cousin."

"Govek, that is too far," Karthoc said so low and deadly it snapped up Govek's spine.

But Govek could not stop. Not now. "Everything that my brethren say about me is *true*, Karthoc."

The snarl faded from Karthoc.

"Every Fades-fucked thing. I am uncontrolled, and violent, and unpredictable. My fury is unchecked and turns my magic into something so foul it is a wonder Rove Wood Clan has sustained me this long. I have not even been trained to control it. None could stand in my way if I truly lost myself."

"Easy, tough guy."

Miranda's voice soothed him through his mind's eye and Govek managed a deep breath. "I am the vile wretch they say I am, Karthoc. And we both know that it's best for everyone's sake that I stay far away."

With that, Govek turned away from Karthoc, walked into the crowd and used Miranda's scent to guide him.

Fuck, *fuck*. What had he said? What was he doing? Karthoc may have been his cousin, but he was still the *warlord*. Treating him so brashly could get him sent to the Foothills before the judgment even took place.

He would lose Miranda.

There was no way Govek would ever let that happen.

A foolhardy plan skipped into his mind, planted itself deep.

He knew what he and Miranda would have to do. It was drastic and foolish and she wasn't going to like it, but they had no other option.

Govek moved through a crowd of orc warriors and into an open area at the center of the trade. Everyone around him was mingling, peaceful. Laughter radiated and smiles abounded.

None of that did anything to lighten his mood.

He scanned, desperate to find Miranda. His eyes locked on her but instead of relief his body quaked with turmoil.

Miranda was talking with Yerina.

CHAPTER

TEN

"So, what do you think of the trade, Miranda?" Savili asked as her mate continued to unload boxes of perfectly ripe fruit. Her baby was happily cooing in the sling over her shoulder and the tension from the ride over had lifted away. "Would you like me to help you get settled?"

"That would be great." Miranda examined the tables again. Most were bustling with multiple orcs haggling and even more waiting. She didn't even know where to start.

"Is there something in particular you're looking for?"

Something she was looking for? Her eyes scanned over the heaps of cloth, and shoes, and small carved items. There was very little food, but it seemed that was because the orcs provided it.

Besides making connections so their lives would be easier after Rove Wood Clan left, it really didn't matter.

Govek could hunt, grow, or make almost everything they needed.

But . . . there was one thing. "Is there . . . anyone at Oakwall that can help with trauma?"

Savili tipped her head, blonde hair catching in the wind, and Iytier glanced momentarily their direction. Miranda felt her cheeks heat as Savili asked, "What do you mean?"

"Like . . . if a loved one passes away or something really terrifying happens and you can't stop thinking about it . . ." Miranda's throat closed again, and she looked away from the woman, took deep breaths, worked the tiny faces of her babies out of her mind.

"Did something terrible happen to you, Miranda?"

God, how to answer that question when she couldn't even catch a breath?

"I'm sorry," Savili said quickly. "I didn't mean to pry." She stepped closer to Miranda and placed a hand on her arm. "We all have some horrors in our pasts that are difficult to speak on."

Some of the tension in Miranda's chest eased.

"To answer you, there isn't one particular person from Oakwall that would be of good help." Savili continued, stroking down her babies back. "We all tend to band together for support. It's a small community, after all. Barely a thousand at Oakwall and only three hundred at Rove Wood. We keep to ourselves. Only trade among each other. Until Tavggol found Viravia in the woods, no one from the outside had joined our clan for almost four generations."

"We barely have visits from other orcs," Iytier said as he took the lid off a crate of apples. "There are only a handful of warriors who we trust to deliver the healing tinctures we make, and they only stay long enough to retrieve them. Not even Karthoc travels to the Rove Woods often. This is the first time he's set foot in the clan in almost five years. He didn't even come to tell us about Tavggol's capture in person. He sent a bird." The bitterness in Iytier's tone was obvious.

Miranda blinked with surprise and glanced toward Karthoc still standing with Govek near the perimeter of the birch trees. They both looked tense.

"Savili," Iytier said tensely, drawing Miranda's attention. His eyes were narrowed on the crowd.

"Oh, Fades spit," Savili said, and Miranda scanned the crowd to find what they were looking at, or rather, *who*.

There was a little group of women gossiping off to the side. Miranda recognized Hilva and the other two. The last woman was new.

She was tall with curves for days and stunning blonde hair that fell in lush waves down her back. Her green eyes were striking, her nose was petite, her lips were full and red enough to make Miranda think she was wearing lipstick.

"Yerina."

Miranda's stomach dropped. What the heck was with Govek being surrounded by all these stunning women?

"Fades be." Iytier dropped the crate he was holding. Likely all the apples were bruised now. His hand raked through his long hair the same way Govek always did, unsettling it from its queue. "I thought Viravia sent a message asking for Yerina to be kept in the village today."

"She did. But *clearly,* Headman Gerald didn't comply with her request," Savili muttered.

Miranda glanced back at Yerina as the woman flipped her hair in the wind. Her long-lashed eyes scanned as if searching for someone. Did she know Govek would be here? Was she going to confront him outright?

The anxiety lacing the back of Miranda's throat hardened and her spine steeled as she readied for the verbal fight that was sure to come. The sensation was all too familiar from her time spent in the group home.

Savili heaved a sigh. "Miranda, I'm sorry. I'm not sure how much you know about Yerina—"

"I know enough." Miranda said firmly. "I know she's Govek's former lover and I know that she's been spreading lies about him. Lies that I fully intend to put a stop to."

"What?" Savili sounded baffled, and her wide-eyed expression betrayed her.

"That's one reason we came to the trade today." Miranda saw no reason not to be forthright with the woman. If anything, Savili could help.

But instead of confidence, Savili said hesitantly, "Miranda, you shouldn't. Yerina can be extremely difficult."

"Savili is right," Iytier said, expression tight. "It would likely be best for you and Govek to go. Come back to the trade a different day."

Miranda narrowed her eyes. "You both *want* the lies about Govek to continue?"

Savili immediately looked to Iytier, and the male raked his hand through his hair again.

Miranda's stomach twisted. Had she guessed wrong? Did they dislike Govek too?

"We want . . ." Savili cut off, patted her baby, who had fallen asleep. Oh, to be little and not have to put up with any of this garbage.

"Can I be blunt?" Iytier asked, his voice low and serious. Miranda nodded, wishing he would get on with it.

"The bulk of us that were Tavggol's closest friends *know* how Govek truly is at heart. We know he would never hurt a woman the way Yerina claims he hurt her."

"We do." Savili assured her with a firm nod. "He made Haysik's cradle. You should see it, Miranda. It's obvious he put incredible care and time into carving it. And I would know. My father is a woodworker."

Miranda's chest warmed at the thought of Govek building a cradle.

He'd done something like that and still didn't think Iytier and Savili considered him to be a friend? Her heart ached for Govek and she wondered how deep his insecurities truly ran.

"So, believe me when I say we've *tried* to change the clan's harsh opinions. It's like it's ingrained." Iytier dropped another box of apples heavily to the ground. "And his penchant for withdrawing completely at the slightest hard glance hasn't exactly helped. He won't even *try* to defend himself."

"Can you blame him?" Miranda crossed her arms. "The way Govek tells it, he never thought *anyone* from this clan has ever been on his side."

"That is not true," Iytier said with a little too much force.

Miranda held up her hand. "I'm not debating the truth of it. I am just saying what Govek perceives. And frankly, even after being here for a few days, I can see how he got that impression. Y'all are either suspicious or angry at him. Not one person *welcomed* him back to the clan. Not one person seemed *relieved* that he'd survived Estwill, only irritated he hadn't managed to bring back more women."

"That's not how I feel." Iytier threw up his hands.

"Perhaps not, but you didn't offer him many kind words when you saw him this morning, did you?" Miranda pointed out. "I'm not saying you don't have a right to be angry at how obtuse he can be. I'm just trying to help you see things from Govek's perspective."

Iytier's green face grew pale and Savili's eyes fell to the ground.

"There've been so many misunderstandings between the clan and him it's completely overshadowed how amazing Govek is. How selfless he can be. I've witnessed that firsthand. He saved me out in the woods. He fed me while he went hungry. He literally gave me the clothes off his back. He's held me when I'm at my worst and made me laugh even when I didn't want to."

He was patient, and kind, and she never tired of being around him. Even now she wished he was standing beside her so she could rub his fist into unclenching and rest her head on his arm and chatter at him about how strongly she felt for him. How much she . . . she . . .

Oh *wow*.

She was in love with him.

Her cheeks heated and her heart hammered, and she glanced up at the two faces regarding her with confusion.

Confusion *and* guilt

Her heart was still pounding from her revelation, but she took a breath, determined. "You say you're on Govek's side, but *he* doesn't see it that way. And honestly, neither do I. No one has *ever* taken his side, but I intend to change that. He's been silenced long enough. And a good place to start is by dispelling all these lies Yerina's been spreading." Miranda's brow furrowed then. "Do you know *why* she's perpetuating them?"

"I assume for attention," Savili said with a heavy sigh. "Most of those who listen think her very brave and valiant for going through what she did with Govek and not calling for a judgment against him. She claims it is to maintain the peaceful trade between our peoples, which makes some feel indebted to her for being so gracious."

"Do you know why she started them in the first place?"

"No," Iytier said. "But I do know she would often play this way. Scorn him so he might bring her more boons to win her back, and he always did. Except that last time as he left for Clairton without telling anyone, and then . . ."

"Hmm . . ." Miranda glanced back toward Yerina and found her curling her hair around her finger, pouting her pretty red lips. "I can imagine Yerina was pretty pissed about that. Especially if she expected him to come back on his hands and knees and he never did."

"He never came back at *all*," Iytier said, his voice low and his expression dark. "And Chief Ergoth told us it was because he found himself too *dangerous* and I was a stubborn fool. Too angry that he left for Clairton without even . . ."

Savili placed a hand on Iytier's arm and Miranda wondered, once again, just how many misunderstandings had led to Govek's alienation.

And how many of those misunderstandings led back to Chief Ergoth?

Savili began to remove the baby sling and passed her little one on to Iytier. "Well, we aren't going to get Yerina to admit anything if we just stand here. Let's just go and see where it leads."

"Sounds good to me." Miranda perked up. She honestly hadn't expected Savili to go with her.

"You sure you want to take this on Savili?" Iytier asked, though he was already adjusting the sling to his height.

"I am. I can handle it, Iytier."

"I don't doubt you"—the male plucked a kiss to the top of his mate's head—"just try not to be too loud."

Savili cast him a mischievous smile. "Never thought you'd give me *that* command."

Miranda snorted, trying to hide her laughter, and not doing a very good job of it. Her eyes scanned the crowd again. She found Govek still talking with Karthoc.

She hoped they would have enough time before he came to join her. Miranda expected the verbal punches to be flying, and she didn't want him bruised any more than he already was.

Miranda followed Savili through the crowd to where Yerina was still talking with Hilva and a few other women from Rove Wood near the center of the trade pavilion. Her hair billowed, her posture was loose and flippant. Her expression was a perfect mix of aloof and bemused.

God damn it. Why did Miranda have to be such a jealous ninny? Why did her abandonment issues have to crop up at the worst times? Govek was imprinted on *her*, not Yerina.

Yerina caught Miranda's eye in the crowd. They flashed with acknowledgment which meant Hilva must have filled her in on *everything*.

Yerina's sharp green eyes trailed all the way down Miranda's body and back up again. She scoffed. Mocking laughter touched her red lips before she turned her attention to Hilva and whispered something into her ear that made the younger woman chortle and stare.

Oh, it was *on*. She and Savili walked over with no hesitation.

"Yerina," Savili greeted cooly. "I don't think you've been properly introduced to Miranda yet."

"No, I haven't, but Hilva tells me *Govek* brought her here." Yerina's voice was high and crisp and grated on Miranda's nerves. "It's good to meet you. How are you settling into the clan? I'm sure it must be a might overwhelming for you."

Miranda bristled and bit back, "It hasn't been bad at all. I've been warmly welcomed by everyone."

Yerina smirked, eyes flickering down Miranda's body. "You do look a state, don't you? It's all right, Miranda. I know that orcs can be rather a lot to handle, even on the best of days. It takes a special kind to keep them content."

If Yerina was going to come out punching, Miranda would too. "Oh, I have Govek plenty content."

Yerina rose her brows slightly. "Oh, is that *so*? Well, I suppose you don't need my advice then."

Miranda tipped her head. "Advice? I thought you would try to give *warnings*."

"She will give you warnings." Hilva cut in and stepped forward even as the other two women from Rove Wood backed away. They were smart enough not to get caught in the crossfire. "And you would be *lucky* to heed them."

"Hilva," Yerina said smoothly, almost cooing. "Thank you for defending me, dear, but perhaps you would be good enough to fetch me something to drink?"

Hilva jerked, clearly put out.

"I'd like a private word with our newcomer. You understand, don't you?"

With a grumble, Hilva conceded. She walked off toward the orc side of the trade.

"Don't think you can get rid of me so easily, Yerina." Savili crossed her arms.

"Of course not, Savili. You're always welcome." She turned her full attention back to Miranda. "Hilva told me you and Govek have been intimate in the past. I assume then that you are here to learn what truly transpired between Govek and I?"

"If by 'in the past' you mean just this morning, then, yeah, we've been *intimate* in the past. And we'll be intimate again in the future." Miranda watched Yerina's face carefully.

But the woman was good at her game, her expression barely flickered. "Your confidence is adorable." Yerina's eyes moved toward the crowd, to where Govek was still engrossed in his conversation with Karthoc. "Hilva mentioned you couldn't have been together more than a handful of days and yet Govek is here. At the trade for the first time in almost a season."

"What's your point?"

Yerina's eyes flashed, and a smile tugged at the corners of her lips. "Orcs come here to find conquests, you know? I'm just surprised that his interest with you waned so quickly."

Miranda's gut twisted despite herself. "You go on and tell yourself that."

Savili cut in. "Perhaps you shouldn't speak of waning interests, Yerina. Govek was with *you* for almost three seasons, and in the end, never decided to make you his mate."

"Oh, but he wanted me to be. He was *constantly* talking

about bringing me to his home. Keeping me all to himself. Worshipping me."

Miranda's heart clenched in her chest.

Yerina's expression was smug. "Oh, he didn't tell you that, did he? That he practically *begged* me to stay with him."

Damn it, she was *blustering*. It meant nothing.

And yet Miranda's stomach wouldn't stop churning.

"I am the only woman who could ever handle him, after all." Yerina flipped her hair and looked down her nose at Miranda. "Who could face him at his utter worst. You have seen it, right? Watched him lose control?"

Miranda balled her fists. "Of course, I have."

"Do you mean that little fight between him and Wolvc? Hilva told me all about that," Yerina said with a shrug. "I don't mean like *that*, Miranda."

Miranda went cold.

"I meant have you let him lose control with *you*? You would know if he did. It's . . ." Yerina sighed, bit her lips like she was imagining it.

Imagining being with Govek when he lost himself.

She'd had that. Yerina had gotten him to lose control.

And Miranda couldn't.

"I thought you said he *attacked* you?"

Savili's voice was loud and broke Miranda out of her stupor. It broke Yerina too, making her glower.

But Savili continued, undaunted. "You've been saying for a whole season that Govek lost control and *hurt* you. And now you speak on it as if it's something Miranda should be envious of. So, which is it? Did he *hurt* you or pleasure you?"

"That is none of your business, Savili," Yerina snapped. "It's between Govek and I."

Savili laughed. "You must be jesting? You made it *everyone's* business when you started spreading your lies."

"I *never* lied," Yerina insisted. "I've only *ever* spoken the truth about Govek. That he lost control, and it was . . ."

The humming sigh Yerina let out made it obvious where her mind was and Miranda clenched her teeth.

"Yerina, I have *heard* you say he attacked you with my own ears," Savili said just as Hilva came up behind Yerina holding a full cup of water.

"Perhaps I embellished a little," Yerina admitted flippantly before looking Miranda in the eye. "Govek and I were so *passionate*. It's understandable that emotions would grow high."

"Your embellishment caused many in Rove Wood Clan to think Govek attacked and hurt you," Miranda said coldly.

Yerina shrugged. "I cannot control what others think and say. I am not responsible for the rumors."

"Govek was alienated because of you."

"I cannot be blamed for that," Yerina said smoothly. "He was an outsider *long* before I gave him my support and comfort. He leaned on me greatly for it. I helped him more than anyone else *ever* has and he won't soon forget that."

"Yes, in exchange for boons." Miranda could feel the rage bubbling up her throat, threatening to make her voice louder. She worked to keep herself calm. There were more people watching now, listening in. If she got hysterical, they wouldn't take anything she said seriously.

"Why *shouldn't* I have received boons from him?" Yerina asked. "All other conquests receive boons in exchange for their service."

"Yes, but *you* weren't a conquest, were you? Otherwise, Govek would have a son right now." Miranda pointed out. "*You* were in a romantic relationship with him. Tell me, Yerina, did you *ever* care about him at all?"

"Of course, I did—"

"Or was it just his boons you wanted? Meat and tinctures." Miranda kept her gaze on Yerina even as she noticed Hilva tensing in the background, as others from the trade began to gather near. "You had quite a good thing going, didn't you? A good transactional relationship."

"That's how *all* orc and human relationships are!"

"Is it? That's not how my relationship with Govek is now. If we ask the other mates in Rove Wood Clan, do you think they would agree with you?"

Yerina scoffed. "You're honestly saying you're with that male and getting *nothing* in return? Then you must only be with him out of pity."

Miranda ignored her goading. "It made you pretty mad when he decided the deal wasn't sweet enough, didn't it?" Miranda spoke loud and clear. "You say he lost control, but you did too, didn't you? He gave you the best you ever had, but on *his* side, it was mediocre. It was so dull for him he broke things off entirely, you poor thing. That must have stung."

"I have *never* been mediocre!" Yerina almost shrieked. "Govek *groveled* at my feet. I gave him the attention *no one* else was willing to give. I was the best he ever had, and he'll want me back. That's why he's *here* today. Because I'm the only one for him, and he knows it."

"He's here because I asked him to accompany me. He never even *mentioned* you when we made our plans,"

Miranda said. "What makes you think he'd ever want you back?"

"You delusional wretch! He *will* come back to me. He'll toss you in the mud." Yerina jabbed her finger at Miranda but wasn't brave enough to make contact. "Just you watch. I'll win him back in the end and then I'll be matriarch of Rove Wood Clan and I'll make your life *miserable*."

"I will never allow that to happen." The low tone shot a shiver up Miranda's spine, and she shot her gaze toward the voice.

Govek had arrived.

CHAPTER

ELEVEN

By the time Govek made it over to Miranda, he'd overheard almost all of Yerina's admission. And so had everyone else in the vicinity.

There were so many orcs and humans gathered around that Govek felt like his flesh was blistered from their penetrating stares, his ears burned from their clamoring voices.

But Miranda reached out to him and he drew strength as he moved to her side. He wished he could pick her up and cart her off into the woods and pretend that none of these other beings existed.

"Are you well, Miranda?" he asked quietly.

"I'm perfectly fine." She gave him a smile that helped ease some of his tension.

"Govek." A light brush against the back of his arm made him shudder. Yerina regarded him with her large, watery eyes that had always caused him to bend to her will.

Never again.

"Govek," Yerina's voice broke. "I've missed you."

"Missed me so much that you spread falsehoods about me."

Yerina straightened and wrung her hands. "I don't know what you've heard but—"

"Why would I *ever* want to be with someone that is so hateful toward me they would gladly ruin my life rather than be near me?"

"No! It wasn't like that. You don't understand. I did it out of *love* for you," Yerina pleaded, her eyes flooding. "I couldn't bear the thought of you finding another before we could make amends. We're meant to be together, Govek. You see that, don't you? I'm the only woman who could ever understand you."

"You understand nothing but my abilities to hunt, craft, and offer you boons." Govek nearly snarled, his blood heating. To think this was the woman he adored for so long. To think he had prostrated himself for her sideways glances. Allowed her to spread vile lies about him for months out of guilt that he'd truly done wrong by her in the end.

He was a fool. He would not be one again.

"I'm sorry, all right?" Yerina stepped forward to take his arm, but he snatched it away from her. "I'll make it up to you. I'll make sure the rumors about you stop. And I promise I'll prove to you that I truly am the best woman for you."

"You could never—"

"Go ahead and try, Yerina. You think you can undo the lies you've spread so easily? I'm willing to bet you'll never manage it," Miranda said.

Yerina's face contorted into rage so vile that Govek

tugged Miranda behind him. "You'll see. I'll prove to both of you that I—"

"What is going on here?"

The booming voice of Headman Gerald rose above all other voices. Yerina came upright and paled, tears instantly halted.

"Yerina." The headman's eyes narrowed into a deep scowl as the crowd parted for him to come through. Fades, every being at the trade was watching this. "I told you to apologize to Govek, and make right the wrongs you have committed, not attack him and his companion."

"I did apologize." Yerina sounded more like a child than a grown woman.

What Govek had *ever* seen in her, he would never know.

"Headman Gerald." Govek's father came forward as well. The headman tensed slightly and Govek knew why. Chief Ergoth's face was flat, his eyes fiery.

He was still seething about Karthoc's warriors being invited to trade.

"What is going on here?" Chief Ergoth asked cooly, and the hush over the crowd was instant. No one even whispered.

Headman Gerald had not lost his voice. "It was brought to my attention very recently that Yerina lied about Govek attacking her."

Chief Ergoth gave Govek a sidelong look before saying, "Are you certain that your source for this is sound? You have proof of his innocence?"

That punch rocked right through Govek. He'd known his father had likely believed Yerina's lies, but having that confirmed felt like fire in his belly. It burned away at his already fraying control.

Cool relief tucked around his arm and he looked down to find Miranda had wrapped him up, was stroking his hand. He worked a deep breath of crisp morning air into his lungs.

"Yerina admitted it to me herself." Headman Gerald crossed his arms over his chest. "Yerina?"

The woman fidgeted. Puffing up her chest, her lip quivered, and her eyes filled with pretty, shimmering tears again. "I . . . only spoke a few mild untruths because I was a little angry. I thought it would force him to confront me, and we would make up. I never thought they would spread so much. You wouldn't even come to the trade to talk to me, Govek. You just shut me out completely. What else was I supposed to do? I cared for you so much! I still do."

She broke into pitying sobs and it made his stomach go sour. No natural tears could look that pretty.

And the truth of it all smacked him.

Fades be fucked. He really *hadn't* done anything wrong. He hadn't gone too far with her. He hadn't hurt her or frightened her. It had all been manipulation—a way to keep him under her control.

But no longer.

"Now, child, please calm," Chief Ergoth said soothingly, and each word grated against Govek. "Your apology is accepted. Please dry your tears."

"Excuse me?" Miranda snapped and all eyes latched onto her. "I think it's *Govek's* choice whether he wants to forgive her."

The way Chief Ergoth looked at Miranda made Govek's blood go still.

"Quite right," Headman Gerald said before Chief Ergoth could make a sound. "Govek, what can we do to make amends?"

Govek's spine straightened. They wanted *him* to decide what to do? He had no idea, nor did he want such authority.

He looked to Miranda. "What say you? You were insulted as well."

"I think that—"

"I am still chief of this clan."

All eyes fell on Ergoth and Govek found him still holding that rage-soaked fire behind his eyes. His face was a mask of pleasantry even as his words were clipped. "I am *still* chief of Rove Wood Clan, and this weighty matter should be decided by *me*."

Govek blinked, thrown off by this sudden change from his father's more congenial and controlled mannerisms.

Headman Gerald sighed heavily, clearly exhausted. "Of course, Chief Ergoth. What do *you* suggest then?"

"I believe the woman being forced to admit her wrongdoing here, in front of so many witnesses, is punishment enough. And I would not risk the peace between our peoples by suggesting anything more severe."

"Oh my god," Miranda said with a shake of her head and Ergoth made a low threatening sound that instantly had Govek's claws extending.

But Miranda continued. "In *addition*, I think it's reasonable to say she isn't allowed at the trades until Govek says it's all right. *And* she should be disallowed from having any contact with Govek."

"That sounds more than fair," Headman Gerald said quickly, looking truly relieved by the suggestion. "Robire? Please escort Yerina back to Oakwall."

"Wait!" Yerina said. "Govek, just let me speak to you in private for a few more moments, *please*."

But Robire, a burly man who was one of the lead guards

for Oakwall, already had Yerina by the arm and was pulling her away. The crowd made a wide berth for them.

The voices rose again, and Headman Gerald called, "That's it then. Let's resume this trade."

Chief Ergoth moved to step toward Miranda, his sharp eyes narrowed on her, his posture radiated his fury.

Govek balled his fists and light sparked behind his eyes as his magic simmered. It didn't fucking matter if Ergoth was his father. He'd punch the chief's jaw clean off his face like he'd done to Wolvc if he dared to harm Miranda.

"Miranda," Chief Ergoth said smoothly, raking the tone over Govek's frazzled nerves. "I would like a word with you. *Alone*."

"I'm sorry, Chief Ergoth, but I'm too tired at the moment. Govek, will you take me home?" Miranda said quickly, her warm hand pushed at the small of his back to force him away. Her prompting won in the end. He could not refuse a direct request from her.

And Chief Ergoth did not try to argue again. There were too many eyes for him to try to force the hand of one of his clan's precious females.

"Huh, looks like Hilva dropped her cup," Miranda said as her eyes lingered on an abandoned mug on the mossy ground.

Miranda's words broke Govek out of his worry and into confusion. "She what?"

"Oh, nothing," Miranda said. "Let's go."

With each step away, Govek gained back a little more control, was able to clear his mind a little further. The whispering voices around them and skewering gazes felt *different* this time. They were not so harsh and hot. They did not churn up his guts so terribly.

There was now no reason for Oakwall to refuse to trade with him, to stop him from moving forward. He could hunt for the humans regularly and obtain everything Miranda wanted. Keep her safe, happy, and whole.

"I cannot believe . . ." Govek shook his head as the scene played out in his mind all over again.

"I can," Miranda said, as they rounded a bend in the path, leaving the trade behind them. No one followed. "People like that always crumble when what they want is suddenly snatched away from them. They say and do more and more crazy things until the mask they wear slips, and they can no longer hide their cruelty."

His brow pinched as he examined her brooding expression.

"Did you see how pissed your dad was when you looked at *me* to make the decision about Yerina instead of him?"

Fuck. "*Don't.*"

She looked up at him with wide eyes and he regretted his harsh tone, but still he had to warn. "*Don't,* Miranda. I wanted to tear him apart."

She hummed, stroked his arm. "Your dad really doesn't like his control taken away, does he?"

He could not recall a time his father had ever *lost* any of his control, so he could not answer that question. Chief Ergoth had always been the pinnacle of authority and lived to ensure the clan prospered.

He had *never* seen him act the way he had just now.

When he threatened Miranda . . .

He tightened his hold on his woman, wrapped his arm about her waist, and pulled her closer to his side. Ground his teeth and balled his fists and tried to work the image of his father's rage directed toward his precious mate out of his mind.

"Well, I do think the 'oozing' was a success in the end." His eyes popped open, and she smirked at him. "Best 'ooze' I've ever had."

"Stop."

"Ten out of ten 'oozes.' Can't wait to 'ooze' with Oakwall again."

"Miranda."

"Or would it be 'ooze' *on* them?"

He pinched the bridge of his nose, unsure if he wanted to groan or laugh. "*Fuck*, Miranda."

"Not a very nice picture I'm painting, is it?" She stroked the arm she was still holding tight. She hadn't let go of him even once. "But don't worry, Govek, you're the only one who can really make me 'ooze.'"

The contrast between pleasure and disgust at the picture she was painting made him growl. "Be careful, Miranda, or I'm going to make you 'ooze' right now."

"That a promise?" she teased, walking her fingers up his arm. He shivered with delight. His mouth began to water. His blood raced and his cock pulsed.

And then her expression fell and flattened.

His gut clenched, but before he had to press her for answers, she said, "So, how come you've lost control with *Yerina* but not me?"

His eyes went wide. "What?"

"She told me how you trusted her enough to lose yourself with her." She skewered him with both her words and her eyes. "But no matter how many times I *ask*, you adamantly refuse."

Of course, he did. He *had* to. Losing control was the *worst* thing he could possibly—

"Maybe you just don't like me as much?"

"That is not true," he grated, finally finding words. "Yerina is *nothing* next to you."

She pursed her lips, expression still unhappy, but she hadn't let go of him, hadn't pushed him away or struck him with insults or raked her eyes over him in disgust.

Instead, she put her arms around his neck.

"What are you doing, Miranda?" Hope swam in his veins, but they were still on the path, right here in the open. If any orcs or women walked back early, they would see.

Unless he carted her off into the woods. Then they would only hear and smell.

Fuck, he wasn't of sound mind.

"I dunno." She scratched at the back of his neck as he leaned down closer. "What do you think I'm doing?"

He tried to graze her lips with his, but she ducked, slunk away. His gut twisted. "Miranda?"

"I want you to tell me . . . what does Yerina have that I don't? What can I do to have *all* of you and not just pieces?"

Fuck. He needed to clear his head, but the honeyed scent of her was far too sweet and growing thicker.

What was going on in her mind? He would sell his soul to read it.

"How come Yerina got to have all of you, and I don't?"

"You're too precious, Miranda. I cannot risk losing you."

"I don't feel precious."

Her words sent a spiral of anxiety through him, and all pleasure dimmed away.

"I don't feel precious, Govek," she said again, her voice firm. "I feel like you can *resist* me, like I don't make you crazy, like I'm the only one who's desperate. What did Yerina have that I don't?"

"She wasn't . . . she didn't—"

"What made you lose control with her, Govek?" she asked, reaching up to cup his face in her hands. She held him firm so he couldn't look away from her eyes. "What did she *do* that made her irresistible?"

"She wasn't irresistible. She was fucking *harsh*." *Fuck,* he couldn't stop the words from spilling. "She was wicked with her complaints. Constant in her demands. She pushed and yanked and scratched until I was in bloody *tatters*. And then I would give in because I was so fucking *lonely— fuck*."

He squeezed his eyes shut and worked the horrible memories out of his mind. Of being so fucking *desperate* that it made him lose himself. Of going to lengths beyond his endurance just to keep her from abandoning him. From being alone again.

"Sorry."

He blinked as Miranda brought him down into her arms. Pulled him to rest his cheek against the top of her head. Her hair tickled his nose and lips as she clung to him, allowing him to use her as an anchor until his turbulent emotions passed.

"I'm sorry, Govek. I didn't mean to bring up all those bad memories . . ." She wrapped her hands around his back and squeezed. Stroked. Fuck, it felt good. "I just want *all* of you. I want to prove to you that you can take me exactly how you want, and I'll never leave you."

I'll never leave you. He fucking *soared.* His blood warmed, his chest fluttered, and his limbs trembled.

And then she began to pull away from him.

"Miranda." His voice was far too close to a whine, and it made his cheeks heat.

But she just smiled at him, stepping away. Toward the edge of the path. His body went tense.

"Let's try something else. Something *I* want."

Something she wanted? "I'll give you *anything.*"

Her grin made his heart flip. "Good, then chase me."

His pleasure snuffed out. *"What?"*

"I want you to chase me." She took another step back, toward the woods. "To hunt me like the predator you are."

"Miranda," he said warningly even as his blood heated. No, *no,* he could absolutely *not* give into this desire of hers. It was too dangerous. Too risky.

Even if he wanted it too.

He reached out to grab her, but she managed to evade him by skittering back a few steps. Blood pounded in his ears as the instinct to give chase flooded his veins.

"*No,* Miranda," he said between clenched teeth. Fuck, he couldn't even look away from her. The mischievous glint in her eye, the way she nibbled at her perfect bottom lip, the blasted gorgeous *smile* she blessed him with, flooding him with heat, raking his flesh with want.

She stepped away and his hands twitched.

Maybe just a little—

No, *no.* He couldn't.

"I'll lose you." His throat was tight.

"You think you can't catch me before I get lost?" she teased, but his strangled expression at the mental image made her smile dim and he wanted to roar with fury over the loss. "Govek, I already told you. I'll never leave you."

He took deep, heaving breaths.

"And you're still under that magical binding, right?" She stepped back again. "So, you *can't* do anything that I wouldn't like."

Fuck, that was *true*.

"I'm not leaving. I just want to play a little game. To get that raw, carnal, sexy *beast* I like so much to come out and play."

The *beast* she liked so much. He trembled, took a step forward.

Her smile came back. "I want my big, rough orc to chase me. Hunt me like you promised you would. Drag me into the dirt and take me *exactly* how he wants."

Oh fuck, *fuck*.

He stepped forward.

The binding *didn't stop him*.

"I want you to pound me—hard. Use my body for your own pleasure. Use your claws on me. Your *teeth*."

His teeth too? She wanted that too? As badly as he did? Would she let him scrape and nip and *bite*?

Would she let him mark her as his?

Fuck, no! He couldn't. He couldn't hurt her.

But she began to unbutton her dress and his mouth went dry. He could taste her on his tongue. His teeth clenched, fangs working against his still tucked jaw.

The honeyed scent of her arousal slammed into him.

"*Miranda*," he snarled, and she shuddered. Her whole body trembled.

His control teetered.

"Come and get me, *tough guy*."

And then she turned on her heel and *bolted.*

And his rational mind evaporated with blistering *need.*

CHAPTER

TWELVE

MIRANDA

Wind whistled in her ears as she ran.

Her feet scrambled, and her muscles danced with adrenaline as he charged up behind her. His footfalls sounded like thunder. His snarling struck delicious pleasure deep into her core. Pulsing, aching.

She only made it about ten steps when he caught her and yanked her to his chest, pulled her against him. His frame loomed over her. The wall of muscle was firm and unrelenting. He dug his nose into her hair and dragged air deep into his lungs. She thought he might be trying to absorb her.

She squirmed, desperate, *fighting* him. He pulled her harder against his torso and snarled against her skin. Goosebumps broke out over her whole body, and heat bloomed in her gut.

"*Fuck*, Miranda." He shook his head as if trying to clear it. *"Don't fight me."*

"And what if I do?"

He made a strangled sound in the back of his throat and loosened his grip. Her heart jumped into her throat.

Instead of using the slack in his caging arms to bolt, she freed her hand and snaked it back between their bodies. Found the hard, twitching length of him. Stroked it from base to tip. Even through his pants, she could feel how hot he was.

His body shuddered against her and his breath came out like a choked wheeze, like he couldn't get enough air.

She grazed her thumb over the soft head of his cock beneath the rough wool. He shuddered again, and his grip loosened even more.

She took advantage of his distracted state and broke free of his grip.

"Miranda, *stop*," he snarled, but she'd already leaped away from him. Out of his reach. He wasn't chasing her this time, and she turned back to find him warring with himself. Uncertain.

"You don't know what's in my head, Miranda," he said between the clench of his sharp teeth. "You don't know what this *fighting* does to me. What horrors it sparks in my mind."

"I decide if they're horrors, tough guy," she said firmly as his eyes bulged. "Tell me what you want."

He swallowed thickly with a shudder. He stepped forward.

She swung around and sprinted away.

Got absolutely *nowhere* again.

He grabbed her by the arm with his huge hand and hauled her back to his frame again. His hand clenched right under her breast. She could feel the prickle of his claws against her sensitive skin, and it shot electric bliss through her body.

Then he tripped her feet out from under her and the autumn woods careened, spinning, swirling colors of bright red and orange. They fell to the ground, and she yipped with surprise at the sudden fall. He caught her in time to cushion it, making sure her cloak protected her body from the chilly forest floor. He cupped the back of her head so it didn't hit. She landed on her back in the damp leaves.

The trees above swayed in the breeze, reds and yellows accentuating his green face as his fangs untucked, his teeth so long and sharp her heart pounded with a mixture of nervousness and desire. His face was a mask of burning want.

She could feel his cock pressed against her thigh. The tip was so fucking close to the junction of her legs. She rolled her hips, and he hissed, squeezing his eyes shut.

"I want you so bad, Govek. Tell me what you want too."

"*Ah, fuck,*" he snarled, body trembled around her. He dipped low, close enough to her neck and shoulder that she could feel the sting of his teeth with every word. *"I want to bite you."*

A flash of white fear and hot longing shot down her spine.

"Right. *Here,*" he snarled, laving his tongue over the sensitive flesh right above her collarbone. "I want to wrap my teeth all the way around your neck and mark you as mine."

Oh fuck, why did that sound so *good*?

"I want to brand your flesh with my fangs, hold you captive with my tusks, and taste your blood on my tongue." He pulled back, leaving her flesh tingling and cold. His brows pinched and his jaw trembled. "I'm a *beast*, Miranda. *A monster.*"

"You are." She ground her hips into him again and his eyes flashed. His black pupils were tiny pricks in the sea of green and gold. "*My* monster. I want you, Govek. I want you to bite me."

He went so still she could *feel* his shock sparking against her flesh.

"You thought I wouldn't want that?" She brought her hands up into his hair so he was forced to hold her gaze. "You thought I wouldn't want to be *branded* by you, Govek. My sexy, strong, amazing man? Amazing *orc*. You thought I wouldn't want *everyone* to know that we belong together? That I've put my whole self into this? My whole *heart*? I trust you with every fiber of my being."

He exhaled against her skin. The heat of his breath curled around her shoulder exactly where his mouth would be curled. Her pussy pulsed as she imagined the sting of it, the tight hold.

And she would be his. Forever.

"Miranda, you smell so *good*," he said, voice laced with disbelief. "How can you smell so *good*?"

"I want this as much as you, Govek. Even more than you."

She grazed his abdomen, then she cupped the hot, throbbing bulge in his pants, smoothed her fingertips over the pulsing length of him from the base all the way to the head. He twitched, shivering and panting with each stroke.

His eyes shut and he groaned. "*Mirrrhanda.*"

Fuck, she *loved* how he said her name. She wanted him *howling* it.

And he would. His eyes opened and her breath caught.

His gaze was scorching. Pure and primal. His jaw unclenched, teeth dripping. Triumphant pleasure flooded his features, and her heart skipped.

"Mine," he said so low and slow that her body jittered. Her pussy clenched, soaking and slick, as she squirmed beneath him. He dragged air into his lungs, his eyes shuttered. "*Yes*. You want it."

"*Yes*." She tried to squirm out of his grip to make him wilder. "*Yes*, Govek. I want *you*."

Damn, did she ever. She'd never wanted anything more. She felt like she would lose her mind.

His voice was so raw it skittered pleasure all the way down her spine just before he yanked up her skirt. His hand cupped her aching pussy, holding it tight, and she gasped at the heat of his palm.

He dipped low, pressed his lips right against her ear. "I'm going to use my mouth on you *here* first." The damp heat of his breath curled around her neck and cheek like it had around her shoulder. Surrounding her. Flooding her senses. "I'm going to clasp my jaw around your core, thrash you with my tongue. Bring you to climax over and *over*." His mouth was at her neck now, heating her skin. It made her quake and tremble. "You'll squirm and buck and *come* against my mouth. I will drink your pleasure again and again until your mind is fucking *gone*."

She lost her breath as fire roared through her core, her legs trembled, her toes curled around the back of his calves as she spread her thighs. He dragged in the scent of her and cursed loudly.

"You are *wicked*, Miranda." He went up to his knees and fisted both sides of her dress, yanking it open. The buttons popped off as they ripped free.

Her body was bared to the chill of the forest and she shivered, but she couldn't tell if it was from the cold or from the intensity of his eyes on her naked breasts. His clawed finger raked along her nipple and it beaded as spikes of bliss radiated through her body. Her breath came in pants. She felt electric.

His voice was a low rumble, building fire in her gut. *"The Fades must have sent you to torture me."*

She shuddered as he traced the other nipple. The sight of his dangerously sharp claw gently circling her sensitive skin was *too good*. She wanted more. "Reward you."

His eyes snapped to hers and he let out a hum of thought that sent delicious waves of tingling bliss throughout her stomach. "I'm going to reward *you* now, Miranda."

Without warning, he scooped her up and hauled her over his shoulder. Her world dipped upside down and she gasped, half laughing, half shrieking as he carried her deeper into the woods.

Oh *fuck*, he was strong. So dang *strong*.

His hand dipped under her skirt and smoothed over her calf, to her thigh, and raking claws between them to part her legs.

She moaned, going boneless as his fingers slid toward her pussy. He was so close. *So close*.

"Wicked woman," he snarled and the sound of it made her clench and buck. She kicked out her legs, pointed her toes. Desperate. Needy. *"Mine."*

"Ooh," she panted, breathless. His long, thick fingers found the edge of her panties and delved beneath, dipped between the folds of her slit. Her hands fisted the back of his shirt as sparks of bliss radiated through her whole body. She bit her lip to keep from screaming.

He groaned, his body shuddered under her, but he kept walking. "So *wet*."

Fuck, she *was*. She could feel herself dripping all over his fingers as they stroked and swirled and danced around her clit, teasing her. She bucked mindlessly as he explored.

And then he swung her down without warning. She yipped as he dropped her, her ass landing on something soft.

A boulder. A huge boulder covered in thick, springy moss.

At just the right height.

He stepped in close, and the bulge of his cock was *right* at her pussy. His huge hands cupped her ass and dragged her into it, grinding her core against his cock. She bucked helplessly, clit pulsing with every rake against the rough texture of his pants.

She wanted his pants *off*.

"Govek, *please*."

"You're begging will win you *nothing*, woman." He leaned in to loom over her. His eyes were fiery swirls of gold. His teeth bright white and so sharp they glittered. His claws were braced right next to her hips.

He leaned in further until his lips were right over hers, but not quite touching. She moved forward, but he evaded her kiss. "You said you wanted me to do whatever I want," he snarled. "I plan to *wring you out, Miranda*. Push you to your limits the same way you push me to mine. Every one of your pleas will fall on deaf ears from this moment until I've had my fill of you."

"Ooh *fuck*." Her stomach quivered. Her whole body was an aching ball of *need*. "*Yes*, Govek! Anything you want."

"Good." He yanked off his shirt and threw it into the woods.

Goddamn, he was a fucking *dream*—rippling muscle, pure masculine strength. His delicious pine scent flooded her nose, stark against the autumn chill. His heat radiated, making her forget the cold.

"I'll have you now," he snarled. *"I'll have your surrender."*

Oh, hot damn. "Yes, *yes*."

He went to his knees.

His face was level with her thighs.

Her skin prickled, her stomach tensed and quivered, her pussy throbbed and her clit ached with want. He pulled up her skirt and the chill of the forest felt *delicious* on her skin.

His claws grazed her slightly, just enough to send spirals of shivering nerves down her back. He forced her legs wide, cut off her underwear with a slice of his claw, and bared her to the woods. The icy air seared her dripping, wet pussy.

"You're *mine*." His voice was back to being that tangible, fluid *bliss*, and she lost all her breath and reason.

"Yes." The word turned into a yelp as he wrapped his hands around her thighs and yanked her, forcing her to rest on her back against the rock. Her body was cushioned by the moss and her cloak. Her head was supported by the boulders flat top. The woods danced their colors above her, the sky was glittering bright blue.

His hot breath hit her lower stomach. Harsh and coiling. She squirmed as his hands forced her knees wider. Heat blazed over her as he drew near. His eyes fixed on her pussy as if mesmerized. Then his mouth opened wide.

Bliss skittered up her spine at the long slow lap of his tongue. She threw her head back, arching into him. "Govek, *yes*."

He raked over her sensitive clit, and she squirmed

against his grip, moaning, breathless, unable to get words out. It was so much she couldn't think, couldn't get enough air.

Waves of pleasure crashed over her as he teased her entry with the thick of his tongue before flattening it up her slit to lick her clit again.

Oh god, she couldn't *move*. Couldn't get away. She snapped her hips and his hands on her thighs tightened. He wouldn't let her move. She was going mad already, and he'd barely started. She wrapped her legs around his torso, kicked into his back. His tongue laved her again, searing hot and blissful.

Spirals of trembling need vibrated into her stomach, bloomed behind her eyes. He skewered his hot, slick tongue between her folds and she tried to thrash, hips desperate to thrust into him.

He wouldn't speed up. Wouldn't delve deeper. Wouldn't lick harder. She whined, pleaded, quaking for more as he methodically dragged her toward her climax. It went on and *on* until she was twitching and aching and *desperate*.

Then he slowly swirled the tip of his tongue around her clit and bright stars flashed in her eyes. Her pleasure mounted. She was going to—*fuck, fuck, fuck.*

Ecstasy radiated up her spine and made her arch into his mouth. Her scream echoed off the trees as her thoughts relented to the climax, releasing all tension and frustration. Her lungs gave a satisfied heave. Her vision spun as Govek pulled her onto him.

Onto his *face*.

"Wait—what?" Her words ended in a shuddering gasp as he slung her thighs over his shoulders, forcing them apart. Her heels dug into his back. Her back stayed against the mossy boulder, supporting some of her weight.

His eyes grew rich and dark. Clawed hands clutching her hips. He opened his mouth impossibly wide. *Too wide.*

Holy fuck! *He could unhinge his jaw.*

He yanked her throbbing pussy forward *into his mouth.*

His teeth prickled a tight ring all around her sensitive flesh. His tusks teased her ass and his fangs gripped right above her clit.

She was seated over him, half her weight on his face. Her hands scrambled to grip the mossy boulder for support as she looked down at her most sensitive place clutched in the mouth of a dangerous predator.

Tingling, aching, *need* blistered right up her spine, pooled in her core. Her pussy twitched and her clit started throbbing again.

His eyes smoldered, and she thought she may catch fire.

And then he growled.

Torturous vibration coiled up from her core, twisted in her gut, rained through her spine and she gasped, hardly able to breathe. Fuck, *fuck.*

He growled *again* and her head fell back onto the moss as a guttural cry burst from her lips. It echoed between the trees, swallowed up by the woods.

His low, vicious snarling broke through her and her hands shot out to grip the top of his head. She tightened her fingers into his hair. Pushed him away, pulled him in for more. She ground her heels into his back as she tried to kick and buck against his vibrating mouth, his caressing lips, his prickling teeth. His hold on her hips was so tight she couldn't even *twitch.*

He howled and moaned and rumbled so deep into her gut her body turned to putty in his hands.

And just when she thought she would go mad from the pleasure, his tongue laved all the way from her dripping core to her pulsing, desperate clit.

Her vision blurred.

He raked over her quivering flesh and forced her to yield. She screamed, voice hoarse already. She thrust her hips and got nowhere. Babbled senselessly, but her pleas fell on deaf ears.

Just like he'd promised.

He swirled and flicked and *bit*. Stinging tightness around her pelvis helped to cut through the agony of her over sensitive clit until she was a pool of ecstasy. Completely limp on the rock. There was no use fighting.

She couldn't escape. He drenched her in pleasure and she drowned in it. Choked.

Tingling bliss built up her spine.

"*Govek!*" she screamed as rapture forced her into another orgasm. He skewered his tongue into her, thick and probing, lapping up every drop. Her vision went white. "Fuck, Govek, *yes*."

His mouth tightened, the bite turned sharp, and it only made her tremble harder. She couldn't breathe, couldn't escape. She didn't want the ecstasy to end.

"*Again.*"

She felt the word more than heard it. It rolled through her stomach and exploded in her mind. She dug her heals into his back, tried to move away. "I *can't*."

"*You will*," he snarled and she lost herself. Rippling, bucking, unsure if she wanted to escape or beg for more. She panted, her eyes rolled back, her head shook.

"Yield!" he roared. His massive tongue drove *inside* her. *Deeper.* He pressed *up*. Skewered right into her G-spot and raked it without mercy.

"*Oh fuck!*"

Her body relented, arching away from the boulder and forcing his tongue deeper into her pussy. She was hurtled, pulled into the depths, surrounded by him completely, absorbed. Her mind seized.

His mouth left her, popped off, leaving her raw and aching. The icy chill made her spasm. Her hands grappled to find him.

He yanked her down off the rock. Onto him. Splayed her hips over his.

His massive cock skewered her with one smooth, effortless thrust that had all air pushed from her lungs.

She threw her head back in all-consuming *bliss* as he yanked her to sit flush against his pelvis. All the way inside her. She felt every twitch and shudder of his cock as his hips trembled.

Then he wrapped his hand around the back of her neck. Yanked her down.

His breath was hot on her shoulder.

His fangs sunk into her flesh.

The bite speared her, forced her eyes wide. Pain melded with pleasure into pure sensation so stark and perfect she was mindless. She pushed into his mouth and he snarled. She couldn't escape. She didn't want to. Thrill poured like magma through her veins. The climax felt *endless.* Everything was raw and tight. She thrust her hips, desperate and wanting more, *more, MORE.*

Her pussy rippled around his plunging cock. His mouth and sharp teeth a perfect contrast to her overwhelming pleasure. The sting was absolutely mind bending.

She couldn't scream anymore. She dragged air over her tongue. Tasted the forest. Tasted *him*—pine and salt.

He roared around her shoulder. His grip on her flesh firming as his teeth sunk deeper. He held her captive. His hands gripped her tight, filled her up. Filling places inside her that had been left void for so long. Empty spots that had been yearning for someone to flood them. Someone to end the bitter loneliness. Someone who would never abandon her. Who would keep her and cherish her and never let her go.

Govek filled all those voids. Every last one.

Liquid heat bloomed in her guts as he came. His whole body vibrated, his cock spasmed inside her, and she was pushed over again. Hurtled into more gut clenching, mind numbing ecstasy.

He released her shoulder. The wound pulsed with the same fervor as her pussy. It matched her heartbeat. His cock twitched inside her, and he moaned low, lapping at the stinging punctures with his soft tongue.

Finally, her mind relented. She went limp, and he flopped onto his back against the chilly forest floor. He pulled her to his chest. Her muscles loosened and twitched. Her pussy clamped around his cock, which was still buried deep inside her.

His heat surrounded her, his thick arms enveloped her body to adjust her cloak and protect her from the chill.

Even through this, he took care of her. Her heart thundered a sweet, intoxicating rhythm that matched Govek's own. She could feel their bodies beating in tandem.

He relaxed against the ground. He adjusted her so he

could kiss the wound on her shoulder again. The action made half of his cock slide out of her. She trembled at the loss, tightening her thighs to keep him inside. His breath hitched with pleasure. His breath heated the bite wound until the stinging turned to tingles.

He lapped at her again, full flat tongue soothing against the cuts. She wriggled against him and nuzzled her cheek into his hair. "Govek, that feels so *good.*"

He hummed in response. The rumble danced more pleasure into her bones.

She could see the bite from the corner of her eye. His tender attention had stopped the bleeding, and she wondered if his magic might be at play. A wide oval of punctures framed all the way around her shoulder. Deep enough they would certainly scar, but not so deep they were dangerous.

He moved her again so her head could rest on his shoulder, right next to his face. His hand covered the entire back of her head. The other tucked under her cloak and skirt to rest over her butt, kneading it softly.

He could go from ruthless to tender in so little time . . . her heart melted.

She adjusted so her hands could roam over his abs, trace the divides and grooves with her fingertips, breathe in his husky spice.

A low whimper pulled her out of her thoughts, and she blinked. Finally, looking up to Govek's face.

Instead of blissful, she found him tortured, brows tight. His gaze was fixed on her shoulder, which throbbed and pulsed with the steady beat of her heart. Hers *and* his. It pounded in her soul.

Govek's breath came out shuddering and raw. His jaw trembled.

He regretted it.

She didn't.

"I hope it scars," she said softly, and his eyes went wide with remorse. She caught his gaze. "I hope it scars so that I'm branded by you. So that anytime anyone sees it, they'll know I'm yours. And I'll remember too. I never want to forget this."

His expression fell from torture to gaping shock so fast she almost couldn't believe it. He blinked his beautiful golden green eyes at her, opened his mouth, but nothing came out.

And then his face crumbled, and he buried it in her shoulder again, hiding himself away as he trembled. Clinging to her as he rode out the storm of his emotions.

Her mind fluttered back to the revelation she'd come to with Savili and Iytier.

"I love you, Govek," she whispered into his scalp, and he began to quake. His grip around her waist tightened, and his breath shuddered. She curled her fingers in his hair and pulled him back gently so he would meet her eyes, see the honesty there. "I love you."

His eyes were flooded, and he plastered a kiss to her lips. His mouth was so soft, so sweet. His tongue bathed her in tenderness even as she tasted her own blood on it. The contrast was so perfect her eyes prickled with unshed tears.

He rained kisses down her face, and she returned them. She kissed the wetness on his cheeks, absorbing as many of his turbulent emotions as she could.

She wanted him to feel nothing but good. Only pleasure and contentment and bliss for the rest of his days. And she was going to watch every one of those days by his side.

CHAPTER

THIRTEEN

They had safely returned to their home and Govek still could not find words.

He watched Miranda cook at the stove. He'd bandaged her shoulder and the white linen peeped through the neckline of her new dress. The other was ruined, but she'd folded it neatly and tucked it safely into the bottom of her trunk. She said she wanted to keep it.

He had tinctures that would heal the injury in moments, but she refused them. She hadn't been embellishing when she'd said she wanted it to scar. And scar it would. The raised white and pink marks would forever remind him of this day.

Fuck, what had he done? He'd lost himself. Given into his most ruthless needs.

And she'd liked it. She'd wanted it. She'd said that . . . that she . . .

His mind couldn't seem to process, so he focused on the food. Foreign combinations of garlic and ginger. His stomach rumbled and his mouth watered.

"Hey."

She turned to face him and quirked a smile as if she knew what he was thinking. "Come over here."

He got up from his chair at the table and loped shakily across the floor. She plucked a quick kiss to his jaw and pulled him by the hand until his chest was against her back. Her sweet scent mingled with the cooking and made him lean in.

Fuck, he shouldn't be allowed to feel this much bliss, contentment, joy.

He nuzzled the top of her head as she turned back to the pan. His body shivered against her as she stroked the arm he'd wrapped around her waist. He needed to find words. To speak. But he couldn't. They just wouldn't come out of his worthless throat.

"This is nice." She leaned into him. "We should cook like this all the time."

He nodded in agreement as his eyes fell to half-mast. He stroked her hair away from her neck. She smelled like paradise made real.

Miranda.

His mate.

He hadn't asked her to be his mate formally yet, but in his mind, she was. He'd thought of her as such for so long now. Maybe even from the first moment he'd seen her fall out of the sky. But humans took a long time to consider lifelong commitments. Miranda had said that her people dated for *years* before marrying.

He would wait to ask. Give her time to settle. Perhaps after the clansman were gone, and they had the Rove Woods all to themselves, she would be ready to carry the full label.

He felt no rush because it truly did not matter. He would never let this woman go, regardless.

His eyes drifted to the little bag at the corner of the kitchen where she had put her evidence, and his stomach twisted. He would rip anyone who tried to take her to shreds.

"Still a bit tongue tied, huh?"

"I apologize," he said, almost as a reflex. His voice was so raw it hardly sounded like his own.

She set down the wooden spoon and turned to face him. "Govek, you don't have to apologize for that. I don't *want* you to apologize for that."

He raised a brow at her, confused.

She stroked his cheek, and he leaned into the touch, soaking up her warmth. "I don't mind you being quiet. It's part of your nature, and I *love* your nature." Her eyes went soft and pink brightened her cheeks. "I love *you*."

His stomach bloomed with warmth, and he was certain his emotions would get the best of him again. He crushed her in his arms, basking in the bright, warm sensation that worked its way through the darkest corners of his mind.

She loved him. This perfect, wonderful woman *loved* him.

"Goodness gracious," she said as her hip bumped the handle of the pan and some of the stew-like meal sloshed out.

"Goodness gracious?" he mirrored, incredulous. Her tone suggested she meant it as a curse.

"What?" She tossed him a sidelong glance as she mopped up the spill. "You cuss all the time, and you can't handle 'goodness gracious'?"

A smile tipped the corners of his mouth. "'Goodness gracious' is not cussing, Miranda."

"Of course it is!" she countered, but her tone betrayed her mirth.

He worked to bring it higher. "It's about as harsh as a dewdrop."

Her laughter radiated through the room, and contentment bloomed in his chest, built a wall of security and sweetness he'd never known.

"Who are you trying to impress with it? Baby bunnies?" His offhand comment caused another round of giggles. The sound was melodic and dreamlike.

"I was a flipping daycare worker," she said, her beam radiant. "I don't use foul language!"

He leaned against the counter, crossed his arms casually. "Ah yes, this job where you sat upon children."

"Oh, hush up," she snapped, though her laughter continued.

"And you do curse, Miranda," he said, leaning in closer. "I've heard it many times. I can prove it."

He bridged the gap between them, dipped his lips to hers. Held her captive with his kiss. Reminding him of the metallic sweetness she'd flooded his mouth with in the woods. Of the bite he'd given her shoulder and the happiness she'd expressed when she'd talked about it marking her as his.

For once in his miserable existence, he didn't feel a tinge of remorse.

He dueled with her tongue, nibbled at her lips. No

longer worried he might cut her. He could control himself with her and if he wounded her by accident, he had no fear he could not make his mistake right.

The security of this was like nothing he'd ever felt before. A weight lifted from his gut. The brightness of his soul broke through the dim.

He broke off the kiss, leaving her lips swollen and her eyes misty.

"Fuck . . ." She touched those reddened lips before letting out another wry laugh. "Okay, fine. I do curse. But it's *your* fault for making me."

"I love you, Miranda."

Her breath caught and her eyes flooded with tears. He touched his forehead to hers and whispered again. "I love you."

"Ah shoot." She wiped at her eyes, voice thick. "I already told you that. And I know you do. It shouldn't be this big a thing."

He chuckled, mingling radiant joy as he dipped and kissed the tears off her cheeks. "You are perfect, Miranda. The Fades must have created you for me."

"Or the other way around." Her voice warbled a little. She put her arms around his neck and tugged him into her. "Sometimes I still wonder if you're real, if I'm dreaming."

"Sometimes, I wonder if I died," he said, musing on that day he lay paralyzed on the forest floor. Listening to her babble about being in a dream. Who would have imagined he would be lucky enough to listen to that babble for the rest of his days?

"Don't talk about your death, Govek." Her concern was so obvious it made his heart flutter.

He raked his fingers through her soft, lush hair, earning

shivers of pleasure from her. Leaned down to her mouth. "I apologize. Allow me to make it up to you."

"The food will burn," she said, even as she tipped her head up to receive his kiss.

"And I'll gladly eat it anyway," he said against her lips.

A frantic knock sounded at the door.

Miranda jumped and knocked her forehead into his nose with a crack. "Oh gosh." She reached up to rub the sting with her gentle fingers. "I'm so sorry."

He could only grin.

The knock hammered again, and the scent registered. Sage. His brows furrowed as he eased Miranda's hand away and went to answer.

Viravia burst in without preamble and shut the door behind her. The hood of her cloak was tucked so tight around her head it was a wonder she'd been able to see, and she threw it off without care as she entered, disheveling her hair. Her cheeks were bright from the cold.

"Viravia, my gosh, hi," Miranda said, but the woman ignored her, forcing Govek's mood to sour.

"Govek, is it true?" Viravia's wild eyes darted to his. "I heard about . . . well, *everything*."

"Are you all right, Viravia?" Miranda came over to the table. She didn't seem as upset by Viravia's dismissal.

And the woman made her amends quickly. "Miranda, I'm sorry for barging in. I'm just all out of sorts."

"Here, sit down." Miranda pulled out one of the chairs.

But Viravia looked to Govek instead. "Savili sent me a message. She told me . . . she told me about the judgment. Is it true?"

"Yeah," Miranda said. "I'm not going to let Maythra get

away with attacking me, but they say Govek was out of line when he broke Wolvc's jaw."

Fuck, he hated the reminder that he'd been so far gone. His fists curled and the one that had cracked the male's teeth tingled.

"Not that," Viravia breathed, allowing herself to be helped into the chair. "The *punishment.*"

Govek's guts plummeted as Miranda met his gaze. "Punishment?"

"You were *told*, weren't you, Govek?" Viravia asked.

"Yes, Karthoc informed me of it."

Viravia sucked in her breath. "You have to call for a lower cost, Govek. This isn't right."

"Okay, hold on, *what* punishment are you talking about?" Miranda stepped between Viravia and Govek.

He let out a long sigh. "Chief Ergoth has insisted that those accused of wrongdoing in this face the highest punishment. If found guilty, I will be forced to go to the foothills." He swallowed thickly. "To the front lines of the war."

Miranda's face went pale, and he reached out to hold her arms lest she fall.

"Do not worry, Miranda." Govek willed her to recover. "I have a plan."

"Yeah." Miranda's face went flat. "The plan is that you won't lose."

He clenched his jaw, still stroking her arms. His eyes flashed to Viravia, and she was obviously stricken. Tense.

"But if . . ." Viravia wrung her hands. "If you *do* lose?"

Miranda shot Viravia a withering look, but Govek found it a valid question and no longer saw need to hide his plans from the woman.

"Should they find against me, Miranda and I will go to the mists. Into hiding."

A deadly silence descended.

"Govek, *no!*" Viravia gasped. She was so pale he wondered if she may faint.

"What are the mists?" Miranda looked between them. "Govek?"

"Govek, that's complete *lunacy*. Even crazier than going to *Estwill*."

"There is no other place that I could escape a punishment. They would hunt me to every corner of this world. At least within the mists, Miranda and I would stand a chance."

"*What* are the mists?" Miranda insisted again.

"They are the edges of our world," Govek said. "Great banks of fog that are a mystery many have tried to solve."

"And that *none* have ever returned from."

"If we stay hidden at the edges and do not go too deep, we will be fine." Govek assured them when Miranda gave him a worried look.

"Govek, you *can't* do this. You must at least *try* to reason with Ergoth."

"He will not listen. He is the one who made this demand of Karthoc."

"But what is Ergoth thinking? He has to know this won't stop the merger."

Govek shook his head. "I do not know my father's plan. I only know that he must have one and that there is nothing I can do to change it."

"Reason with *the warlord,* then." Viravia was shaking and her voice quivered. "You're his cousin. He can't possibly be so heartless as to want to see you *killed*."

"What is done is done, Viravia." Govek found it telling that Viravia did not even question Ergoth's sanity when he tried, once again, to put his only living son to death.

"*Please*, Govek," Viravia pleaded, coming to her feet. She reached for him. "There has to be another way. You must become chief of Rove Wood or we'll be forced to merge. I can't leave . . . I have to stay . . ."

Viravia collapsed, head in her hands as she began to sob. Govek's stomach twisted in confusion, and he glanced at Miranda, unsure what to do.

Miranda did not hesitate to step forward. She placed her hands on Viravia's shoulders and gave them a little squeeze. "This seems like more than simply not wanting to merge, Viravia. Can you tell us what's going on?"

Viravia's head snapped up, her eyes round with fear, her lips trembled and her cheeks were soaked. "I-I'm sorry. I'm sorry I can't—"

"You don't have to." Miranda rubbed Viravia's shoulders. "Lord knows I have my own secrets. Look, if you really don't want to leave the Rove Woods, couldn't you ask Oakwall if they would take you in?"

Govek thought it a fine suggestion until Viravia pointed out the obvious.

"He . . . he would *never* let me."

Chief Ergoth would never leave her behind. The babe in her belly was Tavggol's only son. The last trace of his brother. His kin, who he loved with his every fiber.

"We will aid you in hiding."

The words left Govek's lips before he realized what he was saying. Miranda's brows rose, clearly perturbed that he'd made this decision without consulting her.

And logic caught up with him then, too. Viravia was less

than a moon from giving birth. The forest was relentless with incoming winter, and he had his own mate to care for.

And yet, this was Tavggol's mate—a woman who had been endlessly kind to him. He knew not what horrors lay in her past, but he could not leave her to suffer and pretend she and the babe meant nothing to him.

Blessedly, Miranda gave him a nod, and he repeated. "You may flee with us for a time, and then once the clan is gone, we can decide where to go. If you want to travel with us to the mists or stay at Oakwall."

"Are . . ." She looked to Miranda, gripping her hand. "Are you certain?"

"Yeah," Miranda said. "We won't abandon you here."

"Oh Govek, Miranda." Viravia's eyes flooded with unshed tears all over again. "Thank you. *Thank you.*"

Govek nodded and Miranda's hands fell away as Viravia stood and hugged her tight. Miranda rubbed her back somewhat awkwardly and promised once again that things would turn out all right.

"I-I'd better go." Viravia finally pulled away from Miranda. "Thank you. Both of you. I promise, once things are more settled . . . I'll . . . I'll tell you everything."

Viravia wouldn't meet Govek's eye as her hand stroked her stomach and Govek's own gut twisted again. He balled his fists.

Had he made a mistake inviting Viravia along?

But the promise was done and, in the end, Govek knew the guilt of abandoning his brother's widow would be far worse than whatever horrors she was running from.

"*And,*" Viravia said, meeting his eyes solidly. "I swear, I will do all I can to ensure the judgment tomorrow results in your favor."

Govek blinked at the intensity in Viravia's eyes, but she left without another word. Miranda all but collapsed into a chair.

"Oh my god. I'm freaking . . ."

Angry that he'd made this offer to Viravia without consulting her? Nervous for what was to come? Upset that their easy plans had been dashed?

"Curious!"

Curious? He shouldn't have been surprised and yet his mate's admission still brought lightness to his chest. Humor to his heart.

He kneeled before her and wrapped his arms around her stomach, pressed his face into her chest. She was so warm, and she scratched lightly at his hairline, sending shivers down his back.

"I'm sorry," he said.

"You have nothing to be sorry for. Sometimes we gotta make decisions on the fly. And I was perfectly capable of negating your offer if I hadn't wanted to go through with it. But . . ."

"But . . ." He looked up to meet her gaze.

"He's your nephew, Govek," Miranda said with a softness in her eyes that reminded him of her face when she was holding little Haysik. "And she's your sister. Kinda."

He buried his face in her chest again, right between her soft breasts. Beneath the clothes, he could smell the faint blood of the mark he'd given her.

She was his, and he was uncertain what he had done to deserve her.

"You think she'll still tell us what's going on with her after we help her?"

Govek snorted. "I could try to force it out of her if you want."

"No . . . I like her too much to do that. And it sounds like we're gonna have her as a companion whether we flee to the mists or not. I'd rather not make her upset."

Fuck. In this one promise, he'd ruined the happy plan of keeping Miranda all to himself in the abandoned Rove Woods.

"I'm sure we can get her to join Oakwall," Govek said. "And I'll keep you here. All to myself."

Miranda laughed—a sweet sound that flooded him, drenched him, pulled him down into contentment. "You'll have to share a little with my babies once we find them and bring them here too," Miranda insisted. His throat tightened at the solid conviction in her face. The unwavering determination that these children of hers really *were* alive here on Faeda somewhere.

They could be. He had no reason to believe they *weren't*.

And yet . . .

"She . . . didn't mention someone who could find them for us. Do you think she forgot?"

"After all that has occurred? It's likely."

Miranda hummed in thought. "Let's remind her after the judgment tomorrow. It's not like we can do much right this second anyway, since the seer still won't talk to me. But after we win tomorrow, he will. I *know* he will."

His whole body went rigid, and Miranda stroked his hair, clearly noticing.

"It's going to be all right. We're going to win. We will find my babies. And then, we'll live happily ever after. *I know it.*"

He looked up into Miranda's solid determination. Her strength drew him in and amazed him. This woman who was so certain in her conviction.

Even as his own instincts clamored with fear.

"You're not going to lose." Miranda gave him another squeeze. "We're ready."

He took a deep breath and nodded, wishing he believed her.

CHAPTER

FOURTEEN

MIRANDA

The hall was absolute *chaos*.

The voices of the orcs as they exchanged their good mornings, found places to sit, and visited were almost a roar by the time the breakfast had finished being served. It seemed like everyone who hadn't wanted to eat here was now showing up. The door was propped open at this point.

And Miranda was so impatient she wanted to gnaw her fingers off.

Instead, she busied herself by going through her little bag of evidence. She reread her note and tried not to stare at Maythra, Rogeth, and Wolvc, who were seated in chairs just as hard and uncomfortable as her own on the opposite side of Ergoth's platform. Maythra's glare was hot enough to burn her to cinders, but Rogeth was constantly fidgeting. He squirmed around and tried to look anywhere but at her.

Wolvc, however, almost appeared resigned. His jaw was bandaged in white linen. His eyes were a little cloudy, like he was drugged. He twitched a few times as if pained, and Miranda wondered just how bad his injury was. Once or twice, Miranda managed to catch his eye and furrow her brow at him, and each time, he simply regarded her with a dejected look she was *dying* to decipher.

Would he tell the truth?

A light brush to her hair caught her attention, and she leaned into Govek slightly, letting his warmth and comfort soothe her frazzled nerves. He'd chosen the chair between her and the clan, blocking her from view for the most part. Didn't stop people from staring, or from trying to crane their necks around Govek's bulky frame to see her, but it was better than nothing.

"You doing okay, tough guy?" They'd been sitting here for a while now. Long enough that her butt was going numb. Govek was already so tense, and the chair seemed too small for him. It forced his knees to bunch up. He kept extending them out for a few seconds to stretch. She stroked her hand down his leg, meaning to be soothing, but the fire in his eyes made her stomach flip.

"I'm well, Miranda," Govek said softly. "Just as I was a few moments ago."

"I wouldn't keep asking if you stopped lying," she grumbled, and he scowled at her. "We're ready. I've got all my evidence, and I know all the proceedings."

Though she kinda wished her plan wasn't quite so . . . argumentative.

There was no way around it. They'd been set up to fail, and she intended to level the playing field.

She *had* to. She had to get justice. She had to overcome or else the seer wouldn't be able to help her. She scanned the crowd for him again.

Still not here.

"Miranda," Govek rumbled, making her shiver. He trailed a finger up her arm and back down to her palm. The gentle caress was so soothing and made her marvel. He'd been so *affectionate* since the trip to Oakwall.

Not that she minded in the least.

She tipped her head a little. "Lean down here. I need to tell you something." His eyes flashed with worry, but he obeyed, and she smacked a kiss to his cheek before murmuring, "I love you."

That adorable little snort of contentment he always did when she confessed her affection broke from him and he pressed his forehead to hers a second before sitting back up. Then he wrapped a hand around her hip and tugged her closer, almost off the chair.

She laughed despite her tension as their thighs bumped. "You want me to just crawl into your lap?"

"Wouldn't mind that." He sent another quick grin at her. He didn't seem worried about this.

But he wouldn't be, since he had a plan whether they won or not. A plan Miranda didn't want to think about. Living in the mists in complete isolation. Always looking over their shoulders. On the run.

Her babies wouldn't thrive there like they would in the Rove Woods. She may not even be able to keep them there. She'd have to introduce them to Oakwall Village and leave them behind. Again.

Just as she'd left them on Earth.

Her stomach twisted.

They wouldn't need that plan because they *would* win. She would get justice.

"Maybe if I ask Chief Ergoth *really* nice, he'll let me sit on you for the duration," Miranda teased, her eyes flitting to where Ergoth was still mingling with the clan down at the first table. The same one Govek had struck with his magic. She could see the black bolts jutting from the charred center, which had a crater the size of a soup bowl. They stretched almost twenty feet before finally petering out.

It looked kinda cool, honestly.

Ergoth continued to chat away with a group of orcs with black hands. Govek had said they were the lead conjurer team, but every now and then, Ergoth would look her direction. And the fury in his eyes made her stomach queasy.

"Why's he so mad at *me*?" she murmured to herself, but of course Govek heard.

"I think . . ." Govek trailed off, and she looked up at him and stroked the back of his hand to get him talking again. "His plan was to have me bear the role of chief but default entirely to his judgment."

"Right." Miranda nodded.

Govek held her eyes. "But he cannot have control over me because *you* hold all of that control."

Miranda's stomach flipped right over, and she let out a little laugh before shaking her head. "Govek, don't make jokes like *that*."

"I am not jesting, woman," he said with enough sincerity that it forced her laughter to die out.

Her blood buzzed and her heart clamored out a rapid pace. "So I guess this means I really *can* tattoo my name on your ass."

Govek chuckled. "I'd let you tattoo much more than *that*. I'd let you brand any part of me you wished."

"Oh my god, Govek," she snapped, and he was

surprised enough at her outburst that she realized his mind hadn't taken the turn hers did. Her eyes flashed down to his groin and he instantly got it, going tense as he realized the liberty he'd just granted her. Before he could worry she might not be joking, she said, "Nope, not going there. *That* is perfect just the way it is."

She stroked a hand up his thigh, forcing a shiver out of him. He snatched up her hand before it got too high.

A loud scoff came from across the platform and Miranda looked up to find Maythra glowering at her. She opened her mouth as if she were about to spout off.

Karthoc burst into the room.

Miranda sat straight along with the rest of the clan as the scowling warlord stalked into the hall with his battle-scarred brother following close behind.

And no one else.

Dang it, *where* was the seer?

Chief Ergoth called a greeting even as he made his way toward the platform. "Karthoc, good morrow to you. I trust the trade went well after we parted ways."

Karthoc's scowl was hot enough to melt all the crystal leaves of the Rove Tree and Miranda was instantly curious about what had happened after she and Govek had left.

"The seer won't be joining us today?" Chief Ergoth asked. Apparently, Miranda wasn't the only one who'd noticed his absence. Ergoth climbed up onto his platform as Karthoc approached, but the warlord stayed on the ground, scowling up at his uncle.

"He still may," Karthoc said. "He was unwell this morning, but he is going to make the attempt."

"I am sorry to hear it." Ergoth didn't sound the least bit sorry. "Let us not delay."

The chief stood tall and stretched his arms wide. His billowing violet robes were even shinier today, catching the light from the nearest bonfire. He had not one white hair out of place from his braids.

The hundreds of once clamoring orcs fell into hushed silence, all eyes on their leader. "My clan! Welcome. I trust we are all rested. It is here, beneath the Great Rove Tree, that we have another judgment. Although it may cause pain to see strife within our great clan, together we overcome."

He followed with a chant in a rolling, deep language that most of the orcs in attendance joined, but she noted that neither Govek nor Karthoc spoke.

"Warlord Karthoc has deigned to oversee these proceedings. It is a great matter that we are deciding on today. Long has it been since such violence has been done to one of our own women." Ergoth turned and met Miranda's eyes. His expression made her back straighten. "I would like to formally apologize, Miranda, on behalf of all in this clan who failed to protect you. I swear it will not happen again."

Miranda tightened her grip on Govek's arm. "That's nice of you to say, but I don't need your protection."

The chief's eyes burned but before he could say another word Rogeth cut in.

"Chief Ergoth."

The young orc butcher sat on the edge of his chair. His fists clenched and unclenched.

Ergoth turned his raging gaze away from her. "Yes, Rogeth, you may speak."

"Can the binding be removed now?" His question came out almost as soon as Ergoth stopped speaking.

"That is fine, as long as no one objects."

Rogeth's eyes darted around the room and Miranda realized that his fidgeting and nervousness may have been because he was in *pain*.

"Come forward, Sythcol," Ergoth called. And while the conjurer came up to the platform, Miranda looked to Govek.

"Tough guy . . . how bad *is* it?"

Govek glanced at her and then let out a long breath. "For me, not bad. I have practice dealing with it, but for them . . ."

Miranda looked over to where Sythcol had just finished removing the binding from Rogeth. The male all but collapsed into his chair, head in his hands, body shuddering.

"But . . . it was that bad for you? At first?" Miranda's throat closed up a little.

Govek nodded.

She hugged his arm tight, brought his hand up to kiss his palm.

Fuck Ergoth and this entire clan. Govek had literally been *tortured*.

Sythcol stopped in front of Govek and rose his black hands to his chest. The discoloration stretched to his elbows, much further than the other conjurers.

Miranda could not see this magic, but the concentration on the conjurer's smooth face told her when the task was done.

Before he stepped away, Sythcol whispered, "I am sorry." His voice sounded tight, and his eyes were lowered.

"You need not be. I've long grown used to this," Govek said, but his response only made Sythcol look more stricken before the conjurer turned away.

"Let us move on. Tell me, Miranda, has Govek informed you of how these proceedings take place?"

"He has."

"Then you know first we will announce the consequences of this judgment," Ergoth said, looking more than a little smug. He kept his eyes on her as he stated, "As we are all aware, this is an extreme case. Attacking a member of this clan is never taken lightly, to say nothing of the attack on one of our women. Therefore, the punishment must also be severe.

"The males in this face the ultimate punishment for warriors of Faeda. The transgressor will go to Avokil with Karthoc. To redeem themselves in battle against the Waking Order."

A shocked rumble passed over the orcs and Miranda examined their faces, tried to catch some of their words. They seemed rather surprised, but no one seemed overly alarmed.

Govek took her hand in his and she glanced up at his tense expression. She couldn't tell if he was offering comfort or needed it. Likely it was both.

And then, Chief Ergoth's lips curled in a smile that made a shudder go down Miranda's spine. "In addition, the punishment will commence *immediately* after the judgment has concluded."

Miranda's blood went still and icy as her mind sparked over that order.

Immediately? Govek would be taken into custody right then and there?

Would they have a chance to escape?

"Govek?" Miranda whispered, her voice broke, and his expression did *nothing* to quell her terror. His cheek twitched and his hand clutched hers so tight it was painful.

Nausea spiraled in her and she worked down the bile in her throat.

They wouldn't lose. *They wouldn't.*

"There are two outcomes in this," Ergoth continued. "Either Govek attacked Miranda and then attacked Wolvc when he came to her defense." Miranda gripped Govek's hand tighter. "Or Wolvc and Rogeth harmed Miranda, and Govek attacked Wolvc when he came upon the scene." Miranda's stomach twisted at the way he worded it.

It dropped completely as Ergoth continued. "Therefore, we are holding two punishments today and deciding two outcomes. One for the attack on Miranda and the other for the attack on Wolvc."

"Wait! So, you intend to punish Govek no matter the outcome?" Miranda went so cold she was almost numb.

"Govek did attack Wolvc in both cases, using his magic to ensure the worst injury would be endured." Ergoth's piercing golden eyes caused ice to skitter in Miranda's veins.

"But he was *defending* me." Miranda rose to her feet and the eyes of every orc in the room bruised her flesh. "Are you suggesting that orcs aren't allowed to defend their women?"

Ergoth's expression twitched, revealing malice for a split second. "That is not in debate here and holds no bearing on the outcome."

"H-holds no bearing?" Miranda snapped just as she felt Govek tug her back into her seat.

"I agree with Miranda."

Miranda craned her neck around Govek and found Iytier standing among the sea of green. Savili sat at the table beside him. She cradled their baby and watched her mate encouragingly.

"Iytier, please voice your concerns," Ergoth said without even the subtlest hint of irritation or worry.

"I find it unsettling that males of this clan could be subjected to our most extreme punishments simply for protecting our mates. Oftentimes, in such situations, there is no time to issue a challenge and action must be taken immediately. Are we all to be forced to go to the frontlines of the war with the Waking Order simply for protecting our women?"

A general clamor of agreement fluttered over the orcs, and Ergoth held up his hand to silence them. "I agree with this."

Miranda was stunned with Ergoth's quick reply and not so surprised when he followed up.

"*However,* we must maintain on the topic at hand. We can discuss this issue at another time. For today, we must maintain the judgment."

Iytier tensed, scowling. "So Govek should be punished today and another orc who is accused of the same transgression tomorrow will not be?"

"Hmm," Ergoth said slowly, his light smile grating against Miranda's nerves. "I see how this is unfair. If you would like, we *can* hold a vote on this."

Iytier glanced down at Savili, who nodded and he straightened. "Yes. I call a vote."

"Fine," Ergoth spread his hands wide again. "All those in favor of reducing Govek's punishment now, before we know if he is responsible for these heinous attacks, please stand."

"Ergoth," Karthoc growled threateningly.

"That isn't what I—" Iytier started.

"I apologize." Chief Ergoth looked genuinely remorseful. This orc's ability to fake contrition unsettled Miranda. "Truly. I must have misunderstood what you wanted. Please, Iytier, word the vote exactly as you will it."

Iytier looked around the room in defeat.

The damage was done. Who would vote to reduce the sentence without proof?

"I . . . call to vote that Govek not be punished for injuring Wolvc while defending his woman."

No one stood.

"*Just* for the attack on Wolvc," Iytier clarified rapidly. "The punishment for the attack on Miranda can still maintain."

She searched the room.

No one stood. Not one.

Miranda looked to Ergoth, who stood atop his podium, chin raised, posture easy. He'd known none of them would side with Govek. He'd known that not one of them would play fair.

Govek and her were officially fighting a losing battle. But Miranda steeled her jaw and straightened her spine.

She would still fight.

CHAPTER

FIFTEEN

GOVEK

Govek's mind reeled. His thoughts spun and his heart raced. He wanted to pick Miranda up and flee.

He'd thought of doing so this morning. They could have packed up a sack on the way out the door and ventured off into the woods. They'd hide among the mists and pretend Rove Wood Clan had never existed.

He should have known the clan would be biased. That they wouldn't play fair in this.

These could be the last moments he spent with Miranda. His love.

Fuck.

"Sythcol, please, come forth to perform the clearing."

Ergoth looked almost *satisfied*. It blistered in Govek's chest.

Yes, his father was meant to put the clan before everything else, but Govek was still his *son*. Should that not count for *something*?

Govek gritted his teeth. It never had counted in the past. He shouldn't be surprised now.

"Chief Ergoth." Miranda sat up straight again with Govek's hand tight in hers. "I request we do not use Sythcol's magic during these proceedings."

Sythcol, who'd been making his way to the alcove at the back of the Rove Tree where the clearing was performed, stopped dead in his tracks, and whipped around to stare at Miranda.

"I don't think how it works is fair," Miranda said, and Sythcol's face twisted with ire.

Fuck.

Govek's rage simmered at the back of his mind. He was already too caught up. He could not face a male looking at his woman the way Sythcol was now. He wanted to rip the conjurer to shreds.

"Govek," Chief Ergoth said loudly. "*Control* yourself or I will have to ask you to be removed from this judgment."

A clamor of agreement rumbled through the clan, but Miranda rose her voice to speak over them. "*That* is exactly the problem, Chief Ergoth. That is exactly why I don't want the clearing used."

His father scowled at her and Govek had to shut his eyes, take deep breaths. Miranda gave his arm a reassuring squeeze, but it did little to quell the rage in his blood.

"You make no sense, nor do you have the right to demand this." Ergoth's voice was clipped.

"Explain, woman," Karthoc said, earning himself an angry rebuke from Ergoth, but Karthoc skewered him with a glower and the chief fell silent.

Miranda got to her feet. "Govek told me that Sythcol's

clearing magic helps everyone to maintain attention on the judgment."

"That is true," Ergoth said. "It is to everyone's benefit."

"Is it also true that it prevents people from interrupting the proceedings?"

"Yes, of course."

"Even if they want clarification or to ask questions?"

The rolling voices of the clan rose higher.

"They do not need to ask questions. All the information they need is presented in proper order so they can make a fair judgment."

"So, they get to draw their own conclusions. What if not *everything* is covered? Wouldn't that mean they fabricate evidence in their minds to fill in those blanks?"

"How dare you—"

Maythra had started to spout off, but one look from Karthoc made her pale and bow her head.

Then Govek turned back to his father and his stomach dropped. Ergoth's eyes were *blazing*.

Govek resisted the urge to pull Miranda back down into her chair, to hide her at his side, as Ergoth stepped forward. "That is a rather lofty and unfair assumption. You are a human outsider. Who are you to judge the great workings of our lead conjurer, Sythcol?"

Miranda was undeterred. "Isn't it true that in the past, just like *today*, Govek has been asked to leave the proceedings before he could speak, and the judgment was concluded without his input at all?"

"That is for the safety of our clan. You are too new and blinded by your biased opinion, but we all know how uncontrolled and dangerous Govek's rage can be." Ergoth swung his hand out. "Just look at our *table*. Sythcol says it will take half a moon to mend. What if that strike had landed on another orc? Or one of the *women*?"

Govek's stomach churned, and he felt like he might be sick. His fists balled and his claws dug deep.

Miranda reached out to cover it. Her touch was so gentle. He breathed deeply.

"What Miranda says is true," a voice called.

Govek looked out over the clan to where Iytier was standing once again.

"There have been many times that Govek was asked to leave before he was allowed to speak and more still that he was not even present for the proceedings at all. Estoc, you have witnessed too, yes?"

What? *Estoc* was here? He'd arrived back from the seasonal communion early as well?

Govek swallowed, unsure if Estoc would be of any aid. They had always been at odds.

Estoc rose to his feet. He was short of stature but had a stocky build. One that Govek realized in an odd turn matched his own proportions somewhat, just on a smaller scale and with far less muscle.

A quiet descended on the clan. A chill.

"Yes, it is true," Estoc finally said. "I have been present for *every* judgment where Govek has stood accused. There have been *many* and most of them have seen Govek dismissed long before he had any chance to defend himself."

Govek sucked in a breath, and fresh air flooded his lungs, clearing his head.

Estoc had *defended* him.

"How has this been allowed to occur without *any* among

you calling the fairness into question?" Karthoc asked, eyes on Ergoth.

Miranda spoke out loudly, her voice echoing around the hall. "They couldn't call it out because Sythcol's clearing magic prevented them from interrupting."

The silence in the hall was deafening, and Govek could hardly fathom the shifting of energy within the clan.

Ergoth said confidently. "This is all complete conjecture. Even *if* the clearing stopped members of the clan from speaking during the judgment, it could not have stopped them from speaking out afterward. None of the clan members ever came to me and asked that the proceedings be redone. Not even Govek himself."

The whispers in the clan began again, but the tones were mixed.

"But would they have? The clearing helped them to draw a conclusion on their own. Their minds were made up by the end, even though the statements were biased. But since they *never* got the full truth, they wouldn't be *able* to see past that, would they?"

The whispers turned to grumbles, and the tone was far less difficult to interpret.

They were angry.

Govek clenched his jaw and stroked his thumb over Miranda's wrist. Were they angry at *her* words or . . .?

Miranda looked back at him, nodded confidently.

She wasn't afraid in the least.

Karthoc spoke, his voice seething. "We will need to discuss this at *length*, Chief Ergoth. But not now. For now, Sythcol, return to your seat. We will not be using your magic today."

Ergoth cut in. "You have no authority to—"

"I have all the authority, Ergoth," Karthoc said slowly. "I could remove you from this entirely. But out or respect for this clan's traditions, I will not. Not *yet*."

Ergoth's chin rose, and he looked to the clan. "What say you, my great clan? Karthoc may have authority, but our community has always been built on equality. You should be the ones to choose."

Karthoc grumbled with irritation but didn't fight it. *Couldn't* fight it. Angering the only males who could create healing tinctures for the orc warriors would only bring him ruin. Govek was struck by the difficulty of his cousin's position in this as Karthoc speared the hundreds of powerful, magic-wielding clansmen with a hard look.

For the split of a moment, Govek's mind flailed and his muscles tensed to bear defeat once again.

And then Estoc's voice rose. "I call to vote for no clearing today. Who stands?"

Govek blinked as nearly all the males within Rove Wood stood. Strong, firm, supportive.

He couldn't catch a breath.

"Fine." Ergoth spat quiet venom. "We will proceed without."

Ergoth whirled away from Miranda, his violet cloaks billowing and shimmery in the bright light of the hall.

Miranda sat down again, close enough that their thighs brushed, but she was still tense, on the edge of her seat, ready to stand whenever the need struck.

Stand for *him*. His mate stood for him in a way that no other member of his brethren ever had.

Fades, he loved her with every fiber of his being.

Chief Ergoth faced Maythra a moment before regarding Wolvc.

"First to speak is *you*, Wolvc. But, from what I understand, because Govek unduly used *magic* when striking the blow, your jaw is shattered and even Hovget's powerful healing cannot reduce the agony."

Bile burned at the back of Govek's throat and the hand that had wounded this male so badly was shaking. Even Miranda's firm grip couldn't stop it.

Ergoth continued. "Since you are unable to speak, I will elect someone to speak on your behalf. Someone who was there that night and can give a firsthand account. Maythra, please rise."

What? *Maythra* was getting her chance to speak now? So early on?

Miranda was on her feet. "I object."

A rolling grumble of irritation rolled through the clan, but Miranda did not budge.

"*Young* woman," Chief Ergoth said. "Do you plan to find issue at every stage?"

"No. Just the unfair ones," Miranda said with a shrug that made amusement rise in Govek's chest despite himself. "I was told that the victims get to speak first. So Maythra shouldn't be allowed to speak before I do."

"Maythra is the only one who can properly account for Wolvc's tale," Ergoth countered.

"I ask that you let his father, Agol, speak for him instead. I'm certain Wolvc has communicated everything to his father clearly, even if Agol hadn't been there to witness it."

What? Govek went cold. Miranda hadn't told him about this part of her plan.

The gleam in Chief Ergoth's eyes instantly unsettled Govek. "His *father*. Well, of course, that is a perfect alternative. I will allow it unless any have objections?"

None rose, but Govek felt the twist of uncertainty clench his mind as he tried to fathom what Miranda intended with this.

If it had been his own son on the stand, Govek would likely have been willing to say *anything* that would prevent him from being sent to war.

But before Govek could find a way to rationally object, Ergoth called Agol to the platform, and the male stood tall, right before him. Agony and fury masked the male's features.

Govek had nearly *killed* his son.

Govek lowered his eyes as Miranda sat down again, close enough that he could feel her warmth, but it did nothing to soothe him this time.

Agol spoke in a flat tone that gave no hint to his true thoughts. "According to my son's account, he was walking with Rogeth and Maythra to the hall when they happened upon Govek and Miranda. Miranda appeared to be unconscious and mostly unresponsive, and Govek was on top of her. Wolvc rushed to intervene and Govek attacked him without issuing any challenge. When Miranda recovered, Govek spun her a different story to make her believe my son and his companions were the ones attacking."

"Shit."

The whispered curse made Govek whip his head toward Miranda. She moved to cling to his hand with both of hers, pulled it into her lap for comfort. Her expression was tense and angry as she regarded Agol.

Clearly, she'd been of the opinion that the male would speak the *truth*. But could he have even known it? He only knew what his son, Maythra, and Rogeth told him.

"That is all?" Ergoth asked, his tone giving no illusion he was *pleased* with this outcome.

Govek burned, looked at the contrast between Ergoth and Agol. Both fathers. Both standing for their sons.

But where Agol was standing to defend Wolvc, Ergoth was . . .

Govek squeezed his eyes shut as his guts rolled. It was for the good of the *clan*. Chief Ergoth was only doing what needed to be done to protect the orcs of the Rove Woods.

But his repeated mantra was not soothing his fury like it had in the past.

"No."

Govek blinked up at Agol's clipped word.

"No," the lead guard continued. "I have more to say." The male's eyes pierced into Govek's for a long moment and behind him, Ergoth's lips curled into a smile. "Although this is the account my son has communicated to me, I have doubts at its truth."

The clan began to murmur again, much louder this time.

"Silence, my clan, be still. Warlord Karthoc, do you not see that *this* is why the clearing is so important? Please, Sythcol, go to your post—"

"Be *silent*, Ergoth," Karthoc snarled. "My decision on that vile clearing is *final*. It will not be used." Then he roared to the clan. "You lot are fucking *grown*! Act like it and be *silent*!"

Everyone went still except Miranda, who made an odd choking noise, and Govek blinked down to find that his little mate was trying to withhold her laughter.

Govek smiled despite himself. He supposed he could see the humor in the regal orcs of Rove Wood Clan being scolded like children.

"Agol," Karthoc said. "Proceed."

"Agol, I find I must remind you that you are speaking for your *son* and not yourself—"

"Be quiet, Ergoth," Karthoc snapped. "My order for silence extends to you as well."

Chief Ergoth's face twisted, but he went silent.

"Now, Agol, finish with your truths." Karthoc waved the male on.

Agol spoke without preamble. "I doubt my son's account because I could scent Rogeth all along Miranda's chin and mouth. Clearly, the male had touched her, likely to silence her. If they had happened upon Govek attacking, why would they need to prevent this woman from screaming for aid?"

The clan remained silent, but Govek could see from their postures that they were thinking this logic through.

"These are simply your own opinions, Agol. Tell me. Could Rogeth have accidentally touched Miranda while he was trying to aid her?" Ergoth asked, ignoring Karthoc's harsh glower.

"It is unlikely," Agol said.

"But not impossible."

There was a tense pause before Agol finally admitted quietly. "No. It is not impossible."

Ergoth tipped his head at the male. "I thank you for your account, Agol. I know this has been very trying for you. Your only precious son was ruthlessly attacked. I think we all here can imagine how *horrible* those few hours wondering if he may live or die must have been."

Govek twisted inside and he shuddered. He couldn't even feel Miranda's comforting grip on his hands.

"Now," Ergoth said, turning his sharp eyes to Miranda. "Let us proceed."

CHAPTER

SIXTEEN

MIRANDA

Maythra's eyes scorched Miranda's body, making her feel like she was suffering through another blazing Earth summer. Though instead of being caused by pollution and global warming, this awful heat was brought on by something far more satisfying—forced silence.

Miranda shouldn't relish the woman's angst so much, but she did. Maythra had been queen bee for far too long, and it was time for her to get squished.

"Miranda, please come forward and explain what you believe happened that night."

Miranda caught her breath, gave Govek's hand one last squeeze and left the protection of his large frame. No longer concealed by his body, she moved to take center stage.

A cold flash prickled along her skin as every gaze in the hall skewered her. It was a lot more daunting to have hundreds of eyes on her than she'd thought it would be. Everyone was so quiet and still as they waited for her to speak. She clutched her bag of evidence; the weight was comforting in the face of this.

Her voice came out a little squeaky. "I had just finished talking with the seer in the woods and was on my way back to the hall—"

Ergoth interrupted. "Why were you speaking with the seer?"

"I don't think that's really your business," Miranda muttered before thinking and earned a dark scowl from Ergoth. Dang it, he already didn't like her and here she was making him even angrier.

"She is right," Karthoc said. "Her business with Evythiken is her own. Move on."

Miranda nodded. "I was returning, taking rest on a log, when someone threw a sweet-smelling liquid all over my face."

"You did not see who this was?" Ergoth asked.

"No. But I heard both Rogeth and Wolvc talking."

"But you did not *see* them throw the tincture on you?" Ergoth asked again and Miranda was forced to concede.

"No. I didn't see them. But I *know* they were there. Afterward I—"

"What motive do you suppose they had for attacking you so unprovoked like this?" Ergoth interrupted again.

"For fuck's sake, Ergoth, let the woman *speak*." Karthoc threw his hands up in exasperation.

"Thank you, but I'll answer." She'd known this question would come up at some point. "I overheard them *all* talking. Maythra, Rogeth, and Wolvc about how they wanted to get me to the hall, show me unconscious to Govek, so that he would lose his head and attack in front of the clan."

There was another rumble as the orcs began to converse.

She couldn't tell from the tone which side they were on, but judging from the fact that Ergoth did not interrupt them, Miranda suspected they didn't believe her.

"I understand that this is what you have heard," Ergoth said, with a genial nod. "But I am unsure that this could be given as a valid reason. A single outburst from Govek would not be enough to change Warlord Karthoc's mind. Am I right, Warlord?"

"Yes." Karthoc said flatly and Miranda's stomach plunged, especially when the voices of the clan murmured their agreement.

She drew a long breath. She'd been prepared for them to cast doubt on her claim, since it was her word against theirs. But her alternative reasoning wasn't much better.

"I have another motive that could have caused this," Miranda said. "Before I left the hall, I accused the lead butcher, Rogeth, of framing Govek for animal torture."

The rumble of the orcs was silenced by Ergoth's swift hand. He waved for her to continue.

"I was told that Govek tortures his kills and leaves lash marks on them. But I'd seen him kill the elk a few days ago, and it didn't have any marks before we delivered it to the butchery. As the lead butcher, Rogeth is the one who could have put them there before he brought it to the hall."

"How dare you accuse me of such a thing!" Rogeth bounded to his feet and Govek let out a low growl. Thankfully, Rogeth was smart and didn't approach. "I would never defile the body of the Fades creatures like that."

"Miranda." Ergoth's face was smooth and calm. She gulped. "Once again, I must ask, do you have any proof of your claims?"

"It doesn't matter if I have proof or not." The collective surprise at her statement nearly helped calm her nerves. "What matters is that I *accused* him of it. In front of the whole clan in the hall. And that is enough motivation to anger him into attacking me right after."

Rogeth sputtered, going pale. "I didn't—I wasn't even *there* when you—"

"Miranda."

Ergoth's voice was smooth and careful and it made Miranda's stomach sour as she met his glittering gold eyes. "Why would Rogeth care so much about this accusation?"

Miranda chose her words carefully, unsettled by the intensity of Chief Ergoth's gaze. "Why, indeed? I can imagine he wouldn't be angry, unless it was true, and he was trying to silence me."

"I did *not* do it," Rogeth spouted. "You make no sense. It sounds as if you are only bringing this up here to try to place blame on others for this torture, when the fault lies only with Govek."

Miranda could tell from the rumbling of the orcs that they all agreed, and her blood went cold. She should have known this line of reasoning wasn't solid enough, but she'd been desperate. Her mind worked for something she could say to counter. *Anything.*

"No torture has taken place in the Rove Woods."

Miranda's heart jumped into her throat.

In the open door to the hall, outlined by the morning light, stood the seer in his white robes. He moved inside, navigating easily despite his blindness. He made his way over to where Karthoc stood.

Ergoth spoke up. "Seer, you are most welcome here today. But please, do not trouble yourself with these proceedings. I know how unwell you have been and how unwell you *were* just this morn."

"Your concern is so touching, Chief Ergoth of Rove Wood Clan, but *alas*, I am perfectly well now and see no better way to spend my morning than listening to this nice little show you have created."

Ergoth straightened, shoulders tense, jaw tight, fists balled. "I do not know what you mean. This is not a *show* but a judgment proceeding of great consequence."

"Yes, and that is why I have come—to impart my wisdom." The seer took a place at the center of the floor in front of the platform. His face tipped up at the chief as if his clouded eyes could see him. "I have truths that need spoken here."

Miranda searched Ergoth's face, but the male was too good at hiding his thoughts. "Speak your truths then, seer. We are glad to hear them."

"No torture of animals has taken place in the Rove Woods."

Miranda's breath caught as triumph worked its way warmly through her mind, even as an odd sense of disappointment warred with it.

The clan became loud once more, but another snarl from Karthoc forced them to quiet.

"This wisdom is from the Fades themselves? *They* showed you these truths?" Ergoth asked.

"The Fades show me nothing," the seer said, and Miranda's disappointment mounted. In the back of her mind, she'd hoped that the seer might come in and simply tell everyone that Govek was not at fault. *He'd* been the one that told her to sit on the log after all. The seer must have known what was going to happen next.

And yet, somehow, she'd known that it would not be that easy.

This wasn't about Govek. Not entirely. This was about her healing from her trauma. This was about getting justice in some small way so she could recover enough to dredge.

And she would not recover if the seer did everything for her.

"I only know that no torture has taken place because we are in the Rove Woods. Acts of malice against healthy creatures would leave a trace. You orcs can commune as well as I. Reach for that truth, and you will quickly find that the only darkness tainting these woods is found within the blight."

"I don't see how you can be so certain of anything," Chief Ergoth asked. "You yourself say that your head is clouded of late."

"Are you calling my abilities into question, *little chief?*"

Miranda blinked at the seer's tone and the orcs seemed to have an even more violent reaction. Their muscles bunched, and their eyes went wide.

"N-no, Great Seer. Of course not." Chief Ergoth managed through clenched teeth. "Very well. Since you say that no torture has taken place, then I will see this as a valid motive for Rogeth to have sought retribution. Even if it is not certain that Rogeth is truly behind this act."

Of course, Ergoth would call it "this act" instead of saying clearly what it was.

Govek had been *framed.*

Rogeth shot up again, "My chief, I *swear* I never—"

"Silence. Now is not the time for this," Ergoth said. "The truth has been brought to light, and we will leave these troubles in the past."

Miranda's jaw dropped. Was he saying they were just going to *let this go*? Years of Govek being framed as an animal abuser, just "poof"—gone—like he hadn't been *wronged*.

"Rest assured," Karthoc said, his voice low, slow and deadly. His dark eyes were trained on Ergoth and the chief grew tense. "*I* will be doing a thorough investigation into who is responsible for deceiving the clan and making them all believe Govek abused his kills."

"F-fine." Ergoth straightened his purple robes. "I wish you well with it."

"And *you* will aid me."

Ergoth scowled. "Since most of the evidence has been *eaten,* I do not see how much more I could do." Karthoc growled and Ergoth hastily replied. "Fine. Yes. I will help. Miranda, you're finished with your account, yes? Let's move on to Maythra—"

"*Ergoth*," Karthoc said threateningly.

"I'm not done," Miranda said quickly. Ergoth was stupid for even *asking.*

Did that mean he was getting desperate?

It didn't matter. She would keep going as if the whole world was against her. She put her entire being into the act of getting justice for Govek. For herself.

Miranda straightened her spine. She was ready. She'd thought this all the way through.

She pulled her dress from that night out of her bag of evidence. "Is Hovget here?"

"Hovget, come forward," Ergoth said, and in a moment, the healer made his way up the stairs onto the platform. The long gray hair that framed his face was disheveled and his clothes were crooked and there were large bags under his eyes.

"This is the stain where the tincture they threw on me was. Can you tell me what it is?"

Hovget took no time. "It's vorial. It is used to aid in sleep."

"Right. You prescribed this to me, didn't you?"

"Prescribed?" he asked, brow furrowing at the word. "I did give you some of it, yes."

A snort came from Maythra's direction and Miranda looked to find the woman smug and satisfied with her arms crossed under her bosom.

"You have something to *say*, Maythra?" She was honestly surprised Maythra hadn't interrupted already. It made Miranda's plan a little more difficult.

She needed Maythra to start talking.

"Rise, Maythra," Ergoth said soothingly. "You may speak."

Maythra took to her feet, hands clasped in front of her. "I just find it very telling that you *admit* to having this potion. That Govek had easy access to it."

"It was offered to *me*." Miranda used a more forceful tone, hoping, praying, it would be enough to goad her. "Not Govek. Govek had nothing to do with it."

Maythra laughed. "*Govek* was the one who requested it for you. Of *course,* he had access to it."

Bingo!

"How could you possibly know that?" Miranda put a hand in front of her mouth as if shocked, hoping that it would hide the smile threatening to quiver at her lips.

"I know everything in this clan," Maythra said with a wave of her hand. "Especially where the women are concerned. And I passed Wellia *multiple* times while she was on her way to deliver this potion to you. So, I know you have been using it quite a bit. Or perhaps did you *lose* some and need a replacement?"

This accusation was said with a pointed look toward Govek and the clan began to chatter again.

Miranda rose her voice to be heard. "I never got a replacement. I never got this tincture at all."

"Don't *lie*." Maythra swept her hands out. "Many here also saw Wellia on her way to your home."

"Wellia." Miranda looked out into the crowd. "Care to speak?"

"Wellia." Ergoth went to the edge of the platform toward the table where all the women sat. "As a woman of this clan, you need not speak if you do not wish to."

"I wish to." Wellia stood and pushed her dark curls back away from her face.

Miranda soared. Her heart hammered. She looked to Govek and found his eyes wide, brows raised.

She knew he never thought this would work. When she'd drawn this conclusion on her own while pouring over all the events surrounding Maythra's attack, Govek had confessed to being confused over how a tiny detail such as this might bear so much weight on the argument at hand. Miranda supposed all those years watching crime documentaries were finally paying off.

"I never delivered the tincture," Wellia said clearly, and her voice was almost drowned out in the end by the clan breaking out into open chatter.

Karthoc roared for silence, but Maythra didn't bother to obey. "That is *not* true," she wailed. "I *saw* you. Three times

I saw you. And Hilva saw too. As did Beleda and Tove. *Tell them.*"

The three stood but Karthoc yelled, "Sit down! Wellia is speaking first."

"I'll come up." Wellia hurried to the platform and stood next to her mate, who regarded her with surprise. She took Hovget's hand and gave it a gentle pat before she looked out over the clan. "I *never* gave Miranda the potion, and the account books at the Healer's House can prove that."

"But I saw—"

"What you *saw*, Maythra, was me *attempting* to deliver it. I went to Govek's home three times to deliver the vorial, but they never answered the door and I did not feel comfortable leaving it since it has such *extreme* side effects when too much is used. As we all know."

"Govek must have stolen it then."

Wellia's eyes were cold. "Perhaps. One vial *is* missing, but it went missing after *you* visited, Maythra."

"Are you accusing me of *stealing* now?" Maythra nearly shrieked. "I was never anywhere *near* the Healer's House!"

"I'm not accusing you of anything. I have no proof. I've been on my own these last few days, so there have been many times I've been out of the room where we store our tinctures. I cannot watch the vials at all times. But I *do* account for them three times daily."

The clan chattered again, but Miranda was standing close enough to Hovget that she could listen in as he leaned close to his mate. "Why did you not tell me vorial was stolen? I could have aided you."

"You've been so busy with your study," Wellia whispered with a glance toward Govek.

"I am sorry," Hovget said gently. "The poison from the boar has been keeping me so preoccupied."

The poison from the boar? Did he mean the poison from Govek's *blood?* Was the *blood* Hovget took from Govek keeping him up studying?

Miranda's curiosity was piqued and catching like a wildfire.

"All is forgiven, my love." Wellia placed a kiss to Hovget's cheek.

"This still proves *nothing!*" Maythra's cry drew Miranda's full attention. "I'm *certain* Govek stole the vorial! I've done *nothing* wrong! Chief Ergoth, you swore you would ensure this played out the way I—"

"Be silent, Maythra!"

The venom in Ergoth's words made Miranda flinch. The whole hall quieted.

There was something in the chief's golden eyes, some vicious glimmer, that made Miranda suddenly itch to run. Go back to Govek. Head for the mists like he planned.

But her curiosity burned too. What had Chief Ergoth sworn to Maythra?

"This is a *very* serious crime you are accused of committing." Ergoth's voice dripped with checked rage. "And you have made far too many mistakes along the way for anyone to think you are completely absolved."

"B-but my *chief?*" Maythra stammered.

"Speak the truth now, and perhaps I can be lenient," Ergoth said slowly. "Did you steal vorial from the Healer's House? Did you attack Miranda in the woods? Was it *you* who has lied before this clan?"

Maythra clenched her hands in her skirts, darting her eyes around the hall. "I-I don't. I didn't—"

"We did."

Miranda's gaze shot to Wolvc. He got to his feet. His body wavered, but his eyes were clearer now. He raised his chin high and looked out over the clan.

"We attacked Miranda." His words were muffled from the bandages and slurred from his injury, but clear enough to make out. Miranda's heart pounded. "Maythra's idea to show Govek as unfit."

"No!" Maythra screamed, but it was drowned out.

Miranda's mind buzzed and her ears rang with the sound of the clan in a complete uproar.

And her eyes found Govek, who had gotten up. He was standing strong and tall and utterly *shocked*. Eyes wide, eyebrows high, mouth almost agape.

Hands unclenched and relaxed at his side.

They had *won*! They had gotten him his justice! It was done!

And yet . . .

The thrill of victory dimmed in her chest. The adrenaline and anticipation of this day ebbed away. Her stomach clenched and her palms sweated.

The faces of her babies flashed in her mind.

They had gotten justice. She should feel better. She should be ready to talk to the seer!

But the heavy, pressing weight of grief clenched in her gut.

Why hadn't it ebbed? Even just a little?

Karthoc silenced the room, and Ergoth said loudly, "I call for a vote."

CHAPTER
SEVENTEEN

Govek's chest swelled with each moment that no one spoke. The stark parallel to the hall's horrible silence after he'd been ordered to Estwill was not lost on him. This time, instead of dark spiraling dread sinking him down, Govek was hurtled to his feet, brought into the light. Hope gleamed brightly in his mind and warmed his chest.

And then Iytier stood. "I side with Govek."

Govek's chest swelled, males who had never spoken to him, males who had offered him only harsh looks and clipped words, stood in agreement. Spoke out to Rogeth's and Wolvc's faults. By the end, the entire clan was on their feet.

The judgment was done.

He had *won.*

A burst of joy flooded him. Elation tingled in his veins. He turned to Miranda, looked into her wide eyes. Wanted so fucking badly to kiss her. To sing her praises. To thank her for the important part she'd played in this. He owed her his life in so many ways.

He managed to keep his composure as she returned to his side, but just barely.

And only because there was a haunted quality to her eyes that unsettled him. His throat worked.

"It is done then," his father said over the general clamor of orcs sitting back down. "Now for punishment."

The punishment. Govek's chest tightened. He would still be punished for attacking Wolvc.

"I want to call another vote."

Iytier again, his voice loud and booming over the orcs. Karthoc bellowed for silence.

"What vote is this?" Ergoth said slowly.

"I call to vote that Govek's punishment for attacking Wolvc be delayed. I vote that we hold a judgment in a few days' time to decide whether protecting a woman is justification for attacking without establishing a formal challenge first. After we get that result, we can decide if Govek should be punished or not."

Ergoth's face contorted and Govek felt like his stomach was going to bubble up and out of his own throat.

His father was blistering mad. Govek had never seen him in such a state.

Terror gripped Govek.

"I second this!" Estoc said. "Stand to vote."

Most of the orcs were already on their feet before Ergoth could say anything to interrupt them. And seeing the unanimous decision again, Chief Ergoth was forced to concede. But his father's face went tight, his posture went rigid, and Govek could see the rage that simmered beneath his skin.

Resignation thrummed a familiar beat in Govek's chest. He would need to stay out of his father's sight after this. Not a difficult task. He'd been doing that his whole life.

"It's done then!" The victorious tone wasn't lost on him. "Govek will not be punished this day."

The rush of that slammed into Govek, and he lost his breath. His every fiber buzzed with the knowledge.

He would not be sent to his death. He would not be separated from Miranda by force.

He dragged his mate to his side and tucked her up close. She beamed up at him, eyes glistening.

Fuck, he was the most blessed male in all of Faeda.

"Sythcol, please come forward to bind Rogeth and Wolvc so that Karthoc can take them back to his camp." Ergoth's voice was tight.

"Wait!" Rogeth cried. "That's not necessary. I'll comply with everything, I swear."

The conjurer came back to the platform slowly, his eyes sorrowful and his hands trembling slightly. For a moment, Govek thought perhaps it was simply from overexertion.

But it dawned on Govek, upon seeing the horror on Rogeth's face, that the lead conjurer didn't want to bind him any more than the young butcher and guard wanted to be bound.

That Sythcol was being forced by Ergoth to commit acts of *torture*.

Torture, and then, after all that, they would be sent to the front lines. To their death.

Would the magical binding still be in place when they were pushed to the front of the battle? Govek trembled, horror gripping his guts.

"Stop." Govek's voice carried much further than he thought it would. The clan hushed in an instant.

Ergoth looked out over the now attentive clan and scowled before turning to Govek. "What is it, *my son*?"

What *was* it, indeed? Govek had spoken without thinking and could hardly find the words to convey what he felt.

Warmth pressed to his chest, and he looked down into Miranda's curious eyes. Govek breathed deep, kept his voice solid so it would carry but spoke to his mate. "I do not think forcing them to death is appropriate."

Miranda smiled.

"It is not your place to decide."

Govek looked up at Ergoth, brow furrowed. His father continued. "They have committed a crime against this *clan* as well as your woman. Attacking one of our few precious women is a *severe* offense. Or do you not agree that harming Miranda deserves punishment?"

Govek's gut twisted but Miranda took his hand up in hers and spoke for him. "I agree it deserves punishment, but even as the person who *was* attacked, I think forcing them to the front lines of the war is extreme. Surely there is another punishment that would be better suited, Chief Ergoth?"

His father hummed in thought, eyes glimmering, and Govek wondered just *why* Miranda had placed this punishment back into Ergoth's hands.

Maythra fidgeted, clearly wanting to step forward, but the two males had stayed back and looked at the floor. Although Wolvc had been the one to tell the truth, Rogeth had not fought it.

Just how much of their plight had been from Maythra's

influence? Did they truly despise Govek enough to get him killed, or had they simply been led astray by a manipulative woman who had, at many times, acted as their mother?

"There is another punishment that may well be better," Ergoth said, going back to the edge of the platform. "My clan, in a great show of leniency, our newest member has suggested a lesser punishment. We will hold a vote to change their fate from death to silencing."

Govek suddenly felt chilled.

"And since this type of conjuring can also be cast upon humans, Maythra will receive it as well."

"What?" Maythra nearly shrieked as she stepped toward Chief Ergoth. Her hands clasped before her, her eyes wild and pleading. "My belov—my chief, you *can't*. Please, I beg you to show mercy. I swear I will *never* speak on this event as long as I live. I will never—"

"Silence!" Ergoth cried and Maythra went quiet, but for a few muffled sobs.

"What is silencing?" Miranda asked softly, searching Govek's face.

He leaned close, more for his own comfort than to help her hear his response. "It is magic that prevents the one cursed from using *any* form of communication. Even hand gestures and writing."

Miranda paled. "Oh wow, is that *better*?"

He thought it likely was better than death, but not by much.

"Let us vote."

"*Please*. My chief, I *swear*," Maythra said, but it was too late. The clan was already rising to their feet, albeit reluctantly.

"It is done," Chief Ergoth said quickly. "Sythcol. Perform the spell."

"W-wait!" Miranda hurried in. "Shouldn't we at least let them have a chance to speak their *goodbyes* before being silenced?"

"Those are not the terms of the punishment," Ergoth said, eyes narrowed.

"I agree," Karthoc said. "I believe letting their punishment wait for a day or two will do no harm."

Many of the orcs voiced their agreement and Ergoth's expression grew dark. "Fine, I will concede. They will all be placed in confinement where they can write their final words and the silencing will be performed tomorrow. Agol, please take them away."

Govek's eyes shot to Agol. The male was clearly stricken and disheveled. It was his son about to be silenced, and Govek could not even fathom the pain of this.

"No," Karthoc said.

Ergoth glowered at Karthoc. "No?"

"I believe, under these circumstances, being able to actually speak their goodbyes to their loved ones is warranted. Unless Miranda or Govek feels that is too lenient."

"I don't. Govek?" Miranda looked up at him and he simply shook his head.

"That is too far, Karthoc," Ergoth snapped. "You do not have the authority to overrule my judgments."

Karthoc scoffed. "How many times do I have to repeat that I have *all* the authority, *dear uncle*. But if you truly feel that this is too lenient, when even those who have been *wronged* do not, perhaps you would like to put it to another vote?"

Ergoth looked out over the clan, at their steely faces, and relented. "No. I see I am in the minority in this. I only feel so strongly because it is my dear son who has been so wronged."

Govek's nose curled up and Miranda snorted as if she were about to start laughing. Ergoth glowered at her but Govek managed to push Miranda behind him before he could confirm Miranda's mirth.

Ergoth turned back to Karthoc. "Perhaps you would comply with having an orc be witness to these conversations. Just to ensure that no lies about my son are spread."

Karthoc looked like he was vacillating between disbelief and irritation. "Fuck, *uncle*, I never knew you cared *so* much about my cousin. From all your past actions, I would have assumed you would *wanted* vile rumors to fly."

Ergoth's voice grew dangerous. "These jests of yours are getting out of line, *nephew*."

"Jests," Karthoc snorted. "Of course. But *very well*, if it stops your complaints, I will have one of my warriors sit with them to ensure topics remain on personal matters."

"And one of my conjurers."

"*Fine*. Now, are we done?"

"Yes. Call one of your warriors to escort them to your camp."

Brovdir came forward without preamble. Ergoth addressed the clan. "I call this judgment to a close."

Brovdir gestured for Maythra to move and she refused so he took her arm. She fought and demanded he let her go, but he barely looked at her as he pulled her out. Rogeth and Wolvc followed without any fight, and Agol took up the rear.

"Ergoth, wait. Ergoth!" Maythra screamed, fighting Brovdir until the hall doors thudded shut, cutting off her words.

And Govek was still inside.

Elation burst through him like crisp spring water flowing over his overheated flesh on a warm summer day. It flooded, drenched, his body trembled under the force of the fury in his gut being drowned out.

They had won!

He instantly caught Miranda in his arms and pulled her in for a kiss, uncaring who saw them. She tasted so sweet, and her warmth was so delightful. He wanted to laugh until his chest burst open.

He wanted to bellow with triumph as a thrill coursed through him. The hall grew brighter, as if his vision had cleared and his mind had been cleansed.

He had won this justice. And not just in his own mind. He had won it in the eyes of his clan.

He set Miranda on her feet and searched her lovely face.

Her expression was a little tight as she patted his hand. "We should get down."

He agreed, leading her off the platform and into the crowd of orcs, most of whom had left their seats now. He scanned the masses, feeling brave enough to do so. They had heard him. He had not been silenced or shamed. They had seen his truths and judged him to be right.

Iytier's face appeared in the crowd, smiling, and nodding confidently. Estoc too, though the male did not smile.

"I'm glad for this, Govek." Iytier clasped him about the shoulder. "Truly."

"Yes," Estoc said. "Those three deserve everything they have coming."

Govek felt light, thrilled. His face hurt from the effort of keeping his jaw tucked while smiling.

"The rest of our clan is returning from the seasonal communion now. They will be here by mid-meal," Iytier said. "I will be sure to tell them *all* of what those three have done and of the outcome here."

"They're going to be Fades-blasted *shocked*," Estoc grumbled. "I know after Iytier told me of all the lies he has uncovered." His eyes slid to where Ergoth was now mingling among the clan. "Our chief has much to answer for."

The venom in Estoc's tone unsettled Govek. He had never heard an orc of Rove Wood Clan speak this way about his father.

He glanced to where Miranda should be at his side, wanting to know how she felt about this shift and found her gone.

Panic sliced through him, and he jerked up, scanning the crowd, used her scent to follow where she was.

And when he found her, he felt no better.

She was standing with the seer. Tense, trembling slightly, wavering.

She was going to have another attack.

"Govek?" Iytier said, but he ignored the male's prompt and forced his way through the crowd.

To get his woman before it was too late.

CHAPTER

EIGHTEEN

MIRANDA

There he was!

Miranda weaved her way through the crowd to where the seer stood near the exit. Her heart hammered. Her limbs felt jittery.

It was time. She was ready. *Finally*.

She made her way over to him quickly. No one stopped her or even noticed.

"Seer—"

"Rogeth did not frame Govek."

Miranda jerked to a halt at the seer's words. Her mind worked to switch gears. "O-okay?"

"But I cannot see who did," the seer whispered.

Miranda shook her head. This wasn't what she wanted to speak on now. "Seer, I think—no, I *know* I'm ready."

He turned his head toward her. His cloudy eyes looked right through her for a few seconds.

"You are close, but you are not there."

Her stomach dropped. That couldn't be right. "But I *won*. *We* won. I got justice here. I feel fantastic. If we dredge now, I know it will work."

The seer's brow screwed up. "You think that momentary elation would stand against bone-deep grief?"

Her jaw trembled and her eyes stung and she couldn't catch a breath. The excitement from winning began to dim. "But . . . but I sat on the log like you told me to and let all this happen. I thought that would get me ready. Or at least ready long enough to dredge."

"You still aren't ready, Miranda."

Frustration snapped her up. "Why did you make us go through all that if it wasn't going to get me ready to dredge? Why make me work so hard when *you* could have just spoken for us and ended it all, even before this judgment started?"

"That is not how the Fades work, Miranda." The seer's voice was unyielding and cold. "I did not know this was going to happen. I do not know what will happen next. I see only what the Fades show and not a speck more."

"Seer, I've been working *so hard*. I don't think about it every hour of the day and I've made sleeping properly and eating well a priority. I've been controlling the grief like I'm supposed to. I even got through the whole day yesterday without thinking about Earth *once*." Well . . . almost.

"Didn't I tell you that avoiding it wasn't the answer?"

Her stomach dropped.

He sighed heavily. "You are not ready. You need more time."

No. *No.* "I don't *have* more time. I have to find them *now*. They need me." Her throat grew tight and her eyes burned. Her mind wailed all the way back to Earth. To the desolation and the heat and the crushing weight and the screaming of her babies in her mind.

They hadn't died there. They *hadn't.*

The seer's brow grew tight. "Do you mean the family you asked after in the woods?"

"Yes. My *babies.*" Miranda tried to keep her voice hush so none of the mingling orcs around them noticed but it was difficult—so difficult. "The kids that I took care of. *That's* what I want to know. I *have* to know what happened to them. It's driving me *crazy* thinking about them calling for me. For help. And that I didn't go back for them. I just left for the ocean and I didn't . . ."

The seer said nothing, only blinked, and she managed to take a few shaky breaths. "They must have made it here like I did. I have to find them. You can tell me where they are. *Please.*"

"That's not what this is about."

"But . . . but that's the only thing that matters—"

"That isn't what this is about, Miranda," the seer said slowly. "The Fades, they want me to know of the *memories* you lost. They will not show me things that you could not possibly know."

Her whole body went cold. Quaking. A ringing sounded in her ears as the world around her dimmed.

"I can only dredge from things that you yourself have experienced, Miranda." The seer inhaled sharply. "And I sense no children within those memories. Only you and . . . *chaos.*"

"No." Her voice didn't sound like her own. "No. That can't . . . you're supposed to tell me . . ."

"I am very sorry, Miranda, for the horrors you have suffered, but what you ask for is beyond my ability."

She could not think. Could not move. Was not even aware that the seer had bid her goodbye and left her standing there, right next to the doors.

"Miranda?"

She had to get out of here. Right now. She had to escape.

"Miranda, are you well?"

Miranda's heart thundered in her ears. She spun and ran out of the hall into the too bright daylight.

"Miranda, stop!" Govek was right at her side, following closely. He matched her stride as she made a fast clip along the path back to their home.

She wished he wouldn't. She wished he had stayed in the hall, enjoyed the win he'd earned, basked in the revelry of his victory.

A victory she would never have.

Earth was gone.

Her babies were *gone*.

They . . . *they hadn't lived.*

Her chest felt like it was being ripped in two, like her heart was cracking apart. Her mind reeled and her throat closed around a wail—

"Miranda, stop!" Govek demanded, even as she picked up the pace. The houses here were vacant, and the stretch leading to Govek's home was lonely. Desolate.

Just like how Earth had been in those final days.

"Miranda!" Govek gripped her shoulders and forced her to turn around. She looked at the middle of his chest, trying to push the burning guilt down so she could speak past it.

Please go back to the hall. Please talk to your friends.

Please celebrate the way you deserve to. Please leave me to wallow and scream and fall apart on my own.

But Govek didn't. It wasn't in his nature. "My *love*." He got to his knees before her. "I—" He stopped when his eyes met hers. She was certain he could see her soul cracking apart as sorrow ripped her to shreds.

It wasn't fair. None of this was fair.

"What did he say? What did Evythiken *say*?"

His voice was clipped with rage and she could not answer him. She couldn't look at him. She didn't want him to be lost in her grief. He should be reveling in his victory.

"Come." He rose to his feet and pulled her along. It helped distract her. The icy air in her lungs tasted too sweet. The world around her was too vivid. The colors were too real. The scent was too lush.

Govek did not say anything until they were home and he'd closed the door behind them. "Speak, Miranda."

She would have laughed at such an order had she been of a mind to do so. Instead, the idea of laughter sent a torrent of horror down her spine. Children's laughter. Young and innocent and turning into horrific *screams*.

"Come here." He took her hand and brought her to the couch. "Look at me."

She did and in his eyes, she saw true heartbreaking worry. Her eyes flooded. "God, I'm so sorry. You should be celebrating. Please, please go back. Don't let me drag you into this."

"Miranda, you could not drag me anywhere, even if your life depended on it. And there is no other place I would rather be than here."

She shook her head, eyes flooding. "You won't think that when I tell you."

"You've heard my worst, Miranda. Listened to my truths about Clairton. You held me through it. I will do the same for you. I will not leave you."

She gulped and looked over at the bare embers in the fireplace. The heat of them barely registered. "I'm jealous."

Govek shifted and his brow pinched as if in disbelief. "I love you, Miranda. I would never even dream of choosing another over you. Not Viravia, or Yerina, or any other in the village. And I certainly do not want Iytier's company over your own."

"No." Miranda pressed her palms into her stinging eyes. Her skin prickled and her muscles bunched as she hunched in on herself. "I'm jealous that you . . . that you *won*. That you got to win."

He was silent a long moment before clarifying. "You hoped that the judgment would not be in my favor?"

"No." She began to tremble. "No, it's not that. I'm so *glad* you won. I'm jealous that you . . . that I can't . . ."

Govek's hands wrapped around her wrists and pulled her palms from her face.

The dam broke, and her tears coursed hot tracks down her cheeks. "I can *never* have that. God, Govek. Earth is *gone* and so are my babies and I'm never going to get any justice for it." She broke off in a sob that wracked her whole body, shivered from the top of her head down to her heels.

And her words flooded out. "It's not fucking *fair*. The people who killed my planet won't ever have a trial or a judgment. They won't ever come to justice. They got to die quickly and uselessly at fucking best, never to know what happened or what they did. Or worse, god, Govek, what if they *lived*?"

The word came out as a wail and she dug her hands into

her knees, rocking and rubbing at the wool skirt as if that might ease the pain. "What if they got to *live*? What if destroying everything but their perfect little corner was the goal and—oh god. They killed all those *babies. My babies*." She covered her face with her palms again. "Josephine and Taylor and Robby. Oh, Robby had a brother who was ten months like Haysik. He'd just started babbling his first words. *I can't—*"

She couldn't get the image of those tiny precious babies out of her fucking head. Their laughter swelled like a sea of fire.

"What if they didn't die quick?" She rocked herself for comfort. "What if they got trapped like me? Without their mommies. What if they screamed and cried and no one came to save them?"

Arms came around her. Warmth. Strength. She clung to it.

"They killed them. *They* did. And I don't even get to know who *they* are. I'll never get to hit them or scream or claw their eyes out or make them see what their worthless, horrible greed did to me. To all of us."

"I'm sorry," Govek whispered against the top of her head, rustling her hair. "I'm so sorry, Miranda."

"It's not fair!" Her voice was so shrill it didn't sound like her own. "Why do I get to live when my babies didn't? Why couldn't they have gotten here too? Why do I have to be the one to live without them? I don't think I can do it, Govek! How am I supposed to just keep going when they suffered, and *I never went back for them?*"

She sobbed so hard she started coughing. Her nose was clogged, her cheeks wet with tears, her eyes burned and her vision was so blurry she couldn't see anything but the precious faces of the babies she'd loved so dearly. "Why did this happen? Why do I have to accept that I'll *never* know? *It's not fair.*"

Govek moved to sit down on the couch and dragged her into his lap. He rocked her and she gripped his shirt in her fists.

"I want to go back," she wailed. "I want to go back and make sure they don't *need me*. What if they lived? Oh god . . . I'm horrible, but fuck, I *hope* they died. I hope it was quick. I can't live with the thought that they suffered. I'm a *monster*."

"You are not." Govek gave her a little shake. "*You are not*."

"I want to check the daycare . . . to find their bodies and . . . oh *god*." The images her mind conjured were too painful. She was going to vomit.

"Breathe," Govek demanded of her. "Just breathe, Miranda. *Breathe*."

"I can't," she whispered like a mantra. "I can't, I can't."

"Try. Just try. Right here." His hand pressed gently into her chest and the pressure helped her take a breath.

"Why didn't I die too?" Miranda pressed her head onto his shoulder. "*It's not fair*."

"I know. I know it isn't. Fades, I wish I had answers, Miranda. I wish . . . I'm so sorry."

The tremor in Govek's voice brought her a sliver of control. Enough to stop the waves of agony from crushing her. She sobbed and shivered and allowed her mind to dip into the blackened chaos. Allowed every emotion she'd locked away to bellow out in one massive surge. Govek was soaked in her sorrow and only held her tighter. He rode it out with her like a buoy in the storm.

She concentrated on her breathing as the grief swelled and ebbed in waves. This grief she'd tried so hard to hide from by creating a new life, by sleeping on Govek's chest, by concentrating on the trade and the trial and every other distraction Faeda could give her.

By succumbing to the desperate delusion that her babies could somehow have survived and made it to Faeda like she did.

Her babies were gone. She wasn't getting them back. She would not be building a new life for them here.

The vision of the future she'd clung to disintegrated, and in its wake, she was left with uncertainty. Of numbing darkness growing behind her eyes. Exhaustion laced with icy cold sorrow.

"Just breathe," Govek said, voice thick. "Just breathe."

"What do I do *now*?" Her voice was hoarse. "Where do I go from here?"

"With me," he said firmly. "You go with me."

She shuddered and coughed to clear the phlegm from her throat so she could gulp air, but she didn't bother with the streaming wetness on her cheeks or under her nose. It didn't matter.

She let out a long breath and whimpered. "I don't deserve you. I should have died, Govek. I should have been the one to die instead of them."

"No," he said so forcefully she felt the word vibrate through her whole body. "*No.* I do not believe that. This was in the hands of the Fades, Miranda. I know it. I can feel it. I'm certain you can feel it too."

He was right. She *could* feel it. Like a pulsing at the back of her mind, the beginnings of a blooming headache she could not escape.

"I don't want to do *shit* for them," she said, anger slicing through her like the jab of a poker. "They *could* have saved my babies, and they didn't. *They let them die*."

He tightened his hold on her. "And you don't have to. In my mind, you have already fulfilled your duty here tenfold. Now you get to choose where you want your life to go."

She already knew where she wanted it to go, but that life was snatched away from her. Ruthlessly destroyed by the seer's truths. "I don't want to choose. I just want my babies back."

"I know," he whispered, and she clung to him.

"I'm just . . . I'm just so *tired*, Govek."

"Then let me cradle you. I will protect you through this, Miranda. Through this and *everything* else for the remainder of your days. You need not do anything you do not want to do, and I will throttle any who try to force your hand."

He pulled her in tight and she rested more heavily against him, eyes swimming again. The tears dripped from her nose onto his perfect green skin. "My hero."

He let out a little warm huff of contentment against the top of her head. "Things I can see. Your beautiful hair, the dying fire, the cups I forgot to wash . . ."

She huffed, eyes heavy as her mind sunk down into the kind of numbness only pure emotional exhaustion could bring. Govek continued to rumble. She went limp against this male she loved so much. She soaked up his comfort as she drifted into unconsciousness.

Miranda couldn't be sure how long she dozed on him, but it was long enough that she felt almost ill from hunger when she awoke. She could taste the need for water at the back of her parched throat. She ignored it and stroked Govek's arm.

He breathed deep, as if rousing, but didn't lift his cheek from her scalp. Her eyes moved to the window to find that the sun was bright and high. The shadows cast by the trees were dark.

"Miranda." He sat up so she could move and stroked her hair. "You are awake?"

"I think so." Her voice was so raw it twinged with every syllable. "How long was I . . .?"

"A while," he said as she adjusted so she could look at his face. Her eyes were blurry, and her nose stung. He tucked her hair behind her ears as she examined his furrowed brow and tight mouth. "You must be hungry now."

She nodded. She touched her stomach and was surprised she didn't find an empty pit. She hadn't eaten anything yet today. She'd been too nervous before the judgment. "Yeah, and thirsty."

"Do you feel . . . better?"

There was a lot of weight in that question. His brow knitted, and his face was a little pale as he waited for her answer.

The searing rage and the icy guilt still gripped her heart and tore through her guts, but it was duller now. Like the blunt end of a blade, instead of the sharp edge.

"No," she whispered. "And yes. And . . . . I don't know."

He let out a strangled sound that shot remorse through her. She reached out to cup his face in her hands. "I'm so sorry. I wish you hadn't fallen in love with someone so *broken*. You deserve someone whole and perfect."

His jaw trembled, and his hand came up to cup her chin firmly so she couldn't look away from his gaze. "Don't *ever* say something like that again. You are *perfect* for me, Miranda. In every way imaginable."

Tears spilled from her eyes anew. "I-I'm sorry."

His face contorted, and he yanked her in, tucked her face into his neck, tightened his arms around her. "Don't be *sorry*, Miranda."

"You should be happy. Celebrating. Not stuck here with me while I collapse."

"There is no use in celebrating without you." His mouth was hot and damp against her shoulder. "I would give up a million celebrations crafted by the Fades themselves to have you."

"You're too good for me." Miranda closed her eyes again. She felt anchored, yet weightless. Fuzzy, but cool. Her muscles were sore from sleeping in an odd position.

"I believe it is the opposite way around, Miranda." His warm breath fanned the top of her head. Her hair felt matted, and her skin was sticky.

But as disheveled as she was on the outside, Miranda could feel the storm inside begin to pass. She knew it would creep up on her again. Healing was not linear. But for now, for today, she'd reigned in her sanity.

As if he could sense it, Govek stroked her back, moving his calloused hands along her arms, shoulders, chest, as if he was brushing her off.

And *damn*, it felt good. It felt like he was wiping away her lingering tension, like he was pulling out the darkness to make room for light.

She let out a long sigh as his fingers splayed into her hair, along her scalp. "W-what are you doing?"

"Soothing," he said. "Is it helping?"

She *really* didn't deserve him. She opened her eyes to meet his. "Yes. It's helping. I love you."

His face flushed, and he leaned in. She met him halfway, eager for his kiss. Their lips met tenderly. Warmly. She clung to his chest.

When they parted, she could still feel his warmth against her mouth. His love. She went boneless.

And then her stomach grumbled. *Loud.*

"I'll make you food now." He rose to his feet and took her with him effortlessly.

"Can I walk? I need to pee."

God, she *really* needed to pee. He set her down, and she rushed toward the bathroom. Her steps were jerky as her limbs protested. How long had she been asleep? She was so sore.

She finished up quickly. The very practical task grounded her, and she rejoined Govek in the kitchen. He was already preparing her meal, and she was too exhausted to do anything but sink down into one of the dining room chairs.

"Thank you." She glanced out into the bright sky. Birds whizzed by the trees, a squirrel hopped from each branch, leaves rained down covering the forest with their color.

Everything inside her was falling apart, but everything outside continued on. Lived their lives. Took every day as it was.

She wanted to do that too. Focus on now and forget everything else. Watch the trees and animals out the window. Breathe in the scent of the bacon Govek was cooking.

To just be here, in their house, in the woods. On Faeda, where nothing could hurt them.

Except Ergoth, she remembered. Chief Ergoth had looked *terrifying* when he lost the judgment. Maythra and her cronies were taken care of, but suddenly, she felt like their battle had only just begun.

"Man," she breathed. "That judgment was . . . *a lot,* wasn't it?"

"Yes," he agreed, beginning to chop up vegetables and throw them into the pan with the sizzling bacon. "It is a bit . . ." He paused, considering.

"It's a bit insane, is what it is." She focused on the turmoil of the clan and finally let her own horrors fall to the wayside once more. "Govek, my impression was that most of the clan had *no* idea of who you really were. Your dad had them all thinking you were some kind of psycho monster. Others were framing you for things you didn't do. Is that . . . right?"

He let out a long sigh, but nodded slowly. "That is my conclusion as well."

"But *how*?" she asked a little too loud. "How is it possible that no one in the clan really got to know you? You were raised here. Wouldn't they eventually come around? Figure it out?"

He was silent a long moment, stopped mid chop. "It . . . may have been my doing."

"Don't go blaming yourself for everything again, Govek."

"No, that isn't what I mean. I . . ." He cleared his throat. "I have always *enjoyed* solitude."

"Don't tell me you liked being alienated. I know it's hurt you."

His jaw went tight, threatening to hide away his teeth. "It . . . has."

She could see how much it took to admit that and got up. Her legs were still stiff as she went to him. Wrapped him up in her arms. Pulled him down for a kiss.

When he pulled away, he had a bird on his head.

"Oh my gosh!" She laughed with surprise and the sharp sound made her chest lighten even as the bird fluttered its tiny brown wings. Its dark eyes blinked at her. It was smaller than her fist. But the little thing recovered from its scare and stayed put, nestling into Govek's hair. "What the heck? Where did he come from?"

"The window's open," he said so casually it made giggles burst up her raw throat all over again.

"Birds just fly in and sit on you whenever you leave your window open? You really are Snow White." She resisted the urge to reach up and touch the precious little thing. "Oh gosh. I hope he doesn't poop in your hair."

"He wouldn't dare," he muttered, though his eyes narrowed.

"What would you do if he did?" she pressed. "Cook him up in the stew?"

He snorted, amusement curling his lips. "That would be a lot of effort for very little reward."

"A one bite reward."

"More like the tease of a taste where my big mouth is concerned." He gently pushed the bird onto his massive finger and untied something from his leg. A piece of paper.

So, someone had sent them a message? "You have the opposite of a big mouth, Govek," she said, thinking of the common Earth term that referred to someone prone to revealing secrets.

"I think I've proven my mouth is *plenty* big." His tone

reverberated through her whole body. "Big enough to wrap around your thighs anyway."

She shivered, the memory spiking heat and curling her toes.

He finished the task of retrieving the note, and the bird took off out the window.

"Who is it from?" She craned around to look, even though she knew she couldn't read it.

"Viravia. She has invited you to have mid-morn meal at the hall with her and the other women who've returned from the seasonal communion."

"I . . . thought she was having trouble getting to the hall for meals?"

He hummed in confusion and then shrugged. "Perhaps something has changed?"

"Maybe." She had never been pregnant, but she could imagine that some days were better than others. "I'm not really up for a big meal like that." She looked out the window again. Her brow pinched. The sun was in an odd spot.

Wait. "Govek, did you just say *mid-morn* meal?"

"Yes."

"But it was mid-morning when we left the hall and then I had a long nap and . . . Govek, what *time* is it?"

He hesitated only a moment. "You slept through the rest of the day and night."

Her stomach dropped, and it was in that moment she realized just how *famished* she was. "I slept through the . . .? Are you saying I slept for almost an entire day?"

"Yes."

Her mind reeled. God, no *wonder* she was so sore. "I'm sorry. You should have woken me up."

"Never." The vehemence in his voice made her blink.

"But you must be *starving,* Govek. And thirsty. And needing to pee. Why haven't you gone to the bathroom yet?"

He met her gaze. The gold in his eyes caught the light and lead her to distraction. His face was loose and calm, jaw untucked, expression so soft and warm it melted the aching in her chest.

"Miranda, there is nothing in the world I would rather do than hold you in your times of need." His voice was a soothing rumble that pushed bliss into every corner of her body causing her heart to soar. "The Fades gifted you to me and I will take on as much of your strife and chaos as I am able. I would harbor the darkest parts of you, Miranda, if it meant I was allowed the honor of watching your happiness bloom."

Her stomach flipped right over. Throat tight. Eye's prickling. "Come here, tough guy."

He did not hesitate to wrap her up, tuck her into his warm chest, and curl around her like a wall of protective muscle. She breathed in his crisp pine scent, stroked her hands down the sides of his back, brought them around to cup his face and pull him down further.

"God, Govek. I love you." She showered his face with kisses, soothed his forehead, and caressed his hair. "I'm never going to let you go."

His voice was tinged with delight as he said, "That is my goal."

CHAPTER

NINETEEN

Govek had not realized bliss such as this existed.

His belly was full, his body washed and clean and now he had his mate cuddled up with him on the couch, nestled in his lap. He rubbed his cheek against her soft hair. The warm scent of the safril tea Miranda had made curled around them, mingling with her sweetness.

He was lost to her. He never wanted this to end.

"What time do you think it is, Govek?"

He grumbled unhappily. "A bit after midday."

"Hm, so like one o'clock in the afternoon? Does that math seem right?"

"You and your math. My mind does not obsess over numbers like yours does."

Her voice was tinged by withheld laughter and he was relieved to hear it after the sorrow she'd overcome. "I'm not *obsessed* with numbers!"

"I think all Earthfolk must have been." He pulled her in further. "Times, ages, speeds, money, distance, dates . . . constant numbers."

"Hey." Her irritated tone was drowned out by her laughter. Fuck, he loved the sound of it—warm and rich. He wanted to cup it in his palms and drink it. "We only did math, like, ninety percent of the time."

He snorted in amusement.

She rested heavily against his shoulder, a deep sigh escaping her parted lips. "Govek, the seer told me . . . told me . . ."

"You do not need to speak on it if it causes you pain." His guts twisted up at the mention of the seer.

"No, I want to. I just . . ." She sat up enough that he could see her dark expression and she murmured. "He told me that he can't show me what happened to them." Her voice grew strangled. "To my babies."

He brought a hand around to cover the back of her head and pressed his forehead to hers. "I am sorry, Miranda."

"I can't believe it. I was so *sure* that's what he was going to tell me." She shook her head against his. "But it wasn't, and I just have to accept that I'll never know."

Fuck, he was a wretch, but her words eased the ache in his chest.

Evythiken did not have answers for her, which meant that she wouldn't seek him out again. She would not be thrown into this chaos—fall apart in his arms, be lost to him so completely that once the sorrow and rage subsided, she slept like the dead for a horrifically long time—again.

He'd clung to her in her sleep, concentrating on every intake of breath. She'd been so still and quiet that without her chest and stomach rhythmically pressing his own he would have thought she'd left him.

She could *never* leave him.

"The seer told me that Rogeth isn't the one who framed you."

He blinked, mind working around this information.

"It's strange, isn't it? I thought for sure it was him, but looking back, he *was* pretty adamant that you had done it." She stroked the back of his head, scratched at his hairline as she thought. "The seer said he suspected who it was."

"Did he give any clues?"

"No, I was . . . I was too caught up in my own stuff. I'm sorry."

"You have nothing to apologize for."

Fuck, he was so glad this chapter was done. Now they could finally move on, together. Miranda's grief could proceed naturally. She would not continue to force her way through it.

A knock sounded at the door.

"You think that's the clan back to convince you to stop the merger?" Miranda crawled out of his lap and his chest tightened at the loss.

He took a deep breath but he couldn't catch the smell of who it was. He went to the door and swung it open. The day was sunny, but the cool air still hit him.

Right before the scent did. Sage.

"Viravia?" he asked. It was undoubtedly her, but she was almost completely bundled up. Only her eyes were visible beneath the thick cloak. A wool scarf covered up her nose and mouth.

"Yes, Govek. Hello. Could I come in?" Viravia leaned slightly so she could look past him into the kitchen.

His response was to step aside to make room for her.

"Hello," Viravia said to Miranda as she entered the room. She pulled down her cloak and tugged the scarf away from her face after he had shut the door tight. "How are you doing?"

"Oof. Tough question." Miranda lifted the mug of tea to her lips.

Viravia blinked rapidly. "I-I'm so sorry, I didn't mean to—"

"No, no, sit down. It has absolutely *nothing* to do with you. It's just been . . . well . . ." Miranda glanced at Govek, but he couldn't offer her anything other than support. It was her story to tell.

"Could I make you some tea?" Miranda shot the woman a reassuring smile. "I don't have *sage* but Govek picked some mint."

"Safirl," he corrected.

"Oh, that's very kind but I'm actually here to . . . well, you got my note, right? It would mean so much if you both would come join us at the hall."

Miranda froze in place where she was mixing up the cup and Govek felt similarly stunned.

"Both of us? I thought your note just said me?" Miranda asked, clearly excited by this prospect even as he had no idea how to feel.

How long had it been since he was *invited* to the hall?

Had he *ever* been invited?

"Yes, both of you," Viravia said with a quick nod. "We're holding the return celebration."

A celebration. He was being invited to one of Rove Wood Clan's *celebrations*?

"What's that?" Miranda came to stand next to him.

"It's a revelry held once everyone from the communion party has returned. The last few arrived this morning," Viravia explained. "Lots of food, drink, and visiting."

"Children," he said, wanting to be transparent. After her breakdown, he could not be sure if Miranda would want to be around them now. "There will be *many* children."

Many *many*. Basically, all of them. His gut twisted. "Are you certain they want me to be there?" He had never been welcomed around the orc sons before.

But Viravia's smile turned soft. "Yes, Govek. They do. I won't lie and say that there aren't a handful who didn't agree with the decision, but Iytier and I have told *everyone* about the outcome of the judgment. And about the misunderstandings that have taken place in the past. And well . . . everything."

He felt flush. What did this *mean?* How should he even *act* with them? He'd always simply walked away, and no one had ever questioned that.

"And . . . you are going to become our chief?"

His gut twisted and Miranda tightened her grip on his arm. She looked up at him, brows raised.

Fuck, should he tell Viravia he refused to become chief now?

Would he still be invited to the hall if he did?

"Govek?" Viravia's tone indicated she was put off by their odd, tense reaction to her simple statement and blessedly, Miranda was able to shrug it off first.

"I'm totally up for celebrating in the hall and meeting a whole bunch of orc kids," Miranda said, catching Govek's gaze. "If *you* are."

"Oh, please, do come." Viravia stepped forward. "Iytier and Savili will be there, as well as Estoc and his mate and children. And *many* others who all want to visit with you."

Many others who *wanted* him there?

He didn't believe it.

He supposed he would need to *see* it to believe.

"All right," he said. "Let's go."

CHAPTER

TWENTY

There were kids *everywhere*.

They climbed up on wagons, called after their fathers, wrestled over tree stumps, and careened down the street like their butts were on fire.

They laughed, and yelled, and played silly games that looked a lot like tag. Every one of them was a rough and tumble boy with green skin and little fangs and bright happy eyes.

Miranda's chest was tight, her throat was thick, and her hand shook, but she also felt so *full* watching them.

She wished that her babies could have lived here and been happy like these children.

While at the same time, she was so relieved to see that orc children were just like human ones. And that they were so well cared for and obviously loved.

She refused to let her own grief taint her view of another child. She refused to let jealousy over what could have been color the joy of what was now. It wasn't fair that her babies couldn't have the blissful life these orc sons did, but that wasn't their fault. It wasn't this community's fault.

She swallowed. Was . . . it her fault? She'd been the one who hadn't gone back to save them.

But . . . would she have been able to save them?

Govek placed a hand at the small of her back and she glanced up at his face. She managed to blink away the tears prickling in her eyes.

"I'm so *so* glad you're coming," Viravia said, her voice muffled under the multiple layers she was huddled under. Her pregnancy must have been making her cold or something because although the air was crisp, Miranda was perfectly fine in the cloak Govek had given her and a thick wool dress.

"How many kids are in the clan?" Miranda asked. There were only twenty women acting as mates and somehow because of that small number Miranda had assumed that there wouldn't be many kids.

But that was obviously *not* the case. There were *dozens* of children of all ages. Apparently, it really was more common to get a conquest from Oakwall than it was to take an actual mate.

"Close to fifty?" Viravia mused. "Perhaps more? I know there are a few pregnant conquests at Oakwall as well."

Oh frick. Miranda hadn't even thought of that. If they merged, how would those babies get to their dads? Would they have to come all the way back to get them? And then carry their newborn over war-torn lands?

Govek's hand tightened in hers as her eyes shot up to him. His brow was furrowed as if he were worrying about the same thing.

"Govek, what is Karthoc's forge like?" Miranda asked as her eyes settled on a few orc kids swinging from tree branches.

"I . . . don't know," Govek admitted, and Miranda met his eyes again. "I have never been there."

"It's horrible."

Miranda jerked her gaze back to Viravia. "You've been to Karthoc's home?"

"Oh—uh." Viravia cleared her throat and Miranda's stomach twisted. Was she getting sick? Is that why she was so bundled up? "I meant in general the world out there is horrible. Every city, orc and human, has high walls surrounding it, blotting out the view. It isn't often safe to leave those walls for any length of time, so the areas around have been stripped barren and inside it's even worse." Viravia looked up at the tree canopy. They were close enough to the hall now that the sky flickered from the Rove Trees crystalline leaves, casting rainbows through the blue. "It's *nothing* like this."

"You traveled around a lot, right? As a trader?" Miranda asked. "It must have been dangerous."

"It was," Viravia answered softly. "It was not an easy time, my childhood. Nor . . . after."

Miranda decided not to pry, and instead, looked over to where an orc was unloading a wagon with his two young boys. Each time they passed one another, arms full of baskets and rucksacks, the dad tried to rustle his sons' hair and the boys would cackle with glee as they tried to dodge without dropping their stuff.

Everywhere you looked, there was happiness—people calling out greetings, visiting in front of their houses, throwing open windows to let in the crisp autumn air.

"Oh shi—uh." Viravia stopped in her tracks and lifted her scarf a little higher on her face. Any more and she wouldn't be able to see.

"What's wrong, Viravia?" Miranda looked around but nothing seemed out of place that could have startled her. The children laughed, orcs continued to unpack, and the hall was within sight with a handful of warrior orcs entering but she couldn't recognize any of them before they disappeared into the hall.

Her stomach twisted as she wondered if the seer was among them.

"N-nothing. I just forgot something at home."

"You forgot something?" Miranda asked, curious. "Do you want us to go back with you to get it?"

"No, no," she said with a wave of her hand. "You don't need to do that. My home is right there."

Miranda glanced and found that Viravia's tree house was, indeed, down the street from them. And she looked the other way and saw the Great Rove Tree just a quick walk away. So close to the hall. Miranda hadn't noticed since they'd only visited Viravia after dark.

"Are you certain?" Govek asked even as Viravia moved away.

"Yes, I'm *fine*. Estoc is already in the hall and Iytier will arrive at any moment. I'll be back shortly. Don't worry," Viravia said rapidly, already heading back down the street.

"All right?" Miranda said quietly as Viravia disappeared. "Is she always that scattered?"

"Scattered?"

"Forgetful, all over the place."

"Not typically," Govek muttered as they continued up the path toward the hall.

Miranda held Govek's hand tight, but kept her eyes on the kids. How they played and laughed and spoke just the same as the kids on Earth. Even though they were a different species, on a different planet, they were still kids who needed peace and love, who deserved clean air and safety.

Miranda's gut twisted, remembering what Viravia had described. "Govek . . . if they merge, what will the kids' lives be like?"

Govek made a little strangled sound and Miranda glanced up to find his face stricken. He'd never been around the children of Rove Wood Clan before. He probably hadn't even *thought* about this, and she couldn't blame him.

And now that he was . . . his expression told her everything she needed to know. She didn't need to make him harbor any more guilt than he already did.

She reached up to the back of his neck and pulled him down for a quick kiss. "I love you."

He huffed, and a tiny bit of tension ebbed from the muscles in his back.

"Govek."

Brovdir walked over to them with a steady gait. His eyes only flashed to Miranda briefly before turning to Govek.

"Brovdir," Govek greeted as his heavily scarred younger cousin stopped to his side. "What brings you to the hall?"

Brovdir's voice was like gravel. The scar around his neck looked ghastly. "Karthoc brought me. With the seer."

Miranda's stomach tightened. Dang it, she was trying not to think about the seer. It wasn't fair of her to blame him for not being able to give her the impossible—she knew that —but logic played no part in grief.

"Karthoc and Evythiken?" Govek said, incredulously. "Why are they here?"

Brovdir shrugged. "Food's better."

"And why did Karthoc bring you?" Govek asked. Miranda elbowed him in the side at his incredulous tone. But he just narrowed his eyes at her and explained. "Brovdir typically dislikes crowded places. I find it difficult to believe you *also* came here for the food."

Brovdir shifted his weight and said, "Brother has plans."

"Plans for what?"

"Ask him," Brovdir said.

"Brovdir!"

Karthoc's call came from inside the hall and the male's face twisted. He scratched at the back of his neck before letting out a deep sigh. "I'm . . . sorry. Must go."

"Yeah, sounds like it," Miranda said. She glanced at Govek and found him looking confused, brow furrowed at the hall doors as Brovdir jogged back over and disappeared within.

"You okay?" Miranda asked, stroking his arm.

"Yes," Govek said. "That's fucking *odd*."

"Brovdir being in the hall with Karthoc?"

"Yes. Something doesn't sit right." Govek began walking and Miranda hurried to match his rapid pace. "Let's go find out why."

TWENTY-ONE

GOVEK

Miranda babbled constantly as they made their way toward the hall doors. It was as if she could read his mind and knew he needed a quick distraction to keep his tension at bay. Knew he needed something to look forward to.

"So, after this, I think we should stop by the storeroom and pick up all the ingredients for a new food I want you to try." She stroked his arm. Her fingertips were like the touch of butterfly wings and made him shiver. "It's called pizza and it's basically flat bread with a bunch of delicious toppings on it. I'm not sure how the bread will turn out, but it can't be much worse than the rolls you made for us, or should I say, the *rocks*."

Govek snorted and slowed his pace. He wanted a few more moments to listen to her, and the hall was far too close.

"I think we should try to figure out what your favorite of

all the things I cook you is. Maybe tomorrow I can make all the best dishes so you can try them together. Then you can choose your favorite. I guess that might be wasteful though, right? Maybe we should invite Viravia and Brovdir over to help us eat it? Man, I forgot to quiz Brovdir about that woman he's seeing at Oakwall. Dang it, now we *have* to invite him over for dinner."

Govek disliked the idea of sharing his time with Miranda. He tugged her closer to his side. "You do not need to invite them, Miranda. I will eat *everything* you make."

"Oh really? That sounds like a challenge." Miranda grinned. "You'll have to pay attention though, cause I'll want to know what you like best."

"I already know what I best like to eat."

Her eyes danced with mischief. "Oh *really*? What might that be?"

"I'll give you a hint." He brushed his lips against her ear, kissed along her cheek. He tipped her chin to his mouth.

"Govek."

He jerked away from his mate. Chief Ergoth stood before him.

"What are you doing here, my son?" his father asked, eyes on Miranda. Govek felt his blood lick with flames as he pushed his mate behind his back. Ergoth puffed in exasperation as he adjusted the sleeve of his shimmery blue robes. "Really, Govek, you *must* act this way? After yesterday, I would have thought you had learned your lesson."

Learned his lesson? But he'd *won* the judgment. He had no lessons to learn from his victory.

None aside from the new knowledge that he may not be

as reviled as he'd thought. Govek straightened his back as his father continued.

"I hope you don't mean to eat in the hall, Govek. You know how everyone must feel after the ruling. The sorrow over Maythra, Rogeth, and Wolvc's banishment is high."

Govek kept his voice firm. "I was invited."

"Invited? Who invited you?"

"Viravia did, and she will be here to join us soon," Govek said.

"I am still chief of this clan, Govek. *And* your father. I demand—"

"Govek! Greetings."

Govek blinked and turned to find Iytier standing behind him with Savili and their baby. The male narrowed his eyes at Ergoth but said, "Have you come to eat in the hall, Govek?"

"Viravia invited us." Govek tucked his jaw up. "She said we might be welcome."

"You certainly are," Iytier said, but his eyes never strayed from Ergoth's face. "Estoc and Jehvlek are already within. I am confident they would like to speak with you. On friendly terms and nothing less."

Ergoth spoke up. "While I agree that a few in the clan would be fine with Govek's presence, there are many more who would be uncomfortable. Govek, I strongly urge you to return to your home for now. Give those who are grieving time to come to terms."

"Those who are grieving *traitors* can do so in their own homes."

It was Estoc. He had just exited the hall and walked over to their small group. Govek had been on the receiving end of the male's ire more than once, but this time, his dark eyes were narrowed on the chief.

Govek had never seen *anyone* look at his father this way.

"Govek was found in favor. He should not be treated as if he were the one being punished."

"I meant nothing of the sort," Ergoth said, his voice flat and his eyes seething. "I think only of the sadness and suffering of my clan members."

"You've turned a blind eye to your own son's suffering enough times. I would think you could manage the act for Maythra's supporters now," Estoc snapped, flooding Govek with the oddest sensation—like he was growing tall, moving higher. He could look down upon his father and know that any rebuke Ergoth attempted could not reach him at this new distance. "Govek, come eat with me."

Govek stood frozen as Estoc went back into the hall. The male was clearly angry, but not at him, right? Or was this meal about to turn into an interrogation? Govek had not been around these males enough to read what their intentions were. They were his *brother's* friends. And yes, they'd gone fishing and hunting, and occasionally, they'd shared a meal together, but Govek had been an outsider in those gatherings. On the outskirts. Watching rather than participating.

And yet his chest lightened at the memory of Jehvlek offering him a place at the campfire. Of Iytier asking him for tips while hunting. Of being amused by one of Estoc's tales.

Would they really have allowed Tavggol to invite him along if they hadn't wanted his company?

"Come, Govek. Let us catch up on old times and enjoy

each other as we once did." Iytier held open the door for him, even Savili seemed pleased. She grinned at him and Miranda triumphantly.

Miranda placed a hand on Govek's arm, looked up at him with questioning eyes and a light smile. He soaked up her confidence and nodded.

He took a deep breath and entered the Hall.

The world inside was much different from anything he'd experienced in the past.

Govek had never been allowed to participate in the revelry after the families came back from the seasonal communion. He was told he couldn't be trusted around the children.

But not one of the children even noticed he was there as they rushed around, yelling and laughing. Celebrating. Their schooling would take a break now and the energy was high.

"Govek," Iytier said, gesturing for him to follow. "This way." He pointed to one of the tables dead center in the hall, and Govek tensed as the eyes of orcs and women landed on him.

He'd always kept to the outskirts, always lurked along the wall. He'd stayed out of sight as much as possible. He could not recall ever walking toward the center of the Great Rove Tree, head high, eyes scanning rather than averted.

And when he did look . . . Blast. The angry, worried faces he'd endured were gone. Confusion lay in their wake. Uncertainty. There were whispers, but the clipped unhappy tones were absent. The hush wasn't allowed to permeate with so many happy children playing around them.

So many *children*. Govek had never realized how many there were. Probably close to fifty. One-sixth of the clan.

"Govek . . . if they merge, what will the kids' lives be like?"

Fuck.

"Sit here, Govek, Miranda." Savili gestured to the bench right across from Estoc and his mate, Roenia. Roenia was nursing their babe, and Govek's mind shifted to a mental image of Miranda cradling one of their own.

He glanced at Miranda and found her features soft and her mouth quirked into a grin. But her attention was on a group of children playing on Ergoth's platform. Two much younger were whooping with delight as they leaped into an older boy's arms.

Miranda was so Fades-wretched beautiful in this moment of happiness Govek felt his entire being soften at it. She had spoken of cameras, magic that could capture a still image. He had to admit that he longed for this to be made real on Faeda. He couldn't count the sights of her he wished to preserve.

A throat cleared and Govek jolted, brought back out of his musings to find both orcs watching him with wide eyes and their women . . . well their women were hard to read, but their smiles made his gut pitch.

He helped Miranda onto her bench seat and Roenia leaned as far toward Miranda as the suckling babe would allow. She held up her hand to her mouth as if that would somehow prevent Govek from hearing. "You two seem to be getting along. Are you playing conquest? Or are the two of you thinking of being mated? Do you plan to stay here in Rove Wood Clan for the pregnancy?"

Miranda flashed one of her best smiles and greeted warmly. "I'm Miranda. Nice to meet you."

Savili chuckled as Roenia flushed and stammered. "I'm

Roenia, and this is Uvion." She touched the babe's head. "I have four other sons as well." She gestured over to a group of about ten running around. There was no way to pick out which were hers.

"I'm Estoc." Roenia's mate cut in. "I'll get the boys over to introduce later. No use trying to talk sense into their thick heads right now. You'll understand soon enough with your own orc babes."

"Maybe," Miranda said with a shrug and a grin that told him he knew just what she was doing to their curiosity.

Estoc kept his gaze on Govek as he muttered, "You picked a woman as tight-lipped as you are, I see."

Govek huffed as Miranda's grin widened.

"Stop pushing, Estoc."

It was Jehvlek's quiet tone that cut the tension. He walked over with his usual smooth glide. His slender frame and careful demeanor gave him an aloof air that had never left Govek feeling completely comfortable. This was the first time he had laid eyes on the male since Tavggol's death, but he met Govek's eyes with ease. "Govek has always been private, so I can only assume his woman is as well."

"He could at least tell us if she's staying," Estoc muttered but dropped the subject.

Jehvlek made no move to sit. "I'll return shortly with my mate. Would you like us to bring meals for you and your woman, Govek?"

"I'll get it once she's settled," Govek said firmly and Jehvlek gave a simple nod before disappearing into the chaos.

Surprisingly, Estoc grinned with amusement. "Ever the

provider. You—" He froze, eyes narrowed on the door. "Fades be fucked."

Govek looked over to see his father walk into the hall. He kept to the wall like Govek usually did and scanned the crowd. When their eyes met, his father glowered, straightened up, and turned away. He moved off toward his platform where the children were still roughhousing.

"You'd think he'd read the energy," Estoc growled under his breath and Roenia patted his arm with her free hand. "He should either explain himself or stay out. He's going to spoil the mood."

Roenia censured him quietly. "Estoc, you promised."

"I know, I know," he muttered. "Sorry, Govek. I know it's not a pleasant topic, but fuck, Ergoth hasn't even . . . sorry. Nothing."

A tense silence followed as Estoc went quiet, though his eyes still narrowed on Ergoth, who had climbed up to his platform and disappeared into his private rooms.

"What do you mean?" Miranda pressed, drawing Govek's attention back. "Ergoth hasn't even what?"

Roenia met Estoc's eyes. "We, most of the clan, have been asking him to clarify some things, like why he lied to keep us from visiting Govek after Tavggol's death, but he's been rather avoidant."

"Guilty is what he is," Estoc snapped, going off in a way that made Govek's brows rise. "He even promoted the rumors that you abused Yerina. That's why so many here believed them."

Govek clenched his teeth so hard he thought they might crack.

"Estoc," Iytier cut in. "You vowed to make this a pleasant meal."

Estoc growled slightly but met Govek's eyes. "Sorry, we're all furious. Karthoc said he'll search out the truth, but what for? We all already *know* the truth."

Govek swallowed and searched the hall to where Karthoc stood beside Brovdir, chatting with a large group of males who were all sitting and eating. Most of the expressions were actually *pleasant.*

Had . . . the warrior's reputation in Rove Wood Clan changed? What had caused that?

"He won't be our chief for much longer anyway," Iytier said, giving Govek a pointed look.

Govek's skin prickled.

He would *not* become clan leader. He was not suited for such a role.

Govek calmed himself by toying with the idea of taking Miranda on a long hunting trip. He'd hide her away from all these complications until they resolved on their own.

Estoc snorted loudly and drew Govek's attention back. "Regardless, most do not think of Ergoth as our leader any longer. Too many vile things have been uncovered. Why even the clearing has—Vaiteg!" The male rose to his feet, eyes flaming. Govek was jolted by the sudden shift that it took him a moment to remember that Vaiteg was the name of Estoc's eldest son. "Get out of that cauldron! Do you want to be turned into stew?"

Govek blinked, trying to pull himself out of his own mind as Estoc charged off to get his child out of the cooking pot. He clenched and unclenched his hands, working to calm his nerves.

Miranda's bright laughter instantly caught his attention. Everyone's really. He turned to find her eyes trained on Estoc. He yanked his son out of the cauldron only to realize it was partially full of raw fish already. The muck splashed out and splatted all over the floor and Estoc's legs as well.

His tension dimmed as Estoc's raging disgust roared over the general clamor of the hall. Vaiteg barely looked bothered.

"That boy certainly keeps us running." Roenia nodded at Miranda with an easy smile. "This isn't even the oddest thing he's done."

"Oh, I'm sure. Kids with that much energy tend to get into the *worst* trouble. And the most hilarious," Miranda said.

"Miranda used to work with children," Savili offered.

Roenia's eyebrows rose. "I bet you have some good stories."

"Oh man, absolutely." Miranda leaned in a bit. "One time this four-year-old, Josh, got into the snack room, which is usually barred from the kids, and ate every pack of fruit snacks we had on hand. Like three pounds of the stuff."

"Oh no!" Roenia said, clearly amused, though Govek heard the note of confusion in her tone at Miranda's Earth words.

"Was he ill?" Savili asked.

"That's an understatement."

"Vaiteg did something similar." Roenia started up her own tale as Iytier got Govek's attention.

"Govek"—his spine locked with tension as he wondered what the male wanted to speak on—"do you remember that fishing trip we took alone last spring?"

Govek blinked, brow furrowed. "Yes?" It had been of little consequence. The clan had needed fish, and Iytier had volunteered his aid. They'd barely spoken. Kept to the task at hand.

"I want a rematch."

Govek blinked. "You what?"

"A rematch. I've been practicing my skill since then and I know I can beat you this time." The male grinned. "Or are you too scared to face me?"

Govek's chest tightened, and he huffed, trying to think of what *exactly* this male was trying to goad him into. "You want to . . . challenge me to a *fishing* match?"

Warmth slipped into his hand and he realized Miranda had laced her fingers with his under the table. She cast him a little smile before going back to her own conversation.

"Why so shocked? You didn't think the one would suffice after our numbers were so close. I only caught ten less fish than you. I'm certain I can get more." Iytier said with a confident nod.

"I . . ." Govek wasn't certain how he should respond to this lunacy. He gave Miranda's hand a squeeze, drawing strength from her. "I did not realize we were competing."

Iytier's face fell. "You what?"

"I did not realize we were having a competition."

"Are you jesting?" Iytier's voice rose, thoroughly flummoxed. "Tell me you're jesting."

Govek shook his head. "I am not."

"Oh, for the will of Fades, I was blistering my balls to beat you and you weren't even *trying*?" Iytier's voice carried, and all around murmured in shock. Some nearest Govek seemed to get up to move away. "Fuck, Govek, that settles it. We're going fishing *tomorrow*. And this time, I want your best."

Govek could not place the fluttering emotion that had begun to gnaw away at the edges of his gut. "Fine. I will rise to your challenge."

Iytier nodded confidently and turned to Estoc, who had just come back over with a bowl of steaming stew. "Estoc, tomorrow, fishing against Govek. Winner gets to boast the title of best spearman in the clan. Are you with us?"

Govek's amusement heightened.

"Fuck, no," Estoc said, settling down across from Iytier. "I don't need to prove myself."

"You too scared to face him again?"

Govek tensed. The last time he and Estoc had fished together had ended poorly.

"Fuck off," Estoc muttered, arranging his mate's bowl carefully so she could reach the spoon. "I'll come watch and be glad to laugh at you while you lose."

Govek snorted as amusement bubbled up in his gut and threatened to split his face.

"We're going to laugh at Iytier?" Jehvlek appeared out of the crowd holding two bowls with his curly haired mate in toe. Roenia and Estoc made room between them so Aralie could stay next to Jehvlek but the separate conversations could be maintained. "You can count me in."

"Shut it, Jehvlek. We're going to *challenge* Govek for the title of best spear-fisher in the clan," Iytier said.

Jehvlek laughed humorlessly. "Good luck with that, but it will be a pretty sight to watch you suffer a humiliating defeat, Iytier."

"You two have no bravery!" Iytier tried to goad them, and Govek had to admit, he would find it far more amusing to have more challengers.

So, after a half moment of hesitation, Govek said, "I will teach you how to spear against the rapids."

The three males fell silent as they turned to Govek, and he clenched his fists. He'd always avoided putting himself in any role that might be misconstrued as dominant and the place of *teacher* unsettled him, but . . . "I remember how you wanted to learn, Estoc. If you agree to the challenge, I'll show you." The male split into an enthusiastic grin that had Govek saying, "Perhaps it will give you an actual chance of winning."

"Ah fuck." Estoc slapped his hand on the table, glowering and grinning at the same time. "I don't know if I'm excited or insulted. You're fucking *on,* Govek. You better get a good night's sleep tonight."

"I'm in too," Jehvlek said with a solid nod.

"Then it's settled," Iytier said triumphantly. "Tomorrow after morning meal, we'll go."

"Yes," Govek agreed, already anticipating the event in a way he'd never had before.

TWENTY-TWO

MIRANDA

Miranda found herself seated at a table, surrounded by four orcs, three women, two babies, and a clan in boisterous chaos.

The room was warm, bright, and smelled strongly of roasting fish. The three fires boasted massive cauldrons all filled with what seemed to be carrot and trout stew. Only about half the children had settled down to eat and those that were bounced around in their seats, wanting to gobble down their grub as quickly as they could.

"Vaiteg! Get your brothers and come over here to eat!" Estoc roared into the crowd, but the dark green boy ignored his father's command and continued to sprint around the room.

"Sorry," Roenia said. "I guess we'll have to make introductions later."

"That's just fine," Miranda assured her. Savili had just

poured a slew of names out so quickly Miranda's head spun. But at least everyone at their table *looked* very different.

Iytier was the closest to Govek in height, but he was lighter in color, though not as light as Jehvlek, who was slender and had a pointed chin. Estoc was the darkest and was much shorter, but had the most muscle aside from Govek. She tried to repeat the names in her head, but knew that she'd be checking with Govek later.

The newest woman was Jehvlek's mate, and she was the exact opposite of Jehvlek. Short, curvy, and dark complexioned. Her name had been impossible for Miranda's brain to keep hold of, but mostly because when Savili had introduced her, Miranda had gotten distracted by some of the nearby children having a roaring competition. Their faces were so fierce, and their volume couldn't match. *So* cute.

All the kids were. And so hauntingly familiar to the children on Earth. Happy, innocent.

Miranda's eyes prickled even as a smile played on her lips.

Two twin boys, probably around three years old, ran out of the throngs and clung to Jehvlek's mate. Their dark hair and light green eyes examined Miranda nervously. One dipped his finger into his mother's soup bowl and messily sucked off the liquid.

"Tovis," his mother chided quietly, pushing her utensil into the boy's hand. "Use a spoon, please."

He let out a sigh so gusty that Miranda was instantly thrown back into a memory of Jacob with his dramatic exasperation every time the daycare cleaned up the reading nooks. He liked his spot just so and would spend a long time putting all his pillows in order again. Miranda had always been impressed with Jacob's attention to detail.

Her eyes stung.

"I know it's a lot," Savili said. "Feel free to ask all our names again whenever you need to."

"Oh, I'll need to," Miranda confirmed, blinking the unshed tears away before glancing to the woman holding her twins. "You were . . . Avery, right?"

"Aralie," she said quietly. "And this is Tovis and Rynen."

"Tovis and Rynen," Miranda said, smiling eagerly at the little ones. Tovis nodded his head, taking a bite far too big for his mouth, and Rynen hid his face in his mother's arm. "They're adorable."

Aralie smiled so sweetly it made Miranda grin. Jehvlek reached over to rustle both his sons' hair before going back to the male conversation. Miranda noted that Aralie looked to Jehvlek often, leaning into him a little for support.

Roenia and Savili, however, barely looked at their males and had chosen to sit next to her and Aralie instead of with their mates on the far opposite end.

Miranda wondered how long each of them had been a part of this clan. Judging by twelve-year-old Vaiteg, she suspected Roenia was very comfortable here.

"All your children are adorable." Miranda looked around at the bustling room. The energy of the hall was completely different now that the children had returned, and Miranda basked in it like a cat in a sun-drenched window, even if it made her sad.

There were probably twenty or more kids under the age of fourteen, all boys, all orc, all incredibly rowdy as they ran around. Some clung to their mothers, others jabbered at friends who were eager to hear their tales, but all ran up and down between the tables. Some were even jumping off Ergoth's platform, though it did earn them a scolding once they were caught.

Miranda clutched Govek's hand and wished she could ask about their ages, and family lives, and routines, and it was stupid because they didn't *need* childcare here. It was obvious the clan took care of them as a community. Raised them as a unit. Cherished them.

Dang it, she wanted to cherish them too.

Her chest tightened, and uncertainty warred in her gut. She glanced at Govek, squeezed his hand, and he met her eyes for a moment. That one look told her everything.

He was as uncertain as she was.

They'd need to talk this over. She didn't want him forced into the chief position out of guilt over what might happen to the children. That wasn't fair to him.

But she didn't want the children to suffer either.

"Where's Viravia?" Savili asked, drawing Miranda's attention. "I thought she would come with you."

"She said she forgot something at her home," Miranda said.

"Should one of us go check on her?" Aralie asked softly. "I know she's been struggling to get around with the babe so big, and I heard there's a blighted boar stalking the west."

"A boar? I was told it was a wildcat," Savili said.

"It's unlikely to get into the clan, but I will go check if she doesn't show up soon," Roenia said, looking mildly concerned. "Perhaps we should all go. Leave the mates to discuss their fishing."

"We should get together tomorrow morning too, while they're gone," Savili insisted.

Govek's hand clenched in hers and his eyes slid to her gaze. She patted to reassure him, secretly loving his clinging. "I'll probably go with them."

"You'll go . . . fishing? Do you fish?" Aralie's brow furrowed. Then the boys slid off her lap and ran off toward another young orc. "Don't get into trouble!" It seemed like a fruitless command to Miranda.

"No, but I like to watch. Govek's so fast I swear it's unreal."

"Well, my skills have gotten better," Iytier said with a confident nod. "I guarantee a good show."

"You want to impress my mate?" Govek went tense against Miranda.

But Iytier wasn't the least bit put off and Miranda couldn't help but smile. "Of course not. I want to impress Savili."

"I'll be impressed if you don't *drown*, Iytier."

"You wound me, woman!"

Aralie cut in. "Perhaps we could all go?" She looked at Jehvlek.

"Of course." Jehvlek nodded. He was more reserved, but when he spoke it commanded Miranda's full attention. His complexion was so light it reminded her of the seer.

She glanced around. The seer was here, wasn't he? She couldn't decide if she wanted to seek him out and ask for more advice, or slink back home with her tail between her legs. Her heart still ached knowing she would never find out what happened to her babies.

"I guess we're going to have a full day of it then," Roenia said, smiling at Miranda. "Viravia will be sad, but I don't think she'll be able to make the trek to the spring in her state."

"We can bring her back a bunch of fish," Savili said with a confident nod.

"Pretty sure she's tired of fish," Aralie said.

"Has she tried it fried?" Miranda asked, remembering how Govek's mind was completely blown after she'd battered and fried the fish he'd caught them.

"Fried?" Roenia asked.

"It's really good. I could make it for you."

"Woman, be careful with your promises," Govek grumbled, and for a moment, Miranda thought he was going to get jealous that she was offering to cook for other people. "You'll never be rid of them after they've had your cooking."

Miranda grinned. "I'll just *teach* them to cook."

"So, you're a good cook then, Miranda?" Aralie asked.

"She's incredible," Govek boasted. The earnest tone made Miranda blush.

"I'm not *that* good."

"I'm horrible at cooking," Savili admitted. "My mother bakes pies for a living and I helped her since I could walk, but the skill just never stuck. One of the draws of joining this clan was that almost all meals are taken in the hall."

"That and your love for me, yes?" Iytier said, narrowing his eyes.

"Eh," Savili said with a shrug, forcing a round of chuckles from the table. Even Govek snorted.

Iytier growled slightly under his breath and Savili looked away, covering her mouth as she whispered into Miranda's ear. "Ooh, I'm going to regret that tonight."

"Or be glad for it," Miranda said.

Savili leaned in as the males began talking among themselves again. The other women leaned in with her. "Glad and dissatisfied at the same time. Why did no one warn me that being intimate was so blooming difficult once you had a babe?"

"Yes," Aralie said mournfully, glancing toward where her twins were playing. "It always seems the moment we're *certain* we have a stretch alone they wake, or need something, or get into trouble . . ."

"Count yourself lucky that you're at least out of the 'must have milk every moment of the day' stage," Roenia said, switching her nursing babe to the opposite side. "It seems this little one will only cease when I'm a dried-up husk."

Miranda pounced. "Oh my gosh. *Please* let me watch your babies."

The women all blinked at her and Savili spoke first. "Oh Miranda, that's a kind offer, but . . ."

She glanced at Aralie and the woman said, "We've done this in the past. Switched off watching for each other from time to time, but it doesn't work very well."

"Orc children are notoriously stubborn," Roenia confirmed. "Aralie tried to watch Vaiteg for me when I was heavily pregnant, and it was a nightmare."

"It was," Aralie said with a shake of the head. "They just don't like to listen to anyone but their parents."

"I have *plenty* of experience with stubborn kids." Miranda was unwilling to let this opportunity pass her up without at least getting a chance. "If you're worried, you can let me host a 'playdate' and stick around until you're comfortable."

"You're really that confident?" Aralie asked, quietly.

"You keep saying you have experience. Was it an orphanage you worked at?" Roenia asked.

"No, I . . ." Miranda cut off, unsure of how to explain this. Should she bring up Earth now? Could she manage it without crying? "Let's just say many of the parents where I used to live were busy working and would ask me to watch their children for them while they were away."

"How many at once?" Roenia asked.

"It was ten per caretaker in the toddler rooms. Three per in the infant rooms," Miranda said. "And then twelve to fourteen per when you got into groups of children over five."

"You would take care of *fourteen* children on your *own*?" Aralie asked.

"That must have been madness." Savili shook her head. "I couldn't even fathom it."

"I loved it," Miranda said wistfully. Her throat closed up a bit, and she managed a breath. "Every second."

Govek caught her tone and turned his attention to her. He gave her hand another squeeze.

"Second?" Roenia asked quietly, making Miranda's chest tighten. Her confusion had Miranda realizing *this* could be the perfect opening. She could and *should* at least broach the topic of being from somewhere very far away now.

But she waited too long and Estoc, seeming to instantly read the tension, took a bite of his stew and loudly proclaimed. "Fucking fish again. Maybe we should have a hunting challenge instead. Govek, you've been in the clan for days. Why haven't you been bringing us some actual meat?"

Tension fell over the table. The friendly nature turned a

little awkward. The knowledge that Govek was the *only* hunter for this clan but still considered an outcast, and the animal torture allegations that had only just been disproved, hung heavily in the silence.

Miranda, determined to end the discomfort, spoke a little too quick and loud. "Govek's been far too busy giving *me* his meat to go hunting."

Savili choked on her stew.

The rest of the table was stunned into silence for a moment before breaking into laughter and exclamations, though none quite as loud as Govek.

"Woman, you will be the end of me." Govek laughed, pinching the bridge of his nose. *"Fuck."*

She grinned at him, satisfaction working to quell her embarrassment. Everyone at their table was back to smiling, though she noted that Aralie and Jehvlek were looking at Govek's grin with shock.

It dawned on Miranda then that perhaps Aralie was *nervous* about being around Govek. Was that why she was clinging to Jehvlek? Judging from her clenched hands and wide eyes, Miranda suspected that was the case. She knew Govek's reputation wouldn't be changed in a single night.

But dang, she'd hoped it would.

She took a moment to glance around the room and found that, thankfully, no one else in the clan was looking at them. The stares that had been pressing when they'd first entered were absent now, and no one even glanced their way as their chatter continued.

And then her eyes found his.

The seer's.

Her stomach clenched, and she almost looked away

before she remembered he was *blind*. There was no way for him to see her staring at him.

He was seated at a table with Sythcol and a few other conjurers, judging by their black hands. He chatted with them casually, and Miranda wished she knew what about.

And then he bid them goodbye, rising from the table.

"Miranda."

Govek's clipped word brought her out of her stupor. "S-sorry. I got distracted."

Govek's expression was flat and unhappy as he looked between her and the seer, who was now busing his plate.

But what Govek thought didn't matter. This was about her and the seer, the reason she survived Earth's apocalypse, the reason she was brought to Faeda.

And she realized in that moment that even *if* the seer couldn't tell her what she wanted to know about her babies, she was still bound to him in ways she couldn't understand. The pull was still there. The drive to be near him. To touch his hand and force him to work out her secret.

Ready or not, it would happen soon.

TWENTY-THREE

GOVEK

"What's so funny over here?"

The loud boom of Karthoc's voice broke Govek's thoughts. The male stood next to Iytier, arms crossed, expression lax. Brovdir stood right behind him, looking extremely uncomfortable and refusing to meet Govek's eye.

What was going on in that male's head?

Iytier piped up, though his voice was a little tight. "Govek and I have planned a fishing competition for tomorrow."

Karthoc's grin widened. "A competition? What stakes are being raised?"

"Bragging rights," Estoc said. Though his face was flat and unhappy, he nodded his greeting to Brovdir, making it clear that his dislike only extended to the warlord.

"When are you going?" Karthoc asked.

"Tomorrow morning," Govek answered after the others

stayed quiet. Even if they disliked Karthoc, he was still their warlord.

"Mind if Brovdir and I join you then?"

"Brother," Brovdir said, his voice even more strangled than normal. He coughed a little, rubbing his neck.

Karthoc looked at him a moment before finally saying. "You're dismissed, Brovdir. Go to the healer and have him look at your throat."

Brovdir bowed and was halfway across the room in the blink of an eye. Govek's eyes followed him as Karthoc quizzed Iytier for details about their fishing trip.

Ergoth lurked at the end of their table.

Govek narrowed his eyes at the chief and the male quickly looked away, appearing as if he was talking with the small group at the end of their long bench.

Why was he so close? Was he trying to listen in to Karthoc's conversations?

"Miranda. Good day to you."

Govek whipped his head around as the seer approached his mate.

Fuck.

"Hello, seer," Miranda said, her voice breaking slightly as she attempted to stand. Govek kept a firm grip on her hand, and she shot him a puzzled look but sat back down.

He'd thought they were done with this. He thought Miranda knew that consulting with Evythiken could only bring more pain. It was too soon for Miranda to go through another trauma.

It was too soon for *him* to have to witness it.

"Miranda. I would like a word with you in private, if you will," the seer said, and Govek's gut twisted into a ball. "Unless your male is vehemently opposed."

"I am—"

"Govek." Miranda's sharp tone and steely eyes stopped him in his tracks.

Was she going to leave him? Over this? He just wanted to keep her *safe*! Why couldn't she see how horrible the seer was to her?

Miranda moved to stand and Govek followed suit, his mind reeling for a way to stop this from happening without Miranda threatening to leave him behind. She brought a leg over the bench.

The seat shifted.

And she *tripped.*

Govek snapped out his hand to catch her, but it was too late. She'd already fallen into the seer. Their skin collided as her hand caught his.

And she collapsed completely.

CHAPTER

TWENTY-FOUR

MIRANDA

His skin was *scalding*. It pulled at hers, stuck to her like glue. She couldn't wrench away even if she had wanted to.

She *didn't* want to. A shiver rolled up Miranda's spine and burst at the base of her skull. Flashes of Earth pierced through her. It was like she was there.

There were the skyscrapers that loomed above her as she walked from the bus stop to the bank for her morning shift. The blaring car sirens. The smell of exhaust and hot pavement.

The smell of stale coffee in the break room at the bank where Miranda had raided the employee fridge for snacks.

The droning clack of computers as the tellers worked away. Pleasant conversation wafting down the hall from the lobby. Mr. Barker had let Ashley take lunch early with Grace.

More sirens.

Sirens so loud and long Miranda felt them vibrating in her eardrums.

Mr. Barker yanked her down the bank stairs to the vault. Shoved her inside. Screamed at her. *"You wait here! I'll be right back with Nichole!"*

The memory came back in a flash of pure white light.

Nichole. His granddaughter, who was working as a barista at the coffee shop across the street.

He'd left to go get her. He'd sworn he would be *right back.*

But he never came back.

And then the bombing began.

Her mind flooded with that white light again. A fog soaked into every corner of her mind.

The mist.

The sight of the barren desolate wastes after she'd somehow escaped the ventilation shaft flashed. The crumbled buildings. The mangled cars. Everything was charred and ashen and pungent with the scent of smoke and baking chemicals.

And Earth, her planet, it was gone. *Gone.*

"Miranda!"

She snapped out of her mind and back into the present world so violently it felt like drowning. The air was too different, too clean, the voices were too low and rumbly. The smell of smoke and fish was strong and curled in her stomach. Bile climbed up her throat.

"You are not of Faeda."

"Get the fuck away from her."

"Govek, calm down! Look. She's *fine!*"

She barely registered the words spoken so loudly. The

growling voices dimmed as she managed back to her senses. She was held up against warmth. A chest.

Govek's chest. She was back with Govek. On Faeda.

Miranda's head pounded, and her eyes watered, but she looked up at Govek. He was baring his teeth at someone, sharp dripping fangs. She reached up to touch the side of his mouth. "Y-you can put me down."

"No," Govek snarled into her ear and she shuddered again. Put her arms around his neck.

"I'm okay," she whispered, a desperate attempt to reassure him. She wanted to reassure herself too.

"Evythiken," Karthoc roared hand on his head. The seer barely flinched. "What the *fuck* was that?"

The sentiment was repeated by everyone around, questions and shock rippled through the crowd.

Miranda's heart twisted as she noticed most of the kids running back to their parents, faces pale. A few were crying. Some orcs seemed dizzy. Others simply stared at her with wide eyes.

Her gaze moved to the group she'd been getting acquainted with. They looked equally disheveled. Aralie, in particular, was pale and shivering. Her boys were tucked into her body, hiding their faces. Her mate had her tight against his side.

Before Miranda could find her words, Savili stammered, bouncing Haysik. "Are . . . uh—are you all right?"

"I'm . . . fine."

The woman gulped, opened her mouth, closed it, and looked to her mate.

"Miranda," Roenia called from the other side of the table. "Are you . . . really from that other world?"

Oh fuck. Miranda's gut twisted as she noted how many

eyes were on her. Not just from their group, but from the entire clan.

She looked up to Govek, and he leaned in close. "Evythiken *projected*."

"Projected?" she whispered, resting her forehead against Govek's face. She felt so heavy.

"I apologize." Evythiken said soft and low. "It was . . . not intentional."

"We saw it in our minds," Govek murmured. "The way you saw it in your own."

Oh *fuck*.

"What the *fuck* are you doing?" Karthoc's roar made Miranda jump and her heart exploded into a frantic rhythm.

But he wasn't looking at her. He was looking at . . . Miranda turned her head to find Karthoc's glare was narrowed on Ergoth, who was at the very end of the table, a few steps away from the long bench that she'd been sitting on.

"What am *I* doing? What is *she* doing with the seer? What was *that*?"

"Don't try to deflect," Karthoc said, pointing a massive threatening finger as he charged over to the male. To Ergoth's credit, he did manage to stand his ground. "I *saw* you push the bench and knock her over."

Miranda felt Govek tense, and she quickly worked to soothe him. "I'm okay."

"Ha! You think I would do something so petty?" Ergoth snorted. "Your bad opinion of me is unfair, my nephew. And even if I *had* bumped it by mistake, I could never have moved it with so many seated upon it."

That seemed logical. The bench spanned nearly thirty

feet and had five other orcs sitting on it aside from their group.

"Quiet."

Evythiken's words flattened the room, dulled it like he'd smothered everyone in a blanket. Even the colors seemed distorted, muted. Miranda clung to Govek, confusion coursed through her overtaxed mind. She squeezed her eyes shut and welcomed the dark.

"You are not of Faeda, Miranda," Evythiken said, his voice crisp, clear. She forced her eyes open again and found him in front of her, breathing hard. "By the will of Fades, what *was* that?"

Miranda gulped, mouth dry, throat closed, but the word came anyway. "War."

"War," Evythiken repeated.

"My world was Earth," she said slowly. Govek's hands moved up her arms, steadied her, cleaving her to his chest. "I lived on a planet called Earth, and we *killed* it. With war."

Evythiken hissed and braced himself on the table. A million voices sounded at once.

"Silence!" Karthoc hollered again, and the venom caused quiet to descend. "Govek, explain this."

"It is as she says. She is not of Faeda."

"Where the fuck did you *find* her?"

"She fell out of the sky before my eyes."

More whispers, too many. Miranda's head spun, and she watched the seer gasp as he clutched at his head and shivered in agony. His muscles bunched, he was twitching, and tears flooded her eyes. He'd witnessed the horrors she'd seen. She'd forced them on him.

On *everyone*.

"Hush," Govek said near her ear, and she shut her eyes again to soak up his comfort. "Let's go somewhere quiet."

She nodded eagerly.

"We cannot go." Evythiken's voice rang out, and for a second, Miranda thought he was ordering her and Govek to stay, but instead, the seer turned to Karthoc. "We cannot *go*."

"Enough with this seer," Karthoc snapped. "We will speak of it later."

"*We cannot leave the Rove Woods!*" Evythiken slammed his hand down on the table and cups clattered. One bowl slipped off the edge and splattered on the stone floor. Stew and ceramic exploded in thick droplets and sharp shards.

"I have *told* you, Karthoc. Too many times. Far too many. But now you must listen. This is a *sign*. The Fades brought her here to show me this." Evythiken drew all the attention in the room. Miranda could feel the eyes leave her and finally she managed to take a full breath. "We are meant to be under this Great Tree. In the Rove Woods. The Fades want us *here*, so they can complete their work."

"I ask you again," Karthoc demanded, storming over to the male. "Here and now in front of these witnesses. What *fucking work*? You spout about it day and night, driving me daft with your demands to bring my legions here. To call the clans to settle in the Rove Woods. To tell our overlord to gather his thousands of orcs, give up fighting for our lives, and retreat to this Great Tree, but *why*?"

"I don't know! I don't know! They just keep *screaming at me*!" Evythiken's voice broke, his body shook, and his hands grasped his head. "*They won't stop screaming!*"

"For fuck's sake! You want me to drive our overlord to stop fighting for our fucking *lives* without just cause?

Without any *reason*? How can I tell any of my males to simply sit and allow the Waking Order to *slaughter* them? You see how mad that is, don't you?"

"They can't reach here," Evythiken insisted. "The Waking Order cannot breach the Rove Woods."

"Explain. *How*?" Karthoc demanded, face contorted, spitting rage. "The Waking Order knows of this place. They will come. They will burn it. There is no one to stop them except for *my warriors*. The Fades won't help us. *Nothing can help us*. We must fight!"

"We can't!" Evythiken pleaded. Still writhing, knees buckling, bracing his weight on the table. "We *can't*. We have to end the war, or our world will be *destroyed. Just like hers*."

Miranda's stomach dropped, and her eyes grew hazy.

Govek swung her up into his arms and carried her out of the hall. The continued fighting between Karthoc and the seer followed them out the door. The words banged around in her head, beating against every corner of her mind, spilling acid into her marrow.

Our world will be destroyed.

"Miranda, look at me."

Govek set her down on a rock near the edge of the path. Thankfully, everyone who'd been outside had already gone into the hall. They were alone, and she collapsed all over again.

"Miranda," he said, soothing, desperate. "Miranda, come back."

"I am." She sobbed. "I am back." And fuck, she *wished* she wasn't. She wished this was just another one of her episodes. That what she'd seen and heard in that hall were only delusions. Conjurings from her mind. That she could focus on the present, on the woods and the clean soil, and the rumble of water and the twitter of birds and know that the horrors she experienced on Earth hadn't been *real*.

But they had been.

"I can't be your savior." Her voice caught. "I don't know what to do. Govek, I don't know what I should *do*."

"You don't have to do anything, Miranda," Govek said, cupping her face, pulling her into his chest.

She knew he was wrong. God, she *wished* he wasn't. But the pull to speak to the seer was still hot in her gut and her hand trembled with the need to take his.

It wasn't done. The compulsion to seek out the seer hadn't abated yet.

"It's not fair." She curled into Govek's arms and tucked her face in his neck. "I don't understand."

"I know," he said, solid and unwavering. "I don't either. But I am here. We are together. We will figure it out, side by side."

His vow made so much of the tension in her chest ease. Her head lightened. Her lips quivered. "What do we do now?"

Govek was quiet a long moment. "Evythiken can figure it out on his own."

Miranda went still at that. She pulled away to look him in the eyes. "What?"

"Evythiken is the seer in this. He's the only one who can speak with the Fades." Govek stroked his warm hands down her arms to clasp her own. "He doesn't need you. You don't have to contact him again."

It was such a simple, straightforward response that Miranda found herself laughing. "What? But aren't I supposed to do what the Fades command?"

Govek snorted. "Miranda, I know you well enough to be certain that you won't follow any commands you don't agree with. Even if they are delivered by the divine. You are far too stubborn and opinionated."

Miranda chuckled wryly, wiping the tears from her eyes. "Wow, thanks."

Govek cupped her face again. The gold in his green eyes glistened in the dappled light. "I love every one of your stubborn opinions, Miranda. I would gladly follow them right to my doom."

"Oh god," she laughed. "That shouldn't be comforting. Why is that comforting?"

"Because you love me," he said, making her laugh again at the arrogance smoothing his brow and curling his lips. "And because you know it means we are in this together. No matter the cost, Miranda, I will always be at your side."

She crumbled and wrapped her arms around his neck, squeezing him tight, surrounded herself with his warmth and light. "I love you."

"I love you, Miranda," he whispered into her hair.

"Miranda?"

Miranda sat upright and found Viravia standing on her stoop just twenty or so feet away.

Man, Govek really picked a spot, didn't he?

The woman took one look at Miranda's tears. "Come in here, both of you."

"Miranda!"

She looked the other way and saw Savili, Roenia, and Aralie quickly approaching. Roenia still had her baby in her arms.

A baby who'd had to see Earth's horrors because of her. All those children in the hall had . . .

"I can take you home, if you prefer," Govek assured quietly.

"No, I . . ." Miranda's stomach twisted. This wasn't how she wanted Earth to come up at *all*. But she supposed it was done now. And it was better not to run away. "It's only going to be worse if I put it off."

Govek nodded slowly and helped Miranda to her feet, dusting her off.

"C-come into Viravia's house," Miranda called to the pale women before looking at Viravia. "If that's okay."

"Of course, come, come." Viravia waved them all inside. In a few moments, the door was shut firmly behind them and they were all huddled in the warm living room of the tree home. "What is going on? Is everything all right?"

Before anyone could answer Viravia, Savili threw her arms around Miranda in a tight hug.

Miranda stood as still as a boulder, eyes wide, mouth dry. "Uh . . . Savili?"

"Was your world really destroyed like that? With fire?"

Of all the questions Miranda expected, *that* wasn't one of them.

Miranda's throat closed up again, but she managed to say, "Y-yes."

Aralie rushed in next, embracing Miranda from the left.

"Her world? What?" Viravia asked quietly and Roenia pulled her aside, spoke to her in low, hushed tones, filling her in without interruption.

Miranda was so grateful her eyes filled with tears again and her chest grew tight and a little choked sob left her, making the women embrace her more. The warmth and strength and sheer *power* exuding from the women soaked into Miranda. It was like nothing she'd ever known.

Govek touched her back, his massive hand covering it and Miranda's finally let her tears fall. Her chest heaved and her vision blurred but the support was still there. Viravia took her hand. Roenia rested her palm on Miranda's shoulders. They were all around her. They wrapped her up so tight she truly felt nothing could harm her again. Nothing.

They stood there for eons, and Miranda's tears dried up. Her exhaustion turned to stillness. Her sorrow turned to quiet relief. Her world shifted, and these strangers shifted too, taking on roles in Miranda's life that had never been filled. Places in her heart that were so foreign and that had been left vacant for so long, she did not even have names for them.

Eventually, they all managed to move to the couches and settled down in silence. Govek pulled her into his lap. Viravia held her hands. The other women surrounded them, murmuring soothing words and patting her until Miranda found her voice.

"I'm . . . sorry I didn't tell—"

"No. Don't. How could one even *begin* with that?"

"We are as strange to you as you are to us, Miranda." Savili kneeled down next to her and stroked her knee.

"No one expected you to just come out with that right off." Roenia stood behind Savili and adjusted her babe, flexing her arm slightly. "Well, perhaps *some* in the clan would. But they aren't worth space in your mind."

"We'll make sure they don't bother you." Aralie's eyes were red rimmed and her voice was thick. She sat next to Viravia and rubbed Miranda's shoulder gently. "Hilva, mostly. Right?"

Savili nodded. "Yes, Hilva's been such a chore. If she

bothers you, Miranda, you just tell us and we'll shoo her off like the gnat she is."

Miranda huffed out a choked laugh, and she felt Govek stroke her hair.

Roenia said, "You know, this explains a lot of mysteries we've been puzzling over." Miranda tipped her head at the woman as she shifted the baby again. "Viravia told us all about your newborn and bottle advice. Knowledge that not one of us had. Not even Aralie, and her mother is the midwife at Oakwall."

"Yes," Aralie agreed. "My mother would love to talk to you, I'm sure. It sounds like you have so much knowledge to add."

Miranda shifted and nodded slowly.

"Look," Savili gave her knee another tight squeeze, "We all saw and heard what happened in the hall. It's pretty clear why the seer thinks you're here." She met Miranda's eyes solidly. "But that doesn't mean your *only* worth is tied up in that insanity."

Miranda blinked, tightness ebbing from her chest.

"Yes," Roenia said, adjusting her squirming baby in her arms. "You are your own person. Just because the Fades brought you here, doesn't mean you don't get to exist on your own terms. Take up your own place."

Miranda licked her dry lips. "I don't even know what place I *should* take."

"You already have one." Viravia squeezed her hands again.

"Yes," Aralie agreed, her eyes hesitantly landing on Govek before they skittered away.

"And you have *plenty* of time to figure out the rest, Miranda," Savili assured her.

"Fades, being companion to an orc is the only useful place for any of us mates, really," Roenia said with a wave of her hand. "Take me, for example. I can't cook. I can't do craftwork. Blast, I can't even stitch up a hole in a shirt. But I can love my babies and keep Estoc in check. No one here expects any more from me. And we don't expect more from *you* either, Miranda."

"That's right," Aralie said with a confident nod. "The males can keep the war. If all you want to do is dole out nursing advice and help keep the peace, that's wonderful." She slid her hesitant gaze to Govek again.

"Yeah, that's *plenty*," Viravia gushed. "No offense, Govek."

Govek snorted with amusement and Miranda shot him a little smile. One that made Govek's face crumble. He kissed the top of her head.

"So tomorrow." Miranda tensed, turning her attention to Savili. "At the fishing competition, we're going to focus on nothing but getting you familiar with the clan." Miranda blinked.

"We'll talk about our holiday celebrations, the communion, how the trades work, what all the orcs *names* are."

"Only the important ones," Aralie assured her.

Roenia snorted. "Don't bother yourself too much with it, Miranda. I've lived here for nearly fourteen years, and I still don't know half the orc's names."

Viravia's brows rose. "Are you serious?"

"What's the point? They all sound the same. Just call everyone dear like everybody else does." Roenia shifted her babe to the other arm.

Miranda smiled, amused that she was being given that advice again.

Savili continued. "And then in the evening, you can tell us how to make this fried fish you were talking about, or we can show you one of our own recipes."

"And give you food poisoning," Roenia muttered, earning a glare from Savili. "Don't look at me like that. None of us are good cooks."

"I'm not *that* bad," Savili countered.

"I can manage to boil things at least." Viravia looked equally affronted. "Throw in the fish and some vegetables and that's stew, right?"

The earnest tone of Viravia's question caught Miranda off guard, and she laughed. The tension inside her eased tremendously.

"I'll teach you to make fried fish."

"Thank Fades," Govek muttered under his breath and Miranda burst into laughter again. The other women laughed too.

"That's cruel, Govek," Viravia said to Govek. "You've never had my cooking."

"I've smelled it," Govek muttered and the woman gasped.

"Oh, that's it." Viravia grinned even as she was affronted, "I'm going to cook tomorrow too and the males who win this fishing competition get Miranda's fried fish and the one who loses eats my slop—er, I mean, my *stew*."

Miranda's smile made her cheeks hurt.

"We're going to end up with enough fish to last the winter," Govek said.

"You want to make that the new challenge?" Roenia teased, adjusting her baby again.

"Fuck, no."

Miranda swallowed. "Could I hold him, Roenia?"

The woman's response was instant. "Of course! Thank you. My arms are dying. This little one is such a cuddler."

Miranda lifted the warm, content baby into her arms, cradling his head in the crook of her elbow. His green face was smooth, his long dark lashes cast shadows on his cheeks. He cooed contentedly as Miranda got him settled in.

"He's so beautiful," Miranda said, looking into the pure face of the sleeping babe. Innocent, unblemished, and perfect. His life was just starting. His journey had only begun. "Thank you. So much."

The women's faces reflected a world of warmth and acceptance that Miranda had never thought she would receive so quickly. That she hadn't imagined she would *ever* have in her life. It filled her up, split her face in a smile, and flooded her eyes with fresh tears.

Viravia took Miranda's hand again, her own eyes misty. "Thank *you*, Miranda. And welcome to Rove Wood Clan."

CHAPTER

TWENTY-FIVE

Govek stirred, waking with a deep breath that tasted crisp on the back of his tongue. The scent of meat roasting flooded his nose.

And he opened his eyes to find Miranda hovering over him.

He blinked, eyes and head still blurry. "Were you watching me sleep?"

"Yeah," she admitted casually, stroking her hand over his forehead. Gentle fingers he hopelessly leaned into. He closed his eyes again and wished the night wasn't over yet so she could come back to bed. Into his arms. "Good morning."

It certainly was. She braced her warmth and weight on his chest as she leaned in to kiss him. The oddity of feeling completely at peace while first rousing was not lost on him. He relished it as he pulled her in closer, drank her up. Stroked his hand down the back of her head.

"How late is it?" he asked, not bothering to open his eyes and look out the window. "Fuck, we're going to be late."

"Probably." She slid off the bed and disappointment flooded him. "I made a breakfast sandwich for you so you can eat while we walk."

"Why didn't you wake me?" His eyes fixed to her curves, which were accentuated by her gown as she walked back toward the doorway. She'd told him she wanted to wear pants, and blast, he probably wasn't going to *survive* if her legs were on display all the time.

He'd find a way to make her some as soon as possible.

"You were basically *dead*, Govek. The only reason I knew you weren't was the snoring. There was no waking you." She shot him a smile that eased the rebuke before she exited the room and went back into the kitchen.

He had his feet on the floor before he realized this woman had been sitting next to him, watching him, likely caressing him, and he did not wake once. Her presence was such a comfort that he felt not a hint of anxiety from it. In fact, he'd likely slept deeper with her nearby, surrounded by her protection. Her acceptance.

Her love.

He gathered his things quickly, pulled on clothes, and washed his face before joining Miranda in the kitchen. The food she'd made smelled incredible. Eggs and bacon and onions. He didn't even mind that the bread was almost as hard as stone.

"Thank you," he said, throat a little thick as the gorgeous woman he loved handed him food she'd made specifically with him in mind while allowing him to sleep in. This was unlike anything he'd ever imagined, even in his wildest yearnings.

These moments weren't passionate or intense like he'd always imagined life with a woman to be. Yerina had painted that image. He'd never known anything else.

But true fulfillment came from this. The quiet moments. The transitions in the day. The gentle touches and mild teasing. The bone-deep knowledge that through even the most mundane tasks, he would have her at his side.

"Are you ready?" She lifted the pack. He quickly took it from her and slung it over his shoulder. She didn't fight him on it, just took his hand and guided him out into the crisp, icy morning. He shut the door, ensuring the new lock he'd made fit snug.

"Do you think Karthoc will show?" she asked carefully, her tension obvious by her tight grip on his hand.

He turned away from the door and focused on her. "I am not sure. But if he does, I will make certain he does not try to interrogate you about Earth."

She pursed her lips, thinking. The women had already vowed not to bring up Earth unless Miranda did first. He wished he could protect her from this agony. He was well equipped to fight for her physical safety, but had no experience combating things he could not see, things that lived *inside* her mind.

He had his own turmoil to deal with. His own pains and truths coming to light. They'd kept him up through the night and caused him to sleep late.

But in the crisp dawn, he was still confident in the decision he'd formed.

"I do not want to become chief of Rove Wood."

She looked up at him, expression easy, holding no judgment.

He took another breath. "Even *if* my isolation was built upon lies." *Fuck,* was it all lies? Had his father *truly* been the cause of all this? Govek shook his head. "Even if that were the case, I still would not want this role. Being a leader . . . it is not something I have ever wanted to do. Controlling others is not how I want to spend my life."

She nodded slowly, gripped his hand tight. "Using *control* is certainly how your father has led Rove Wood Clan, but it is not the only way to lead."

His brow furrowed, confusion lighting him.

Her smile softened. She reached up to stroke the hair on his forehead and he relished the simple touch. "I have no doubt, Govek, that you would find the right way to lead your people, should you choose to do it. But I also think that, after everything, you are in no way obligated to give up the life you want because of another's demands."

She stroked her hand down his arm, taking his hand in hers. "I want you to know that no matter what you choose, I will support you. All I ask is that whatever decision you come to with Karthoc, you *both* take the children of Rove Wood Clan into consideration."

His whole body quaked, and he leaned down to press his forehead to hers. "I will, Miranda. *Thank* you."

"I love you," she said, and he kissed her, praising the Fades at the same time.

Blast, they really didn't despise him after all.

They walked on for a short span, the light breeze rustled the trees, the dawn brightened into blue sky and dazzling autumn color before Miranda broke the silence.

"Who would be named chief if both you and Ergoth

died?" She flinched, let him go and looked around. "Knock on wood. Where's some wood?"

He watched, completely flummoxed as she went and rapped her fingers against a tree trunk. "What are you doing?"

"I mentioned your death, so I'm warding off the bad luck. The knocking scares off evil energy."

He paused for a moment before saying slowly, "I know that. I'm well aware. Did one of the *women* tell you to do that?"

"No." She came back to his side. "No, it's an Earth thing."

"That is a *Faeda* thing," he insisted. "Sometimes knocking can dispel magic. Especially negative magic. I thought you said you did not have magic on Earth?"

"We don't. But lots of people believed in energies. Both good and bad." She paused, taking a breath to search his face. "I guess you have it here too, huh? The same superstition. That's really weird. Maybe the Fades really did create the humans on Earth."

She said it so casually, but it struck him right through the gut.

"You should finish up your food." She tapped his half-forgotten sandwich, and he dutifully continued eating, relishing each bite, even as he considered what other parts of Faeda culture had been passed on to Miranda's world. What other connections would they share as their relationship progressed?

He could not wait to find out.

"Mostly, we did the knocking thing with the little kids." Her eyes unfocused as she fell into her memories. "Some of them, a lot of them really, had a hard time when they made small mistakes. Like tripping or spilling juice or coloring outside the lines. It got them distracted cause almost *nothing* was created from wood on Earth anymore. By the time they found their wooden thing and knocked on it, they'd forgotten about their mess-up entirely."

She had so many wonderfully sweet stories and he longed for the day she could share them without tears flooding her beautiful eyes.

It would take time. Mourning. She was in the thick of it and he knew of at least something small that might aid her.

"Would you like to speak a bard for them?" he asked. "For the children you lost."

"What?" She tipped her head, blinking tears out of her eyes.

"In my culture, we speak final words to those who depart. The rituals are long but hold great power, and once done, the Fades call their soul to come and sleep with them. They live in peace and harmony while they wait for waking and rebirth."

"That's beautiful," she said, as she hugged his arm again. She looked back to the tree canopy. "But the children I watched weren't even from here."

"I do not think the Fades would discriminate. I truly believe they made your people too, Miranda. The humans of Earth were also their creations, so of course they would allow the babies you loved to join them here on Faeda." He met her wide eyes. "In a way, that would make them closer to you as well. You could sleep easy knowing their presence was around you."

Her eyes flooded then, tears dripping down her face. "Oh Govek, that's so . . . . Okay. Yeah. I would really like that." She paused in her stride to embrace him around his stomach, squeezing him tight. He relished the feel of her clinging to him. "Thank you, Govek. So much."

"Of course, Miranda." He hid his beaming smile against the top of her head, lest she take his deep pleasure the wrong way. But blast, this felt so good. Caring for her. Soothing her. Teaching her of his culture and using it to help bring her peace. It made him feel as if she truly belonged on Faeda with him, rather than simply being planted here by the Fades. Like her world and his were becoming one.

They continued on in easy silence, weaving through the trees toward the spring he and Iytier had agreed to have this competition at. Govek remembered the last time he was here with Iytier. Tavggol had only just left to try to do trade with Clairton. Govek's tension had been high, his thoughts muddled and unfocused on the task at hand.

And Iytier had thought they were competing.

The truth of it still made mirth bubble up in his chest and he chuckled over the ridiculousness of it.

"What is funny?"

Karthoc startled them both as he appeared out of the thick woods on their left. He'd been tromping through the forest rather than taking a path.

The warlord's expression wasn't overly tense. His eyes lingered on Miranda. "Woman, I wish to apologize to you."

Miranda clutched Govek's hand in surprise, and the sensation mirrored what was in Govek's own chest. His cousin was rarely moved to remorse. Karthoc was oft more like a boulder barreling down a steep slope, crushing everything in its path and not looking back.

But the warlord lowered his head this time. "My arguments with the seer should not have been allowed to leave our camp. I regret bringing them out so openly, and that you felt discomfort enough to leave the hall."

Miranda glanced up at Govek, lips pursed. "Are you more upset about us being uncomfortable or that we all now know that Evythiken is fighting for you all to stay in the Rove Woods?"

Govek tensed as Karthoc's expression darkened, but the male lowered his head again with a deep sigh that vibrated through the surrounding trees. "Both. Fuck, the blasted orcs won't leave me *alone* now."

"And for good reason."

Evythiken made his way out of the tree line. Govek's guts twisted. Had the seer not done enough already?

Karthoc growled low. "I thought I told you to stay at the camp."

"And I thought I told *you* I would not," Evythiken said smoothly. He looked far less disheveled than he had the day before. He inclined his head toward Miranda. "Good morning to you both. I come to exchange pleasantries with Miranda."

"You come to muddy up the only reprieve I have in this whole mess," Karthoc muttered. "Your *pleasantries* are schemes."

"I think we can both agree that the scheming belongs to Ergoth."

Karthoc snorted, but met Govek's eye. "Yes, and I want to assure you we'll be hosting one of those *judgments* of Rove's soon, Govek. Perhaps tomorrow."

A shiver threatened to roll down Govek's spine. He could never have imagined that his father would ever be on the hard end of a judgment.

"Rest assured," Karthoc said, clearly noting Govek's

discomfort. "You needn't worry about it. You don't even need to show up if you don't want to. Plenty of males have already come to me with complaints. Waves of them. Fucking *forests* worth. I've got Sythcol and Brovdir compiling them as best they can."

"*Sythcol?*" Govek said with a shake of his head. The lead conjurer had always followed Ergoth's commands. He even invented the clearing *and* the binding under Ergoth's orders. "Are you certain he's trustworthy in this?"

"He is," Evythiken confirmed, rubbing at his temple. "He feels badly used. He is . . . satisfyingly vindictive."

"Satisfyingly vindictive?" Miranda repeated, brows raised.

"Miranda, I wanted to tell you I stripped your memories from the children's minds."

Govek could feel her sag with relief even as she tightened her grip on his arm. "Really? You can do that?"

Evythiken chuckled. "Of course, I can. Especially when it is willed by the Fades. Which it certainly was. This message is not for our young to experience, but for *everyone* else."

"Everyone else?" Miranda asked and Govek's guts began to twist up.

Fuck, wasn't she *done* with this? Why did she keep pressing?

"I have much to impart on you, but later. Let's keep today light while we still can."

"Agreed." Karthoc clapped his hands together. "I want to hear nothing of mergers or clans or Fades or bloody *prophesies* until after the winner of this fishing competition has bragged to the entire clan. Now, let's get going. The weather won't keep."

Miranda curled her fingers around Govek's arm as they set out again. He relished it even as his mind worked for a way to tell the seer to fuck off and leave them in peace.

All he wanted was Miranda to *heal*. *Was* that really such a grand request?

Before long the pool came into view. A deep span of blue water surrounded by mossy rocks and a few fallen trees. It was part of the Spring of the Fades and thus often had many fish. Most of it was only waist deep, and the bottom was rocky, but slick.

Iytier and Estoc were already there with their mates and sons. Setting up blankets for their women to sit upon. Estoc's four older boys were taking turns jumping from a boulder twice their height onto the sandy ground while Roenia bounced their youngest, who was fussy.

He walked Miranda over. Savili spoke first, drawing the attention of the males. "Hello, Miranda, good morning. I'm so glad we got another pleasant day for this."

Govek could feel the tension leave Miranda in a rush as they approached the women. "Yeah, it would be pretty miserable out here in the rain. Viravia couldn't make it?"

"She wanted to rest, but she will join us for the cooking later," Savili said.

"She's still got half a moon left before the babe comes, poor thing." Roenia patted her little one's bum. She gave Govek a smile that stunned him. Drew him abruptly into the realization that being greeted warmly by the women of Rove Wood was an oddity he would have to get used to. "Govek, Warlord, Seer, good morning."

"Govek, what kind of spear are you using?" Estoc asked gruffly, giving up on smoothing out the blanket as Roenia plunked down unhindered.

Govek's brow furrowed as Iytier's attention turned to him, obviously eager.

"Good morning to you too, Estoc." Karthoc's tone was laced with amusement, and Estoc wouldn't even look at him. "You look very chipper, as always."

Estoc turned away purposefully. "Vaiteg! What are you chewing? Spit it out *now*."

Karthoc grinned, clearly amused by Estoc's distaste, as the male stormed off toward his son, who instantly dashed into the woods away from his father. Estoc cursed and broke into a sprint after him.

Before he could ask, however, Iytier cut in. "What spear *did* you bring to use, Govek?"

Govek snorted. "I'll just make one here."

"Are you serious?" Iytier muttered, eyes narrowed.

"Yes." Govek shrugged. He'd made so many of the blasted things in his life he could do it one handed and blindfolded. "What of it?"

"Oh, he's gonna make Estoc *so* mad," Roenia said to Miranda, though loudly enough that the males could hear. "My mate spent *hours* this morning going over each of his fishing spears, trying to choose the best one. I had to talk him out of bringing them all. Now Govek leaves it up to chance? Ha!"

Govek grinned.

"That's what he's always done. Is that not the norm?" Miranda settled down on the blanket where Roenia patted.

"No," Savili laughed, adjusting her baby so she could sit down next to Miranda. "It is *not* normal."

Govek's chest lightened as Miranda's mirth lit up the forest. Her smile was radiant, and her relaxed posture soaked into every one of Govek's muscles.

"There you are, Jehvlek!" Iytier bellowed as the male and his family appeared out of the woods. "We thought you'd decided you weren't good enough to face us."

Jehvlek met Iytier's taunt with a lewd gesture, but both males were grinning.

"Be good!" Aralie called as her twins hurried off to join Estoc's boys. Govek's eyes followed the young ones, soaking up their chatter, basking in their delight.

They were so alive. So vibrant. He realized then why Miranda enjoyed children so much.

"Evythiken? Are you well?" Aralie called and Govek glanced behind him to see the seer clutching his head.

"Fine," the male grated before he walked off into the woods.

"Should we help him?" Miranda looked at Govek.

"He'll be fine," Karthoc muttered, clearly undaunted. "This happens all fucking day. Nothing we can do to help anyway."

Miranda looked stricken, but before Govek could think of words to ease her worry, Karthoc demanded, "Let's get this going. Govek, hurry up and make your spear."

"What?" Estoc said, as he appeared out of the forest carrying his son over his shoulder like the boy was a rucksack of dried beans. His voice almost shrill as he followed. "You're going to *make* your spear? Right now?"

Govek snorted his amusement and walked over to snap a branch off the nearest birch without much thought.

Iytier burst with laughter and met Govek's eye. "This is why I like you, Govek."

Estoc cursed and barely noticed his son squirmed from his grasp and went to go roughhouse with the other boys.

"Language." Roenia snapped at her male and he went mum.

Govek felt his muscles relaxing as a chuckle rolled through him. He caught Miranda's eye, and she beamed at him, her pleasure so radiant that it brought his own higher.

This was from her. He was *here*, in these woods, with these males, feeling like this because of *her*.

Govek stalked over, bent down, and plastered a kiss to her lips. Kissed her with every breath of passion he had in him. Left her panting and flustered.

When he straightened from his smiling, blushing mate, Estoc stomped over to his own woman. He glowered at Govek before kissing Roenia.

Govek, unsure of how to respond to that, looked at Miranda and found her shaking from withheld laughter. He did not understand until Estoc stood back up and said. "Trying to show me up in everything, aren't you, Govek?"

Fades, was *everything* a competition to this male? Govek had to admit that he wasn't the least put off.

Miranda gave his hand a squeeze as she lost her battle against laughter and Estoc stormed off, yelling over his shoulder. "Hurry it up, I'm starting *now*."

Roenia pressed her fingers to her lips and whispered to Miranda. "I don't know if I should thank you or not . . ."

Miranda cackled.

"Go right ahead, Estoc," Iytier called. "I don't mind giving you a head start if you need one. I'm sure Govek doesn't either."

"Fuck you!" Estoc snapped, though he stopped at the edge of the pool to wait.

Iytier kissed his woman as well, though with much less passion than Estoc had. Jehvlek also followed suit, and then they all moved into the water. Govek carved his spear as he went, using his claws to sharpen the wood, readying it without needing to take pause.

The water was cold as it lapped around Govek's legs. They all picked spots a good distance from each other and Estoc's children set up baskets on the bank for them to throw their fish into.

They began spearing without preamble, and Govek found that his concentration was easily broken by the laughter of the children. He watched between strikes, as the sons raced each other to the fish that didn't make it into the baskets. Estoc, Iytier and Jehvlek were all missing on purpose to give the boys more to do. Govek followed their lead.

Govek could hear the swell and taper of Miranda's voice as she chatted merrily with the women. Expertly bouncing both the babies on her lap as she exchanged advice and told stories.

Some of Earth. Lighthearted ones he'd heard before about some of the children she'd worked with—sassy two-year-olds and boys who liked to hide in the oddest places and the struggles of getting them to sleep for their naps.

Estoc's second youngest, Yavil, raced around trying to keep up with the older boys. He noted the frustration as he failed to get to yet another fish before his kin. Govek's memories swelled to his own frustrations in his youth. To the constant disquiet he'd tried so hard to stifle.

The boy stomped his feet and proclaimed how unfair this game was and Estoc spoke up. "Change the rules. Younger boys, stand at our baskets and try to catch them before they make it inside. Don't let them slip through your fingers. Older boys, keep racing to catch the ones that don't make it in."

Govek felt his throat tighten.

How odd this was. To see this boy vent his frustration without being silenced or told his outburst was wrong or frightening or crude. To have his father advocate for his son instead of pushing him away.

Govek wondered what his life might have been like had he simply had a different father.

He felt Miranda's eyes on him, and he met her gaze, took in the warmth of her smile. Allowed himself a breath to bunch his fists and slink out his claws and let the anger burn in his chest.

And then he released it and went back to his spearing.

The day weaved long. The baskets filled steadily, and the friendly banter drew him to distraction when he should have remained vigilant.

"Ha! I've hit fifty," Jehvlek said triumphantly.

"I've got fifty-*three*!" Estoc said, only to have his face fall. "Fifty-three fucking *fish* that we're going to have to eat. Why didn't we go hunting for hare?"

"You wouldn't have won at hare either, Estoc." Iytier grinned. "I've got sixty-one."

"The hall's going to smell like fish for moons," Savili said.

"The hall? Try the whole *clan*." Miranda laughed.

Roenia added. "They'll probably smell it all the way over in Oakwall."

"We could ask Sythcol if he needs it for his conjurings?" Aralie offered.

"What conjuring requires so many fish?" Roenia asked.

"Don't ask!" Iytier called over. "We'll just leave them on his doorstep. He can figure it out from there."

"Best we leave it tomorrow," Estoc said. "So the stench will cover our trace."

Govek bellowed with laughter. "Fuck, Estoc, you're a genius."

"Hey," Estoc said sharp, "Govek, you didn't say your count."

Govek grinned.

Miranda said, "Maybe we should wait two or three days and leave them on Ergoth's . . ."

The scent caught Govek too late, like drenched fur and oozing pus. Thick, rotting.

Blighted.

Panic seared his spine, shook his limbs, and he barreled out of the water, toward the bank, toward the women who were not yet on their feet in alarm. They didn't know what was coming, but they couldn't sense it.

But they did see him. Aralie instantly bounded to her feet and rushed away from him in panic. Roenia and Savili stood too, backing away. The males roared, demanding to know what he was doing.

And Miranda stood alone, her eyes wide with shock. Unprotected.

He'd only just made it to the bank when the boar burst out of the forest, heading right toward them.

CHAPTER

TWENTY-SIX

The squealing roar punctured through the air and rattled in Miranda's skull. Her mind went blank, breathing stopped. Her muscles bunched with panic.

The screaming beast twice Govek's height charged toward them. A massive, disgusting pig with black fur and a humped back. Foaming mouth. Beady red eyes. The stench of rot burned her nose. Its hide was covered in swollen, oozing welts.

"Miranda!"

The terrified screams brought her back to her senses, and she plunged to the left, bolting for cover with Roenia's babe still in her arms.

"Oh Fades! Miranda!"

She whirled toward the voice and found Roenia and Savili scrambling toward her with terror-stricken faces. Roenia got to Miranda first and snatched her baby back.

"Here!" Aralie yelled from behind an oak trunk. The other women bolted for it, but Miranda turned, stupidly, helplessly.

Where was Govek?

The beast was *right there*. So big, Miranda couldn't comprehend it. Its head towered over her. Its mouth was gaped, drooling, with jagged yellow teeth.

Govek made it to the beach first and scrambled toward Miranda. Eyes wild.

The pig turned away from her and charged for him.

Miranda's throat burst with a scream as Govek caught the creatures' tusks in his hands. They were longer than his whole torso and sharp enough to skewer him. Water sprayed in arches around the pig's sides as it pushed Govek deeper into the spring.

Govek roared. Somehow, he leveraged himself against a boulder and hurtled the beast onto its side. Water splashed so high she lost sight of him. Her heart exploded in panic.

The beast snarled and flailed its legs in the air. Spraying water. She couldn't see Govek. Was his head under? Was the pig on top of him? Was he going to drown? She couldn't see—

There he was! He was trying to leap around the creature, to get behind its head. But then the pig got back onto its feet. Its head plunged forward, yellow tusks skewering the air toward Govek. He barely managed to dodge.

There were black spikes near the base of the tusks, thick cords of rope had them tied on securely.

Just like the one that had skewered Govek the day they met.

Her stomach dropped.

"Govek! Get back!"

Miranda couldn't tell which of the orc males had yelled. She couldn't see anything but Govek as the beast was on its feet again. It swung its deadly tusks, ready to skewer him.

Govek dodged again but slipped on the rocks. He couldn't get traction. Oh god, oh god!

"Govek!" Miranda wailed helplessly. Govek's eyes snapped to hers for a split second. Long enough that the pig caught him with the end of his tusk.

She heard the crack. Felt it in her own chest.

She'd killed him! Oh god, she was so—

If Govek felt pain, he didn't acknowledge it. He dove into the waist deep water, scrambling back as the beast swung his head. It charged. Sliced its deadly tusks through the air again. She could barely see past the waves, could barely make out Govek's green blur.

"Help him!" she screamed at the other males. Karthoc sprinted in. The others had already gathered up their children, and were dragging them deeper into the safety of the woods.

Miranda started into the icy water, eyes back on Govek. She couldn't look away again, but she was so terrified of what she might find.

"Here!" Karthoc raged at the beast. His voice ricocheted off the trees and coiled in Miranda's gut. "Come for me!"

It was like the pig didn't even hear him. It was so blind in its pursuit of Govek. Its eyes bulged and its screaming squeals raged, and Miranda slipped on the rocks, fell to her knees in the icy water. But she got back up and kept trying.

She could not let him die.

The cold barely registered as she went deeper. Her lungs

burned, her muscles quaked as she tried to keep her balance. She slipped on the rocks again. Almost there.

Miranda lunged forward and snagged the beast's tail. She fell, splashing into the spring as she went under. The pig's back leg whizzed through the water right next to her head.

She burst back to the surface and scrambled away from the deadly hooves. Blood pounded in her ears. Her hold on its tail tightened like a vice, and she yanked hard.

The beast screamed.

It turned toward her.

"Miranda!" It was a woman's scream, but she didn't know who. She couldn't bring herself to look. She let go of the pig's tail and struggled away, slipped again, unable to get traction. Her knees gave out.

"Miranda!"

Govek's roar punctuated through her soul, and she turned.

The pig was right behind her, its red eyes fixed. Drool and pus and rot sprayed from its screaming mouth.

Govek slammed into its side and it fell.

Water exploded in front of her. Govek and Karthoc both straddled it. Their claws dug into its hide. The pig wailed and the unholy sound caused Miranda's ears to ring.

Govek unhinged his jaw, stretched his mouth impossibly wide, and dug his massive fangs deep into the creature's neck.

Blood sprayed from the artery, flooding the air with its metallic odor, turning the water red. Govek slashed again with his hands, slicing deeper through the vein in its neck.

Fuck, he was *covered* in blood. From head to toe. What of it was his? She couldn't tell.

He and Karthoc held the creature down as it fought to its last. Iytier and Estoc rushed in to help even as the pig's twitches stilled. Its eyes clouded. Its nose bled.

Govek slid down from the creature's back, shaken and wobbly. He loped toward Miranda with murder in his eyes and yanked her arm, dragging her through the icy water and back to the bank. She followed blindly, trying to catch up so she could get her hands on him. See his side where the tusk got him.

He stopped only when they reached the center of the bank. He rounded on her, ran his hands over her arms. Her sides. Through her hair. Eyes searching.

"I'm okay." Her voice came out choked. She gripped his shirt and tried to pull it up. To check where he'd been hit. "A-are you? Govek, are you—"

A deadly growl left his lips. His eyes spat venom. *"Never again. Don't ever do that again."*

"But you almost . . . you were . . ." Tears coursed down her cheeks. Govek's thumbs came down to wipe them away.

The sticky feel of the boar's blood on her face barely registered as Govek's eyes widened and he snapped away from her, backed up. She felt his warmth leave her like an eclipse. Her body shook almost violently.

He was completely *covered* in blood—chest and face coated, arms bright red all the way to his biceps. His fangs dripped, sharp rows of points disappearing into his still gaping maw.

"Oh god, fuck, Govek, are you okay? I mean . . . I mean —holy shit." Miranda staggered toward him, but he backed up again. "Is . . . is your mouth . . .? Oh god your teeth . . .?" He'd just torn out the creature's throat with his fangs. That couldn't have been good for them. And the damn pig was *rotting*. Had he been poisoned? Would he get sick?

His eyes widened, and he spun around. He shuddered and curled in on himself slightly. He tried to wipe at the blood as if it mattered.

"Govek, look at me. Are you okay? It got you in the side. Let me see!" She rushed around to face him and thankfully—for his sake—he didn't try to hide again. "Let me see your side. Is your mouth okay? Your jaw?"

She pulled up his drenched shirt and looked at the dark mark on his green hide. There was no break in the skin, barely the start of a bruise. She wanted to collapse with relief, but instead turned to his mouth. "Open up. Let me see."

His eyes widened, but she pinched his chin until his skin went almost white under the pressure and he helplessly obeyed. None of his teeth appeared to be missing, and he was able to open it just fine.

"Okay," she breathed, panic coming down. Her body shuddered and her eyes flooded, and her throat choked up. "You're okay. You're okay. Right? Nothing hurts?"

He remained frozen.

"Govek, talk to me. You're covered in blood and I can't tell if any of it is *yours*." She scrambled her hands back over his chest. "Is it? It's not, right?"

"I'm . . . fine," he said slowly. "It's the Fades Spring."

"What? It's the . . ." Oh fuck, she was so stupid. She forgot the spring healed orcs. Relief made tears sting her eyes.

He stepped back.

"Don't you dare!" She closed the gap again.

She started to tremble as the adrenaline faded. God, that

boar had been so close to skewering him through the stomach, and even if the spring could heal, there would be no coming back from that. He'd have been dead *instantly*.

"W-we should go to the doctor anyway." Her eyes burned. She wanted to hold him, to wrap him up, to run her hands over his chest and prove it really was undamaged. "M-make sure-sure you're all right—"

"I'm all right, Miranda." She was sobbing now and couldn't hear him very well.

She ripped at the tie of her cloak, fumbling with the stupid knots like she always did. It was soaking wet, only making the task more difficult.

"What are you doing?" His tone was tinged with bafflement.

She couldn't get the words out. She ripped off her cloak, turned the leather side toward him and pressed tight into his chest, covering up the blood. Like not seeing it would help calm her down. What the fuck was wrong with her?

"Miranda." He watched her struggle. She couldn't get the damn cloak to stay up and stopped trying. Just let it fall to the rocky ground.

"N-no more fishing."

He was silent a long moment and it let her gather herself before he muttered, "What?"

"You aren't allowed to go fishing ever again!" She wailed, far too loud. Her voice echoed in the woods. "Or hunting! Do you hear me?"

"Miranda—"

"You almost died." She sobbed harder, tucking her face into his chest, uncaring that she was now getting covered in sticky blood. "Don't ever, ever do that again, Govek."

"Okay," he whispered. Still hovering around her when

she wanted him to hold her, squeeze her tight. "Okay, Miranda."

She reached up around his neck and pulled him down, forced him to rest his head against hers. He muttered something about getting her bloody and she snapped. "I don't fucking care. You better hug me right now or I'm gonna turn myself into a backpack and force you to carry me around everywhere for the next month." She might do that anyway.

He huffed out a sound she couldn't place. Something like a laugh or maybe a whimper. His weight curled around her, settling heavily on her head and around her back. She felt his palms on her shoulders and against the back of her head.

"Fingers too, Govek," she demanded, harshly. "Claws and all." He hesitated but did. Very lightly. "I'm never going to forgive you for this. When we're old and gray and on our deathbed, I'm still going to remind you of how bad you scared me just now."

"Yes, my love," he whispered into the top of her head. His weight crushed her a little and she relished it. "I will not fish in the afterlife either, if it will appease you."

"Damn straight you won't," she said, uncertain if she was laughing or crying. "Why'd I have to fall in love with a fucking orc! Why couldn't you just use guns like normal people!"

"I don't know what a gun is, Miranda." His voice warbled with humor.

"Bows and arrows then. Keep yourself at a nice safe distance and shoot things from really, really far away." She moved back a little, rubbing the tears from her eyes. "Goddamn it, Govek."

"Is everyone all right?"

Miranda was jarred out of her haze.

Dang, she was surrounded by people right now. Most of them were only twenty or so feet away. They came out from behind a huge tree. The adults had their full attention on their families as the boar tainted the water red. The children were mostly distracted too. Either crying in their mothers' skirts or looking to their fathers for support.

Estoc's eldest, however, burst in excitedly, "Father, I want to touch it! Let me touch it!"

"For the will of Fades, Vaiteg, if you ask to touch it one more time."

"Look, father!" the boy pleaded. His exuberance got a few of the younger kids to look up, releasing a little fear. "It's *amazing*. And did you see Govek? He was like—rawh!" The boy exuberantly acted out Govek ripping out the boar's throat, tiny fangs and all.

Miranda smiled. She couldn't help it.

"I wanna do that when I come of age! I want to hunt a boar."

Estoc glowered at Govek as he said to his son, "No."

"Aw, father, *please*!"

"Are you all right, Miranda?" Savili approached, her hands trembled around her whimpering babe. "You aren't hurt?"

"I can't believe you ran in there, Miranda!" Roenia said. "That was so foolish."

"Yes."

Govek's single word spiked a torrent of shivers down Miranda's spine. Oh shit, he was *big* mad. She would have to make this up to him *majorly*.

"I'm sorry," she said, mostly to the women because

saying sorry would not put much of a dent in Govek. "I just . . . got caught up."

"I'd do the same for Iytier," Savili said.

"The fuck you would!" Iytier raged from where he stood in the water next to the boar as he examined its tusks. "If I ever catch you running after a boar, you'll have the Fades to answer to."

Savili ignored him. "I have an extra dress, Miranda. Come on."

"This is the same as you saw, right, Govek?" Karthoc pointed to the spikes tied to the animal's tusks. "When you were in the outer woods?"

"Yes." Govek let Miranda go and waded back into the water to examine the boar. Savili pulled her behind a nearby rock and helped pull her gown off. Roenia brought the new one.

Fuck, it was cold. So damn fricking icy cold!

"Look at this. It's like the rope is fused to the tusks," Iytier said.

"It smells odd," Karthoc muttered. "What is that? It's not blight."

"It's . . . familiar," Govek said quietly. "The last had it too. This odd stench. Is it goblin poison?"

Miranda finished dressing and came around the bolder just in time to see Govek's expression go slack.

"Iytier . . . scent here. That's . . . it can't be."

The male leaned close to the boar's tusk and his brow furrowed. Then he shot back with wide eyes.

"*Fades be fucked!*"

"What?" Karthoc said. "What is it?"

"Magic," Iytier said. "*Orc* magic."

"Who?" Karthoc asked just as Govek had made it back to the bank.

He swung Miranda up into his arms. Held her tight. A chill sliced at her scalp as he barreled through the woods. But not before he raged over his shoulder to answer Karthoc's question.

"Ergoth!"

CHAPTER

TWENTY-SEVEN

GOVEK

G ovek kicked the door to the hall so hard it nearly flew off its hinges.

"Where the fuck is he?"

His roar sliced through the clan instantly bringing many of the orcs to their feet. He must have looked insane—covered in blood, wreaking of blight, eyes wild as he clutched Miranda.

Glowers and demands to explain himself from the males blasted Govek and licked the flames of his rage higher. He didn't give a shit what the clan thought of him. He had attention for only one being in this room.

Ergoth.

The vile chief scrambled up from his precious little throne and narrowed his worthless beady eyes in Govek's direction. "Govek! How did you survi—how dare you bring your anger and strife into this hall—"

"I challenge you!" Govek roared so loud that Miranda covered her ears. The words echoed around the hall and ricocheted up the Rove Tree, reflected into the crystal leaves and rained down upon the whole of the clan.

"You *what*?" Ergoth began to laugh. Govek trembled with the need to rip his mouth off his face. The only thing that stopped him was Miranda held securely in his arms.

His mate. She was all right. He needed to breathe.

"I challenge you," Govek said. "For sending a boar and nearly killing my mate—"

"A boar? What is this about a boar?" Ergoth said. "You're covered in *blood*. Did you hurt her?"

"The boar attacked while we were fishing, there were *children* present," Miranda said. And thank Fades because Govek's throat was constricting. "You could have gotten them killed."

"Is everyone all right?" Hovget rose from one of the center tables. Wellia followed suit. "Was anyone hurt?"

"Yes, Hovget, please, go and check over those who were attacked. Quickly," Ergoth said.

"How dare you feign concern when *you* were the one who sent it!" Govek snarled as Hovget went still. Govek needed to calm, needed to get his raging inferno under control before he lost his ability for reason.

But *fuck*, Ergoth stood there looking so *smug*. He smoothed his robes, and turned up his nose, and barely bothered with the fact that he'd nearly destroyed the only thing Govek cared about in the whole world.

"Govek." Miranda stroked the side of his face. His breathing was so labored it made his head dizzy. "Tough guy, you've got this."

He squeezed his eyes shut and concentrated on her soothing fingers.

"My son. You know not how your accusations wound me," Ergoth said, filling Govek's mind with poison. "I have ever done right by you, but you accuse me of *this*? Of sending a boar to kill you? How could I even do such a thing?"

"You did. With your magic. The blight cannot hide the scent of it. I know it too well. The magic on the boar might be tainted and dark, but it is still *yours*." Govek trembled, teeth gnashed. "Just the same as the magic on the boar that attacked me on the way to Estwill."

He'd been too muddled at the time—too distracted—to place the scent, but now the memory was *clear*.

His father had been trying to kill him this *entire time*.

Govek's spine straightened as Karthoc burst into the hall behind him.

Ergoth scowled. "Karthoc! You have no right to—"

"I have every right. I was attacked in the woods just as the others were with their *mates and children*," Karthoc roared. "Attacked by a boar *you* sent."

"I don't know what lies my son has told you, but I would never have risked the lives of—"

"Govek speaks the truth!" Karthoc yelled over the crowd. "I was *there*. I smelled it and can confirm that it is Ergoth's magic that lingers on the boar that tried to kill Govek. It sought him *blindly*, wanting no others but him." He pointed a finger to Ergoth. "You sent a boar to kill your own *son*!"

"How *dare* you accuse me of this!" Ergoth walked to the edge of his platform. "With no proof but your own senses."

"The boar is preserved. *Any* can go and check it, even the *seer*."

"The seer is *false*," Ergoth countered with a flippant wave of his hand. "Even *you* say that he is muddled of late. That his prophesies are warped and wrong."

"You vile scum—" Karthoc started.

"Karthoc speaks the truth."

Hovget's voice punctured the room, silencing it once more. Wellia stood at her mates' side, looking confident in her support.

Govek leaned into Miranda for support of his own, twisted up at the horrors of what could have been.

He'd almost lost her. Again.

Fuck.

"Healer, I suggest you hold your tongue," Ergoth said. "This does not concern you."

Hovget continued, undaunted. "I did not want to believe it at first. Even still, I don't. But in light of this, I can no longer stay silent for you, Ergoth, even if you are my chief—"

"You don't know what you're inferring, Hovget. I have never silenced you."

"Against Ergoth's direct order, I took blood from Govek." Hovget's voice rose to stop Ergoth from speaking over him. "From the wound a blighted boar made on Govek's flesh. I gathered the poison that was planted within him and examined it thoroughly."

"I ordered you *not* to interfere," Ergoth cried over the clan's voices. "How *dare* you go against my command?"

Hovget lifted his head and faced Ergoth. "I found Rove Wood magic within the poison. *Your* magic."

The blanket of stillness that settled over the hall grew suffocating, nauseating. Govek's thoughts narrowed on a single conclusion that tore him apart and stitched him new.

His father really *had* sent that boar to kill him.

And Govek was barely shocked. In fact, the knowledge was cleansing. It flushed out his head and helped him see clearly—see every horrible thing Ergoth had done, every unfair judgment, every cruel word.

From this moment forward, Ergoth was no longer Govek's kin.

Govek balled his fists, blood zinging. He centered his gaze on Miranda, his true family. He touched his forehead to hers. Soaked up her determined expression. The fire in her eyes. Her damp skin was hot with fury as she drew the same conclusions he did, as the whole clan did.

Hovget was still speaking. "And I have kept the sample. I can bring it here, now, to prove my word."

"*My* word is the only one that—"

The orcs tensed, eyes narrowed, and the energy in the hall turned dark. Equality had been the driving force behind Ergoth's control.

And now it would bring his downfall.

"We do not *need* to bring proof into our great hall." Ergoth changed tactics, slithering around like the disgusting serpent he was. "We have *better* methods. Sythcol, bring the clearing. We will hold this judgment *now*."

"No." Sythcol rose to his feet as he spoke the single, clear word. So simple and yet with such power.

"I am your *chief*," Ergoth said. "You will do as I command."

"No longer," Sythcol said, holding his slender chin high.

His posture radiated with the power that Govek had always admired. The control over his strength that Govek longed to carry within himself. "Did you think, after what happened during Maythra's judgment, that I wouldn't examine the methods used by the clearing? That I wouldn't examine the herbs and magics? You should be ashamed of how you twisted our minds."

"I did *nothing*," Ergoth insisted. "And even if I had, *you* were the one who always used the clearing."

"Yes, after *you* created it and ordered me to do so."

Govek went very still. Ergoth had invented the clearing?

The voices of the clan rose with agreement and Ergoth's eyes went wide before he snapped back into place, straightening his robes. "You twist my words harshly, Sythcol. I am not to blame for this. It is true negligence on your part to *not* look into it before implementing its use. After all, *you* are the lead conjurer of this clan. I am merely its leader."

"You told me the clearing was to help concentration."

"And that is what it does."

"No, the combination of herbs you used *strip* thoughts. It doesn't aid them. It strips them and allows anything *you* desire to take its place. The first words spoken are *branded*. I am studying it now, uncovering its depths as we speak."

"Only now? Are you saying that after I gave it to you, you used it without bothering to even look at it?" Ergoth's eyes gleamed. "That seems more negligence on your part than mine."

"I *trusted* you," Sythcol said loudly as he gestured wide. "We *all* trusted you. But no longer. I will never blindly trust again. Not you or anyone. I will ever seek to find deeper truths on my own and guide my magics with clear purpose.

I will never allow any other to play on my conscience and coerce me into performing acts against my better judgment."

"I have *never* wanted you to do anything less, Sythcol," Ergoth said, his expression that perfect mix of pure pity and remorse. It socked Govek right in the gut. Ergoth *lied* so easily. Why had he never seen that before? "And if you were ever given the impression I did, then I apologize."

"You have manipulated us all using this clearing. You forced us to follow your every whim."

Ergoth's face went slack, as if he were truly wounded by the accusation. "Of course I didn't. You followed me of your own wills. Because of the *good* I have done. Tell me" —Ergoth stretched his arms wide to address the clan— "Who created the ability to vote as a group? Who implemented the storerooms? Who increased the production of crops and allowed magic to flourish? Who kept Rove Wood pure all these many years? Why, more than *half* the mates currently residing in this clan joined during *my* reign."

Govek clutched Miranda tight, despising the insinuation that Ergoth had *anything* to do with her decision to stay with him. To love him.

And judging from the tension of the other mated males, they felt the same.

Iytier suddenly appeared in the door and stormed into the room. Jehvlek followed close behind. They stood at Govek's side and his tension eased as the warmth and strength of their support humbled him.

"Ergoth, how *dare* you try to kill—"

"Stand down, Iytier. This does not concern you."

"Doesn't concern us? Our *mates* were at the spring," Jehvlek snapped. "Our *children*."

"I don't know what you think, but I would *never* have sent that boar. You all know how precious your sons are to me." Ergoth insisted so vehemently that a rumble of confusion swept through the clan. "Someone has framed me for this act."

"Framed you the same way Govek was framed for the torture of his kills?" Jehvlek asked. "Evythiken tells us Rogeth isn't the one who did it. So, tell me, *Ergoth*, who is truly responsible for that heinous deception?"

Ergoth's cheek twitched under his eye. "Are you trying to imply that *I* mutilated the animals?"

"You were the first to know about them, weren't you? Govek was ordered to report all his kills directly to you as soon as he brought them in. What was your reasoning for that?" Jehvlek's voice carried as the clan fell into a hush again.

"To ensure they could be butchered while fresh," Ergoth said between the clench of his teeth.

"Would not the preserving magic have been enough for that? Rogeth and his butchers worked in the butchery *every day*. Was there really such need to interrupt your work as our chief just to ensure Govek's kills were addressed immediately? Or was there another reason *you* wanted to see his kills first?"

Govek's stomach clenched, and his palms sweated, and the pieces snapped into place so easily, so firmly, he could feel the jolt down his spine.

Iytier cut in before Ergoth could respond. "And what of all the lies you have told us about Govek? About his unchecked fury and his demands that we stay away from him? Did you really think we would not eventually discuss among ourselves and discover your deception?"

"You wouldn't have." Govek found his voice beyond his shock. The clan turned their full attention to him, but this time Govek felt not a single desire to shrink away or vent his fury. Instead, his words continued cold and clipped and even. "You wouldn't have, because the clearing forced your silence."

"You will be *silent*, Govek!" Ergoth raged as his body shook and his teeth gnashed. His mask was dropping away and Govek stared as the true face of his father broke through.

He found his voice, drawing from decades of his father's manipulation. "Calm down, *Ergoth*. Control yourself."

Ergoth's face contorted. "You wretch, how dare you—"

"All my life you've demanded *I* control myself, but that was only to control the *clan*, wasn't it? To taint their opinion of me."

"You have no right to speak among this clan."

"Why shouldn't he?" Iytier demanded. "He is next in line to be chief of Rove Wood."

"He will *never* be chief!" Ergoth pointed his finger at Iytier. His *clawed* finger. Govek could see the tip of it starting to slink out. "You think I would ever let my vile traitorous spawn come into power here? When the role should rightly go to Tavggol's perfect child? You would have Tavggol's son robbed of his rightful place by this disgusting monster?"

Govek felt each word like the slice of a blade, cutting deep and twisting until his insides were turned to mush and he could hardly find the will to stand.

"You're the monster!" Miranda cried.

"Be *quiet*. Everything I fucking did was for this clan!" Ergoth took the tray of food next to his throne and shattered it, splattered its contents across his podium. "Every speck of this food is from *me*. Every magic is from me. Every trade and success and joy *you* feel is by *my doing*. I brought light to this clan. I am the reason you thrive. This clan would be *nothing* without my rule.

"And now you want Govek? That abomination of the Fades born with power beyond your reckoning? He'll gain control and become a *tyrant*. Do you not see how having magic and strength is *dangerous*? You bring your own doom! Even *Corine* couldn't face him. His warrior *blight* would not even be known for *years* and *still* she left him. She would rather risk *death*, abandoning him than bear to even hold him after he was birthed from her womb."

"My god," Miranda said, her exclamation somehow cutting off Ergoth's tirade. "Maythra said the same thing, and now I know where she got it. Govek was a *baby* when his mother left."

"She left because she knew he was *vile*. She *knew* that he would grow to have a bulging hideous warrior frame and could not bear to raise a child so monstrous."

"*You* just admitted no one knew Govek would have a warrior build until years after his birth." Miranda's voice was loud, steady, and it *radiated* through Govek. Brought clarity to his mind. "Why did you reject him before you knew?"

Fuck . . . all these years. Why had he not seen . . .?

Miranda continued. "Tell me, Ergoth, did you banish him to the outskirts of Rove Wood Clan when he was seven because he was a *warrior* or did you *always* despise him?"

Ergoth really had been responsible for all of it. Every. Last. Thing.

Govek went cold from this truth.

"I did what I had to do to protect this clan!"

"It wasn't for the clan. It was for you! Because you couldn't *stand* that your mate left because of *you*!"

"It was not me! *It was not me!*" Ergoth roared through the clan, swept them all up in its spiral. "No woman would *ever* leave me! I am the chief of Rove Wood! Second only to the Fades themselves. Corine should have scraped at my feet, slaved over my whims. She was meant to worship me as a good woman should. It is *Govek's* fault she left, not mine! *Not mine!*"

Govek was going to vomit. His whole body shook so violently he was nearly forced to set Miranda down.

"I built this clan," Ergoth raged, eyes bloodshot and bulging. His claws were fully extended now. "Every scrap and being in it belongs to me, and no one will fucking take it from me."

A surge of power coursed through Govek's body, ripped away his anguish, tore out his fear. His own claws snapped out unheeded and Govek relished it.

He stepped forward, bold, determined. "I challenge you, Ergoth. Your time etching malice into this clan is *over.*"

Ergoth's eyes flashed, as if coming back to himself a moment. "You can't—"

"A challenge has been issued, Ergoth." Karthoc's voice was a pool of rage. "By the laws of our kind, you will *fight* or you will yield."

"I will not! I demand to select a champion!" Ergoth said so confidently that Govek wondered if this had been his plan all along. To elect someone to fight Govek in his stead. Perhaps *many*.

But a deadly hush settled over the males of Rove Wood. Ergoth had destroyed himself already and was too delusional to see it.

Karthoc snarled. "You coward. You will fight your own battle."

Govek cut in. "No. I will accept it." He gave Miranda's hand a final squeeze, earning her strength in return as he stepped forward to address the clan. "Any male here who wants to *fight* on Ergoth's behalf, step forward now. Step forward and I will fucking cut you down and throw you out of the Rove Woods along with him."

No one twitched.

"You cretins!" Ergoth snarled, shaking wildly in his fury. His hair came undone from his queue. His face was so dark it was a wonder it didn't pop. "I am your *chief*. You will stand and fight. I command it!"

Not a single orc stood. Not one of them spoke on his behalf.

Govek's chest swelled, and his mind reeled, and his thoughts turned to the stark similarities between now and that night that Ergoth ordered him to Estwill.

"Karthoc. Warlord. *Nephew*." Ergoth raised his chin so high Govek could see into his nostrils. "*You* will fight for me. You are duty bound to answer the—"

Karthoc bellowed laughter so loud it thundered through the room. "You are a fucking *fool*, Ergoth. Your *Rove Wood* rules don't apply to me. You must fight your own battle and I have a mind to challenge you when Govek is done! If there is anything left of you."

"You'll have to get in line after me." Miranda's

seething tone sent a shiver up Govek's spine, and he could not tell if he was more terrified by his mate's fury or impressed.

He reached to touch her cheek once more before he stalked toward Ergoth's pretentious platform. Govek's blood turned to pure energy as he barreled toward his father. His eyes pinned the male. The chaos of his mind swirled dangerously high. Govek struggled to comprehend what he was feeling.

All he knew was that his claws were aching to sink deep into something *other* than his own palms.

Ergoth held up his hands as he attempted his holding magic, a desperate effort to stop Govek's advance.

But the magic was barely a glimmer in the back of Goveks mind. Hardly a prickle along his flesh. Govek used his rage like a shield and Ergoth's magic was *nothing* against his furious power.

Ergoth's eyes widened in shock, and he took a step back. His hands fell as he changed tactics. He address the clan again. "How dare you abandon me this way! I have only ever done *good* for you! I was saving you from having a tyrant for a chief. You all *know* Govek needed to die. You all *know* how vile he is! You wanted him as your leader? To follow in my footsteps? To *steal* this clan away from Tavggol's son? The rightful ruler?"

Govek stormed up the steps, barreling his weight onto the wood. For the first time in his life, the platform welcomed him, beckoned him. He felt not a drop of hesitation as he approached his father.

Ergoth spun to face him and screamed. "Get away from—"

Govek lifted his foot and slammed it into Ergoth's chest.

The male flew backward, hurtled to the ground below. Ergoth slammed onto the stone, gasping and writhing.

And Govek felt no better for it. Instead, his chest only tightened and the foot that had struck his father broke out into pins and needles. The swirling turbulence in his mind popped in an instant. The desire to waste one more motion on this sniveling male was gone, disgust rolled into his stomach.

Govek lowered his foot, watching his father swing back around to his hands and knees. Ergoth tried to rise to his feet, but he tripped on his own opulent robes.

Further violence would only make Ergoth the victim and Govek the monster all over again.

So Govek looked to the clan, found the males tense, wide eyes engulfing their faces, fists balled as if they were prepared for Govek to go mad.

Instead, Govek stepped back away from Ergoth's revolting form. A hush fell over the clan. A calm Govek had never sensed from them before.

Ergoth gasped and sputtered. Rage contorted his face when he saw that his once loyal males were not instantly coming to his aid. He rose to his knees. "Seize him, you fools. I did not accept! I did not accept the challenge! You see? You all see how vile he is? He attacked his own father—"

Miranda appeared from nowhere and the crack of her palm across Ergoth's mouth was so loud it reverberated through the hall. His own cheek began to prickle and burn. Ergoth started to speak again, and Miranda spat on his face.

Somehow, after everything, *that* was what stunned Ergoth into silence. His eyes glazed, his quivering hand hovered above the wet glob running down his cheek.

Govek swung down from the platform and picked Miranda up before his brave little mate could start battering Ergoth further.

"All those who choose to remove Ergoth from his role of chief, stand," Sythcol said loudly.

A symphony of clattering bodies and feet as the entire clan rose soothed the anguish from Govek's chest. He tucked Miranda in close, soaking up her warmth, and looked into the strength on her face.

"You want *him?*" Ergoth raged, finally managing to rise. His hair was a tangled mess, and his eyes were wild. "You want the fucking male who butchered the whole of Clairton? You will regret this!"

Govek shuddered, stepping back further. His mind slipped into memories he wanted to forget, of rage and blurs of color, followed by agonizing clarity and carnage. Human men slaughtered, bloody pieces of them strewn about. His body covered in that blood. *Their blood.*

"The whole of?" Karthoc snapped. "You mean the twenty fucking soldiers who were packing up the remains of the town?"

"The remains?" Iytier asked. "What do you mean by remains? By twenty soldiers?"

"Silence!" Ergoth spat, but no one seemed to hear him except Govek.

Iytier continued. "Ergoth told us that Govek slaughtered everyone in sight, including women and children. That he razed the town against your orders."

"I said silence!"

"You will be silent!" Karthoc roared. "You dare spread such lies about your own kin? To say he murdered *children*?"

"He may as well have! How many sons would I have now if he hadn't driven Corine away!"

Govek went very cold only to have warmth wrap about his neck, his chest.

"Govek," Miranda said into his ear. Her tone soothing, strengthening.

"You think that justifies sending a boar to kill him?" Karthoc's voice was a tangible thing, whipping up the clan into a whispering frenzy.

"I have only ever done right by this clan!" Ergoth said. "I have been faithful and loyal and worked too fucking hard for everything I created to pass to this vile—"

"This is the truth!" Karthoc said, his voice echoing above Ergoth's. "We found Clairton abandoned. Scouts had warned them we were coming and they wisely chose to leave. Only a few hands of males were still cleaning up. All soldiers. And yes, we slaughtered them. We *all* did. Govek was in battle rage with the rest of us. But there were no women or children."

Govek's stomach heaved, and he closed his eyes as his body shook.

There had been no children *that* day.

But if there had been . . . if there had . . .

"Govek, tough guy, breathe for me." Miranda stroked the back of his neck.

"Lives are lives!" Ergoth snarled. "And you will have a *murderer* as your leader."

"Better that then a traitor! Govek killed only in self-defense after they tortured your son to death!"

At that moment, the hall doors burst open again. Estoc led Brovdir and two other burly orc warriors into the room.

Karthoc waved them to follow and stormed through the

hall toward Ergoth. Govek found himself carrying Miranda toward the wall of the hall, to the dim spot where the stairs up onto the platform were located, watching, waiting.

Waiting for Ergoth to be taken away.

Govek may never see him again. His throat closed even as his mind scrambled. He fought for something to say, to make sense of the growing dread in his gut.

This couldn't just be it.

"Ergoth, you have been stripped of your role. You have attempted to murder your own kin. You have deceived your clan and abused your power. You will be held at my camp until adequate punishment can be chosen."

"No!" Ergoth wailed as Karthoc took up the male's hands and wrenched them behind his back. He did this so easily, taking action where Govek was frozen stiff.

"This clan is *mine*. They belong to *me*!"

"Govek," Karthoc said after binding his father's hands with a length of rope. "Do you want to take him?"

This was really it? This was all? He'd take Ergoth to Karthoc's camp and then what?

What would happen from there?

What punishment could Ergoth suffer to *ever* make any of the tortures Govek had endured heal?

"No," Govek barely managed. Ergoth's face contorted and Govek felt his entire body contorting with it.

What good would hauling off this male do now?

Govek would recover *nothing* from spending a moment more in his wretched company.

Ergoth was screaming something as Karthoc dragged him away but the clan was so loud it felt like it would rupture Govek's ears.

He saw Iytier start toward him in the crowd. Estoc too.

A few other males from the clan were also looking eagerly in his direction.

They wanted answers. Wanted to voice opinions. Wanted to add more chaos.

"I need to go," Govek managed. Looking for an escape, searching. He found it atop Ergoth's platform. At the back stair that led to the private space none could enter without permission.

"Then let's go," Miranda said instantly.

TWENTY-EIGHT

GOVEK

Her acceptance was all he needed.

Govek turned and stormed through the door at the back of the platform. The wood creaked and groaned under his feet. He wished each step would rip it apart. He wanted to remove every vile trace that his father had ever been here in the Rove Woods.

The spiral stair was too narrow to carry Miranda, so he put her down and followed her up, climbing higher until they reached the viewpoint.

"Wow," Miranda breathed, going to the gorgeous view at the balcony. The sun was too bright and the colors were too vivid. Govek froze in place, afraid he would see Karthoc leading Ergoth away if he looked.

Desperate for something to vent his rage on so his magic would not spiral out of control, Govek pounded over to the mead shelves. He ripped open the doors. His hands quaked as he slashed through the bottles, ripping them from the shelf and shattering them in sickly sweet splatters all over the ground. It drenched his legs, shards of glass nipped at his flesh.

Boar blood mingled with the drink. The rotting stink concealed the saccharine luxury.

"Are you cut?" Miranda asked, as if his outburst was hardly worth considering. She started to approach, mindful of the glass.

"Stop," he demanded, flush with embarrassment over his rash actions. His hands quaked. And he looked to find tiny pricks of red in his palms where his claws dug deep. "I'm fine."

Miranda's eyes darkened and she murmured, "You're not."

He shuddered at her statement and raked a hand over his face, tore at his hair. His fingers were sticky and wet, and his nose flooded with the fermented stink, reminding him of the last time he was here with his father. *Fuck*, this was the last thing he wanted to be covered in. Why was he so blasted *stupid*?

"Here," Miranda said, and he opened his eyes only to squeeze them shut again as cold liquid poured over his head, washing the mead away. He opened his eyes to find her holding a pitcher of water. "Do you feel better?"

"No," he grated. Fuck, he didn't even *know* what could douse the flames.

But there had to be something. He swung Miranda up into his arms and carried her away from the glass while searching the space. There was a door in a nook at the back of the tree. Partially hidden by a thick branch. He settled Miranda on the ground before going to it.

The door was plain but guarded by magic. He could

scent Ergoth's revolting energy from it. Pungent and sweet. The same as on the boar.

If only he had recognized the scent of his fathers magic all those days ago outside the Rove Wood, before he found Miranda.

But how would things have been different? He would still have had to come back here.

There was magic around the door, but not on the frame. Govek lifted his foot, the same one he'd used to kick Ergoth off the platform, and slammed it into the wood. Splintering it with a single thrust. It took a few more hits to work the door free. He was gasping and shaking by the end.

And found the interior filled with Ergoth's stench and rolling waves of his magic. The small workspace loomed before him. There was a desk in the center, a table to the left, cushioned chairs, and a window seat.

He forced his way in and gritted his teeth against the sight. Walls of shelves littered with scrolls, all labeled—potions, conjurings, building plans . . .

Govek yanked down those scrolls and threw them on the desk. Nearly tearing through them in his haste.

But he found *nothing.* Nothing of consequence. Nothing of value.

He blindly yanked down more scrolls, making a tattered mess of them in his search for *anything. Something* that would explain why Ergoth did this. *Why* the male despised him.

It couldn't only be because his mother had left after his birth.

How did that single event shape an entire life of lies? Did Govek deserve to believe himself *vile* for every one of his twenty-eight years because his mother had decided not to raise him? Just like the mothers of so many other orcs?

"Govek?"

Miranda had come in, her eyes coaxing, her posture easy. He shuddered under the weight of her light.

"That's it?" he grated.

She tipped her head, waiting.

"That's fucking *it*?" he asked, looking around the half-destroyed room again. What did he hope to find here? What answers did he seek? He longed for an ease to this agony looming in the back of his mind. It soaked into his gut, grinding him up inside.

"A whole fucking lifetime of feeling worthless and powerless and *furious*." Govek swiped his claws against the scrolls that littered the desk. He tore into them and they fluttered to the ground. "And *this* is how it ends? *That* was his motivation for *torturing me*?"

"I'm so sorry, Govek," Miranda said softly.

He shook so much he felt his limbs might vibrate off his body. "What the *fuck* do I do now? How can anything ever make up for *this*?"

"I know," Miranda said, her eyes haunted. "I know."

His chest squeezed, tightening around his heart. She did know, didn't she? He'd watched her feel this. And *fuck*, he wished that made it better. That he could find a solution for both of them.

He went to her, jerked her into his arms, and curled around her.

"They want to punish him, but what's the *point*?" He drank in the freshness of her scent and let it drown out the stench of his father's odor. "What will killing him or banishing him or forcing empty apologies from him even *do*?"

Miranda brought her hands up around his waist, buried her face in his chest.

He squeezed his eyes shut as brutal, violent images assaulted him. "Should I *fight* him, Miranda? What would that cause but more pain? Would crushing his face to a pulp or ripping apart his limbs make this endless burning agony diminish? Or would it just *increase it*?"

Miranda tightened her hold, soothing him with her touch.

"And what's left after *that*?" His voice broke and his eyes burned. "Fucking *talking*? Fucking going to ask for an explanation? Just so he can twist up my words and justify his actions and push me back into the role of monster all over again?"

Govek saw it so clearly now, how Ergoth effortlessly contorted him into a vile wretch from a few simple statements.

And now it was a part of him and Govek wasn't sure how he would ever let it go.

"I know." Her voice was hot against his chest. "It's not fair. I'm so so sorry."

She did know. She knew because this is exactly what Earth was for her. No chance of justice. No way to turn back time. Endless questions and a lifetime of trying to work past the anguish, knowing answers would probably never come.

He clasped his hands under her ass and dragged her up to him, pressing his forehead to hers. So, they could be equal in this. Face to face. Side by side. Walking this path together.

"What do we do now?" She'd asked the same question

just one day before. Of course, she wouldn't have an answer to it.

But she pulled back from him, pressed her warm, soft hands to his face, and met his eyes with determination. Her gaze burrowed deep into his soul. "We *live*, Govek."

He exhaled and the tension in his chest eased.

"We live the *best* life we possibly can. We do exactly what we want, on our own terms, and build up our own fortunes. We relish in bliss *despite* everything we had to go through, and the horrors others forced on us. We prevail through it. We *thrive*."

His eyes were burning and blurry, but he couldn't blink to clear them. He was too fixated on this woman. This little human who had so much strength and love and built so much joy inside him.

"We'll thrive *together*, Govek. Just like you promised to be by my side, I vow the same to you." Her hands stroked his cheeks. "We'll laugh in the faces of those who thought they'd broken us. We'll build our joy so high they can't even dream of cutting us down. So far above that their evil words and deeds won't reach."

His gut twisted, bile rose in his throat and his mind flooded with the gruesome images of Clairton. "What if Karthoc was wrong?" Miranda's brow furrowed. "He said I wouldn't have killed children, but I don't *know*, Miranda. My mind was gone. I do not even remember killing the men. I just slashed and fought until I eventually came out of my magic-laced rage to discover that I was surrounded by carnage. What if . . . what if I had—"

"Stop. You can't blame yourself for things you never did. That's exactly what your father *wants*. And it isn't thriving."

He shivered and closed his eyes.

"I'll help you. I'll be right beside you every step of the way. And you'll be beside me. Helping me. We'll do it together. Build ourselves back up *together.* Just like we both promised."

"Together." The word soared out of him.

"Every time you think you're unworthy, I'll remind you of what *I* see when I look at you," Miranda said, and he opened his eyes. Her expression was so soft, her eyes sparkling, her warmth soaking into him. She stroked her fingertips along his temples, down over his chin. Her touch grounded him.

"And what I see is someone strong, supportive, and loving. I see the male who carried me through my worst panic, held me when I had nightmares, saved me from a boar and a wildcat and so many other horrors. You have laughed with me, eaten with me, and built your life around mine so effortlessly I wonder if it's real."

"It *was* effortless," Govek agreed, his throat choked and his voice ragged. He could hardly think past the bloom of warmth in his chest. "You slid into my life and routines so easily I cannot fathom how you were not there already. I cannot live without . . . Miranda, I . . ."

"I love you too, Govek." Her eyes flooded and so did his. He couldn't breathe, he was so full. "I love you, and I'm here with you. And we will walk this path together. Because it's the *same* path, Govek. Our lives are entwined, forever."

"Be my mate." He choked on the words. He wished he could be more eloquent, more clear. He wished he could speak words that would make her feel the way hers made him feel. But he couldn't.

And he didn't need to. Because her face lit with joy and tears. Her arms tightened around him and all the breath left him with her exuberant response. "*Yes*. Yes, I'll be your mate. I always was."

He crushed his lips to hers and drank her up. She brought her hands up around his head, into his hair, holding him tight. His joy was finally something tangible. It built in his chest and rolled through his muscles.

She was his. His mate. His love.

Now and forever.

TWENTY-NINE

MIRANDA

G ovek swung Miranda around and plopped her down on top of the desk, not once breaking the kiss.

Her head spun, and her thoughts whirled. The aching need that swelled in her gut was drowned out by the taste of him, the feel of his hot skin on hers.

She was going to be his forever. *Forever.*

It didn't seem long enough to her. She wrapped her arms around him, pulling him close, as he kissed a trail down her cheek, to her neck. Licked her frantic pulse. She shivered, writhed. Her thighs parted.

He gripped her dress and yanked it over her head, tossing it onto the floor. She wanted Govek next to her skin. She helped him where she could.

His head was back at her neck, breath teasing her ear. Electric skitters raced down her spine as he exhaled heavily.

She felt the sting of teeth as he nipped the bandage over her neck and shoulder. He pulled it free.

The dark red scabs from his bite were visible at the corner of her eyes. They tingled under the intensity of Govek's gaze as he examined them. He dipped in and lapped at them with his wet tongue.

Her back arched, and her eyes popped open. Her skin prickled with the intimacy of the gentle teasing of his tongue. The mild sting mixed with zinging pressure drowned out all her rational thoughts.

Oh fuck, it shouldn't feel this good.

She was going to make him bite her all the time. Her whole body would be littered with his marks.

He was slow, easing his tongue over the injury. He bathed her wound so gently it made the room spin. So slowly, it made her daft. Her head felt like it was full of spun sugar.

He trailed kisses and licks down to her breasts. He yanked the damp covering free and bathed her nipples until she was panting. She squirmed and writhed. Her harsh demands that he hurry up were ignored.

His gaze slid to hers, gold and green and raging fire. She lost her breath.

This male loved her. He wanted her. He would never let her go. She relished that truth as he worshipped her body. Ran his big, calloused hands roughly over her sensitive flesh, down her sides, over her navel.

She moaned as he parted her legs further, delved his fingers into her folds, slipping easily around her slick clit. Electric pleasure danced up her spine, making her body twitch. She burned for him, ached for his touch.

He returned his mouth to hers and drank up her whimpers of pleasure. He pressed the bulge of his cock against her pussy.

He still had his fucking pants on.

She reached around, desperate to get them off. Her fingers slipped and fumbled with the ties—like they always did.

He chuckled into her mouth, flooding her with his spicy taste, the warmth of his amusement. She was drunk off it.

He moved to help her and simply snapped the damn tie off. Her breath hitched as his cock sprang free. She shifted, thrusting her hips to beckon him.

He pressed deep into her in one incredible surge, filling her up, stretching her to her limit. She dug her fingers into his ass, wanting him deeper. Demanding more.

Instead, he forced her to lie down. Her back pressed into the scrolls he'd littered on top of the desk. He put a massive hand in her hair, palm nestled atop her forehead. He held her steady as he withdrew.

She groaned, unable to reach around him at this angle, to hold him. She caressed his chest instead, dug her fingers into his skin. "Govek, *please*. Harder."

He hummed with pleasure but set out a deliriously slow pace. She bucked into him as best she could, wrapping her legs around him, digging her heels into his ass, willing him to *move*.

He gripped her hair and pulled her head back. The sting felt so fucking *good* but barely compared to the shuddering, rolling, longing that his gaze speared through her.

His eyes were pools of light and warmth. They glittered in the dim of the room. His brows were set with bliss. His lips parted. He looked at her with reverence, worshipping her.

Pleasure danced in her veins. Heat skittered through her stomach as he pressed in deep. *So deep.*

She couldn't bring herself to even blink. He caught her up in his slow thrusts, his gentle caresses. His love. It flowed around her in waves. Lapped and churned and built until she was consumed by him.

The tension grew. Her fingers clawed at his chest. The spicy scent of him flooded her senses. He thrust deep, grinding against her clit. Delicious heat flushed her body, rose up the back of her throat.

Her body tightened and his slow, measured thrusts dragged her over the edge. A cry spilled from her lips as ecstasy skittered up her spine, soaked into her head. Tingled across every limb.

Through it all, she didn't blink, didn't look away from Govek as he too fell over the edge, drowning in pleasure. His shuddering roar spiking more bliss in her. He moved both hands down to yank her hips close. Pressed deep. She felt totally consumed. Completely absorbed. He touched her soul.

He fell forward, bracing his elbows on the desk as his body continued to shudder in aftershocks. She wrapped him up in her arms, soaking up his warmth. Every time she twitched, he did too.

He nuzzled the side of her cheek, trailing kisses along her jawline, lapping his tongue down her neck. He grazed his lips along the bite mark again. It made her blood sing and her eyes mist, and she turned her head to kiss his ear, murmuring. "I love you, my mate."

He hissed, groaned. His body shuddered with pleasure that forced him back up as he rained kisses all over her face. "My mate. Mine."

"Yes. My mate," she agreed, just to make him squirm

again. She relished that she could make this powerful male collapse.

His beaming smile looked so goddamn good on him. She would spend the rest of her life getting him to smile like this. Every day. All day.

"I'll take you home." He lifted her into a seated position. Her legs were still spread around him. Her breasts were firm against his chest. She shivered, squirming, wondering how he could have so much self-control. "We will have a bath, a meal, and a good night's rest."

He stepped back, picked up his bloody, tattered clothing. He muttered a dark curse as he tried to pin his pants shut to no avail. He'd torn them too badly.

Her hands moved to her bodice, and she found it irreparable. Her bra too. Shoot, this dress belonged to Savili. She snorted. "That was a bad idea, wasn't it?"

"We'll get more from the storeroom." He chuckled dryly. "Again."

"Doesn't really help now, though. How will we get home?"

"You can use my cloak." He shrugged out of it. Her cloak had been forgotten at the spring. She hoped she could get it back. It was the one he'd given her when she'd first met him.

Who could ever have guessed they would be here now? She felt so warm and full she wanted to collapse with joy and never stop.

"And you'll go naked?" She giggled. "Just letting your bare ass shine for all to see?"

"Already gave them one show today," he said. "What's one more?"

"Oh my god." She laughed, her body going flush. To think he could make jokes about all the insanity they'd been through. "Govek, you're terrible. I love you."

He chuckled, plucked a kiss to her forehead and went to fetch her dress. It had landed next to a row of trunks by the window seat. Something must have caught his eye because he reached over and popped the lock off as if the metal was made of chalk.

Her eyes widened at the heaps of gold coins within. Govek went still.

"Is that . . . money?"

"I don't know. Orcs have no use for jewels and precious metals. Only goblins mine it."

She gulped, wondering what that implied. She knew nothing about goblins. "Did Ergoth steal it?"

"Unlikely," he said before he snapped open the next one. It was filled with opulent fabrics—purple and green and bright blue silks. "We can use this, I guess."

"I think your bare ass would be less conspicuous," she quipped, earning a grin from him. "What's the last one?"

He popped it open and, lo and behold, leather—hats, shoes—and a few pieces of cotton clothing.

He lifted a shirt and shook it out to judge the size. It would be way too small for him, but he could probably make it work. He handed her one of the other shirts before searching through the rest, obviously looking for something bigger, but to no avail.

"This is good quality," he said, fingering the stitching of a pair of leather slacks. "I could make two pairs for you from this. You still want trousers, yes?"

She grinned at the image of Govek sewing her new clothes like the sexiest of seamstresses. "Is there *anything* you can't do? You're skilled at pretty much every trade necessary to survive." She trailed off as his smile showed tension.

How many hours had he spent stitching up his own clothing? Teaching himself to carve? To cook? Even to fish and hunt?

By himself. All alone in his home on the outskirts of the clan. Out of necessity. Not want.

The depths Ergoth had gone to isolate Govek were horrifying. She wrapped her arms around him, wishing she could take all his pain away. He leaned in to nuzzle her chest.

She stroked his wet, sticky hair back. God, they needed baths. Needed to wash away this awful day. She moved her hand down to brush his arm.

"You should do me a nice favor and skip the shirt." She traced his muscles with her fingertips. "I'll keep you warm for the walk."

His haunted eyes heated, and he hummed with pleasure. The deep rumble quickened in her veins and made her squirm. "Woman, keep that up and we won't be getting home at all."

"You promise?"

He gulped, eyes fixed to her lips as if he were going to kiss her again. "Fuck, woman. Don't tempt me." He continued to go through the chest before he paused, leaning back on his haunches. "You know, we haven't fully discussed it yet."

Her brow pinched. "What?"

"Having sons."

Her breath caught in her throat. Sons. *Children.*

He searched her face. "Is it too soon?"

She wrapped her arms around her stomach, "I . . . don't know." He waited, his expression so easy and unjudgmental that she was able to gather her thoughts. "I've always wanted them. *Always*. But . . ."

Guilt warred in her, churning her stomach. Logically, she *knew* there was nothing she could have done for her babies on Earth. She *knew* that. But . . .

"I . . . think I need more time to process. To heal. Is that okay, Govek? Will you wait for me?" She chewed her lip.

But she shouldn't have even been worried because Govek's expression softened in that way that always made her heart thunder and he reached out to pull her into his frame. He pressed his forehead to hers, let his warmth soak into her. She wrapped her arms around his neck and held him close.

"I would wait an eternity for you, Miranda. My mate."

"My mate," she whispered back, and he hummed out a breath that was laced with such warmth and pleasure that it all but melted her. Then he slowly moved away.

And their foreheads stuck together.

"Oh god." She laughed as they finally came apart. She rubbed at her sticky forehead. "We're disgusting." Boar blood, sweat, wine . . .

He chuckled and turned to dig around the bottom of the chest.

"What are you looking for?"

He pulled his arm out with a green bottle in hand. "This."

"What is—hey!" She yipped as he poured the contents on top of her head. "What was that for?" Tingling prickles laced over her skin, and she scratched at her arms. "What the heck, Govek?"

He smirked at her, having poured the rest of the bottle onto his own head. Her eyes widened as his skin went from sticky and red from boar blood to smooth and clean. Even his hair looked fluffier, boasting bouncy looking waves.

"What is this?" She took the now empty bottle from his hand. "Cleaning magic?"

"Yes." He sounded a little breathless. She glanced up to find him ogling her. His hands went into her hair, smoothed through the now unknotted locks. He tipped her face up to his view and breathed, "Fuck, Miranda. The Fades did me the most incredible service when they brought you to me."

Her heart fluttered, and she kissed him again, sweeter this time. His lips were clean, and his taste was unfettered. She wanted to drink him up, but he broke away.

"We really will get caught here if we do not leave soon," he grumbled, pulling another pair of pants out of the chest and judging the size. "And if it's *Sythcol* who finds us, we'll surely regret it. That tincture I wasted is very difficult to make. Takes him many moons to work up."

"I mean, what else should it be used for if not cleaning off?"

"A jar that size is usually used to clean the entire hall."

"Are you serious? Jeez, why did you use so much? How filthy was I?" She looked down at her skin and found it completely unmarred. She felt smooth and perfect. Like she'd just had a whole day of pampering at the spa.

"Once opened, it must be used quickly or it loses its effects. Enjoy being cleaner than you ever have been." He grinned. "Because I plan to dirty you again very soon."

She beamed. "Right now?"

He snorted. "Put on your clothes."

"Fine, fine."

They readied together, working in their easy tandem. The effortless nature of it brought her so much joy—a soul-deep contentment that radiated undertones of bliss as they pulled on shirts and pants and covered their bodies.

But their hearts were still on full display.

Govek looked damn good in these clothes. He could only get the bottom two buttons of the shirt closed, which left a generous view of his muscular chest, and the pants were so tight around his ass they must have been stitched by the gods themselves, otherwise they would have torn open already. She was tempted to demand he never wear properly fitting clothes again.

She reached out and gave his butt a squeeze as they exited the office. He shot her a surprised look.

"You sure you won't go naked for me?"

He huffed, trying to look irritated even as his expression was drenched with pleasure. "Perhaps *after* I get us to the ground."

"Get us to the ground? Aren't we going to take the stairs?"

"And get waylaid by every fucking orc lingering in the hall?" He went to the balcony railing. "Fuck no."

"Don't tell me you're going to do what I think you are." Her stomach dropped.

He looked over the edge to examine the route he was obviously planning to climb down. Then he turned and held out his hand. "Come, my mate. Or do you not trust me to keep you safe?"

"Oh, you jerk. You had to put it like that, didn't you?" She let him swing her up into his arms. She clung to his neck as he climbed over the railing.

"I'll never let you fall, Miranda," Govek vowed. "I will never hurt you."

The intensity of those words struck her. The meaning behind them. Her heart melted at the solid look in his eyes. He truly believed it. *Finally.*

She kissed him hard and fast. "I love you, Govek. Now take me home."

THIRTY

MIRANDA

"Ergoth is begging for a word with you, Govek." Karthoc said from his chair at their kitchen table. He looked far too big for the spot. Just like Govek did in his own chair next to him. Miranda wondered if there was a way to make the furniture in their house a little bigger.

Their house. She relished how that felt. Her apartment on Earth had never felt like this. The glass on Earth had been clearer but the afternoon sunlight that streamed into her and Govek's treehouse was so much more beautiful than anything she'd ever had on Earth.

"He'd better not hold his breath."

Miranda warmed up the fish soup Savili and Viravia had left on their doorstep, though it seemed no one had much of an appetite. They'd brought her cloak back too. It was clean and dry and undamaged. She was so thankful to have it back.

"You really don't want to confront him? You could easily reissue a challenge. Pummel the male the way he deserves."

"No, let him rot."

"That I will do. I have him tied up and gagged."

"You can't use the silencing magic on him?" Miranda asked.

"We could . . ." Karthoc looked at Govek. "Do you want to?"

"No, not yet," he answered before meeting Miranda's gaze. "The silencing is permanent. Once cast, it can never be undone."

"Oh." Miranda's gut twisted. "Have . . . you put it on Maythra and the others yet?"

"No. Sythcol requested we hold off, and I agreed," Karthoc assured them, and Miranda sighed with relief. "Ergoth was furious when he found out Sythcol refused. Makes me wonder what it is those three are hiding that *Ergoth* would like to keep hidden."

Miranda wondered that too. "Has he tried to use magic?"

"No. We have his hands bound too tight," Karthoc said, "and Sythcol is reluctant to use that binding spell on him, made a vow to himself to never use it again. I don't want to force him to break it unless I absolutely have to. I need to keep him on my side."

Govek's brow screwed up in confusion and Miranda mirrored the sentiment. But before either could ask, Karthoc continued.

"Ergoth is going fucking mad, trying to convince us to give him a judgment. When we ungag him to eat, he babbles constantly. He shifts between begging and playing upon sympathies to outrage and fury. It's . . . unsettling. Not even Evythiken can say what his true emotions are."

Govek snorted, obviously amused. "Then we should let him continue in his anguish. Keep ignoring him for now."

Karthoc chuckled. "Fine, fine. But I still expect you to be the one to select his punishment. If you don't want to use magic, I think cutting out his tongue would be fitting."

Miranda tensed at the brutality of that offer but tried not to let her feelings on the matter show too much. If Govek wanted that, she would support it. Ergoth certainly deserved it and more.

"No. Do not. Let me think on it for a spell."

"Suit yourself."

A knock sounded at the door and before anyone could move, it swung open.

The seer stood in the doorway.

Miranda's gut clenched as he moved inside. Her mind flipped through a million thoughts. What was he planning now? What had he needed to tell her?

Was she . . . ready to dredge with him yet?

Despite everything, she still wanted to. The need burned in her chest as pure and crisp as that blinding white light she kept seeing in her mind.

"Greetings, do you mind if I join?" The seer closed the door behind him so the heat wouldn't escape.

Govek scowled, glancing between the seer and her. She knew he was struggling with this, knew he worried about her. She worried too, but not enough to drown out that bone-deep *urge* to take the seer's hand. It simmered in the back of her mind, and the closer the seer got, the closer she came to boiling over.

So, Miranda gulped and said, "Come on in. There's plenty of soup."

Evythiken's face went tense and Karthoc piped up. "You aren't planning on actually *feeding* us that soup, are you?"

Miranda would have been insulted if she'd been the one that made it. *Or* if it wasn't so obviously disgusting.

And yet . . .

"Savili and Viravia made this for us," Miranda said, torn now on what to do. "We should at least *try* it."

"The fish has gone off," Govek said.

"What? How do you know?"

"The scent. They must not have used the fish from today."

She dropped the ladle. "Why didn't you *tell* me?"

"You seemed happy to have something to do," Govek said softly.

"Oh, for crying out . . . ." Miranda trailed off as Karthoc tried to hide his snickering. "This is your fault, Karthoc. I would be *doing* Govek right now if you hadn't shown up two minutes after we got home."

Karthoc was roaring with laughter now. Govek too.

Miranda managed over the males' loud mirth. "Come on in, seer. Have a seat. I promise not to give you food poisoning."

He came and took his place next to Karthoc while Miranda moved the pot off the stove and put a lid on it to cover the smell.

"Miranda," the seer said, when she moved to wipe down the counters. "Come and sit. You know we need to talk."

She tensed. She did know that, and she was ready.

"Can't this wait? We've been through a trial, Evythiken."

"That depends. Karthoc, do you still plan to *leave* day after tomorrow?" the seer asked.

Miranda tensed. *Oh, god, for real? That fast?*

"I see no reason to stay. The matter of the clan was settled today, and I have four traitors in my midst to deal with."

The matter of the clan was settled?

Did that mean that when the clan voted Ergoth out, they'd also voted Govek in?

Without Govek's say on the matter?

Miranda looked to Govek, only to find him just as flummoxed as Karthoc was.

Govek cut in. "Karthoc, I need to discuss the role of chief—"

"Govek, beg pardon, but my conversation is more time sensitive," the seer said flatly.

"More time sensitive than the leadership of Rove Wood Clan?"

"My ability to have this conversation at all is dependent on the reprieve the Fades have given me from their vicious, eternal screaming," the seer said slowly, each word punctuated. "If they start to roar at me again, I will be unable to dredge with Miranda at all, let alone give her the details of what that dredging will entail."

Miranda walked over to stand next to Govek and put her hand on his shoulder. "Do you want to go talk to Karthoc while I discuss things with the seer?"

"No." Govek's response was firm and instant. "We do this together. You can go first."

She grinned as he pulled her down into the chair next to him. By the time she was settled, her anticipation was high all over again. "All right then. I guess go ahead, seer. What's going to happen?"

"That depends on *you*, Miranda." The seer drummed his fingers slowly on the wooden table. "You have blanks in your memory. Things that do not make sense from your time on Earth. I can see the gaps, the places that need to be filled. You *do* want those filled, don't you?"

"Yes, I do." Miranda gulped, her heart beating rapidly in her ears. "I want to know why *I* was the one to survive. And how I made it out alive to begin with. Everything was . . . well, you saw it."

"Yes. I saw it, indeed." The seer huffed out a long breath. "There are guards in your mind, Miranda. *You* are the one preventing yourself from remembering."

"How do I fix that?"

"At this point, you don't." The seer shifted. "You have done all you can in the time allotted. I will have to push through what remains by force."

"By . . . force?" Her hands began to tremble against the tabletop. Govek took one in his, covering it entirely with his warmth.

"Yes. There will be repercussions to breaking down those walls, Miranda," the seer said slowly, still drumming that steady beat. "It will be violent. Brutal. I can feel the fracturing inside me already. It will fracture your mind too."

"Fracture my mind?" Miranda's heart drummed faster than the seer's fingers could pound. "Like they'll break my brain or something?"

"I do not know that, but I do know that there is *death* here. Danger. The severity of this dredging will ripple consequences through the entirety of your being. Your very existence is balanced with it."

A silence descended as Miranda forced herself to process that statement enough to formulate a response.

"No." Govek's voice was sharp and left no room for argument. His expression was tight and his body was taut.

She'd known this was coming. She'd seen it in him. The defiance. The fear. But he'd kept it at bay before. She'd hoped he would be able to until the end.

Because no matter what he said she couldn't stop this dredging.

"Govek," the seer said low.

"No!" Govek said. "I will not take the risk. *She* will not take this risk. Fades be fucked, I'm not risking the life of my mate for your whims."

"They are not *whims*, Govek," Evythiken said, his tone jarring. Miranda's head swam and her heart raced. Her fingers twitched as he continued. "And your mate feels it. Don't you, Miranda?"

Miranda nodded slowly, combing back through those horrible moments on Earth. She looked into Govek's eyes, *saw* the anguish there, but she could not stop. Not when she was so *close*. "I need to know. I've been saying that this *whole* time. Why didn't *I* die with them? I survived and everyone else *died*."

"That's a lie." Evythiken's voice was a sensation. Tangible, alive.

"They didn't . . . die?" Miranda's stomach dropped and her skin broke out into a cold sweat.

Had her babies lived after all?

"No!"

Govek's roar was punctuated by his fist slamming into the table. The corner exploded, fracturing apart.

"You will not do this!" He barreled to his feet,

bellowing so loud it licked up her spine and sparked fire in her mind. "I will not allow it."

"You don't get to decide that," Miranda said, her words clipped, her fists balled.

"Yes, I do! You are my mate!" Govek cried. "You are the woman I am bound to care for. The woman I am imprinted to. It is my responsibility to keep you from harm, and *this will cause you harm.* It has already! Too much!"

"This is what I am *meant* to do!" Miranda yelled back, getting to her feet as well. He still towered over her, but she skewered him with her glare. Slashed him with her words. *"You* don't have any say in this. The only reason you have me *at all* is because I was brought here to do *this*."

"I don't care why the Fades brought you. You are *mine* now. *My mate*! And I will not let you run headlong into danger while I am here to stop you!"

"I'm not a possession you can control, Govek! I choose who I want to be with! And if you don't want to support me in this, then maybe we *shouldn't* be mates!"

Her heart seized, but it was too late. The words had already left her lips.

Govek's face crumbled, his hands shook violently, and a strangled sound left his throat.

And then he turned on his heel and burst out of the door. He ripped it off its hinges all over again and disappeared into the woods.

Miranda stared after him, throat thick, guts twisting. She thought she might vomit. Her eyes burned and prickled and tears spilled from her eyes.

"Miranda."

The seer's voice wrenched her gaze from where Govek

had disappeared. The seer's face was a mask of pity and Karthoc wouldn't even look at her.

Her lip trembled, and she turned away, grabbing her cloak. She left through the back door.

She was mostly up the hill to the falls before she began to openly sob.

THIRTY-ONE

GOVEK

"Govek, hold for me."

Govek ignored his cousin's demand and continued to pound through the woods, leaves and twigs crunched under his feet. His claws dug harshly into his palms as his terror mounted.

"Govek, for fuck's sake!"

Govek couldn't think, couldn't breathe. He wanted to rip the whole forest down.

Because of Miranda.

He couldn't lose her.

"Do not make me tackle you!"

"Fuck off!" he snarled, still going.

"You really want to leave your mate to her own devices right now?"

Fuck no. He wanted to go back and blast sense into her. To hold her tight and demand she bend to his will. To force her hand. To hide her away where no other could ever find her.

And destroy everything they had built in the process. Destroy the trust he had gained.

But *fuck, he could not lose her.*

"Govek." A hand gripped his shoulder and turned him around. Karthoc pushed him, slammed his back into a tree. "Fucking *stop*! You're not in your right mind. You're going to lose that woman if you don't—"

"I'm going to lose her if I stay!" Govek pushed Karthoc off, only to have Karthoc grab him again. "I'll destroy our trust if I yell at her. Now let me fucking *go*."

"No!" Karthoc bellowed. "I won't let you go. You *love* that woman. She lights you up, Govek. And this dredging with Evythiken will happen whether you want it to or not!"

"Don't you think I *know* that?" Govek raged. "I watched her fall out of the fucking *sky*. I know that this is what they want her to do, but why did they make me love her? Why did they make this such agony on her? On me? I *hate* them for what they are forcing on her, and I want to praise them to the ends of the mist for giving her to me. How can they expect me to just stand next to her and *watch* as she suffers through this? How can they ask for me to just *let* it happen?"

"You aren't meant to stand by and watch, Govek."

"What the fuck else am I supposed to do?"

"You support her."

Karthoc's words stopped him cold, made him tremble.

"You are her support, Govek. That much is *very* clear. And if she has any hope of coming out of this, she will need you by her side once again."

Govek made a strangled sound when he tried to argue,

so he just shut his mouth and raked his hands through his hair. His palms were bloodied and raw from his claws.

He couldn't lose her.

He wouldn't.

"It is a difficult trial, being imprinted. The longing to take command of *everything* is thick through it. The raging need to protect is like an inferno, but you must fight it, or you will lose her, Govek. Of that I can be certain."

He may have lost her already.

"Maybe we shouldn't be mates." Fuck!

"You know, I've always envied you, Govek."

Shocked, Govek straightened, eyes wide. The male was looking up at the trees, eyes softer than usual.

"You live here, in these blessed woods. With only the day's hunt and the cold of night to haunt you." Govek tensed and his cousin cut in. "I know that's not the whole truth of it, but I liked to pretend that it was."

Karthoc stopped and looked Govek dead in the eyes. Their depths soaked into his gut, brought Govek to attention, reminding him that this male lead legions and showed him exactly how he was able to accomplish it.

With pure truth and open determination.

"I saw how that bastard Ergoth was treating you *years* ago, but I was too caught up in war to delve further. I should have. I am truly sorry."

Govek was stunned. He searched his cousin's face for a glimpse of the hardness he saw so often behind the congenial mask of Ergoth's apologies, looking for any similarities between the tones and expressions.

The only similarity he saw between Ergoth's saccharine lies and Karthoc's gruff regret were the words themselves.

Karthoc put a heavy hand on Govek's shoulder. "I

promise, Govek, I will never allow anything like this to happen again. I vow to look out for you from this moment on. The way I should always have done."

Govek swallowed thickly. "You speak as if you are forty summers my senior rather than four."

Karthoc snorted, tension breaking.

Govek sought to ease it further. "I could have left at any time, Karthoc. I could have joined you at your forge or another clan, and I chose not to. It is not your fault, nor was it your place to force me away."

Karthoc huffed out a laugh. "Fuck, sometimes I wonder who is truly wiser. Are you certain you don't want to lead your clan?"

Govek blinked rapidly in shock.

"Don't fuck around. I know you haven't changed your mind. I can see it written all over you. Tell me I am wrong?"

"You are not wrong. Even in the face of all these uncovered truths, I do not *want* to be a leader."

"You are far different from me." Karthoc looked out into the woods. "I would have wanted to take control over those who oppressed me. I would have wanted to take their power as they took mine."

Govek's gut twisted at the thought.

"I know," Karthoc said with a nod. "You don't want that. I can tell. But I want to hear the words clear. Do you want to become chief of Rove Wood Clan, Govek?"

"No," Govek said. No hesitation, no regret.

"Then you will not. I have already made the move to put Brovdir and Sythcol in command. Two chiefs with equal power, working in tandem."

Govek was flummoxed. He could not believe what he heard.

"You disagree?"

Govek worked the idea over in his mind. "No. I do not. I think it will work fine."

"Good. So do I."

They stood in silence for a long time, staring off into the beauty of the Rove Woods. Wind whistled through the trees and a chill descended on the land. A chill that had ebbed from Govek since Miranda had come into his life. One he was facing all over again. His throat burned.

"I will ask you another question, Govek," Karthoc said, still looking up to the tree canopy. "You have two options. Either you *risk* losing your mate and support her as she moves through her fate, or you *certainly* lose her by fighting against her. Which do you pick?"

Govek's stomach dropped. He knew instantly what he had to choose.

Karthoc examined his face for a moment and then looked away. "I was in your place once, and I chose wrong. I let my pride get in the way and I have regretted it every moment since. My every *breath* is laced with it. I do not want that fate for you, Govek. It is a horrible one."

Govek was stunned once again. His mind worked to form a picture of Karthoc's words.

"After Clairton, you told me you had broken your imprint on Yerina, but it could not have been a true imprint, then. Because the real ones, the ones that go deep and hook right into your soul, those *never* break. No matter how hard you try."

"You . . . were imprinted?" Govek asked. "You had a *mate*?"

Karthoc looked away, eyes brooding, and Govek

realized this was not the question he should be musing on. These were not the truths he should be seeking.

Miranda's face flashed in his mind. Her imprint hummed in his chest and beckoned him.

He and Miranda were both pushing forward in tandem the best way they knew how. Supporting each other as their hearts and souls stitched and became whole again. Together. Side by side.

That healing wasn't easy, but it was worth it. Govek sucked in a hard breath and pushed past his own selfish fear.

Could he really deny Miranda her chance to *heal*, her chance to do what she thought was right, simply because he feared the risks? Or worse, would he force her to face her fate alone? Would he ever forgive himself if he abandoned her in her most vulnerable moments?

The walls in his mind cracked open and soaked his body in warmth and light.

Never. He would *never* abandon her.

"Karthoc! Govek! *There* you are!"

Brovdir rushed toward them through the woods, eyes frantic, claws extended.

"Brother, what is wrong?"

"It's Ergoth!" Brovdir said. "We ungagged him to eat, and he muttered an incantation in the wind."

Govek's whole body went cold.

"He's sent a *wild cat. To kill Miranda.*"

THIRTY-TWO

MIRANDA

Miranda collapsed on the log next to the falls, screamed her rage into the vicious hurtling water, and buried her face in her hands. Her cheeks were soaked. Her eyes were swollen and stinging, and her throat burned.

Everything was crumbling apart. Just like Earth.

What was she going to do?

She wanted to scream at Govek, hunt him down so she could shake some sense into him.

Hold him and coax him into agreeing with her.

She'd told him she didn't want to be his mate anymore.

What had she done?

Another sob broke. What was she going to do *now*? She *had* to talk to Evythiken. *Had* to know what had happened to her on Earth. It would drive her *insane* if she didn't. She could never stop thinking about it.

But if she lost Govek . . . she wasn't sure she'd ever recover from that, either.

Was she really going to have to choose? She brought her knees up and rocked herself.

"Miranda, there you . . . Fades, are you all right?"

She gasped, sprang up, and tried to wipe her tears away.

Viravia was there. Right behind her. Cupping her stomach with one hand and holding a basket full of colorful leaves and grasses with another.

"Oh gosh, uh . . ." Miranda's voice came out stilted and choked. "I'm . . . w-what are you doing up here? How did you even . . .?"

Viravia cupped her stomach. "It wasn't easy, but I'm not an invalid."

Miranda's brow screwed up. Hadn't she been struggling to walk from her home to the *hall*?

It didn't make sense.

"I was gathering flowers for you when I saw you running up here alone and . . . what happened? Where is Govek?"

"Gathering . . . flowers for me?" Miranda said, unwilling to talk about Govek yet. She could barely think his name without her eyes flooding with tears.

"Yes, you've been through a trial. Both of you."

She was right, damn it, Govek had gone through *so much*, and she'd treated his worries like trash.

And he'd tried to force her hand.

What was she going to do?

"Oh, Miranda, here. Sit. Tell me what is wrong?"

Viravia brushed her off a bit and settled them both on the log at the edge of the cliff. The waterfall was painfully beautiful on this sunny day. Its blue water plummeting into the mist. The green pool forty feet below clustered with ripples and waves. The gray rocks jutting up were jagged and dangerous.

Just like her emotions.

"Oof," Viravia said, eyes wide as she looked over the cliff. "This is awfully close to the edge."

Miranda's lips tugged into a little smile. "I like to live dangerously."

"You certainly do." Viravia rubbed her belly and finally pulled her eyes away from the drop that was less than two feet away. "The view is beautiful."

"How did you even get up here? You can't even get up your own stairs."

Viravia flushed and looked away for a second. "I . . . may have been embellishing my weakened state a bit."

"A *bit*?" Miranda shook her head. "Why?"

"Well . . . lots of reasons." She looked back toward the tree line. "I . . . have a favorite spot up here. A grove of cherry trees just a short walk that way." She gestured to the right. "I come up almost every day to think and to get away from *Maythra's* incessant nit picking. I never got to thank you for getting her out of my hair."

Miranda chuckled humorlessly. "Don't mention it."

Viravia smiled gently. "What has happened? What is wrong?"

Miranda finally calmed enough to get the words out. "Govek and I . . . fought. I said some horrible things."

"I'm sure nothing unforgivable."

"I told him we shouldn't be mates."

"Oh . . ." Viravia's lips thinned, and she murmured. "That's . . . why? What was this fight about?"

She exhaled out as much tension as she could. "About my *reason* for being here. I'm supposed to have the seer help me remember the parts of my past I've forgotten, but the seer . . . he told us today that it's going to be dangerous, that he sensed death."

"Death." Viravia's face paled.

Miranda nodded. "But I *need* to do it, Viravia. I can feel it *all through my body*. It's the whole reason I was brought to Faeda to begin with and Govek does *not* get to just decide I shouldn't because he's *scared*."

Viravia was quiet a moment, processing.

Miranda pushed up from the log and began to pace. "And if he was so against it, why the heck didn't he *say* something? I've been working toward this the *entire* time we've been here. It's nothing new, and he had plenty of time to stop me. Instead, he waits until *now* when we're almost *done* and just blows up at me! How is that fair? Why does he get to choose? He doesn't! This is *my* life."

"You seem very determined," Viravia said quietly. "Would you have listened if he'd brought it up?"

Miranda stopped her pacing.

"I won't pretend that I know him like you do. Fades, I think you've spent twice as much time with him as I have total in the last three seasons. But the Govek I know is . . . quiet. He would gladly keep his thoughts to himself rather than cause strife."

"But . . . I'm supposed to be his partner in this. His equal. And now it just feels like he wants to *control* me."

"I know what that's like," Viravia said, lowering her eyes. "I'm sorry you had to go through that."

"Was . . . Tavggol controlling?"

But Viravia didn't answer. "I can understand why he's scared, though. Evythiken brought up your *death*. That's terrifying. I'm surprised *you* aren't more hesitant after hearing something like that."

"I just . . . I don't think the seer meant *my* death."

"Are you certain? Did you clarify with him?"

"Well . . . no," Miranda conceded and then she lowered herself to the log next to Viravia.

"You may have this invisible drive to do what the Fades have commanded of you," Viravia said. "But he doesn't. Instead, he's *imprinted* to you."

"Yeah, he told me all about that," Miranda said. "The drive to protect me and be near me and all that."

"It's much more than that. The imprint *connects* you to him, makes him feel as if he and you are one. Some of the shallower ones can be broken, but deep ones, ones that hook into the soul, they can't be. If you pass, he will mourn you to the end of his days. He will never recover from it." Viravia looked away. "It's a horrible fate. I've seen orcs who have lost mates who are shells of themselves. And Govek has lived his whole life in rejection. I'm sure he's terrified to lose you."

Miranda's gut twisted and her throat closed up, but she still managed. "So, what? I roll over and let him bundle me up in our house for the rest of our lives? I let him take all the control out of guilt over what he might become if I die?"

"No." Viravia's voice was firm. "I do *not* mean that. I'm only telling you this, so you feel more open to *communicating* with him and working together to alleviate his fears."

"How am I supposed to do that when he flies off the handle and runs away?" Miranda threw up her hands.

"You calm down and then come back together," Viravia

stated, expression flat. "It sounds like he was *very* worked up. Do you think he could have been burying his true feelings for a while?"

"He had every opportunity to . . . to . . ." Miranda stopped and thought back to all the pained expressions, worried tones, and begging. To his words every time she recovered from one of her spells after touching the seer.

"Come back to me. Don't leave me."

He had been scared. Every time she'd fallen apart, he'd pulled her back to him. Helped her out of it. Dragged her back to sanity.

And he'd been scared the *whole time*.

"But . . . but he should have *said* something. I can't read his mind."

"You don't have to," Viravia said. "All you have to do is tell him he can come to you with *any* concerns. And *when* something like this happens again, because we both know it will, you let him vent and then go confront him. Rationally. Make him sit down. Give him something to gnaw on to stop his raging so you can get your side of things out. Tell him you won't listen to him until he uses a normal volume and reward him with your full attention when he does. Then you *compromise*."

She looked Miranda right in the eyes. "And if he won't compromise with you, after trying *everything*, that's when you leave."

Miranda's mind reeled from all this advice. "Wow, Viravia. Thank you for all this. Really." She took the woman's hand. "I'm glad to call you a friend."

"Me too," she said with a smile, squeezing Miranda's hand back. Then her eyes fell. She stroked her stomach.

"Being with a temperamental orc is difficult, requires more patience than I *ever* imagined."

"From how Govek talks, I imagined Tavggol didn't have an angry bone in his body," Miranda said with a small smile.

Viravia looked up, face pale, eyes stricken. "You know that . . . thing that I promised to tell you once all the insanity was over?"

"Yeah, I remember."

Viravia drew in a deep breath, held her stomach tight and met Miranda's eyes. "Tavggol is not the father."

"Wha—I. What? Then who?"

Viravia puffed out a breath, her eyes flat, her posture straight. "Karthoc."

Before Miranda even had time to process that single word, a sharp cry sounded from the path.

A wild cat loped toward them, teeth bared as it drooled. Eyes clouded, fur patchy and oozing. The stench was overwhelming.

They both leaped to their feet. Viravia gripped Miranda's arm. The cat continued to growl as it moved nearer. It stalked closer, muscles tight, as if ready to pounce.

Miranda's heart scrambled up into her throat. Her mind reeled. She froze in place. Govek had told her not to run.

"Oh!"

Something wet splattered Miranda's feet and ankles and she glanced down to find Viravia's water had broken.

"Oh no," Viravia squeaked. Miranda's mind grew frantic. Her breath caught. They couldn't run. Couldn't hide.

Govek was too far to save them.

The cat was too close now. So near that the rotting stench of the blight made her eyes water.

"When it jumps, we have to dodge." Miranda's voice trembled and adrenaline thumped in her ears.

"I-I don't think I—"

It was too late. The beast screamed and sprang toward them. Miranda shoved Viravia with all her might and jumped the opposite way.

She landed on top of the log.

Wind whistled right above her. Something grazed her arm, grabbed her skirt, and dragged her down toward the edge of the cliff.

She clung tightly to the log, then the dirt. Her knees went over the edge.

The tension on her skirt snapped away.

There was a yelp, and moments later, a splash.

Miranda gasped, scrambled, clawed her way back up over the log to solid ground. She whirled around.

The cat was gone. It had fallen off the cliff.

Viravia was gone too.

And then her scream sounded, and it was the most beautiful sound Miranda had ever heard until she *found* her.

She'd fallen and now clung off the edge.

"Oh god!" Miranda scrambled over the log. Viravia hung by a root, face contorted with the effort.

Miranda snatched up the woman's wrist, pulling. She dug her heels into the ground. She had to save her. She had to pull her up.

She wasn't strong enough. "Oh god! I can't!"

"I'm slipping!"

"Govek!" Miranda screamed his name into the woods, hurtled it into the wind, but the falls ate it up.

He said he would hear her *anywhere.* Please!

Miranda clenched her fingers around Viravia's wrist, dug her feet into the crumbling soil, but the cliffside gave way.

They both fell.

THIRTY-THREE

GOVEK

Govek could not think, could not breathe. His tongue tasted of bile; his legs exploded with prickling energy. He hurtled himself through the woods, to his home.

He never should have left her.

The door was already off the hinges, and he ripped his way into the house. Stormed from room to room. The floorboards should have cracked. He nearly overturned the bed in his haste to find his mate.

"Where the fuck is she?" he roared. His eyes bulged and his teeth gnashed and his blood boiled in his veins. "Miranda!"

"Govek!" Karthoc snapped just as Govek barreled into the bedroom, searched the bathroom.

She was nowhere. *Nowhere.*

She had left.

Had she left *him*?

Karthoc was frozen in the entrance to the bedroom. His eyes transfixed to the bed.

"What is *that*?"

Govek followed Karthoc's eyes to one of Miranda's dresses. "That is my mate's."

Karthoc snarled. "No, it's not."

He snatched it up and Govek almost slugged the male right in the jaw as he brought it to his face and dragged the scent into his lungs.

"*What the fuck?*" Govek snarled, working with every drop of his control not to slaughter the male.

"This belongs to my *mate*."

Govek went cold.

Brovdir burst in behind. "What? It's . . ."

"That was given to Miranda by Viravia," Govek said, working around each word as anger cooled in his gut to make room for shock. "*Tavggol's* mate."

"*Tavggol?*" Karthoc snapped. "No. It can't. This was hers. No other but Miranda and my mate have worn it. There are no other scents."

The air stilled as Karthoc scented the dress again, unhinged his jaw to get the smell full into his mind.

"Tavggol's *widow*," Karthoc snarled low, deadly. "*Is my mate*."

These words blasted around in Govek's head. His muscles froze, refused to budge.

"That can't be," Brovdir croaked.

Karthoc snarled. "Where the *fuck* is she, Govek? You tell me where she is *now*."

"I have to find Miranda—"

Karthoc took a threatening step forward and Brovdir

rushed in, placing a hand on his brother's chest. "Calm. Be rational."

"Her house!" Karthoc cried, turning on his heel.

He couldn't deal with Karthoc right now. Fuck, he could barely think through this mess, and he *had* to find Miranda. The saber cat would—

Govek couldn't even imagine it. The fear spiraled in him. It was so thick in his mind.

"I just heard her!" Karthoc said as he pounded back into the house. "She said *my name*, soft but clear. I feel it." He stormed out the back door with Brovdir rushing after him.

Govek did the same. He dragged air into his lungs, trying to pick up the now dissipating scent.

It went up the hill to the falls.

Karthoc was beginning up the hill already and Govek snapped. "Miranda went this way, but your mate could not get up this hill in her condition."

"Condition?"

"She's pregnant." Govek reminded Karthoc. Karthoc knew that Viravia was pregnant with the next heir to the clan.

But then realization slammed into Govek so hard he saw stars.

"She's . . ." Karthoc's tone was quiet and rough. *"She's pregnant."*

Lightning spiked Govek and he whipped around to see Karthoc's face go flat.

"Is it . . . was it Tavggol's or . . ."

"Brovdir, *shut up*," Govek screamed at the male. Words he never thought he would have to say to his usually silent cousin. Brovdir went instantly pale.

"*I heard her.*" Karthoc charged toward the path to the falls.

Viravia could not even make it up her own stairs, let alone climb this hill.

A scream cut through his gut. The call was thick, vibrant, alive. It rolled in waves so strong Govek staggered.

Miranda had called for him.

She was in danger.

His thoughts winked out, and he flew up the hill to the falls.

THIRTY-FOUR

MIRANDA

"Just breathe." Miranda's hands trembled as she dug them into the soft, damp ground. Her sinuses flooded as she tried not to sob. "Breathe, Viravia."

The woman's cry rose and she writhed as the contraction spiked through her. Miranda braced against the cliffside as Viravia lost her senses, threatening to roll them both off the tiny shelf of dirt they'd landed on. It was barely large enough to fit Viravia and Miranda was forced to claw into the cliffside. She dug her toes into the crevices between slippery rocks. The water raged fifteen feet below them, bellowing mist. The rocks and boulders were jagged, threatening instant death if she lost her grip.

The contraction eased and Viravia gasped and sobbed. Miranda leaned against her, trying to give her own muscles a moment to relax.

"I'm sorry," Miranda choked on the words. She couldn't

cry now. She needed to concentrate. "I'm sorry I pushed you."

"I-it's all right," Viravia gasped, eyes squeezed shut. "Better that than eaten."

Miranda let out a half chuckle despite herself. The wild cat had fallen but she couldn't get a good enough grip to look and ensure it was gone. What if it was climbing up behind them? What if it was getting closer?

Miranda clenched her jaw. She couldn't panic now. The cat must have fallen. It must have been battered by the rocks. Taken downstream.

Just like they would if she didn't keep hold—

Viravia screamed as another contraction hit her. This damn baby was coming too fucking *fast*.

"Govek!" Miranda screamed again, bellowing into the air around her. "If you don't fucking come *right now*, I'll never forgive you!"

She wouldn't have a *chance* to even try to forgive him because she would be dead.

Tears coursed down Viravia's cheeks. "I didn't trick Tavggol."

Miranda warred between the need to know and telling the woman to conserve her energy.

"I knew of the Rove Woods." Viravia shuddered. "From . . . Karthoc. I knew it would be safe for . . ." She touched her stomach and tears streamed from her eyes. "I just couldn't let him die like I *knew* his father would. Bloody and battle crazed in a hopeless war. They would both *leave* me. I couldn't . . . I wasn't strong enough to . . . you understand? Please, Miranda, you have to . . ."

"Hush," Miranda said softly. She wished she could

squeeze the woman's hand, wipe the sweat from her face, soothe her with a caress. But she was too busy convincing her muscles not to give out. The rocks under her feet were crumbling. "I understand."

She did. Miranda knew the lengths *she* would go to save the ones she loved.

"Tavggol knew. I told him everything in the outer woods before he took me back to the clan. He was so kind. He treated me as a sister." She broke off, sobbing, unable to breathe. And then a contraction hit her, and Miranda pushed against her with all the force she could, desperate to keep her from writhing off the cliffside.

"Breathe!" It was the only advice she knew to give a laboring woman. "Just breathe, it will pass. Govek, *please*."

"Oh Fades," Viravia pleaded as the contraction ebbed. "Hear me, I beg you. Forgive me for all I have done. Please spare my son!"

Her wailing broke Miranda. She wanted to thrash the gods that had led them to this. Vent her fury at them. How dare they put her through this? Her and Viravia both. *How dare they*?

"Miranda!"

Relief struck, and she nearly lost her grip on the slippery rocks "G-Govek!" Her voice broke, tears flooded her eyes, and she couldn't get out another word.

"*Fuck*!" He was *right there*. She couldn't look up without the risk of slipping, but she could feel him. Moving above her. "Hang on! Don't you fucking let go."

"Wasn't *planning* to," she snapped, irritated and amused and so fucking *grateful* he'd made it. "Hurry up!"

"Ovinia!"

The roar was so potent and loud that Miranda couldn't tell what orc had bellowed it.

Viravia's eyes snapped wide. "No! No, he *can't*!"

"Karthoc, what the *fuck* are you—!"

Something slammed next to Miranda, and she lost her grip. She screamed, arms cartwheeling as she desperately tried to stay mounted. The raging of the river flooded her mind.

Someone gripped her arm, and she was yanked back, pressed into the muddy cliff then jerked upward by her wrist.

"Get her, Govek!"

More hands dragged her up. Into warmth. A chest. Her terror exploded as the scent of musky pine flooded her nose. She burst into sobs, going almost completely limp.

"Hush," Govek said into her hair. He clung to the cliffside with one arm and cradled her in the other. She gripped his neck so tight it was a wonder he could still breathe. "I have you. Hold tight. I need both hands to climb."

"V-Viravia," she managed as he climbed up.

"Karthoc has her," Govek said, and Miranda buried her face in his neck. He made quick work of the climb and finally, blessedly, they made it over the edge. Over the log. He carried her to safety. Away from the falls. Away from certain doom. "Hush, Miranda. I have you. You're safe."

She clung to him, refusing to budge, digging her nails into his back.

"I need to check you," Govek demanded, running his hands along her body. "Are you hurt? Are you wounded? Let me look. Let me see."

She refused, only tightened her grip and buried her nose

in his neck and sobbed the way she'd wanted to since she'd first seen the cat.

"I was so scared," she wailed and Govek stopped trying to check her and hugged her tight instead. *"I was so scared."*

"I'm sorry." His breath was hot against the top of her head. "I'm sorry. I should have been faster. I shouldn't have left you. I'm sorry."

"Don't ever leave again!"

"I won't. I won't," he vowed, clinging, "Fuck, I love you."

"Let me go!"

Miranda came back to her senses as Viravia's furious scream blared over the raging of the falls. She jerked her head up to find the laboring woman scratching and clawing at Karthoc as he carried her over the log to safety. The male's jaw trembled. His breathing was labored. His face was contorted as if he were trying to hold back tears.

"Ovinia," he breathed. "I found you."

"Get away from me!" Viravia snapped and pounded her fists against his chest and tried to claw at his face. Karthoc grabbed her wrists to stop her, though the hold was so light and tender she ripped out of it a second later.

"Put me down now!"

"I have to get you to a healer," Karthoc said, his voice thick. "The babe is—"

"He's not yours! He's not fucking yours!" Viravia snapped.

"Ovinia—"

"That isn't my name!" She wailed, though her fight was ebbing. "Let me go. You have to let me go."

Karthoc's face grew tight, stricken, he shook with the

force of his emotions before he said low, "*Viravia*, I can scent that he is mine." Viravia sobbed even harder and Karthoc shuddered, stroking her face. "And you are my mate. My light. I would raise a thousand of your babes sired by other orcs and men if it meant I won you."

Viravia went still for a moment, eyes wide as the words soaked into her. And then she began to sob again, then cried out as a contraction hit her.

She writhed and Karthoc was forced to lower her down, kneeling at her side. He gripped her hand as she worked through the agony. "You are strong." He brushed her hair out of her face. "You are brave. You can do this."

"Karthoc! I found the saber cat!"

Brovdir burst into the clearing. The poor male skittered to a halt, taking in the scene—a woman screaming in labor on the ground, Karthoc looming over her, and Govek clinging to Miranda, everyone caked in mud and grime.

"I-I—"

"You found the saber cat? Where?" Govek snapped and Miranda was instantly tense. Oh god, what if it came after them again?

"Yes," Brovdir said. "It's dead. Downstream. Battered to death on the rocks."

Relief flattened her.

"Downstream and battered . . . Miranda?"

She looked up into Govek's terror-stricken face and she forced herself to explain. "I-it charged us and . . . and . . ."

He snarled. "Did it touch you? Are you hurt?"

Miranda shook her head as he looked her over again. "It ran past. It fell, but we did too. Oh god."

He crushed her to him again. She relished it. The heat of him. The pine smell.

"How dare Ergoth do this?" Govek snarled so low and deadly Miranda shuddered. What did Ergoth have to do with this?

"Get away," Viravia said to Karthoc, trying to push him away again. "Don't touch me."

"We must get you to the healer," Karthoc begged but he did pull his hands away from her. "Let me lift you."

"Don't touch me!" the woman wailed before screaming in pain as another contraction descended.

"Let me," Brovdir said, low, thick. Karthoc rounded on his brother as if he were going to challenge him.

"Let him! Brovdir, please take me," Viravia begged and Karthoc's face crumbled so piteously Miranda felt her own eyes prickle.

The male trembled, unable to speak. He nodded to his brother and Brovdir scooped her up in an instant, running down the hill at a faster clip than Miranda thought was safe.

"She told me she hated the war."

Karthoc's voice was devoid of emotion, his eyes fixed to the place where Brovdir had disappeared.

"She told me she wanted me to stop fighting. I laughed at her. Called her a . . ." Karthoc shuddered, raked a hand over his face. "I said *horrible* things to her. Vile threats. She left me after . . . I never knew she was with *child*."

"Would that have changed your mind?" Miranda asked, as Govek's grip tightened around her. "If she'd said she was pregnant, would that have changed your mind about the war?"

Karthoc's face twisted, but he didn't find words. And he didn't need to. She could see the truth in his dark eyes. Back then, it would have done nothing. He was too drenched in power. Soaked through with blood and pride.

He turned away and stormed down the hill after his brother.

Miranda cleaved to Govek, closing her eyes as she tried to think.

Govek nuzzled the top of her head and carried her down the hill without a word.

CHAPTER

THIRTY-FIVE

"Fuck." Govek paused halfway down the hill, his legs shook too badly to continue safely while carrying Miranda and he certainly wasn't going to set her down.

She clung to him as he loped over to a nearby rock and collapsed on top of it.

He pulled her closer, pinned her. He couldn't seem to get enough air into his lungs.

She'd nearly died twice this day. *Twice.* "*Fuck,* Miranda, you're going to be the death of me."

"It's been a lot, hasn't it?" Her voice broke as she began to ramble. "Too much. God, how many near-death experiences do we need in a twenty-four-hour period? In a lifetime. Goddamn, I've fallen off *two* cliffs already, Govek. That's two cliffs too many. I never even want to *look* at a cliff again. It's clear they have it out for me."

He relished the sound of her voice. Soaked it up. She was alive. She was all right. At least all right enough to jabber endlessly at him. He smoothed his hands over her skin. Over every scrape and cut. She was abraded in multiple places on her legs and even though they weren't bleeding, he wanted to heal them. To get tinctures on them.

"I need to get you home." He pressed his forehead to hers.

"I'm sorry."

He froze, moved back to search her face. Her eyes were flooded, and it made him want to crumble.

"I'm sorry, Govek. I'm so sorry. I didn't mean to say that . . . about not being your mate anymore. I should never have said that. I'm so—"

"I love you," he said, his chest tight from how full it was with relief. He pulled her into a tight embrace again. "I love you. I am sorry too. I should not have fought with you. I should not have left."

"You were scared . . . scared of losing me." She pushed away from him, and took a deep breath. "You have to *tell* me when you don't think something is right. Before you get to that point. Promise me."

"I . . . will." Fades, he would try. "I didn't want to push you away."

"I know." She rested her forehead against his chin. "I know you didn't. You have had a lifetime of being silenced, and I'm too stubborn and determined. You go quiet and I steamroll over you. We match so well in every other way but this one."

He tensed, gulped.

"But . . . we'll work it out. I want to be with you. It will be worth it."

"*Yes.*" Fuck, he was so relieved. "Yes, we will work on it. Together. I swear it."

She wrapped her arms around his neck. Kissed his cheek, his nose. His mouth.

She tasted like bliss and his blood heated up all over again.

When she pulled away, he whispered. "We need to get home." They had much to discuss now, and he wanted to get her clean.

"I don't think I can walk. I'm sorry. I want to. I'm just really shaky. Maybe in a few minutes I could—"

"You should dredge with Evythiken."

She went still and so did he. He hadn't meant to say those words. It was the last thing that mattered right now.

And yet it was the strongest vow he had sworn to the Fades while racing up the hill to her. He'd raged at them. And lamented. And given them his word that he would stop fighting them in this if they would just *save* her. His mate.

He'd almost lost her again.

The sight of her hanging off that cliff, precariously close to death. *Fuck.*

The Fades had saved her.

"Govek?" She had moved her fingers into his hair. Stroked the sides of his face. Massaged and caressed and gifted him enough calm to finally speak.

"I vow"—he forced the words out past his fear—"that I will support you when you dredge with Evythiken." He squeezed his eyes shut. "I know it's what you need to do. I know that, I just . . . I can't lose . . ." he broke off, voice thick.

Her warm hands tightened around his face and forced him to meet her solid gaze. She poured warmth and strength into him through her eyes. "Govek, I'm *never* going to leave you."

Fuck, why did that feel so much like a lie?

"I love you. With every part of myself. And if we are ever separated, I will be fighting tooth and nail to get back to your side. I will always return to you." Her fingertips massaged the hinge of his jaw.

He wanted to believe her.

But he couldn't. Not completely. He knew she would always *want* to return to him, but the ability to do so was out of her control. It was in the hands of the Fades.

He knew that. It terrified him. Shook him to his core.

And he would have to let her go through with it anyway.

"You said Ergoth sent the saber cat? How?"

"Magic. Like with the boar." He adjusted her so he could pick her up. "He will not get away with what he has done to you."

He would think long and hard about coming up with an adequate punishment.

"To both of us." She was still stroking his face as he managed to his feet.

"Yes." Fuck, Ergoth had done *so much*.

And yet . . . "If the vile male hadn't banished me to Estwill, I would never have found you, Miranda."

"Don't give him credit for that," she muttered. "I would have found my way to you, no matter what. Fades or not, we're meant to be together."

His heart soared. "Yes."

He began the descent down the hill, and his mind centered on what must be done. What *she* would have to do.

"You aren't . . . scared?" he asked her quietly. "To dredge with Evythiken?"

She huffed out a little laugh. "Oh, I'm plenty scared, but what scares me most is trying to go on *without* knowing. I have to know." She met his eyes again. "I have to fill in those blank spots. I can't move on and heal from all this without it. It will haunt me."

"I know." His throat was thick, his eyes blurring as they prickled. "But *swear* to me you will come back to me. *Promise* that you will not lose yourself in this act. *Vow* that you will spend the rest of your days at my side, that we will heal together, raise our sons together, grow old, and return to the Fades *together*."

She bridged the gap between them, pressing a searing kiss to his lips. The smell of her mingled with the crisp, clean scent of the forest and helped clear his mind. Her lips teased his, her tongue delved into his mouth. He was consumed by her. Praised by her. Relished her sweet taste and her gentle nips and her endless love. He kissed her like this was the last they would ever share. Basking in her. Wishing she could be absorbed into him.

He broke off when she was shuddering. Her eyes misty. Her lips swollen.

It was time to take her home.

As he wrapped her up and continued to carry her down the hill, he was brutally aware she had never actually made the vow.

THIRTY-SIX

MIRANDA

"He's beautiful, Viravia."

Miranda sat at the edge of a bed in a small room within the healer's house. Bright morning sunlight streamed through the windows, giving the illusion that the world outside was just as warm as it was inside the bedroom. The crackling fire at the foot of the bed was merry. The blankets were fluffy and soft. The walls were painted with flowers and animals.

And the tiny baby in Miranda's arms was fast asleep. Miranda had never had the privilege of holding a little one so young before. On Earth, illness and pollution kept babies, along with their caregivers, isolated for many months before they were exposed to the world.

He was so precious and tiny—little green hands clinging to her fingers and black nails so small it was a miracle all by itself. He smelled incredible, sweet and clean.

"He's perfect," Viravia said softly, her tone reverent.

Her love for her little one transcended all boundaries and spilled from her face as she reached for her babe again. Miranda handed him back to her without hesitation. Had she been holding her own newborn, Miranda wasn't certain she would have let anyone hold him, perhaps not even Govek.

Viravia set the baby to her breast and the little one began to nurse with gusto. The slack expression on the new mother's face indicated that she felt no pain, and from the light clicking Miranda knew the baby was swallowing. Her milk hadn't come in fully yet but expressing produced a little.

Enough to put both Miranda and Viravia's minds at ease. She was producing, the baby was latching. At this point, the bottles she'd prepared would probably gather dust on Viravia's shelves.

"He's going to *thrive*, Viravia." Miranda hoped her confidence would soak into the worried mother. "Or should I call you Ovinia?"

"No," Viravia said softly as she stroked her baby's plump cheek. "Ovinia is gone. She was gone the moment I found myself pregnant. I can't go back, Miranda. I can only go forward. You understand, don't you?"

She did in some respects, but not in others. Viravia had accepted Karthoc's gifts for her and their child. The bedding and the babe's blanket were from him. He'd brought all of her meals so far. He sat out on the healer's porch, staring off into the woods, shoulders slumped, eyes vacant.

Viravia would not let him in.

But Miranda could not judge the woman. Viravia had spoken a little of the difficulties she'd gone through at Karthoc's forge. Of the trials she'd been forced to face and how hard she had tried to convince the male she had once loved to see her side.

Karthoc had much to make up for. A few blankets and meals weren't going to cut it. It would take a long time and a lot of therapy.

They didn't even have therapists in this world.

"How are you feeling now?" Miranda said. "Are you still sore?"

"Not at all," Viravia said, casting a relieved smile. "The delivery was a trial, but the orc medicines are a *dream*. I'm completely healed."

"Good," Miranda said with a nod.

"I . . . want to apologize again." Viravia met Miranda's eyes. "For lying to you . . . about this. And to Govek, but I am not sure he's willing to hear it . . ."

Miranda pursed her lips, uncertain if Govek would be receptive to an apology right now. Though not for the reasons one might expect. "He truly isn't mad about it, Viravia. Not after I told him that Tavggol knew."

Viravia licked her lips, eyes going earnest. "He truly did know. I know I don't have any *proof* that he did, but—"

Miranda held up her hand. "You don't *have* to show him proof. He believes you. He remembers a bunch of things about your relationship that he didn't realize were weird at the time."

Viravia blinked, brows rising. "Like what?"

"Like the fact that the two of you didn't touch each other very often."

Viravia blushed. "He *noticed* that?"

Miranda laughed at the woman's shock. She couldn't help it. "Not at the time, but now that he's with me, he realizes how odd it was. He also recalls how often

Tavggol willingly left you to go hunting with him or travel to Clairton. To say nothing of the risks he took trying to strike up that trade." Miranda looked down at the baby.

Govek had told her that if Viravia was Tavggol's true mate, carrying his son, he would never have risked his life in such a way. He knew his brother well, and nothing could have pulled him away from his mate's side.

Miranda would not argue. She didn't know Tavggol, but she also knew that Govek was likely projecting his own feelings on the matter. It felt wonderful knowing she was Govek's priority, but clearly, for some relationships, other responsibilities took a higher place. Karthoc was sitting out on the porch, barred from meeting his son, for that very reason.

"I am certain that this evening, after . . . the dredging." Miranda shifted in her seat. "Govek will be in a better place to receive your apology, but trust me when I tell you he truly harbors no ill will toward you."

Viravia relaxed slightly, nodding. Her little baby had fallen asleep at her breast, nursing lazily. The love that poured from the woman into her babe made Miranda's eyes well up.

"Are you going to be okay? With the dredging, I mean?"

Miranda smiled weakly, unable to respond because truthfully, she wasn't sure. Her stomach clenched and her mouth went dry. "I know it's what I have to do. I know that if I don't, it will haunt me for the rest of my life. It's just . . . I worry that if something happens, Govek will . . ."

Dang it, she really didn't want to *cry*.

Viravia clasped her hand and gave it a tight squeeze. "Govek has supporters here. He didn't see it until very recently, but now that he has . . . They'll take care of him, if something happens. I promise."

Miranda forced herself to smile.

A gentle knock sounded, as if on cue, and Wellia opened the door. "Miranda, Govek asked me to fetch you."

Far too soon. Miranda squeezed Viravia's hand tight, bid her goodbye, and followed Wellia out.

Govek was chatting with Karthoc quietly as Miranda crossed the porch that circled the healer's tree and started down the steps. They both stopped in an instant and turned to face her. Karthoc's eyes were so hauntingly hopeful it was difficult for Miranda to stop herself from giving details.

"She's well," Miranda assured him. "She and the baby both."

"She's getting enough rest? Does she need more to eat or drink?"

Miranda saw Wellia roll her eyes at Karthoc's questions. He'd likely been driving the woman mad with all his demands.

"I think she's fine," Miranda said.

"But—"

"We're going, Karthoc," Govek said gruffly, but he patted his cousin on the back affectionately before taking Miranda's arm and guiding her back through the woods. To their home.

"What were you two talking about?" Miranda asked, wanting a distraction from the tension growing in her gut. "Before I came out?"

"His plans. For the merger."

"He's still made Sythcol and Brovdir the new chiefs, right?"

"Yes."

She pressed her forehead into Govek's arm and wondered how that would work out. The two males seemed like complete opposites to her.

But she didn't have the bandwidth to worry about it now.

It felt like far more than a day ago that she was dangling off that cliff. That Ergoth had tried to kill them both. A lifetime had passed them by in just a few short hours, and now another bright, chilly afternoon had descended.

She wished the dredging was already over so she could relish it. Look into these woods and know she would never leave them. Hold Govek's hand and be assured they would be together for the rest of their days. She wanted to get excited for her future. For the home and life they would build.

But she couldn't. Not yet.

"So, I was thinking." Govek placed a hand on her back. "After this, we should do some more 'oozing' at the trade." Miranda's eyes widened, but he continued, "You can argue with them about math, and smack them with a salmon, and we can see if anyone is willing to trade for tools so you can finally get around to tattooing your name on my ass."

Miranda laughed helplessly. Dang, they really *had* gone through a lot. But they'd had so much fun too.

There was so much laughter between them.

"I love you, tough guy." She held his arm tight.

"I love you, Miranda."

Their house on the outskirts came into view and the laughter died away, but the tension wasn't nearly as high as it had been. Govek took her hand and guided her into the house.

The seer was already inside, lounging on the couch.

"Hello. I hope you don't mind that I came inside to wait. Your door is still torn off, so I figured you wouldn't care."

Govek grumbled, but Miranda patted his hand and then went to join the seer. As she settled next to him, her anxiety grew so high she was almost vibrating from it.

Govek sat down beside her, crowded in, and pulled her against his chest. She leaned into him for comfort.

"So . . . um." Miranda gripped Govek's hand and pulled it around her waist. The seer sat up, leaned forward to rest his elbows on his knees, his cloudy eyes blinked. "How does this work?"

"You just take my hand." He readjusted and held up his large white palm to her view. "And the dredging will begin."

"Right," Miranda said as he reached out to her. Her stomach turned nauseous, and her mouth went dry. "Okay." Her whole body thrummed with the yearning to take it. Her palm heated, and her fingers twitched.

She couldn't bring herself to move.

Govek, noting her hesitation, asked gruffly, "Are you certain?"

Fear trembled through her, but longing did too. The soul-deep need to fill in these gaps. To discover the truth. To finally *know* what happened.

And what to do next. To know why she had really been brought here to Faeda.

To her new home.

"Keep hold of her, Govek," the seer said. "It will help tie her to this world."

Her stomach plummeted and Govek tightened his grip and all the terror and determination mounted in her mind.

She arched her neck, looked into Govek's eyes. "I love you."

His throat worked and he managed, "I love you."

She reached out and took Evythiken's hand.

~

SHE WAS FLYING through the air. Air that was brisk before suddenly turning stagnant, polluted. Mud and char coated her tongue.

Miranda's body rose higher, spiraled upward. Her hair whipped around her face, eyes streamed.

She saw the Pacific Ocean again, or where it was meant to be, rather. The endless boiled sand. The stench of rotting fish was so strong she felt like she was drowning in it. She couldn't get a breath.

She was on the cliffside, teetering, looking down at the dead Earth. She was surrounded by carnage. She began to scream but could not make a sound, wanted to look away but could not control her movements.

She scratched and fought and pleaded and the memories burned on anyway. She could feel dirt beneath her feet, her sticky skin, her matted hair. Her mouth tasted of mud, and her nose was burned from the bleach she'd used to keep the dogs at bay.

Her body jerked, flung around, forcing her to face those dogs again. Those rotting *monsters*. Those horrible wretched beasts that had chased her endlessly. Screamed at her. Snapped at her. Threatened death.

But they weren't dogs now. They weren't animals.

They were light.

A beam of white light.

Her mind scrambled to make sense of what this was. What she was seeing. She writhed and fought and continued backward through her memories. Working in reverse, running down the hill. To the cars she'd raided. To the milepost signs she'd passed.

To the camp she'd made the night before. Huddled on the ground. She clutched her bag. Eyes wide in the darkness with nothing but the endless howling horror of those dogs. All around her. Distant but close. Corralling her. She couldn't move. Couldn't speak.

But it wasn't howls, it was voices. Wailing *voices*.

"Keep going. Keep walking. Move."

She didn't want to move. She wanted to lie down and accept her fate. Follow everyone else she'd ever known into the abyss. Where she was meant to be.

She was supposed to be *dead*.

She wailed and screamed and walked across the endless desert. Walked *backward*.

There was *nothing* for *miles*.

Nothing but endless wasteland.

And road signs pointing her ahead to the ocean.

"Go to the ocean. There are people at the ocean."

It wasn't a sign.

It wasn't a fucking sign.

It was light. White distorted light.

Screaming at her.

Blaring right into her mind.

She worked backward still, all the way back to the city, which was no longer a city. To the buildings that were dust. To the roads that were rubble. The stench of ash.

To the vent.

No, no, no! She couldn't go back inside! She couldn't go

back into that vent. Please, god, anyone, don't force her back inside!

But she already was—crushed, panicked, scrambling, and screaming.

Something tugged her, pushed her.

A body. A body made of light.

The eyes were like fire and she couldn't look at them. Couldn't look away. She had to get out. It was too tight. She couldn't breathe. The vent was too small.

The light drew nearer, and went into her, forcing her apart at the seams.

She continued backward in time.

Her body began to deteriorate.

Her flesh blistered.

Her hair sizzled.

Her saliva boiled.

She screamed and screamed and *screamed.*

Her body was a husk. Burned alive.

She had not escaped the explosion.

She had not survived the inferno.

She was dead.

She had died with everyone else.

She had died with her *babies.*

And then the Fades brought her back.

Her skin had melted, her organs had ruptured.

She'd burned alive in the vent.

And the Fades fixed her and prodded her and forced her to see truths so vile she'd imagined they were signs, whispering wind, howling, rotting *dogs,* just to make it seem logical. Better.

Her brain could not fathom that she had been brought back from *death.*

But she had.

And she'd gone to extremes to cover up that truth.

Now it was forced on her. She could no longer hide from it. She had to accept it for what it was.

The Fades were *real*.

The seer had seen it now.

Her job was done.

The light evaporated.

Everything went black.

CHAPTER

THIRTY-SEVEN

GOVEK

For four days, Govek did not eat. He barely slept. He sat at Miranda's bedside, watching, waiting. Willing her to stir.

But she didn't. She wouldn't. She remained in a deep sleep.

"Govek." Hovget hovered in the doorway of the bedroom Govek shared with her. The healer had just finished examining Miranda.

Who was completely fine but *gone*.

"Govek, you need to eat," the healer said quietly. "Eat while I clean up a little."

Govek's home was basically destroyed. *He'd* destroyed it. After Evythiken had awoken. After he had *told* Govek what he'd seen, while Miranda lay lifeless in his arms. Like she was dead.

Because she had died.

And now she was stuck there.

Fuck.

"Govek. Water at least."

"Get out," Govek snarled. He'd said those same words to Evythiken all those days ago. After he'd told him what the Fades had done.

They had used her to send the seer a message.

She'd died, and they'd resurrected her.

She had burned alive.

Burned alive.

Just like Tavggol.

His stomach rolled and he would have vomited if there was anything in it.

Footsteps sounded, growing nearer. "I told you to get out, Hovget."

"And he did. But *I'm* not so obedient."

Govek jerked toward the sound of Karthoc's voice. He scrambled to his feet.

His cousin looked around the room. "Fuck, Govek, what have you been doing?"

Govek's voice was thick and came without thought. "Mourning."

"Mourning?" Karthoc looked on his mate. Govek stepped forward to block him.

He hadn't even been able to *touch* Miranda since he'd moved her to their bed. Only watched longingly as Wellia cleaned her, dressed her, and kept her well. How *dare* Karthoc think he could just set his eyes on Miranda without thought?

"Govek, she's *breathing*. She's not dead."

"Get out, Karthoc."

The male skewered him with steely eyes, anger

snapping so quick Govek had not seen it coming. "She is *breathing*."

"Don't look at her!" Govek rushed him, but Karthoc side-stepped easily.

"Govek. She is not fucking *dead*." Karthoc stormed to Miranda's bedside and grabbed her perfectly slender wrist in his vile fingers. "Touch her! She's—"

"Get your hands off her." He grabbed Karthoc by the neckline of his shirt and threw him across the room.

"You touch her then." Karthoc staggered back but stayed on his feet.

Govek wanted to. Fuck, he *longed* to touch her.

But she was unconscious. She was gone. And his mind was in worthless tatters. The blinding light of the Fades rippled under his skin as his magic spiraled out of control. The conjuring he cast shattered parts of his home at random. His couch, his plates, the mantle on the fireplace. Even parts of his walls.

He couldn't control himself.

And Miranda looked so . . . he heaved. Her eyes were closed, her chest was barely moving. Even her scent seemed dim.

Fuck, *fuck*.

Govek stared at the wrist Karthoc had touched. Searching to make sure there were no marks. Desperate. It was half off the bed, hanging over the side. He wanted to move it back under the blanket. To make her comfortable.

"Easy, tough guy."

The memory of Miranda's sweet voice made him ache. His hand shook as he carefully nudged her fingers with his thumb.

She was so *warm*.

He collapsed to his knees beside the bed, unable to restrain himself. He took her hand in his. Turning it over, stroking her palm, her wrist.

She was warm. Not dead. So warm.

He pressed her hand to his wet cheek, the sight of her blurry as his eyes burned and dripped. He rocked, willing her to move.

But she didn't. She wouldn't.

But she also wasn't dead.

"Govek, what will Miranda say when she wakes up?"

Govek took a shaky breath, looked around the destroyed room. Almost everything was broken. His clothes, the furniture. He'd clutched the bed frame so hard the wood had cracked.

"She's going to be *furious* with you for not eating or drinking properly. And how will you care for her in this condition?" Karthoc continued, unyielding.

Fuck, his cousin was right. With a shaky hand, Govek reached up and gripped the cup on the nightstand, downing the water in a single gulp.

His mind grew clearer.

"Here."

Karthoc forced a strip of dried meat into his hand and Govek's mouth watered. It *could* water now that he'd had something to drink. He gobbled it down and Karthoc replaced it with another.

After a few moments, Govek was able to take the bowl from Karthoc, eating rapidly. Not tasting it, not even seeing it. Just shoveling food into his mouth.

His shaky limbs stilled. His mind cleared.

Fuck, he was a mess.

"You should bathe too." Karthoc took the empty plate.

"You smell as sour as a carcass on a hot day. Worse than one of Savili's fish monstrosities."

Govek was torn between leaving Miranda's side and being clean for her.

Would she wake up?

Fades help him. She *had* to wake up.

"Go." Karthoc shoved Govek toward the bathroom. "I'll stay with her."

"Don't touch her."

"I won't."

Govek swallowed again and loped on shaky limbs to the tub, kept the door open as he washed as quickly as he could. Karthoc fetched him a change of clean clothes, and by the time Govek was dressed, his mind was clear. He downed another cup of water without hesitation, and gobbled up another bowl of mystery food.

"She has to wake," he said, finally having the energy to talk. "I don't know how to wake her."

"It just takes *time*, Govek. Evythiken said it would. Do you want me to bring him in?"

"*No*," Govek seethed.

"Fine. I won't. But you're going to have to be patient then." Karthoc gestured around the room. "And fuck, clean *up* this mess. Do you want your mate to awaken and be distraught?"

Govek instantly began to clean, fixing and mending, folding things and putting them away. Karthoc aided him.

"Why didn't he fucking *tell* her?" Govek's question slipped out before his mind had even caught up with him.

"What are you on about?" Karthoc shut the lid of the trunk by the bathroom door. It sat askew from a broken hinge.

"Evythiken," Govek said, hardly able to get the name out without rage tainting it. "He should have fucking *warned* her about what she would see. He said he'd felt death. He had to know it was hers he felt."

"Would you have let her do it if he had?"

Govek clenched his jaw. "I never should have let her do it at all."

"Govek," Karthoc said low and slow. "Let me impart some wisdom that I have gained from deep loss. If you try to force your mate into *anything*, you will lose her. If you fight against her, she will have no choice but to flee. Evythiken did not tell you because he knew if you fought Miranda on this, you would lose her. Forever. She would never forgive you for stopping her from doing what she was meant to do."

"But I lost her anyway." Govek's voice broke. "At least if she was furious, I would still *have* her."

"You do have her, Govek. And one day, soon, I am certain she will wake. You will be stronger for it. And let me tell you that a mate who feels nothing but fury and hate toward you is not *having* her. It is only agony. *Worse agony than you feel now.*"

Govek turned to his cousin and finally looked at him. He found Karthoc gaunt and tense. His bloodshot eyes focused out the window. His jaw set tight.

His cousin was right. He was living firsthand what it was like to lose a mate from mistreatment. Govek could not fathom what it might be like to have Miranda alive, well, caring for his babe, and refusing to let him get near. *Choosing* to reject him.

Govek went to Miranda's side and took her hand again. He collapsed to his knees and nuzzled his cheek into her palm. If he closed his eyes, he could almost pretend she was caressing him on her own. "Viravia has not . . . relented?"

He heard Karthoc swallow. "No." His heavy sigh flooded the room. "I can only pray that the Fades will show me the way to earn her forgiveness. That they will light the path back to her heart."

Govek nodded, still cupping Miranda's hand to his face.

"I should go," Karthoc said, "Return to the healer's—"

Stomping sounded as a male burst into the room, came to the bedroom door.

Brovdir stormed into the room, gasping. His panicked eyes landed on Karthoc. "She's gone!"

"What?" Karthoc's voice was a rough whisper.

"Ovinia—*Viravia* has gone!"

"Where?" Karthoc rushed to the door.

"We don't know! She masked her scent," Brovdir said as he followed his brother out.

Govek remained in the silence, still reeling from this. His exhausted mind could hardly keep up with what had transpired.

He looked down at Miranda's form. Her *sleeping* form. She was not dead.

He gave into the urge he had been resisting all this time and climbed into the bed with her, curling his body around hers.

Fuck, she was warm. Her heat soaked into him, and he squeezed his eyes shut tight. He imagined she wasn't limp. That her mind wasn't far away from him now.

He whispered, "I love you, Miranda. Please, wake up."

She didn't stir as he rubbed his cheek against the top of her head, her soft hair. "Please, wake. Come back to me."

He'd done this before, called her back from her

nightmares. Her delusions. He used those words now. "You are here. With me. In the Rove Woods."

He felt a twitch.

His eyes burst open, and he examined her close. She was still limp. Still unmoving. But he was *certain* she'd just tensed. He was sure.

He curled around her again. "You are with me. In Rove Wood Clan. You are not on Earth. You are not in a vent."

Her eyes fluttered.

His heart pounded in his ears.

"Miranda." He cupped her face. "Miranda, come to me. Come back to me. Open your eyes, *please*."

Her eyes fluttered open.

He exhaled so hard his lungs felt deflated.

Her body stretched. A smile worked onto her face as Govek collapsed.

"I was having the best dream," Miranda said, her voice husky, her face cuddling into his chest. "But this is so much better."

"You've—you've been—" She was *awake*. She was fucking awake. She'd come back to him.

Miranda jerked up then, looked at him, placed her palms on his cheeks so she could brush his tears away with her thumbs. Her brows were furrowed with concern. "Oh, Govek. What's going on? Are you sick?"

"You were gone for four days."

Her eyes widened, and he collapsed, sobbing into her chest, riding out the storm against her. He released every drop of tension and fear and doubt he'd held inside him for far too long.

"It's okay," she murmured against the top of his head. "I'm okay."

He could not get control of himself. He needed to feel her. Absorb her. Be one with her. He leaned in and collided his lips with hers, drinking her down.

She met him eagerly, delving her tongue into his mouth first, humming with pleasure. She pushed her hands under his shirt and stroked her fingertips down his chest.

Fuck, it had been far too long, but now was *not* the time. He forced himself to push her hands away. He gently stroked her hair, looking deep into her eyes. Those gorgeous, hazelnut eyes. Finally seeing them.

"*Fuck*," he managed as his throat closed again. He didn't want to even blink the tears away. "I thought I'd lost you."

"I'm sorry," Miranda said, her own eyes filling with tears. He brushed them away with his thumbs. She'd woken up smiling, and now he was making her cry. "I'm sorry. I remember now . . . the dredging and . . . and . . ."

"I know." He nuzzled her face, kissed her forehead, wrapped his arms around her so he could rock her. "I know. Evythiken told me all of it."

"Oh god," Miranda whispered. "That was . . . I didn't think it would be like *that*."

"I know."

"I didn't think." She gulped, tightened her grip around him. "There . . . really was nothing I could have done."

His chest lightened, and he looked into her eyes again. He stroked her hair back from her face, her tears off her cheeks.

She trembled. "I . . . died with everyone. We all did. Together. I couldn't have saved them." Her voice cut off in a sob and Govek wrapped her up tight. "I couldn't have.

And it was *instant*. No pain. Just gone. It was the healing they did that hurt . . ."

Fuck! They'd hurt her?

And they had used his mate badly.

How should he address them now?

"Fuck them to the depths," he seethed between clenched teeth and Miranda tensed, moving in closer. Held him until her sobs died away.

Miranda cupped his face. Her beautiful eyes soaked into his soul. He relished her. Cherished the feel of her body pressed to him.

"Govek, even though it hurt, I'm so glad they did it."

His breath caught in his throat.

She stroked his cheeks tenderly, down to his tusks. She eased his turmoil with memories of that first time she'd touched him. Examined him. That first taste of being caressed with tenderness.

"They brought me back, Govek. And it was unnatural. It went against the clockwork of time. It fractured my mind because of how unbelievable it was to me, but they didn't kill me," she whispered. "Humans did. We killed our own planet, Govek. We brought about our own destruction."

He shuddered, pressed his forehead to hers. "I'm so sorry, Miranda. I wish I could take away that pain. I wish you never had to endure that death."

"I don't."

He blinked and Miranda smiled into his face. Her gaze softened as she stroked him again. "Govek, I don't wish that for a second, because that *death* brought me here. To this world that needs saving."

Govek wetted his lips. "Evythiken . . . I forced the truths out of him and wrote them down for you. So that you don't have to see him to know what lies ahead for this world. For Faeda."

He didn't want her to see him. He didn't want that male anywhere *near* her.

But he would allow it if she wanted it.

"Thank you so much," Miranda said. "But that's not the most important thing now. That task is for him. My job for Faeda is done. And it was a horror, but it's brought me here"—she stroked down his face again—"to you."

She forced him to look at her. Take in the gravity of her words. The sincerity. "I would endure a thousand deaths like that if it meant getting to meet you again. Getting to call you my mate. Just as you said you would go through a thousand hardships."

She broke down, her eyes flooding with tears. "I'm so grateful to them, Govek. I'm so sad that Earth is gone, but so, so grateful I've been given a second chance. I swear I'm going to make the most of it. I won't take it for granted for even a second."

Govek crushed her to him. His lips found hers again. He couldn't bear to hear her cry for another moment. For the rest of her life, he would do everything in his power to keep the tears from her eyes. To ensure happiness was the only thing she ever felt again.

"I love you, Govek," she said, and he felt that love in every part of his being, soaking into his soul.

The Fades had given him this. This joy. This love. They'd saved this woman and brought her to him. He wasn't sure a lifetime of reverence would be enough to thank them.

But one thing he did know, he would cherish their gift— his mate, Miranda—with every fiber of his being.

And then Miranda made him the promise she couldn't so many days ago.

She looked into his eyes, soaking him with her love and light.

"I vow to you, Govek, I will be with you for the rest of our lives."

GOVEK

Govek gripped Miranda's hand as they walked through the warrior's disheveled and noisy camp.

Everything was in chaos. Some of the males were already packing to leave, but most were fighting in a makeshift dueling ring. They challenged each other to bloody battle and fought viciously to win.

The prize being the chance to stay in the Rove Woods.

"Why?" Miranda asked. She flinched as one male landed a particularly nasty punch. "Won't they *all* be coming back anyway?"

He took a deep breath of the glorious, crisp air, looking at the brightness of the trees, felt the hum of the Fades deep beneath the ground, beckoning and soothing.

"I guess there is war out there . . . isn't there?" Miranda said softly and Govek nodded.

"There is, and some of the clans they will need to move are particularly entrenched."

Change was coming to these woods and to their land of Faeda. Govek could not imagine how different the Rove Woods would be once *every orc* on this side of the Wyin Mountains was moved into their borders.

But according to Evythiken, it would be better than the horrors the land outside would soon sustain.

"They are remaking us." That is what the seer had said to him before Karthoc dragged him off to hunt Viravia. *"And all we can do to ensure our survival through the chaos is get out of their way."*

And out of the way meant under the Great Rove Tree.

Fuck, it was going to be *thousands* of orcs. Would it even be possible?

"Govek." Brovdir moved out of the crowd. His eyes were dark and his posture slumped. Govek felt some guilt over his cousin's plight, knowing that Karthoc had forced Brovdir into the role of chief because Govek had refused to take it.

"See him?" Brovdir winced over each word. He had to talk too much. He constantly had to bark orders now.

"Yes," Govek said, though it came out strangled.

"You okay?" Miranda asked as Brovdir led them further into the camp. "I can go in with you if you want."

"No." Govek stroked Miranda's hair back behind her ear. He did not want her anywhere *near* this. He was glad that Sythcol had put up a glamour so that none could hear anything from within the tent.

"He's ready," Brovdir managed. "Gagged."

Gagged. And sitting in squalor inside a rough leather tent over muddied ground tied to the center pole so he could not escape, bound with the same magic that had blistered Govek in his youth.

The once-great chief of Rove Wood Clan had been reduced to a level even Govek had never been subjected to.

And now Govek would deliver his punishment.

"Thank you, Brovdir," Govek said before patting Miranda's back. "Wait with her for me."

Brovdir nodded. Miranda let him go and he pushed through the cloth exterior into the dimly lit tent. It was stuffy inside, with no windows and a door that shut tight. The only light was a sliver at the top where the fabric was pulled together.

Ergoth's hands were bound behind him, the pole dug into his back. His legs curled up beneath his slender frame. He was dressed in trousers and no shirt, and Govek realized he had never seen Ergoth in anything but his opulent robes before.

He looked small.

His back was to Govek, and the male straightened. Govek inhaled sharply and walked around to face his father.

For the last time.

Ergoth's skin and white hair were both clean, obviously washed recently, judging by how damp it was. They'd cut it close to his head to make the care of it easier. That one change in appearance somehow accentuated his wrinkles, displaying the heavy bags under his eyes, the whites of which were so bloodshot they looked almost entirely red.

Ergoth's green skin was pale. His breathing jagged against the tight rope gag that silenced him. And his gaze spat wild venom at Govek as he knelt in front of the male who had caused him so much grief over the course of his life.

Govek forgot the words that he'd planned to say for a moment, but the tightness in his chest ebbed. The fury churning at the back of his mind cooled, and he released his tension.

This male could do *nothing* to him now.

"You know," Govek said slowly, his voice light and smooth. "Karthoc wanted to rip out your tongue."

There was a flash of anger in Ergoth's eyes, and Govek swallowed at the reversal of power here. He was in control and Ergoth was lost to his fury.

And this brought him no comfort.

"I told him not to," Govek said. "I didn't think that punishment was good enough for what you've done."

Ergoth straightened, his pupils tiny pricks.

Govek snorted. "And no, I do not mean death either. That would be far too easy, wouldn't it? To let you return to the Fades you so greatly praise. The beings who supposedly favored you above almost all others. Do you truly think they would be glad to see how you have abused your power?"

Ergoth bit his gag, chewing at the rope, trying to dislodge it.

Govek reached out to slice it away. Sythcol's magic prevented Ergoth from doing harm and that included verbal magic or incantations. All Ergoth could do was hurl powerless insults, words that held no control over Govek any longer.

There was truly nothing Ergoth could do to him.

The male spoke the moment his mouth was free. "So, you aren't so much a coward than you cannot bear to hear the *truth*."

Govek's brow twitched as he worked to keep his emotions at bay. "And what truth is that, Ergoth?"

The male growled. "The truth that you are *evil*. Far more wicked than I could ever be. What son would *ever* want to punish his own father this way? What child would relish his parent's suffering? Your mother was right to abandon you. You are a wretched abomination."

Govek's brow furrowed, his head tipped.

"You think Miranda would want to be mated to a male who promoted this *torture*? Does she know that I have been denied real food? That I'm forced to relieve myself while bound? Does she know you want the male who sacrificed so much and worked so hard to raise you to suffer so horribly for only a few simple mistakes?"

Ergoth certainly could smell Miranda outside the tent, but Govek could scent her too. Her sweet honey and strength. He breathed deep, holding that courage in his lungs as Ergoth's words continued to roll over him.

"She will leave you for this. What woman *wouldn't*? But perhaps if you offer a reprieve, she might not be convinced you are a complete monster. Perhaps she could find it in her heart to forgive these vile acts if you allow me a final say in my own fate. If you do the right thing and give me a fair judgment, which I should have had *already* instead of being forced to sit here in the muck."

"You think the clan would side with you?" Govek asked, no longer shocked by Ergoth's delusion. "After everything you've done? Even Maythra has turned her back on you. We offered her and the other two a reprieve from the silencing in exchange for the full truth, and she took it without a moment of thought. She told us you incited her to attack Miranda. Said that you swore you would protect her no matter the outcome, but you didn't uphold your vow."

"She's a wretch and a liar," Ergoth spat. "She'd say whatever she needed to get out of her rightful punishment."

"Her punishment for attacking Miranda or for betraying *you*?"

Ergoth's face contorted into a glower that revealed the truth.

"You've never done anything for anyone in this clan unless it benefited you. You manipulated us all."

"I *made* you all. They will see that in time. They would be nothing without my guidance. They would have nothing if I had not been there to steer their hands through these gruesome times. I alone have been the one capable of preventing horrors from descending upon this fair clan.

"Your mother would be *sick* to see what you've done," Ergoth spat. "To see you punish the only male that ever cared about you. To see you torture the great leader that led this clan to glory. The moment you rid me of my rightful place in this clan, the Fades will abandon it. But it's not too late, Govek. It's not too late to change your mind. To set me free. I demand you look into yourself and see what is right."

Ergoth finally broke off, panting. Eyes wild.

And Govek felt nothing but amusement.

Govek said with a shrug, "Is that all?"

Ergoth's mouth slacked, his rows of sharp teeth, the same as Govek's, just more easily hidden, finally on full display.

"All these years, I've let your *lies* consume me. But that's all they are, aren't they? You worked so hard to trap me inside them. To keep me in your clutch. To control me, just as you have controlled everyone in this clan."

"The clan followed me because *I* am the best ruler they have ever had. I have led this clan to *glory*."

"Perhaps. In some ways, you have brought glory to this clan. Your accomplishments here *are* vast. You created the vote and proper judgments. You increased the trade with Oakwall. Food production has been incredible, and the forest is thriving through organized communions you orchestrated." Govek met Ergoth's gaze. "But no one is going to remember that *you* started *any* of it."

"Of course, they will! It is in the historical scrolls for all to see. I've had birds sent to every clan outlining my practices so their scribes could—"

"I am going to have them removed."

Ergoth went pale. "What did you say?"

"That is your punishment, Ergoth, what I have decided for you. The scrolls outlining all of your good deeds will be burned and every vile corruption you have orchestrated within this clan will be outlined for all to see. The binding that was little more than torture, the silencing that you used to cover your tracks, the clearing that warped our minds, all the *lies* you spread. Only *that* will be attributed to your name."

"You can't do that." Ergoth's voice shook. His eyes were wide. "You cannot just rewrite *history*."

"It's already being done. Sythcol is performing the task now with his conjurers. Birds are being sent to the other clans." Govek got close, looked into Ergoth's eyes. "And *you* will soon be dragged around the continent to each and every one of them. You will be forced to listen while Karthoc speaks the *truth* of what you have done here in Rove Wood Clan to every orc who will listen. It will be written down in their clan histories. It will be sent in scrolls with Evythiken as he travels across the mountains to the overlord. And there, in the overlord's great keep, with the entire history of our race, your crimes will remain, painting you the vile monster you tried to make me.

"The image you worked to create is *gone,* Ergoth of Rove Wood. And not one being in all of Faeda will ever believe your lies again. *That* is why I allowed you to keep your tongue. That is why you will not have a magical silencing. Not because of mercy, but because it will be far more torturous for you to be able to scream, and wail, and lament and have all ears turn away from you, see through you. They will hear you and be unaffected. Uncaring. Just as I am now."

Ergoth's body shuddered as if racked by fever. His mouth gaped.

His voice was gone.

Govek got to his feet. "The power you once held over me is broken. The monster you thought you turned me into has only made me strong. Strong enough to fight you and win."

"No," Ergoth managed. "No, you aren't.

"This is my final goodbye." Govek truly felt this to the very depths of himself. "And know that I will never think on you. You will never haunt my mind. I am going to thrive with my mate. And once I leave this tent, you will never occupy my thoughts again."

"*I own you,*" Ergoth managed past his shock. "This clan is mine. You are mine! Even your mate is mine! I will have it all again."

Govek chuckled, honestly amused by Ergoth's desperate final words. "Not anymore. The Fades have abandoned you and so too do I."

And with that, Govek exited the tent.

His whole body felt light. His mind was bright.

The flap closed behind him.

He was free.

Miranda looked into his beaming face and grinned. She tugged him down for a kiss. Held him tight in her loving embrace. He lifted her from the ground, relishing the sweetness of her mouth, the feel of her hands in his hair, the love that she surrounded him with and that he gave back to her. Together. Eternally.

From this moment forward, they would thrive.

EPILOGUE

"Miranda, if we don't get ready, we really are going to be late."

Winter had fallen in the Rove Woods. The snow was thick on the windowsill of their new home. The fire crackled warmly in the hearth.

Miranda's heart was full in a way she never thought possible. Especially after a season of being in this new world. Three months and *everything* had changed.

And it would keep changing. Drastically.

"Are the boys up yet?" She sat up to stretch. Govek sat heavily on the edge of the bed and stroked her hair back. His eyes were soft in a way that made her heart flutter. "What time is it?"

"You and your morning math." He braced his weight at the edge of the mattress so he could nuzzle her hair, nip at her ear. A kiss fluttered across her forehead before he captured her lips. She was in heaven right here in their warm cabin, surrounded by snow and the subtle smell of wood smoke and hard, burned bread.

"They are waiting for us, Miranda," he said into her ear, making her shiver. His voice still spiked heat in her. "The boys are already at the hall."

Her eyes bulged. "What? You let them go on ahead without us?"

"You were sleeping like the dead, Miranda."

"What if they get lost? And what about the sink holes?" She pulled herself to the edge of the bed so she could get dressed. The wood floor felt like ice under her feet as she gathered up her clothes from the trunk at the foot of the bed.

"Sink holes have only opened up on the outskirts of the clan, Miranda. And they know their way to the hall. They've been living with us for two moons." His tone was laced with both humor and exasperation.

"We adopted them so they're our responsibility. It's so cold and slippery outside. They could get hurt."

"They've gone through *much* worse, Miranda," he reminded her. "They can handle a single walk on a snowy day."

"But they shouldn't have to anymore!" She yanked her thick wool dress over her head and quickly put on a pair of trousers he'd made for her. "They have us now. We have an obligation to—"

He yanked her back into his embrace and held her between his legs while he sat on the bed. His arms caged her, and he splayed his hand around the back of her head so she was forced to meet his eyes.

"Our sons are *fine*, Miranda. Young orcs need independence."

"Yenvir is only *two*, Govek."

"And Orin is seven, more than capable of protecting both of his younger brothers."

The reminder that Govek had also been seven when he'd been banished from the clan hung between them.

She forced her rapid heartbeat to quiet. The transition into adoptive parenthood hadn't been as smooth as she'd expected it to be, and surprisingly, Govek seemed more capable than she did most of the time.

Watching Govek care for and cherish their new sons only made her adore him more. Her chest warmed and her panic ebbed. "I love you."

His face softened, and he pulled her down for a deep kiss, one that turned far too passionate, far too quickly, and left her squirmy and raw.

She pulled back slightly. "We've got the house all to ourselves, don't we?"

He nodded.

She laughed. "That was your plan, wasn't it?"

"Maybe. But you slept *late*. We don't have time."

She trailed her hand down his firm chest and his breath halted, eyes falling to half-mast. "Are you *sure*?"

He hummed as if considering.

And then her stomach grumbled, and the decision was made without her consent.

She yipped with laughter as he hauled her to her feet, carrying her toward the kitchen with a beaming smile and a loud proclamation. "My mate must be starving to death to have her stomach growling so loud."

He plunked her down at the new table he'd made. Their new house had been a nightmare when they'd first moved in with the boys, but was now much better after their many months of combined work. They now had a couch that was big enough to fit all five of them at once. A kitchen arranged so she could cook with ease and countertops at the right height for Govek. Bigger windows that displayed the gorgeous white woods surrounding them.

And curtains for privacy since they were much closer to the clan now and visitors were far more frequent. Roenia's and Aralie's boys were always dropping by to play, to say nothing of their parents. She half expected Iytier and Savili to come up the path for a visit right now.

"Your stomach is so desperate I bet it would accept the bread I made."

"Not on your life," she said as he went to get her something to eat. "But don't you dare throw it out. I'm taking it to Trinia later so we can laugh at it. Maybe we'll try to trick Brovdir into eating it again."

"Vicious woman." He scooped scrambled eggs out of the pan on the stove and onto a plate. He'd clearly cooked for the boys already. "You'll be making that slight up to me later."

"Mm." She squirmed, making him cast her a heated look. "I can't wait. You sure not now?"

"Damn, woman," he cursed, making her smile. He'd taken to using some of her Earth words lately, and she adored it. "You're going to ruin me."

"I've already spoiled you," she said as he brought over the food. She ate without complaint. "Might as well go all the way."

"I can think of no better way to die," he said as she quickly finished. He fetched her cloak. "We need to go. Otherwise, they'll all show up and move into the wrong houses."

"I'm sure Sythcol would straighten them out if they

tried." But she got up and let him pull the cloak over her. The same one he'd put over her shoulders so many times before. The same one he'd given her when she'd first arrived in Faeda.

Then he took her hand and guided her out the door, into the bright daylight. It was a lot later than she had thought. Probably close to noon.

The pathway was littered with the tiny footprints of their sons. They'd clearly been out playing in the snow for a while. Probably with Estoc's kids, judging by the number and size of the prints. Their friendships had blossomed greatly in the season since all the upheaval.

And she was happy to know no one in her little family had suffered a near death experience since. Not even once.

Though that didn't mean there hadn't been a fair amount of drama. Especially where their new chiefs were concerned.

Once they'd made it to the main road, she could see just how frantic and bustling everyone was. They all rushed around, yelling and getting ready.

It had been like this for half a moon now, and she couldn't help but find it a little funny. To think that the Rove Wood orcs, who had been so standoffish and judgmental of their warrior counterparts, would now be doing everything in their power to ensure their welcome was warm and the new homes were ready.

As they walked, she gripped Govek's arm, growing a little anxious from the excitement around them. "What do you think it will be like with so many new faces?"

"I suppose you'd have a better answer to that than I." He patted her hand. "Since you had to learn everyone's faces just last season."

"Yeah," she griped quietly. "I still don't know everyone's names. I really am going to start calling them dear."

"Don't you dare," he growled low into her ear making her shiver. "I'm the only dear you get to have."

She grinned at him.

"Govek! Hold for me?"

Govek slowed his walk and muttered under his breath. "Ah fuck. Sythcol again."

Miranda shot Govek a wry look. "He is doing *your* job."

"Don't start." Govek was genuinely irritated, and Miranda let it drop as Sythcol joined them. He started quizzing Govek about where they could get more firewood since they'd apparently run out.

The males of Rove Wood Clan often sought Govek for council and neither Brovdir nor Sythcol would make decisions without running them by him first. No judgments were held without Govek's presence. No inventories of supplies were concluded without Govek's approval. And not a single one of the trades had taken place without Govek at least stopping by for a brief moment to chat with the headman and keep up friendly relations.

And Sythcol was the main reason for that. The male ruthlessly dragged Govek into every nook and cranny of this clan. Miranda was glad he put his talents to good use because he really could be a criminal mastermind.

"Just take a bundle of logs from every house already set." Govek almost snapped, obviously exasperated. "This wouldn't have happened if you hadn't given them five instead of three to begin with."

"But are three bundles enough?" Sythcol asked, tapping

his charcoal pencil against the linen scroll he always had on hand. "With winter so harsh this year—"

"For fuck's sake, do you think five will be much different from three? It's just to get them started." Govek pinched the bridge of his nose. "They're *warriors*, Sythcol. They'll cut their own wood long before they freeze to death."

"Right. Thank you, Govek. Your input is greatly useful and appreciated."

Govek growled at the male's genuine compliment and Sythcol was smart enough to not press his luck further. He shot Miranda a quick smile and went back to work.

Miranda grinned up at Govek.

"Go ahead and smile, Miranda," he said, though the mirth in his tone betrayed him. "I'm never going to take that title."

"You wanna bet on it, tough guy?"

He snorted, knowing better than to make bets with her. He'd lost too many times.

As they walked closer to the opposite edge of the clan, she felt anticipation roll into her gut. She gripped his hand tightly. "Do you think Karthoc won over Viravia?"

"I'm not sure. But he was very determined."

"Viravia was pretty determined *not* to let him." She gave his arm a gentle caress.

He hummed. "I suppose we are going to find out soon enough." He grinned down at her mischievously. "Do you want to *bet* on it?"

Her heart flipped over. It wasn't legal for someone to be so flipping handsome when they smiled. "I think not. Not with how confident you look right now."

He shrugged. "I suppose I could be wrong. He was a fool not to bend to his woman's will from the beginning."

"Like you bend to mine?"

"Exactly."

Her smile turned sly. "Hmm . . . I'm not sure I would agree."

He forced her to halt and lifted her chin. The gold in his eyes glittered with equal parts amusement and irritation. "Care to repeat that?"

"I dunno," she said coyly, tipping her head in his hand to increase the caress. "Maybe I want you to bend a little more."

His low growl spiked heat through her entire body. "Careful with your teasing, woman, or I'll be bending *you* over the nearest boulder and making you forget everything we planned to do today."

She laughed and pulled him down for a kiss. One that went far too long and left them both panting.

"Fuck, woman," he said, forcing her along as pleasure radiated off him. "We really will be late."

She grinned with delight.

They hurried along the paths that felt warm, despite the snow. Greeting orcs who now considered them friends. To the Great Rove Tree that had been carved with both Miranda's *and* Govek's names.

They belonged here. In Rove Wood Clan. They had both made it their home.

A sharp but beautiful cry sounded from the tree above, and Miranda turned to look. Most of the birds had left for winter outside of the little ones they used to send messages, so she was surprised to hear such a loud, unusual call.

Her eyes went wide, and her heart pounded.

"Govek . . . is that . . ."

Her mate turned to look and tensed. For good reason.

Up high on a branch above them, with the Great Rove Trees crystalline leaves glittering behind it, sat a gray heron-like bird. Its sharp yellow eyes peered down at them curiously. Knowingly.

A Riabell.

Although grief still struck her occasionally, she hadn't had any attacks or flashbacks since she'd dredged with the seer. Her mind was clear most days. Her sorrow wasn't as overwhelming.

Keeping busy chasing after three young orc boys and setting up the clan to host thousands more was a good distraction.

That and the knowledge that her babies on Earth had not suffered. There had been nothing she could do to save them, and she reminded herself of that every time guilt tried to creep up on her.

She would live well in their honor. Cherish every day she had been given back. Remember them fondly in her happiest moments so they could live on in her memories.

The Riabell let out another low, lovely cry and her heart warmed. Aching.

"Miranda?" Govek's voice betrayed his worry.

But she patted his hand and assured him. "I'm okay. It's okay." The bird's call didn't sound like a warning siren at all. Not anymore. "It's beautiful."

He visibly relaxed next to her. His expression softened, and she smiled. She turned away from the bird and looked up into his perfect face with his untucked jaw and his green and gold eyes glittering.

"Are we ready?" she asked, holding his hand in hers.

He gave her a squeeze. "Yes. We're ready."

Hand in hand, step by step, hearts beating in tandem, Govek and Miranda walked with purpose, together with the support of the clan behind them and the promise of peace before them.

They welcomed the merger of Karthoc's warriors with open arms and began the first steps to fulfilling the Fades commands.

THE END

THE TRILOGY IS OVER BUT MIRANDA AND GOVEK'S STORY CONTINUES IN THIS FREE NOVELLA!

The Orc Outcast's New Babies:

With the turmoil of their first few days in Rove Wood Clan finally behind them, Miranda and Govek settle into a quiet routine as they prepare for incoming winter.

But that routine is completely turned on its head by the arrival of three orc children.

The young boys are dirty, tired, and have no caretaker in sight. Miranda is instantly smitten and although Govek is reluctant, he cannot deny his mate anything. Even if that means he's forced to confront traumas from his own past that parallel the struggles of these young orphan orcs.

As the five of them get acquainted, it becomes apparent that the boy's past is even more mysterious than they realized. And when the full extent of their hardship is revealed, it threatens to break the new family apart.

Follow this QR Code or go to
https://www.aurorawintersromance.com/rm3-sign-up
to subscribe to my newsletter and you'll get this free, sweet and cozy novella.

THANK YOU READERS!

Thank you so incredibly much for reading my debut trilogy about Miranda and Govek. I hope you loved them as much as I did. If you did (and even if you didn't) please consider writing a review. Reviews are the lifeblood of indie authors and your support of my books means the world to me.

For the last two years I've been living and breathing these characters and I'm so sad to see their chapters come to a close but so excited to continue working on the next books in this series. Next up will be Brovdir and Trinia's story in The Orc Chief's Baker. Keep an eye on my progress for this novel on my Instagram @aurorawinters.romance. I post lots of character art (both sweet and spicy alike!) and almost weekly progress reports on my writing projects there. I also have a patreon, patreon.com/AuroraWintersRomance, where you can see full versions of my NSFW character art.

I'd also like to take a moment to thank my wonderful husband who fully supported me through this entire journey, happily watched our daughter when I was pouring over projects, and constantly encouraged me. I couldn't have done this without you!

Another sincere thank you to Daisy who spent countless hours helping me edit the books and giving feedback on video calls. The books would not be what they are today without your advice! And to Jennifer who constantly cheered me on and inspired me with her endless excitement.

A big thank you to Lacey Braziel at Lacey Braziel Edits for your expert line and copy editing. Your support was endless and I'm so grateful to have worked with you on this project. I can't wait to continue working with you in the future!

And a final thank you to Cassie Weaver at Weaver Way Author Services for your awesome beta reading, proofreading, and formatting. Thank you some much for your help with my endless stream of formatting updates. I'm endlessly grateful for you.

And once again, thank you to all of my readers! I appreciate every single one of you.

LET'S STAY IN TOUCH!

Sign up for my newsletter on my website, www.AuroraWintersRomance.com and get monthly updates and exclusive art for my subscribers.

Or follow me on Instagram @AuroraWinters.Romance. Where I post almost daily updates about my writing as well as character art and all kinds of other fun stuff.

WHAT'S UP NEXT?

Book four in my Orc Mates of Faeda series follows two characters we've seen featured in the trilogy; Brovdir, Govek's cousin, who has been thrust into the position of Chief of Rove Wood Clan against his will, and Trinia, the baker of Oakwall village who will do anything to keep her bakery afloat, even play conquest to a certain orc chief.

Follow me on Instagram @AuroraWinters.Romance to get regular updates about this books progress!

About Aurora Winters

Growing up in the Pacific Northwest meant many rainy days spent on indoor activities and from a young age one of my favorites has been creative writing. I was penning monster romance stories in high school between classes before I even realized it was a genre and still have many of those original drafts. (Which will never, ever see the light of day again because they are truly cringe worthy!)

It was only recently that my writing grew from a personal hobby into a dream of publishing. When I'm not obsessing over my writing, I can be found wandering through the woods with my daughter and husband, taking pictures of pretty leaves, and throwing sticks for my little dog, Dash.

Let's keep in touch! Join my newsletter at www.AuroraWintersRomance.com.